THE FAULT BETWEEN US

Praise for Stephanie Landsem

The Fault Between Us is a captivating family saga, rich with a cast of characters readers can root for. . . . Historical facts, beautiful descriptions, and genuine sisterly bonds come together under Stephanie Landsem's masterful pen, culminating with terrifying events taken from the pages of history. Bravo!

> **MICHELLE SHOCKLEE,** award-winning author of *Appalachian Song*

This is a compelling and inspiring story of love, loss, and redemption.

> **LARRY E. MORRIS,** author of *The 1959 Yellowstone Earthquake*, on *The Fault Between Us*

A riveting spy story and a nuanced look at the way religion can either justify prejudice or fuel moral action. Liesl's adventures will keep readers hooked to the last page.

> **PUBLISHERS WEEKLY** on *Code Name Edelweiss*

Code Name Edelweiss kept me reading long after midnight. . . . Stephanie Landsem does a masterful job of showing how easily and insidiously hatred and prejudice can grow—and what our response to it must be. Well done!

> **LYNN AUSTIN,** bestselling and award-winning author of *Long Way Home*

Stephanie Landsem's newest . . . is thrilling, vivid, expertly researched, and all too timely. Liesl . . . is a compelling character and readers will root for her.

> **SUSAN ELLA MACNEAL,** author of *Mother Daughter Traitor Spy* and the *New York Times* bestselling Maggie Hope series, on *Code Name Edelweiss*

Part John Steinbeck and part Mickey Spillane, this well-researched historical novel is a tale of inspiration and hope. Highly recommended.

HISTORICAL NOVELS REVIEW on *In a Far-Off Land*

With her signature blend of luminous prose and immersive historical detail, Stephanie Landsem draws readers into the dazzle and darkness of 1930s Hollywood. From beginning to end, I was riveted by this masterful retelling of the parable of the Prodigal Son and moved by the poignant exploration of the power of grace in the midst of shame.

AMANDA BARRATT, author of *The Warsaw Sisters,* on *In a Far-Off Land*

Fans of Susan Meissner and Kristina McMorris will be spellbound by Landsem's gorgeously researched historical . . . a lyrical and thematic treatise on redemption, loss, and love, wielded with such surprising grace the reader will have many breath-catching moments.

RACHEL MCMILLAN, author of *The Mozart Code,* on *In a Far-Off Land*

With everything I crave in historical fiction, Landsem's *In a Far-Off Land* immerses the reader in a world long forgotten yet achingly familiar. Old Hollywood meets *The Grapes of Wrath*, and the redemption, romance, and regret are all beautifully written and deliciously authentic.

AMY HARMON, *New York Times* bestselling author of *Where the Lost Wander*

the FAULT BETWEEN US

STEPHANIE LANDSEM

Tyndale House Publishers
Carol Stream, Illinois

Visit Tyndale online at tyndale.com.

Visit Stephanie Landsem's website at stephanielandsem.com

The Fault Between Us

Cover design by Libby Dykstra

Interior design by Brandi Davis

Edited by Kathryn S. Olson

For information about special discounts for bulk purchases, please contact Tyndale House Publishers at csresponse@tyndale.com, or call 1-855-277-9400.

Library of Congress Cataloging-in-Publication Data

A catalog record for this book is available from the Library of Congress.

ISBN 979-8-4005-0204-0 (HC)

ISBN 979-8-4005-0205-7 (SC)

Printed in the United States of America

31 30 29 28 27 26 25
7 6 5 4 3 2 1

Dedicated to

Mom and her sisters, for sharing their stories

Jeanette Claire Wetzel, née Reardon

Mary Bridget Langan, née Reardon

Marlyn Benson Perry, née Reardon

Joan Marie Floyd, née Reardon

God is our refuge and our strength,
an ever-present help in distress.
Thus we do not fear, though earth be shaken
and mountains quake to the depths of the sea,
Though its waters rage and foam
and mountains totter at its surging.
The LORD of hosts is with us;
our stronghold is the God of Jacob.

PSALM 46:2-4, 8

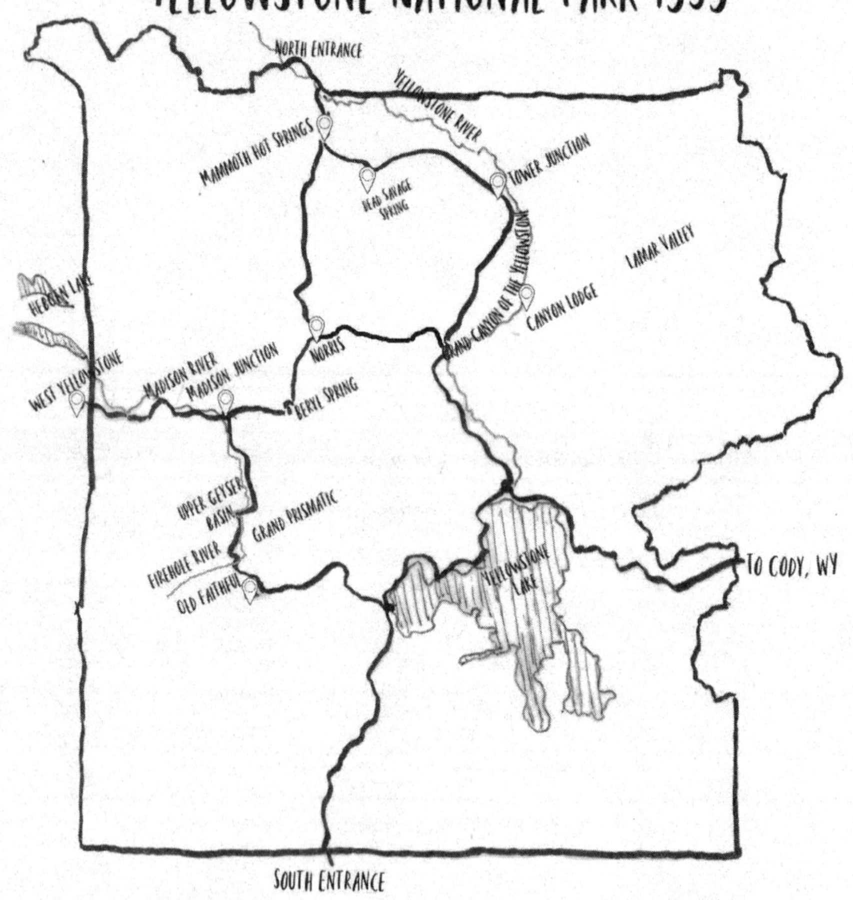

YELLOWSTONE NATIONAL PARK 1959
NORTH ENTRANCE
YELLOWSTONE RIVER
MAMMOTH HOT SPRINGS
DEAD SAVAGE SPRING
TOWER JUNCTION
GRAND CANYON OF THE YELLOWSTONE
LAMAR VALLEY
CANYON LODGE
HEBGEN LAKE
NORRIS
WEST YELLOWSTONE
MADISON RIVER
MADISON JUNCTION
BERYL SPRING
UPPER GEYSER BASIN
GRAND PRISMATIC
FIREHOLE RIVER
OLD FAITHFUL
YELLOWSTONE LAKE
TO CODY, WY
SOUTH ENTRANCE

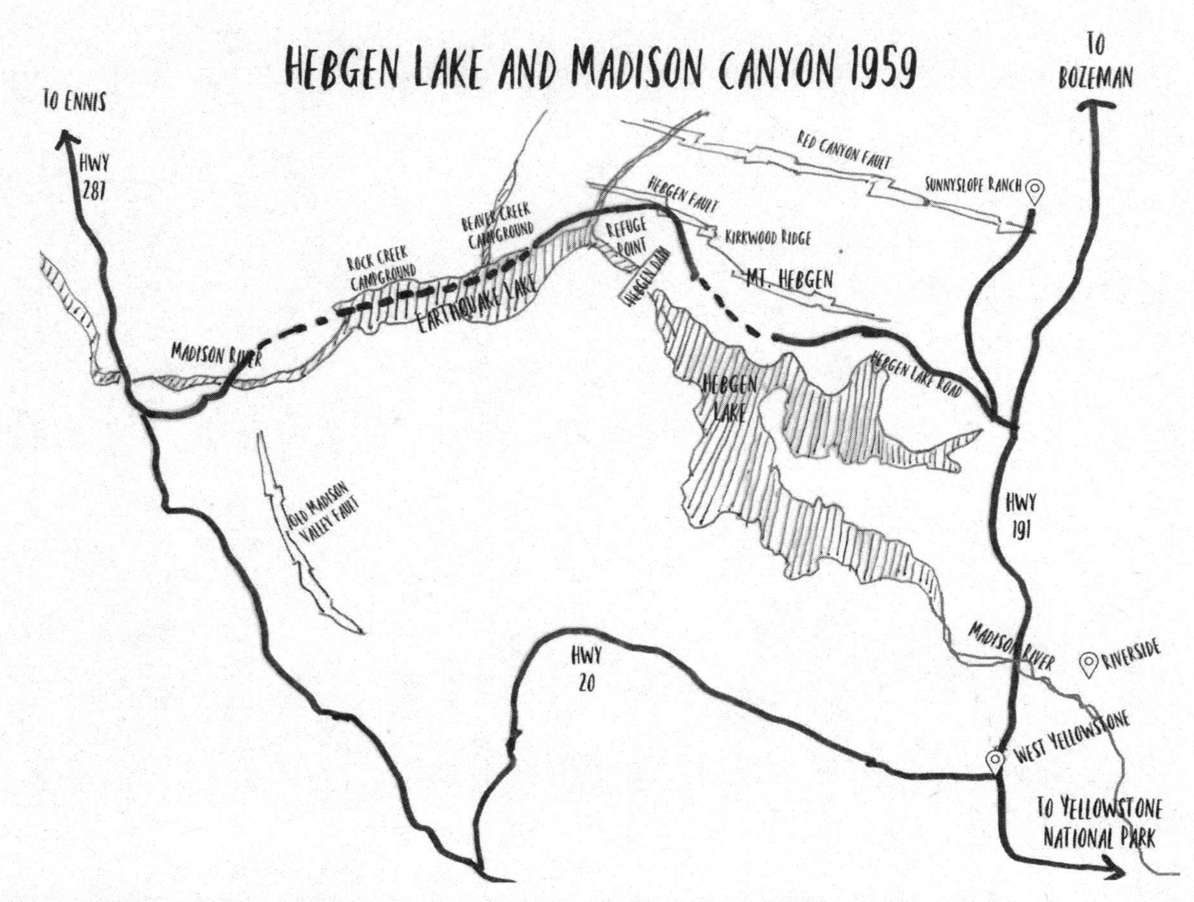
HEBGEN LAKE AND MADISON CANYON 1959
TO ENNIS
HWY 287
TO BOZEMAN
RED CANYON FAULT
SUNNYSLOPE RANCH
HEBGEN FAULT
KIRKWOOD RIDGE
BEAVER CREEK CAMPGROUND
REFUGE POINT
ROCK CREEK CAMPGROUND
MT. HEBGEN
HEBGEN DAM
EARTHQUAKE LAKE
MADISON RIVER
HEBGEN LAKE
HEBGEN LAKE ROAD
OLD MADISON VALLEY FAULT
HWY 191
MADISON RIVER
RIVERSIDE
HWY 20
WEST YELLOWSTONE
TO YELLOWSTONE NATIONAL PARK

prologue

CLAIRE

January 1942
Willmar, Minnesota

The day Mother left, Claire got a gold star for her report on Yellowstone National Park.

She couldn't wait to get home. She tugged at Bridget's hand to keep her from dawdling on the cold walk from Willmar Elementary to their house on First Street. The sharp wind bit at Claire's cheeks and gray slush seeped into her Mary Janes. Dad would come home from work tonight and tell Claire he was proud. Mother might even smile like she used to. Claire burst through the kitchen door with her report in one hand, Bridget's mittened fingers in the other.

Something wasn't right.

Dad was home in the middle of the day. He and Mother sat at the kitchen table. Mother wore her church coat and the pretty hat with the feather, and Dad held baby Frannie on his lap. Claire's report with the gold star fell to the floor.

"I want a cookie," Bridget demanded as she took off her coat.

"Not now, Bridget," Claire told her. Bridget was just six and maybe she didn't see that something was wrong with Dad's face and Mother wasn't looking at them.

"Claire and Bridget," Dad said, and his voice sounded hard, like it did sometimes at night when he and Mother were talking and Claire was supposed to be asleep. "Your mother has something to tell you both."

Mother didn't say anything. Bridget's hand searched for Claire's. Claire grabbed at her sister's cold fingers and laced them with her own. She felt like maybe she was getting a stomachache.

Mother looked at them finally, and her face looked like she had an ache in her stomach, too. "Girls, I'm going to live in another town. I have a job there."

Claire didn't understand at first. Who would take care of them when Dad was at the store? Who would make dinner and wash their clothes and feed the baby? Unless . . . Claire's stomach pinched even more. "Are you taking us with you?"

Mother didn't answer.

"You're staying with me," Dad said. "All three of you."

"I'll come back to visit," Mother said.

Dad frowned when Mother said that.

"Kiss me goodbye." Mother bent down to them.

Bridget kissed her—because she always did what Mother and Dad said—but Claire didn't want to. If she didn't kiss her, maybe she wouldn't go. Mother leaned down and pressed a kiss on Claire's cheek. Her lips were sticky with lipstick and she smelled like the perfume she kept on her dresser and hardly ever used.

"I want a cookie," Bridget said again, but this time her voice was weak and uncertain.

"Claire," Dad said, "take Bridget upstairs and both of you change out of your school clothes."

Claire brought Bridget to the room they shared and helped her out of her dress and into her playclothes. Was Mother leaving because she hadn't been good? Maybe Claire hadn't taken care of baby Frannie as much as she should have. Claire put Bridget's shoes on and tied her laces. "Stay here," Claire said. "I'll be right back." She ran down the stairs with her heart pounding.

Mother stood beside the front door with a suitcase in her hand. "Marie," Dad's voice had that bad sound again. "I meant what I said."

"Daniel, it's not fair." Mother's voice sounded like she was going to cry.

Dad made a sound in his throat. "I'm thinking of the girls."

Mother turned the doorknob and pulled at the door.

Claire's eyes prickled and her chest felt like it did when she held her breath for a long time. Mothers didn't leave their children. Claire pushed past Dad and wrapped her arms around Mother's legs. "Mommy," Claire said. Claire hadn't called her mommy since she was littler than Bridget. "Don't go, please. I'll be good. We'll be good I promise." Claire rushed on. "I'll take care of Frannie at night when she cries. And—and I'll do the dishes in the morning before school, I promise."

"Claire," Mother's voice was a whisper. "I have to go."

"No," Claire said. "You can't." Mothers and fathers stayed with their children and they all lived together.

Dad untangled Claire's hands and pulled her back. Claire struggled against her dad's hold, a sob working up her chest. "Please, don't go," Claire said. "Please don't go."

But the door shut and Mother was gone.

The sob broke free and hot tears blurred her sight. She would come back. She'd change her mind. She'd miss them. Wouldn't she miss them?

Dad sat down on the stairs and pulled Claire into his lap. He held her tight and whispered, "Don't worry, sweetheart. We don't need her. I promise you, we'll be fine without her."

chapter 1

CLAIRE

August 1959
West Yellowstone, Montana

Claire was in the back aisle of Eagle's Store reading the label on a box of Gerber cereal when she heard about the drowning.

"His father had to identify him after they pulled him from the river." Tom Eagle's voice carried through the shelves crammed with souvenir knickknacks, western jewelry, and fishing tackle.

Despite the stuffy August heat, a shiver of cold crept up Claire's spine and her hold tightened on the squirming four-month-old in her arms.

"Imagine having to see your son like that," Helen Eagle said sadly.

Claire had lived on the outskirts of Yellowstone National Park for over a year, but it was still shocking how many ways tourists got injured—and died—in the Great American Wonderland. She felt a stab of sympathy for whoever had lost their son in the river as she put the Gerber's back on the shelf and picked up the Pablum, which was ten cents cheaper.

"His poor mother," Helen Eagle went on. "She's lost so much already."

Claire's sympathy turned to a jolt of realization. Whoever Tom and Helen Eagle were talking about wasn't a tourist. The poor family was local.

Jenny let out an unhappy howl. Claire moved her baby to her shoulder, tucked the box of baby cereal under her arm, and made her way around displays of glassware and moccasins to the front of the store.

"Mrs. Wilder," Helen Eagle said as Claire put her purchase next to the old-fashioned cash register. "Will this be all?" Helen Eagle wore a white apron over a striped housedress, her gray-streaked hair gathered in a tight bun on the top of her head. Her dark eyes were as sharp as a magpie's as she looked down from her perch behind the high counter.

"I couldn't help but overhear," Claire said. "Who was it that drowned?"

Helen Eagle and her husband exchanged a look Claire couldn't fathom and Helen hesitated as if she didn't want to share the news. "Dell Henshaw," she finally said in a curt voice.

"Oh, no." Claire had only met Dell the one time, back when he and Red had been friends. He was so young . . . and his sweet wife. Her heart squeezed hard in her chest. "Poor Beth." Jenny began a stuttering cry, and Claire bounced gently to soothe her. "I'll stop in and give her my condolences." Even if she didn't know Beth, it was the kind thing to do.

Helen jabbed at the cash register. "That will be forty-eight cents."

Claire juggled Jenny and opened her purse, fished out two quarters, and glanced up. "Where did it happen?"

Helen's mouth pursed into a knot and she looked away as if she hadn't heard the question. Claire slid the coins across the counter with a pang of annoyance. How long must she live in West Yellowstone before she graduated from outsider to local? Everyone from the Eagles to the gas station attendant treated her like an interloper no matter how hard she tried.

Tom Eagle's weathered face creased in a frown. "In the Yellowstone."

Claire couldn't hide her surprise. "What was Dell doing up there?" The Yellowstone River was at the northern edge of the park, at least fifty miles from where they were now.

"Perhaps you should ask that husband of yours," came Helen Eagle's terse reply.

Claire's eyes widened and heat flooded up her neck. What was Helen Eagle implying? Jenny started to fuss with a stuttering cry that meant she would soon be wailing.

Tom Eagle handed her two cents and ignored his wife's jab. "I wouldn't go over to Pete Henshaw's place if I were you, Mrs. Wilder. Not with how things are."

Claire's grip tightened on the pennies. Red and Dell had once been friends, but they weren't now. Could that be what Helen and Tom were getting at? She raised her brows and gave Tom Eagle a politely enquiring look. "What do you mean?"

Tom Eagle glanced at his wife. Helen's mouth pinched and she glared at him. He shrugged. "Best not poke the bear, is all I'm saying."

Claire left Eagle's Store with a crying baby and a sickening turn in her stomach. Jenny's sobs rose to a fever pitch as she crossed West Yellowstone's Main Street to where she'd parked the truck. The street was lined with cars, campers, and yellow tour buses making their way to the park entrance for a day of sightseeing. Tourists dressed in madras shorts with cameras slung around their necks crowded the western-style boardwalk, children begged for ice cream, and a horse snorted at the hitching post in front of the Slippery Otter saloon.

She climbed into the Chevy truck—mottled with rust spots and faded blue paint—and settled Jenny on the seat beside her. "We'll be home soon, sweet pea," Claire promised as she turned the key in the ignition. Her daughter was hungry, tired, and possibly needing a diaper change. When Red got home from work tonight, she'd ask him about Dell Henshaw . . . and whatever it was that Helen Eagle was implying.

The engine caught, sputtered, and died.

She tried again. This time, the engine revved for a hopeful moment . . . then clunked to silence.

"You need a hand, Mrs. Wilder?" The gravelly voice came through her open window. "I'm sure Helen will let you call Red from the store phone."

Claire looked out the window to see Grace Miller standing on the sidewalk. The woman wore men's jeans and a long-sleeved shirt even in the August heat. A well-worn cowboy hat shaded her lined face and two silver braids glinted in the sunlight.

She did indeed need a hand, much as she hated to admit it. "Mrs. Miller"—Claire raised her voice over Jenny's cries—"would you mind holding Jenny for a moment?" Claire scooped Jenny out of the hot-as-a-furnace cab and deposited her in Grace Miller's arms. Miraculously, Jenny's cries ceased and Claire let out a breath of relief. Her daughter was always fascinated by a new face, even a scowling one like Grace Miller's.

"Well." Grace Miller looked down at Jenny's tear-wet cheeks and wide blue eyes. "I think she likes me."

Claire reached into the truck bed for the crescent wrench, her thoughts returning to Dell and Beth Henshaw. And Red. Grace Miller had lived in West Yellowstone all her life . . . but it didn't seem right to pry about the Henshaws. Or about her own husband.

As if Grace Miller had read her mind, she shot Claire a sideways glance. "Shame about Dell Henshaw."

Claire nodded.

"Pete and Iris lost their older boy in Korea," Grace Miller said. "Now with Dell gone, it's just the two of them."

Claire stopped her task with a rush of sympathy. "Oh, how horrible." To lose not only one but both of their children.

Grace sighed. "And Beth, a widow so young."

Claire pushed up the heavy hood of the truck, propping it with the metal rod like Red had shown her, her thoughts on the couple she'd met almost two years ago—the summer she'd come out to Yellowstone and met Red. She'd seen in an instant that Beth and Dell were crazy about each other.

"You know Beth's parents disowned her when she married Dell?" Grace Miller went on as if Claire had asked her to elaborate. "So did her uncle." Grace rescued her leather stampede strings from Jenny's grasp before she was able to get them to her mouth. "'Course, Wormsbecker isn't known for his soft heart."

Claire climbed up on the truck's front bumper and leaned over the engine to reach the carburetor. She was well acquainted with Walt Wormsbecker's hard nature, but she hadn't known about Beth's parents. Claire hit the carburetor none too gently with the wrench. And she didn't know what had happened between Dell and her husband to end their friendship. When she had arrived in Riverside—newly married to Red and blissfully happy—she'd set up housekeeping and suggested to Red they invite Dell and his young wife over for dinner and a game of bridge. "We had a falling-out," was all Red said. The way he'd avoided her eyes and went silent kept her from asking more. She knew some things were hard to talk about.

Grace Miller came around the truck to watch her. "Dell and Red used to be as thick as thieves before all that business, you know."

Claire froze, the wrench raised for another blow to the carburetor. *Thick as thieves. Best not poke the bear. All that business.* Why did it seem like the residents of West Yellowstone spoke in code and she didn't have the secret decoder ring? She bit down on the urge to ask about *all that business*. Red should be the one to tell her what Grace Miller—and Helen Eagle—were hinting at.

Claire climbed back in the cab. Her denim pedal pushers were smeared with oil, and her sleeveless cotton blouse was damp with sweat. She turned the key and tapped the gas pedal. The engine sputtered, caught, and roared to life.

Thank the Lord. She revved it a few times to be sure. She just wanted to get home and get Jenny down for her nap, then get dinner ready for Red. Even if they hadn't spoken in years, Red would grieve for his one-time friend. She slid out of the truck and held out her hands for Jenny.

Grace Miller wasn't ready to give Jenny up.

Grace smiled down at Jenny's wide-eyed stare and talked to her in a slightly higher-pitched voice. "Heard your daddy and Dell got into it at the Slippery Otter a couple nights ago."

Claire frowned and glanced at the West Yellowstone watering hole across the street. That couldn't be. Red didn't go to the Slippery Otter, and he would have told her if he'd had an argument with Dell Henshaw. Wouldn't he?

She took Jenny from Grace Miller's hold and held her close, her heart tripping up a notch. The question left her mouth before she could stop it, ending her attempt to not pry. "What night was that, Mrs. Miller?"

Grace's brows went up in surprise. "Sunday evening, from what I heard."

The sick drop of her stomach made her falter. She turned abruptly and settled Jenny on the bench seat of the truck. "I need to get her home. Thank you for your help, Mrs. Miller."

"Nice talkin' to you, Mrs. Wilder," Grace Miller drawled.

Claire put the truck in gear and jerked into the flow of tourist traffic. Her mind spun with questions. Shouldn't she know her husband better than Grace Miller and Helen Eagle? Her father's words—uttered just before he refused to walk her down the aisle to marry Red Wilder—echoed in response.

You don't even know him, Claire. Don't make the biggest mistake of your life.

chapter 2

RED

Red sat at the bar in the Slippery Otter with a beer he didn't want, surrounded by people he didn't particularly like. He forced a gulp of beer past the knot in his throat, the bitterness lingering in his mouth.

Dell was dead. The stupid kid.

This day had turned sour as soon as he rode Rosie into the Sunnyslope Ranch this morning and saw David Endicott's baby-blue Cadillac. Sunnyslope was one of the bigger spreads near West Yellowstone and on most days, a good job for somebody like him. Walt Wormsbecker had a nice setup overlooking Hebgen Lake with a three-story ranch house, a bunkhouse, and a couple of guest cottages. He ran two hundred head of cattle and thirty horses, but the boss's real money came from the fishing trips and big-game hunting he provided for tourists.

Most wranglers and ranchers hated tourists, but Red didn't mind them. He'd been a city kid once, and when he'd found Montana his life had changed. Everybody deserved to see the wide-open spaces. No, it wasn't tourists that got Red hot under the collar—it was phonies like David Endicott. Men who wore expensive cowboy hats and shiny boots but didn't know one end of a horse from the other.

The sun was coming over the Absarokas when he tied Rosie's lead rope to the rail and went to the pasture to get the mounts they'd need for the day. As much as Red disliked Endicott, putting up with him was part of his job. He led Flick—a sure-footed mule who could carry a heavy load—to the rail just as Bucky came over with a sick look on his face.

"It's Dell," Bucky said, his voice breaking.

Red's jaw went tight. "What about him?" If that kid got caught and was in jail, Red wasn't going to bail him out. Not this time.

Bucky looked down at his boots, his throat working. "Wormsbecker just got word over the shortwave. He drowned."

Red's gut turned over and he put a hand on Flick to steady himself. "Where?"

"In the Yellowstone."

Red had expected that answer. He'd warned Dell about that river, but the kid hadn't listened. He met Bucky's gaze and they both looked over at the baby-blue Cadillac.

"Do you think . . . ?" Bucky glanced back at him.

Red shook his head. No way to prove it, and who would believe him, anyway?

He went back to saddling Flick. Poor Pete and Iris Henshaw had another dead son. A rush of anger—of regret and guilt and a storm of emotions—swelled through him. *Dell, you stupid, stupid kid. Why didn't you listen?*

Red led the group of hunters up Mount Hebgen, trying not to think about Dell or his parents or Beth. Wormsbecker came next, pointing out spots for the six-day hunt Endicott had booked in October. Endicott rode beside his father-in-law, Ian Meyer, a decent man who had hunted with them last year and bagged a nice-sized elk. Bucky brought up the rear with a portly accountant type named Topper who looked like he'd never sat on a horse before.

The trail was shadowed and the sun low in the sky when they returned to the ranch. Endicott gave Flick a jab with his fancy cowboy boots, spurring his mount past Red as if they were in a race. "Next time I want a real horse," he groused as he slid out of the saddle. "Not this donkey."

Red gritted his teeth. Flick was a mule, not a donkey, and deserved better treatment.

"Come with us to the Slippery Otter, Red." Meyer tried to smooth things over. "I'm buying."

Red was hot and dusty and wanted nothing more than to get away from Endicott and get home to Claire and Jenny.

"That's mighty kind of you, Ian." Wormsbecker jumped in. "Red and Bucky will take care of the horses and meet us there." Red opened his mouth to refuse but Wormsbecker stopped him with a hard look and leaned close, lowering his voice. "You gotta make sure they leave thinking they've made friends with the wranglers."

Red let out a silent breath of defeat. He couldn't afford to defy his boss.

Now, he sat at the bar, thinking over his last conversation with Dell. Red took another sip of his beer and caught Wormsbecker watching him. His surly look said he expected Red to make nice with the clients.

Bucky was a few stools down, listening to Topper, so Red shifted his attention to Meyer. "How's that granddaughter of yours, Mr. Meyer?"

The older man grinned. "You remembered." Last fall Meyer had talked a blue streak about the girl. "She's a real firecracker." He slid a color photo of a bucktoothed ten-year-old out of his wallet. "Luckily, she's a lot like her mother."

Red admired the picture. "Cute as a button."

The older man beamed. "You have a family, Red?"

Red jerked a nod. "Wife and a little girl."

"Got a picture?" Meyer asked.

Of course he had a picture. He pulled out his wallet and the photo of Jenny, taken just a couple weeks ago when she turned four months. "Prettiest baby in the world," he said, unable to hide the pride in his voice when he showed the black and white.

Endicott leaned around Meyer and snatched the photo from Red's hand. "Well, now, Red"— he looked at it with raised brows—"I didn't know you were a family man. Let's see one of your wife. Is she pretty?"

Red's pulse tripped up a notch. Wild horses couldn't get him to show Claire's picture to Endicott. Red reached to rescue Jenny's photo from Endicott's critical gaze, but the man raised the picture over his head, just out of Red's grasp.

Red clenched his jaw and a wave of heat went up his neck. "Give it back, Endicott."

"That's Mr. Endicott to you," Endicott answered with narrowed eyes. "And say please."

"Knock it off, David," Meyer said, his voice holding an edge of warning.

Endicott ignored his father-in-law and kept his eyes on Red. "Say it."

Bucky pushed back his stool and stood, letting Red know without a word that he was there if Red needed him.

Meyer laid a hand on Red's shoulder. "Some things aren't worth fighting for, son."

Red wanted to disagree, but he knew Wormsbecker was watching. Heck, everybody in the bar was watching to see if Red kowtowed to this bully. His fists clenched as he considered his options. Give Endicott the fight he was asking for and lose his job. Or swallow his pride and keep bringing home a paycheck. He glanced at Meyer. The man was right—Endicott wasn't worth it. "Give it back, Mr. Endicott," Red finally said, his voice tight. "Please."

Endicott flicked the photo into a puddle of beer on the bar.

Red grabbed at the photo, but the liquid had already flooded over Jenny's bright face, turning the picture into a muddy blur.

"And anyway," Endicott said in a voice loud enough to carry all the way across the Slippery Otter, "she's not the most beautiful baby in the world. Not by a long shot."

Red's vision went dark at the edges. Some things weren't worth fighting for, like Meyer said. But some things were.

Red's fist connected with Endicott's jaw with a satisfying crack.

That was for Jenny.

Endicott rounded on him, but the big man was too slow and Red got a second hit to his gut.

That was for Claire.

Topper came at Red, but Bucky stepped in and slowed him down. Red felt a rush of heat through his veins. He pulled his fist back one last time. And that—he slammed it into David Endicott's nose with a satisfying crunch—was for Dell.

By the time Sheriff Eagle showed up at the Slippery Otter, Endicott had an ice pack on his nose and Wormsbecker was in a cold fury. "Red," his boss said as the sheriff directed him and Bucky into the police cruiser, "don't bother coming to work tomorrow. You're fired."

chapter 3

CLAIRE

It was eight o'clock and Red wasn't home.

Claire looked out the kitchen window as she dried the dish from her solitary dinner. The sky pinked in the west, shadowing to periwinkle blue over the Gallatin Range in the east. She peered down the trail to the river, hoping to see Red riding Rosie home through the twilight. The aspen trees shivered in the breeze, but no Red.

She tried not to think of Dell Henshaw drowning in the Yellowstone, or Helen and Tom Eagle, or Grace Miller. Or about Sunday night when Red had taken the truck to the ranch after dinner. To see about a mare, he'd said. He came home after she put Jenny to bed. They sat at the kitchen table, Red playing solitaire and Claire teasing him about how he always lost. "Might win this time," he said, like he always did. Not a word about the Slippery Otter or Dell Henshaw.

Red would have a perfectly good explanation for Grace Miller's gossip and Helen Eagle's cold comments.

When he got home.

When Claire married Red, she knew her life would be different than how she grew up in Willmar, with Dad coming home from the store every night at exactly five fifteen, and Flo putting dinner on the table at five thirty. Red's job was unpredictable. He could be tending to a lame horse, or a fence that needed mending.

She wasn't worried.

Claire paced to the bedroom to check on Jenny. She was sleeping peacefully, curled up like a little bear cub. Claire touched her soft hair, the red hue so like her father's catching the last of the evening light. Claire went out the back door to the pasture. Marigold nickered, and ambled over to the fence. "Hello, beautiful." Claire laid her cheek on Marigold's soft neck and breathed in her horsey scent.

Her heartbeat slowed and she let out a long breath.

She couldn't have been more surprised when Red had a horse waiting for her when they arrived in Riverside. Her own horse. "When—how?" she asked him, dazzled by the mare's golden coat that caught the sunlight, her creamy white mane and tail. "I bought her last fall," he said, "for your wedding present."

"Last fall?" Claire asked. That didn't make any sense. "When I went home to Minnesota and told you I wasn't coming back?"

He looked down and smiled at his boots like he did when he was pleased with himself.

Claire stared at him, then back at her gift. She'd come to Yellowstone for a summer of adventure. Falling in love with a cowboy hadn't been in her plans. Then she met Red Wilder. Red had asked Claire to marry him a dozen times during their whirlwind romance. Each time he asked, she'd said no. Of course she said no.

Red kept asking.

Marigold nuzzled her shirt pocket, looking for her evening carrot. When Claire got on the bus to go back to her life in Minnesota—to her sisters, her students at Tara School, her father—she told Red goodbye in no uncertain terms. But Red hadn't given up. He bought her a horse, and the next spring drove to Minnesota and asked her one last time to marry him, standing in the gray spring snow outside Tara School.

She'd said yes.

Claire fished the carrot from her pocket and Marigold gently took it from her palm with soft, whiskery lips. Red hadn't given up hope for her—for their life together.

When ten o'clock came, Claire paced from the kitchen window to the front door. She tried to pray. Why was it so easy to see God—to speak to him—in the beauty of a sunset or the majesty of the mountains but here in the dark her words felt empty and useless? She switched on the radio, keeping the volume low so she wouldn't wake Jenny. Most days, it didn't bother her that the phone had been disconnected, but tonight she wished she could call Sunnyslope and find out what was keeping Red. Or at least phone Bridget for a long talk to take her mind off where Red could be at this late hour. She and Bridget hadn't had a good talk since Christmas—and even then, the price of long distance made for a rushed conversation.

The hollow emptiness of homesickness came over Claire like a flood, the silence of the house reminding her how alone she was in Riverside. She would write to Bridget. That might be just the distraction she needed. She took out her stationery and the fountain pen Dad gave her for her eighteenth birthday.

Dear Bridget . . .

She stared at the words and thought about Beth Henshaw. The poor girl's story wasn't very different from her own. Beth had come out to Yellowstone to work on her uncle's ranch and met Dell there, the same summer Claire had worked at Old Faithful and met Red. According to Grace Miller, Beth had married against her families' wishes, like Claire. They had both started their married lives in new and unfamiliar places, as outsiders.

But Beth Henshaw's story hadn't had a happy ending.

Had Beth's father warned her, like Dad had warned Claire? Had he told Beth she was making a big mistake? Did Beth have a sister or friends she could turn to?

After their hurried wedding, Claire and Red had left for their new home in Riverside and she hadn't been home for a visit since. Between the bills and a baby, it just hadn't been possible. Now—in the lonely house—home sounded heavenly. Her old bedroom and long talks with Bridget. Flo's cheerful gossip and home-cooked meals. Her friends and familiar surroundings. It would even be nice to see Frannie.

A knock on the door made Claire jump, scattering her stationery to the floor.

Her heart pounded against her ribs. Red wouldn't knock.

She made herself take a deep breath and stood on shaky legs, telling herself she wouldn't open the door to find the sheriff with his hat in his hands, terrible news written on his face. She walked across the tiny sitting room toward the front door and pulled it open.

Bucky stood in the glare of the porch light. He took off his hat and looked at his boots. His pale blond hair was plastered to his head and a stark tan line crossed his forehead. She waited, mouth too dry to speak, her pulse pounding.

Finally, he got the words out. "Red won't be home tonight."

Claire swallowed. "Where is he, Bucky?" *In a river? At the bottom of a cliff? In the hospital at Mammoth?*

Bucky finally managed to get out, "In jail."

Claire leaned against the doorframe, relief rushing through her. He wasn't dead like Dell Henshaw. *Thank God.* Then, consternation. Jail? That couldn't possibly be true.

"I would have come by earlier but . . ." Bucky twisted his hat in his hands. His knuckles were red, and as he raised his face to the porch light she saw a cut on his lip. Bucky's voice dropped to a mumble she had to strain to decipher. "Red's gotta stay 'til morning, Sheriff said."

Claire wanted to sit Bucky down and demand a full explanation—*Why is he in jail? What happened?*—but Bucky looked so miserable already. "Have you eaten?" she asked instead.

Bucky shifted his weight from one foot to another as if given the choice between a homemade meal and escape, he'd take escape.

"Wait here." He might as well eat Red's dinner instead of heating up a can of Campbell's soup like he did most evenings. Claire took Red's plate from the oven and wrapped it in a towel. Bucky got out a thank-you and bolted toward his house across the road like a bear was chasing him.

Claire shut the door and leaned against it for a moment. Her thrumming pulse slowed, but heat rose up her neck. In jail? She'd never even known anyone who had been in jail, and now her husband was incarcerated? Claire walked to the kitchen, and crossed her arms over her chest, her thoughts tumbling. Helen Eagle's accusations, Dell's death, Grace Miller. Red in jail while she was home alone, frantic with worry and alone with a baby.

With jerky motions, she gathered her fallen stationery from the floor. *Dear Bridget.* She certainly couldn't write to her sister about this terrible day. She wouldn't know how to begin and she couldn't possibly tell her sister Red was in jail. The heat of her anger drained away, leaving an empty ache for the comfort of home and her family. Her father and her sisters and friends. For goodness' sake, Jenny hadn't even met her aunts and grandpa yet.

Claire stood in the silence of the empty house as the idea of home gained purchase in her mind. Dad wouldn't mind wiring her the money for her ticket. She could take the bus to Livingston, and she and Jenny would be on the train home by tomorrow afternoon.

Home.

She went to the bedroom and quietly opened the closet door. She pulled her suitcase from the top shelf. The sleeveless summer dresses in tropical prints and polka dots that Dad had sent from the store went in first, then a hostess dress she'd never worn, but it would come in handy at home. Claire tossed in a few pairs of shiny pumps, their matching handbags, and some cotton gloves. Jenny's outfits were next—thanks to Dad, she had more pretty dresses than any baby needed—and a stack of diapers.

Claire snapped the latches closed. Red would just have to understand, that's all there was to it.

chapter 4

BRIDGET

Willmar, Minnesota

Bridget made one last notation on the patient chart and thanked the Lord her shift was over. Her feet hurt, her shoulders ached, and she was hungry. All she wanted was a big serving of Flo's Wednesday night meatloaf, then she'd take off her girdle and settle into bed with her book.

"The heart attack in four didn't make it," Bridget informed the junior nurse at the desk as she signed off the floor. The middle-aged man had come in by ambulance to Willmar General last night. "Notify his family, please, Harmon."

"Oh, please, Reilly," the junior nurse said with a catch in her voice. "Can't someone else do it?"

"Harmon," Bridget said firmly, "getting weepy won't help anyone." Bridget hadn't become the youngest supervising nurse at Willmar General by getting emotional about her patients. She was duty bound to be a good example to the junior nurses—at least until her last shift tomorrow.

Bridget said goodbye and pushed through the double doors into the humid August dusk. Most summer evenings, it was a pleasure to walk the six blocks home after work, but with the way her feet felt tonight she wished she'd learned how to drive. Her regret doubled when she saw Chuck Reed lurking under the streetlight.

"Bridget." Chuck stepped forward with a hopeful expression on his handsome face. "Can I give you a ride home?"

Bridget mustered a polite smile. "No, thank you. I enjoy the walk." Chuck fell into step beside her. She stopped with a sigh and looked up at him. "Really, Chuck. I meant what I said." They'd met when Chuck brought his mother in with a broken ankle, and Bridget had enjoyed his company on a few dates . . . until he started to get serious. She'd broken things off in the usual way, but Chuck didn't get the memo.

"Is this about you going to Yellowstone?" Chuck said. "Because I'll wait."

"Goodness no." Bridget's gaze met his brown eyes. This wasn't about Yellowstone, and she didn't need a lovesick man waiting for her. She wasn't like Claire, ready to rush to the altar with someone she hardly knew. "Like I said, Chuck, I'm just not interested." She brushed past him, ignoring the crushed expression on his face. Of course she felt bad for him, but it had to be done.

Ten minutes later, Bridget quietly let herself in the front door of the three-story house where she'd lived all her life. She hoped she could sneak in, get the plate Flo had left in the warming oven, and get upstairs before she saw either her father or Frannie. She'd taken one careful step on the polished wood floor of the foyer when her hopes went out the window.

"I'm not a child!" Frannie's voice came from the kitchen.

"Then stop acting like one." Dad sounded fed up.

Good grief. They were at it again.

Bridget peeked around the doorway. The kitchen with its polished Kenmore stove and buttercup-yellow refrigerator was spotless, but the air brimmed with tension. Dad stood beside the kitchen table, his arms crossed and looking exhausted. He was only in his fifties, but his hair had gone white earlier than most men. Raising three girls on his own would do that, he was known to say with a laugh. Dad wasn't laughing now.

Frannie faced Dad like a boxer ready for the bell, wearing her standard getup of rolled denim jeans, an oversized men's shirt, and sneakers. She was more petite than either Bridget or Claire, but what she lacked in size, she made up for in fight. "I can make my own decisions, thank you very much."

"Like the one that got you kicked out of summer school?" Dad shot back. "And how are you going to get into teachers' college with that on your permanent record?"

"I'm not going to that stupid college," Frannie spit out.

"This is about that juvenile delinquent, isn't it?" Dad asked, and Bridget stifled a groan.

Frannie's voice increased like someone had dialed up her volume knob. "Jonny's not a delinquent."

"He got you arrested," Dad snapped back.

Frannie stamped her foot. "We were having fun."

"No daughter of mine is going to go around with a bunch of lunatics."

"What about my rights?" Frannie's voice peaked on a high note of indignation.

"Your rights?" Dad scoffed. "What a bunch of baloney."

Bridget stepped into the kitchen. This needed to stop before Frannie got herself grounded for life.

"I hate it here and I hate you!" Frannie bolted from the kitchen, pushing past Bridget and pounding up the stairs. The door to her room slammed and muffled sobs filtered through the heating vent on the ceiling.

Dad sank into a kitchen chair and rubbed a hand down his face. "Her rights," he muttered, then looked up at Bridget. "What am I going to do with her?"

Bridget didn't have an answer. Frannie had been a handful since she turned sixteen, as if the magic number had released a monster.

When Claire was here, at least they'd been able to reason with her. "I'll go talk to her."

Dad gave her a tired nod. "Good luck, sweetheart."

She went up the stairs and let herself into Frannie's room. Her sister was lying on her pink chenille bedspread sniffling, and two flounced pillows lay across the room on the floor. Bridget dredged up a kernel of sympathy, remembering the little girl she and Claire had dressed and walked to school, holding her hand to cross the streets. Why had Claire left Bridget with this mess?

Frannie threw a third pillow across the room. "He hates me."

Bridget sat down on the bed and smoothed Frannie's short blonde hair away from her tearstained face. When was her little sister going to stop being such a baby? At eighteen, Bridget had been studying to get her nursing degree, not failing high school and getting arrested for climbing the water tower. Her courses and then working at the hospital had required her to grow up fast and keep her emotions under control. "That's ridiculous and you know it."

"It's true." Frannie turned her face to the wall and her voice went to a whisper. "I'm the reason Mother left us."

Bridget stared at the back of her sister's head, too stunned to answer. They never spoke of Mother. And how could Frannie blame herself for something that happened when she was a baby? She pulled at Frannie's shoulder, a sudden emotion welling in her chest as her eyes smarted. "Frances Marie Reilly, that is absolute nonsense."

Frannie blinked and two tears ran from the corners of her eyes.

Bridget swallowed hard. This wasn't the time to get sentimental and certainly not about something so long ago nobody even remembered it. "Mother didn't leave because of you or me or Dad or anyone."

"Then why did she?" Frannie whispered.

Bridget didn't know. And it didn't matter. "It doesn't help to go digging up the past." It was what Claire always said, and Bridget believed it, too. "And anyway, we're just fine without her."

Bridget wiped the tears from Frannie's face with a corner of the crisp cotton sheet, then leaned down and kissed her forehead like she'd done when Frannie was small. "Go to sleep now and don't forget your prayers." She covered her little sister with the bedspread. "Things always look brighter in the morning."

When Bridget finally settled down with her book in her bedroom across the hall, the predictable plot and romantic settings didn't let her escape her thoughts. What had got into Frannie, talking about Mother? Did she really blame herself for their mother leaving, or was it just another way for Frannie to be dramatic?

Bridget slipped the bookmark into the pages and turned off the lamp. She'd take her own advice and hope that things would look better in the morning.

Bridget woke early, washed her face, and dressed in her nurse's uniform for her last shift at Willmar General. Downstairs, Dad sat in the dining room in his suit and pressed shirt, looking like he hadn't slept a wink. The newspaper was folded in front of him instead of open to the baseball scores.

"Morning." Bridget grabbed the toast Flo had put out. "Do you need anything at Rexall's?" She had a list of sundries she needed for her trip, then she had an appointment at the hair salon before her shift started.

"Bridget." Dad motioned to the chair opposite him.

Bridget glanced at the door. She really had so much to do today.

"It's important."

"Is this about Yellowstone again?" He wasn't going to fuss about her trip now that everything was arranged, was he?

"It's about Claire." He pushed an envelope across the table. "Got this in the morning mail."

The envelope was addressed to her but already opened. She felt a twinge of irritation. She would have shared the letter with Dad, of course, but would it hurt to let her read Claire's letter first? She pulled the single sheet from the envelope and a twenty-dollar bill fluttered to the table.

Bridget read through the few lines and glanced up at her dad. "She says she's fine."

"I don't think she is."

Neither did Bridget. The letter was like the rest they'd been getting for the past six months—woefully short and uninformative. "She wants you to take back the money, of course." Dad insisted on sending money every week and every week Claire sent it back.

Dad took the letter back, as if he could read something more between the lines of perfect cursive. "When she went out to that place with Millie, she wrote pages of news every week. And sent photos. I only have one picture of my grandchild. And this." He waved the single sheet. "Something isn't right."

Dad always referred to Yellowstone—where Claire had gone to work for a summer with Millie two years ago, and where she'd met Red—as *that place*. When Claire came home after that summer, Dad hugged her like she was returning from war and told everyone that she had got that adventure out of her system.

He'd been wrong.

Claire had put her toe in the water, and then promptly jumped in over her head.

Bridget tucked the letter back in its envelope, leaving the money where it lay. "She's busy with Jenny. That's all." She didn't want him to worry about Claire until she knew what was going on.

Dad picked up a piece of toast, then set it down on his plate without taking a bite. "It's not right to raise a baby without family, Bridget. You tell Claire that. She needs to come home. I can give Red a job at the store and they can live here until they find a place of their own."

Bridget raised her brows. It would be wonderful to have Claire back home, especially if Bridget's plan for September worked out as she hoped. But Red working at the menswear counter of Reilly's Department Store? Taking orders from Dad and living under his roof?

She didn't know Red well, but that suit didn't fit. Still, it wouldn't hurt to ask Claire about it.

"I'll mention it, Dad." She hoped that was all he needed or she was going to miss her hair appointment.

"Promise me, Bridget." Dad reached across the table and gripped Bridget's hand. "Promise me you'll bring your sister and Jenny home." His voice was somehow desperate and demanding at the same time.

Bridget felt the beginnings of alarm. "I'll talk to her, Dad."

He didn't loosen his grip. "And if Red won't come"—his worried eyes met hers—"you bring Claire and Jenny back without him."

Bridget stared at her father. "Dad, I don't think—"

"Red will come around if he really does love her," he insisted.

Bridget considered her Dad's reasoning. If Red loved Claire, of course he'd want what was best for her. But would this be best for Claire? Living at home with Dad and her new husband? She wasn't so sure.

"Bridget," Dad said, this time gentle and pleading. "Promise me."

She felt a wrench of dismay. She never could defy Dad like Claire and Frannie did. His gaze met hers and her resistance crumbled. "I promise, Dad." She wanted to take the words back as soon as she spoke them. "I have to go."

"One other thing, Bridget," Dad said, opening his newspaper and turning to the baseball scores.

What could it be now? Bridget hoped it was something easy like reminding Flo to bring his suit to the cleaners.

"It's about Frannie." He looked up at her and Bridget had a sinking feeling she wasn't going to like what came next. "She's going to Yellowstone with you."

chapter 5

CLAIRE

Riverside, Montana

Claire woke up alone after a restless night and her gaze fell on the packed suitcase next to Jenny's crib. Of course she couldn't run home to Minnesota. If she went home—without Red—Dad would get it all wrong, just like he did about the bear.

When Claire first settled into Riverside, she wrote long letters to Dad and Bridget and Frannie twice a week. She told them all about Marigold and the river out their back door. She described how she and Red fished for their dinner, and how she helped Red skin and cut up an elk that would feed them all winter. Claire thought maybe Dad would finally understand how she loved her new life, the new person she'd become—and he'd see how wrong he was about Red.

Then she'd made the mistake of writing about the bear.

Dad had telephoned her in a panic in the middle of the day. "What's wrong?" she asked him, her heart climbing into her throat at the long-distance call during daytime rates. It had to be an emergency. "Is it Frannie?"

It was about the letter he'd just opened. "I'm coming out," he said, his voice tense. Claire could practically see the anxiety in his eyes, the deep furrow on his brow. "We'll find you a new place to rent, a safer place—I'll pay for it myself if Red can't afford it."

She winced at the very thought. "Dad, don't be ridiculous."

"You were alone, Claire," he went on. "You could have been mauled—killed. What were you thinking?"

"Red taught me how to shoot."

"So you shot a bear?" Dad shouted down the line.

"I shot *toward* a bear," Claire corrected. "And it was just a black bear." She'd been home alone while Red led a six-day elk hunt for Wormsbecker. It was a stupid mistake, leaving a bushel of apples on the back porch overnight, and when she heard the bear grunting and crashing around, she knew she had to scare him off. She didn't want a bear thinking her house was his cafeteria. She grabbed the loaded shotgun, cracked open the back door, and shot at the sky. The bear wailed and clattered down the steps, hightailing it back to the river. It took twenty minutes on the telephone to calm Dad down. Claire couldn't let him come out and humiliate Red—not after what happened at the wedding.

Since then, she'd kept her letters short and sweet—the weather, thank-yous for the gifts of dresses and shoes, and inquiring about Bridget and Frannie. Nothing to worry about. And when she couldn't pay the telephone bill, it was a small mercy that Dad couldn't call to check on her.

She slipped out of bed as Jenny started to wake. She'd wait to go home with Red, when they could afford to buy the tickets themselves. She shoved the suitcase under the bed and went to make coffee and warm a bottle. An hour later, when Jenny was fed and dressed and Claire had started on the laundry, Red finally walked in the door.

He looked terrible. His copper-colored hair was tousled and his eyes were shadowed with fatigue. She glanced at his hands and saw that his knuckles were red and swollen. He swallowed and looked down at his feet like a student caught cheating on a test. "I'm sorry, Claire."

Claire picked up a basket of wet diapers. Was that all he was going to say?

Jenny let out a squeal.

"I'll get her," he said, the relief on his face obvious.

Claire carried the basket out the back door. She'd had a dozen conversations in her head while she'd waited for him. Had he been at the Slippery Otter on Sunday? What did he know about Dell's death? And what on earth had happened last night to land him in jail? But now, her tongue seemed to be stuck to the roof of her mouth.

Red followed her outside, Jenny in his arms.

She put the basket on the grass and turned to see Red watching her like he might watch a skittish horse. They never fought, not in the year and a half they'd been married. She didn't want to fight now. Not when he was looking so miserable. Not when his friend had just died.

"I heard about Dell," she said, instead of giving him the third degree. "I'm sorry."

Red looked past her toward the river. Emotion played over his face, something Claire couldn't read. Grief and regret, perhaps. "He was a good man."

She waited for him to tell her more. About his friendship and how he felt about Dell's death. To open up to her and let her in. To tell her why he'd got in a fight and what secrets he was keeping from her.

She wanted to know his heart, but he was hiding it from her.

He didn't meet her gaze. He kissed the top of Jenny's head and put her into Claire's arms. "I need to get cleaned up and get to work."

Claire had eggs ready for Red after he took a shower and changed into clean clothes. He sat down at the table, but didn't look at her when she put a steaming cup of coffee in front of him. "Jenny slept through the night again," Claire said to break the silence. She didn't say she'd hardly slept a wink.

Jenny, as if she knew they were talking about her, squealed from the spot on the couch where Claire had propped her. Red took a gulp of the hot coffee and nodded as if everything was normal.

She put his eggs on a plate and brought them to the table. They were burnt at the edges and the yolks were hard, but he bolted them down.

"Good eggs," he said.

The white lie made her bristle. She took a sip of her coffee and gathered her courage for one more attempt to get him to talk. "I'm going to the Henshaws' today, to give them my condolences."

His fork stopped halfway to his mouth and his gaze shifted to her. "You don't have to do that, Claire."

She didn't have to, or she shouldn't? "It's the polite thing."

He put down his fork. "They're not that kind of people, Claire. Best to leave them be."

His face was blank, and she was positive now that he was keeping something from her and it had something to do with Dell Henshaw. She picked up his dirty plate and empty coffee cup and brought it to the sink without answering. Suddenly, going to the Henshaws' seemed like just the thing to do.

Red put on his hat and kissed her cheek. "Left Rosie at the ranch. Got to catch Bucky to get a ride to work."

Claire went to the bedroom and settled Jenny on the bed to kick her legs and roll from her front to her back like the *Better Homes & Gardens Baby Book* said she must do at least twice per day. Claire pulled her suitcase from under the bed and began to unpack her dresses.

When she'd first met Red, his quiet nature struck her as romantic—like Gary Cooper or John Wayne in the movies. She'd found out when they married that his silence was also frustrating. Red didn't like to talk about certain things—money, her father, his past. When they came up, he found a reason to see to the horses, or go to work, or just go quiet. Whenever he avoided her eyes like he had today she got a tight uneasiness in her stomach.

Claire opened the top drawer of the dresser to put away Jenny's things. *Best to leave them be,* Red had said about the Henshaws.

But why? Beth was grieving, and Claire could offer her the hand of friendship. She put the suitcase back on the top shelf and picked up Jenny.

After fiddling with the carburetor, Claire got the truck started and drove to Eagle's for a condolence card. "We can't show up at the Henshaws' empty-handed," she said. Jenny squealed in what sounded like agreement. She left the truck running and picked out the first pretty card she saw. Helen Eagle looked at her purchase with raised brows. "That will be ten cents, Mrs. Wilder." Jenny squirmed in Claire's arms as she slapped the dime on the counter and asked for her mail. She shoved the two bills and a letter from Bridget into her purse and left with a polite thank-you to Helen Eagle.

Back in the truck, she wrote a short message inside the card. *If there's ever anything I can do to help, anything at all, let me know.* She drove with one hand on the steering wheel, the other on Jenny, to the Henshaws' place on the north end of town. When she reached the dilapidated two-story, the curtains were closed and no laundry hung on the clothesline. If it wasn't for the red Ford truck in the driveway, she would have thought the house deserted.

Claire felt the prickle of gooseflesh on her bare arms. *Best not poke the bear.* Her heart sped up as she carried Jenny up the uneven sidewalk. The front door opened as she reached it. Claire had seen Iris Henshaw in passing, but other than the streak of white running through her dark hair, Claire hardly recognized the woman looking out at her. Her skin was sallow, her cheeks sunken, grief was written on her face and in the droop of her shoulders. Claire cradled Jenny close as a swell of compassion pinched her throat. To lose a child, she couldn't imagine. Two children was unthinkable.

"Mrs. Henshaw," Claire managed to say, "I'm so sorry about Dell."

Iris Henshaw's expression didn't change, but her red-rimmed eyes riveted on Jenny. The door swung open a few more inches and Beth appeared behind her mother-in-law.

Beth looked nothing like the laughing girl Claire remembered meeting. Her heart-shaped face was deathly pale, her caramel-colored hair fell limply over thin shoulders. "Mrs. Wilder?" she said, her voice uncertain.

"Please, call me Claire." Jenny squirmed and made a stuttering cry as Claire tried to think of something more to say.

Iris broke the silence, her voice a painful-sounding rasp. "Is this your baby?" She reached a trembling hand out to Jenny, who stopped wiggling and regarded her with a round-eyed gaze. "So pretty."

"Would you like to hold her?" Claire said without thinking, wanting to offer what comfort she could.

She held out her arms and Claire set Jenny in them. Iris clutched her close. Jenny let out a squawk of complaint. Suddenly, the door opened wide and Mr. Henshaw loomed over Beth and Iris. He was a big man, bald with heavy dark brows and a fleshy face.

Beth shrank back a step, her eyes downcast.

"Mr. Henshaw," Claire said quickly. "I'm Claire Wilder, and I—"

"I know who you are," he interrupted with a growl. "You're not welcome here."

Claire took a half step backwards, the contempt she saw in Pete Henshaw's gaze sparking a flicker of fear. She was only trying to be kind. She straightened her shoulders and leveled her gaze at him. "I came to see Beth," she stated firmly. Claire held out the card to Beth, half expecting Pete to snatch it out of her hand. Beth took it with a murmur of thanks and slipped it into her dress pocket.

"Iris"—Pete Henshaw's voice went from disdainful to gentle as he spoke to his wife—"give the baby back."

Claire reached for Jenny, but Iris's arms clenched, holding Jenny closer. "Dell is such a good baby," she crooned.

Claire's pulse sped up. Jenny stuttered a cry.

"Iris." Pete Henshaw's voice was soft as if he were talking to a child. "You aren't thinking straight. This is Red Wilder's baby."

The woman loosened her hold and Claire snatched Jenny back, stepping out of Iris's reach. Iris's arms fell limply to her side and her face crumpled.

Pete Henshaw turned a furious gaze on Claire. "Can't you see you're just making it worse?" He crowded Beth and Iris out of the doorway. "Leave us be, Mrs. Wilder."

Claire stepped back, more than ready to leave Pete Henshaw's unjustified animosity, Iris with her vacant gaze and how she'd clutched Jenny so tightly. Now she saw what Tom Eagle had meant. She'd poked an angry bear.

The door slammed shut in her face.

Claire walked back down the steps, as dignified as she could manage with a baby squirming in her arms and beginning to wail. She settled Jenny in the seat and thanked the Lord she'd left the truck running. She'd hate to have to wrestle the carburetor in the Henshaws' driveway.

As Claire pushed in the clutch and ground the gears into reverse, the front door opened and Beth slipped out. She looked over her shoulder as she hurried toward the truck. "Mrs. Wilder," she said quickly. "I just wanted to—"

"Claire," Claire said, as if that were important in this moment. "Please."

Beth nodded and glanced back at the house. "Claire, I'm sorry about Pete. And, well . . ." She swallowed. "About what happened with Red and Dell."

Was she talking about the falling-out Red mentioned?

Beth rushed on. "I told Dell he had to come clean, but he—"

Claire didn't see Pete Henshaw come out of the house until he was right beside Beth. "Iris needs you, Beth." His hand went under Beth's elbow and he jerked her away from the truck.

Claire watched as the man practically dragged Beth back to the house and shut the door behind them. She sat for a moment, looking at the empty-eyed windows and the sagging porch. What was that about?

The truck wheels threw gravel as Claire backed out of the driveway. She drove through town and turned toward Riverside, her thoughts spinning as fast as the truck's tires. What did Beth—and apparently everyone else in West Yellowstone—know about Red that Claire did not?

chapter 6

CLAIRE

It would serve Red right if Claire showed up at Sunnyslope Ranch, demanding answers.

She pulled up to their little house in Riverside instead, with Jenny asleep next to her. Careful not to wake her, she lifted her from the truck and carried her up the steps to the front door. The house sat on a small rise, close to the river and surrounded by buffalo grass and sagebrush. The outside might once have been yellow, but the paint had faded to the color of curdled milk. Three concrete steps led to the front door and the single picture window had a crack repaired with brown tape.

As Claire eased open the door, a business card fluttered to the floor. Claire settled Jenny in her crib and went back to retrieve it.

The card bore the National Park Service emblem and the words *Lem Garrison, Yellowstone National Park Superintendent*. On the back side, a scrawled message. *Red, call me.* Odd. Red didn't have any dealings with the superintendent. Claire put the card on the counter for Red to see and lit a burner to heat up the leftover coffee. After her disastrous visit to the Henshaws', she needed a quiet moment to read

Bridget's letter before starting on the rest of the day's housework. She retrieved the mail from her purse and poured a cup of coffee. The two bills—one from the feed store and one from the electric company with a red stamp of *Overdue*—went into the drawer to deal with later.

She slit Bridget's letter open with a butter knife and pulled out the single sheet of heavy stationery. As her gaze fell on Bridget's elegant cursive, she dropped the knife on the table with a clatter. She read the few sentences again.

Bridget was coming to Yellowstone.

In her usual concise manner, Bridget wrote that Mammoth Hospital had advertised an opening for a nurse and she'd been hired there for the rest of the summer. She couldn't wait to see Claire, meet Jenny, and visit the magnificent national park Claire bragged so much about. That part was wonderful.

It was the last line that had Claire shaking her head in disbelief.

Claire flipped over the envelope and frowned at the postmark. Bridget had mailed this letter two days ago, and yet she said she'd be in West Yellowstone at three o'clock . . . on Friday.

Tomorrow? Claire stared at the words. How could she be coming tomorrow?

Bridget was the opposite of impulsive. Her sister planned everything from her weekly hair appointments to what books she would read next. This was not a spur-of-the-moment trip. She had a job and a place to live that must have taken weeks to set up. So why hadn't she given Claire more time to prepare?

When the Reillys had houseguests—Grandma Reilly or Dad's sisters—they were treated like royalty. The week before a visit would be a flurry of activity. Flo would rope Claire and Bridget into making the house spotless. She'd plan elaborate meals and everyone would wear their very best clothes. How was Claire supposed to get ready for a visitor in one day?

When Claire arrived in Riverside as a new bride, Red had carried her over the threshold and put her down in the little house with a long kiss. "It's not what you're used to," he said as she caught her breath. "I love it," she told him without a qualm. Who needed fancy appliances and matching furniture when you had the rushing river and mountains that drew your gaze upwards like a prayer? "It's our sanctuary," she told him, and it was all they needed.

Now Claire stood and walked through that sanctuary, seeing it with Bridget's eyes.

The little house had been a holiday cabin for fishermen several decades ago and consisted of a large main room that was both living room and kitchen. Claire didn't worry about how to arrange the furniture, because all they had was a tattered sofa covered in a wool blanket where she and Red cuddled up on cold evenings.

The kitchen was scrubbed and tidy, with an aged Frigidaire, a gas range with two burners, and a chipped enamel sink. A pine table and four chairs served both for eating and as a desk where she paid bills and wrote letters. The window treatments were curtains made from the white kitchen towels she'd received as wedding gifts, and the floor was a scuffed and scarred linoleum.

Would Bridget see how perfectly happy they were here? Or would she only see what was lacking—the wing chairs and wallpaper, the throw rugs and draperies?

There was more to consider than Bridget's opinion on her home decorating. Claire would have to cook something other than elk stew—Red's favorite and the only dish she could make with any skill. For goodness' sake, they didn't even have a working telephone, which Bridget would consider utter privation and highly unsafe living this far from civilization. Not to mention they absolutely must take her sister to see the sights of Yellowstone, and they could hardly do that in a truck held together with baling wire and a prayer.

If Dad had been ready to jump on a train because a bear was on the porch, what would he do once Bridget reported back? And report back she would. Claire loved her sister, but she was a terrible tattletale. Claire looked at the letter again, this time parsing the words with a growing suspicion. Perhaps Bridget hadn't merely forgotten to let her know of her plans. Could she be dropping in unannounced on Dad's orders?

Good gracious, she wouldn't put anything past him.

As much as she loved her father, she knew he wasn't an easy man. The clerks at the store lived in fear of his disapproval, and whenever he ate a meal at a restaurant, he had a complaint for the manager. His idea of the perfect husbands for his daughters were men who lived in Willmar and had the wherewithal to purchase big houses, new-model cars, and closets full of nice dresses from Reilly's Department Store. Men like Luke Charpentier.

If Dad really was behind this ploy of Bridget's, it wouldn't take much for him to decide Red wasn't taking good care of his daughter and granddaughter. She could see it now, Daniel Reilly showing up on their doorstep with his checkbook, more than willing to humiliate her husband by outfitting Claire with new appliances and a matching sofa and love seat.

Claire couldn't let that happen. She'd simply have to show Bridget—and therefore her father—that Red was taking good care of his family. Not by the beauty of the river or the freezer full of elk and trout, but in a way that would convince her sister.

Jenny's happy yelp pulled her from her thoughts. Claire poured her cold coffee down the drain and went to the bedroom. Jenny smiled and cooed, always at her most adorable right after her nap. Claire put a rubber mat on the bed and laid Jenny on it, tickling Jenny's cheeks with her eyelashes until she giggled. "Let's change your diaper, sweet pea." She wet a washcloth in the bathroom sink and grabbed a folded diaper and the powder.

As Claire unpinned the wet diaper, she considered what she must do before tomorrow. "We'll need groceries," she told Jenny as she kicked and cooed. Claire washed Jenny with the washcloth, and applied powder. "And we absolutely must get the truck fixed." They couldn't take a tour of the park if they had to whack the carburetor at every stop.

With Jenny's dry diaper in place, Claire pulled her rubber pants back on. The wet diaper went in the diaper pail and she propped Jenny on the couch, a pillow on each side to keep her upright. As Jenny's bottle warmed, Claire pulled open the drawer of bills. Most married women she knew were given an allowance, but Red was happy to put her in charge of the entire household budget. "Do whatever you think is best," he said. She checked the account book and saw the balance was zero, as she knew it would be.

She got out her pen and started writing a list.

Don, of Don's Auto in West Yellowstone, had told her it would be thirty dollars to fix the carburetor, and she'd need another twenty to pay the overdue phone bill and get hooked back up to the party line. She added twenty more dollars for gas and ten for groceries. Several other bills were woefully overdue, including the feed for Marigold and Rosie. How could she get more than a hundred dollars? Red would get paid tomorrow, but they needed most of that money for rent. She stared at the list as if the answer would jump out at her.

Claire took Jenny's bottle from the pan and checked the temperature of the formula on her wrist. She sat back down at the kitchen table with Jenny in her lap. Her thoughts jumped from one scenario to another as Jenny ate, all of them ending with Red being humiliated. When Jenny had taken her whole bottle and was milk drunk and drowsy, she put her on her shoulder and walked outside. "What are we going to do?"

Jenny burped in response.

Claire surveyed the small domain as she patted Jenny's back. A shed full of hay and horse tack. A watering pump and trough. Marigold at the far end of the pasture, the sun gleaming off her golden coat, and Red's pack mule, Bess, dozing beside her. Claire didn't know anyone well enough to borrow from—except for Bucky and he never had any money—and the bank was out of the question. The only assets they owned were the truck and the horses. Bess didn't count, as she was old and blind in one eye.

Claire stopped mid-pat. The horses.

Marigold.

As if she heard Claire's thoughts, Marigold lumbered across the pasture, her ears twitching. Jenny squealed and held out a plump hand to Marigold's searching nose. Claire let Jenny tangle her fingers in Marigold's mane. Marigold was worth at least a hundred dollars, and Claire had the bill of ownership in her name.

Claire walked back into the house. She sat down and looked again at the list, then again at Bridget's letter. Her throat constricted.

Dad had been horrible to Red at their wedding. The look on Red's face as her father made one last effort to stop Claire from walking down the aisle . . . She never wanted to put Red through something like that again. She walked to the kitchen window and looked out at Marigold.

How could she give up the most wonderful gift she'd ever received? A gift that proved she'd left Claire Reilly behind? Her chest tightened at the thought of losing a horse that was like a best friend to her. And even if she could give her up, how could she possibly explain such a thing to Red? The day he gave her Marigold, he'd been bursting with pride—his blue eyes alight with hope.

Marigold and Red and the hope for their future. They all fit together.

She had to make a choice. Let her father's critical judgement come down on Red—again—or let go of Marigold, and break Red's heart and her own?

chapter 7

BRIDGET

Bridget watched the sun-burnished terrain flash past the train window.

She and Frannie had boarded last night in St. Cloud and passed a fitful night sleeping in the upright chairs. When Bridget woke, it was to see the sun rising over the landscape utterly unlike the rolling green hills and sparkling lakes of Minnesota.

"Look, Frannie." She elbowed her sister. Rock pinnacles striped in pink and scarlet flanked deep canyons of olive-green foliage, and golden buttes reflected the sun. "Isn't it marvelous?" If she could drag Frannie out of her sulks, maybe this trip wouldn't be wretched.

Frannie stubbornly kept her eyes shut. If sulking was a subject in school, Frannie would get straight As.

Bridget had tried her best to save Claire from a month of Fran's pouting. "We can't just drop a houseguest on Claire, Dad," she'd said. "She has a baby to take care of."

"Your sister's not a houseguest," Dad said firmly. "She's family. And Frannie can help with Jenny."

Frannie was going to be as much help as a case of measles.

At the thought of their arrival in West Yellowstone, Bridget's stomach did a little flip that had nothing to do with Frannie's pouting. She'd played a mean trick on Claire, showing up without warning.

But Claire hadn't given her any choice.

It was bad enough her sister hadn't come home for Christmas like she'd promised, but when she refused to have Bridget come out to help with the baby, Bridget was shocked. "What do you mean, don't come?" Bridget said when Claire called a few weeks before her due date. Why wouldn't Claire want her sister—a registered nurse—there to help with a newborn? But Claire was adamant. "We'll be fine." Bridget couldn't very well insist, but the unease she had about Claire since her out-of-the-blue marriage grew to worry over her sister . . . and her choice of husband.

Bridget tucked her concern away in the back of her mind as she made plans for her next career move—her application to work at Mayo Clinic in Rochester. It was a prestigious position and one she'd dreamed about since nursing school, as did every other nurse in Minnesota. Then, Claire's letters went from long and newsy to short and unremarkable, Dad got worried, and so did Bridget.

When she saw the notice for a temporary nursing position in Yellowstone National Park, it was the perfect solution. She could find out if Claire really was fine, and wouldn't a month working at Mammoth Hospital be just what she needed to make her application to Mayo Clinic stand out?

Bridget shifted in the uncomfortable chair. Claire had every right to be angry with her, showing up practically unannounced and with Frannie in tow, but what was done was done. She reached into her handbag and pulled out her book. Bridget was settling into the familiar plotline—intrepid young nurse goes on adventure, meets a dashing unattainable doctor—when Frannie sat up and rubbed her eyes.

Frannie glanced at the cover of the novel. "Jeepers, why do you read that junk?"

Bridget frowned. Couldn't Frannie manage a civil *good morning*?

"Because I enjoy it." What was wrong with a predictable plotline and a happy ending?

"You're reading about some silly nurse when the world is going to end in a mushroom cloud. Don't you even care?"

Bridget rolled her eyes. "Talk to me about caring when you save lives every day like I do."

Frannie got up in a huff. "I'm going for a walk."

"Suit yourself." Bridget went back to her book. Not even Frannie could get into trouble on a moving train.

An hour later, Frannie came sashaying down the aisle, holding on to the seat backs as the train swayed around a curve. She plopped herself down beside Bridget, her face unnaturally flushed. Bridget looked at her suspiciously. "You've been gone awhile."

"I met some people, been talking to them." Her words ran together.

Bridget leaned closer and sniffed. For the love of Pete. "Have you been drinking?"

Frannie gave an unconcerned shrug. "What are you going to do? Tattle to Daddy?"

Bridget clenched her teeth and turned to the window. Dad had made her responsible for both her sisters—one to keep out of trouble, and the other to bring home. How was she going to manage that while also working a demanding job at the hospital?

She glared at Frannie, who was asleep again. Maybe she and Claire had babied Frannie too long, treating her like their little doll. Instead of growing up, Frannie was rebelling—climbing the water tower, drinking with strangers. Bridget took out her rosary. She'd pray that Frannie would come to her senses before she got herself into some real trouble.

Frannie woke up an hour later and raised her brows at the rosary Bridget still held in her hand. "I suppose you were praying for me?"

"Don't you need prayers?"

"Freud says prayer is an infantile neurosis," Frannie declared with authority.

Bridget raised her brows. "Do you even know what that means?"

Frannie's face got that stubborn look. "It means it's just mumbo jumbo. I've prayed for lots of stuff and never got even one thing from God. He's either not listening, or he's not there."

Bridget's irritation came rushing back. "God hears your prayers, even if you don't get what you ask for, Frannie. He loves you." She frowned in consternation at her little sister. "You know that, don't you?"

Frannie didn't look convinced. "What about all the people who die in floods and fires? What about Buddy Holly and Ritchie Valens? Don't you think they prayed God would save them, and he didn't lift a finger. Doesn't sound like love to me."

The train jerked and the brakes screeched. Passengers around them stood and began to gather their belongings as the conductor announced they were pulling into the Livingston station.

Bridget gathered her things, glad she didn't have to answer Frannie's ridiculous question. They disembarked, and she paid a porter to transfer their suitcases to the bus, then bought them both breakfast while they waited for the call to board the Greyhound to West Yellowstone.

An hour later, the bus wound through deep green valleys with steep slopes blanketed in trees, and Frannie was looking a little green around the gills. She moaned and covered her mouth with her hand.

Bridget passed her the waxed paper bag she'd packed for just such an emergency. "Serves you right."

"Some nurse you are," Frannie muttered.

Frannie didn't even manage to vomit discreetly.

chapter 8

CLAIRE

Claire stood with Jenny in her arms, anticipation warring with anxiety as she watched the passengers disembark from the Greyhound bus outside the Depot. Red stood beside her, as silent as a statue and just as stone-faced.

Red had barely spoken to her since she sold Marigold.

Claire had met him outside when he came home from work on Rosie. "We had to get the truck fixed, and the telephone," she told him as he slid off Rosie and looked with disbelief at Bess alone in the pasture.

Red followed her into the house, cleaned from top to bottom and smelling of vinegar and scrubbing powder. She held out Bridget's letter as proof. "We needed groceries, and money for gas and to make things nice." Red ignored the letter, his gaze on the braided throw rug she'd bought to cover a hole in the linoleum floor, the new curtains on the front window, a used table and lamp beside the couch.

"Red," Claire said, her throat thickening and alarm rising in her. "Say something."

"You sold your wedding present . . . to make things nice?" he said. It wasn't anger in his voice but something worse. Hurt. Betrayal.

He'd got it wrong, but she couldn't tell him that. She'd sold Marigold for Red's sake, so that her dad wouldn't come out here and humiliate him. But they never talked about Dad or how he'd treated Red at the wedding. "You told me to do what I thought best," she said finally. Claire waited for him to tell her he understood. He had to know it broke her heart to let Marigold go.

He shifted his weight from one foot to the other, his throat working like he was going to say something. He shook his head and swallowed. "I'm going for a ride."

"Red, wait—"

Claire watched him leave, her chest tight. Couldn't Red understand she'd done the only thing she could?

When he came in from his ride after dark, she took his dinner out of the oven and sat with him while he ate. He helped her with the dishes like he did every night, and she tried to ask him questions about his day at Sunnyslope, but his one-word answers only made the divide between them wider. "Are you coming to bed?" she asked him at ten o'clock when she turned off the radio.

"I'll stay up for a while," he said, not meeting her gaze.

Now, as they watched the passengers come off the bus at the Depot, Claire's mouth went dry and her stomach flipped. How was she supposed to prove to Bridget that they were perfectly happy, with Red glowering beside her? And how was she supposed to repair the hurt she'd caused her husband under Bridget's sharp gaze?

When Bridget stepped off the bus and into the late-afternoon sun, Claire stood on her tiptoes and waved. "It's your auntie Bridget," she told Jenny.

Bridget made a beeline toward them through the crowded Depot. She looked like she'd just stepped out of Reilly's summer catalogue in a pink linen traveling suit that hugged her hourglass figure. When she reached them, she threw her arms around Claire and Jenny and squeezed. "I missed you so much."

Claire squeezed her sister back. "It's wonderful to see you," she choked out.

Bridget stepped back, her hands on Claire's shoulders. "You look terrific." She glanced to where Red stood with Jenny. "Hello, Red." She passed him her handbag and held out her hands for Jenny. "Give me that sweet baby girl."

Claire had dressed Jenny in an outfit Bridget had sent, and she looked adorable in the blue taffeta dress and shiny Mary Janes.

"She is perfectly gorgeous." Bridget kissed Jenny's pink cheek and gave her hair an assessing look. "Is she going to be a redhead, too?"

"I hope so," Claire said, and meant it. She hoped every one of their children had Red's copper hair. She sent Red a smile and hoped he'd smile back.

Instead, his brows came together in a puzzled frown as his attention went back to the bus. Claire followed Red's gaze to where a group of young men and women shouldered backpacks and yelled insults at each other. A familiar face separated from the group.

"Frannie?" Was Claire imagining things? When she'd left home, Frannie had long, blonde waves pulled back from her face with barrettes, and wore full skirts and saddle shoes. The girl walking toward them had a short pixie cut and wore teal pedal pushers and a form-fitting sleeveless blouse. It was Frannie, but she looked less like Claire's little sister and more like she'd just stepped out of a teen magazine.

Claire raised her brows at Bridget. Her sister sent her an apologetic look and mouthed *Tell you later*.

"Hi, sis," Frannie said in a bored voice. "Hiya, Red."

Claire stepped forward. "What a lovely surprise." Because what else could she say? She pulled Frannie into a hug that her little sister quickly shrugged away. Then they bustled to the truck while Red loaded the luggage and Frannie shouted vigorous goodbyes to the group who had come off the bus.

"Why didn't you tell me she was coming?" Claire whispered as they squeezed into the truck with Claire next to Red, Bridget beside her with Jenny on her lap, and Frannie next to the window.

"If you had a telephone . . ." Bridget whispered back.

Claire leaned past Bridget to smile brightly at Frannie. "How was the trip? Did you sleep at all?" Frannie mumbled something as Claire's thoughts raced ahead. Had she made enough dinner for an extra person? Where would Frannie sleep? She glanced at Red, who hadn't said two words since her sisters arrived. His hands were clenched on the steering wheel and he stared straight ahead.

"You're going to love it here." Claire continued to talk to Frannie as if she wasn't sulking. "We live right on the Madison River. We can go there after dinner."

"A river," Frannie retorted. "Whoop-di-doo."

Claire and Bridget shared a glance. Bridget rolled her eyes as if to say *See what I have to deal with?*

Jenny chose that moment to let out a squeal and demand Bridget's attention. "Tell me how this little one is sleeping," Bridget said. "Is she eating well? I do wish you'd chosen to breastfeed. At least tell me you're up-to-date on her immunizations?"

"We have doctors here, Bridget." Claire made herself adopt a teasing tone even as she felt a flash of irritation. This was exactly why she didn't let Bridget come out when Jenny was born. She could manage perfectly well on her own and didn't need Bridget looking over her shoulder every second. "And I read the baby book you sent me from cover to cover." She patted Red's leg beside her. "We both did."

Red didn't say a word, but made the turn to Riverside.

Claire's stomach fluttered as the home she'd made with Red came into view. The house looked wonderful, set among the deep green of the trees, the impossibly blue sky above, the late-afternoon sun sparkling off the Madison in the background. Like a postcard. But would Bridget see it that way? "Here we are," Claire said. "Home sweet home."

She watched Bridget's face. Her polite expression flickered. Frannie didn't even try to be mannerly. "Holy moly, Claire, it's smaller than our garden shed."

"Frannie," Bridget scolded. "Don't be rude." She forced a smile. "It's lovely, Claire."

Red put the truck in park with a jerk.

"Please tell me you have a television," Frannie grumped.

"We have the great outdoors," Claire retorted.

Bridget passed Jenny to her, then carefully climbed out in her skirt and heels. "I'm sorry." She glared at Frannie. "She lost her manners somewhere between Willmar and Livingston."

"Gosh," Frannie groused. "Nobody can take a joke around here."

Inside, Claire gave Bridget and Frannie a tour of all four rooms—the kitchen and the living room, the bathroom, and the bedroom—her smile firmly fixed in place.

"So cozy and cute," Bridget said with a pasted-on smile.

"Where am I going to sleep?" Frannie asked, looking at the couch with a frown.

Claire bit her tongue, tempted to tell her little sister she could sleep with the mule. She had planned to make up the couch for Bridget, but now didn't know what to do.

Red came in with an armload of suitcases and spoke for the first time. "Claire and Bridget can share the bedroom," he said. "Frannie can have the couch."

Frannie groaned.

Bridget objected. "Where will you sleep, Red?"

"It's a nice night," he said, his tone clipped. "I'll camp outside."

If Bridget hadn't noticed Red's ill temper in the truck, she certainly did now. She gave Claire an uncertain look.

"He'll be as cozy as a bug," Claire assured her sister. She had the feeling Red was counting the hours until he could be in the company of Rosie and Bess instead of Bridget and Frannie.

chapter 9

CLAIRE

Dinner with her sisters didn't turn out as Claire hoped.

The chicken tetrazzini recipe that *Good Housekeeping* had promised would impress her guests turned out to be a gluey mess, and the Jell-O salad didn't set properly. Red was as talkative as a stump and Frannie sulked. Claire filled the silence with questions about home, pretending all was well.

"Dinner was delicious," Bridget said as if it were the truth.

"I'll take care of the dishes," Red offered when they finished eating the icebox cake Claire had made for dessert.

"Goodness, Claire," Bridget said, standing up with her plate and taking it to the sink. "You have him trained well."

Claire saw Red's jaw twitch. It was just something people said, but why did Bridget have to rub him the wrong way at every turn?

Frannie left her plate on the table and went to the living room where Jenny was on a blanket, kicking and wiggling. "I'll stay here and play with the little ankle biter. That way, you two can complain about me."

"Grab your sweater," Claire said. "It gets chilly when the wind comes up."

Bridget took up the sweater that matched the slacks and blouse she changed into for dinner, but she hesitated before following Claire. "Is it safe?"

Claire stopped halfway out the back door. "What do you mean?"

"I mean, do we have to worry about bears?" she asked. "Or . . . snakes?"

Claire couldn't help but laugh at her sister's expression. "Come on, scaredy-pants. I'll protect you."

Bridget followed Claire out the door, past the horse shed and the pasture where Rosie and Bess were swishing their tails and grazing. The sun was sinking behind the mountains, the blue of the sky deepening, the breeze rippling the silver grasses like waves. It was the prettiest time of day. Claire told herself the tension she'd felt since Bridget came off the bus would disappear as soon as they had a good talk.

Bridget picked her way along the trail, looking carefully at each clump of buffalo grass. "Stop worrying," Claire said. "Rattlesnakes are more afraid of you than you are of them."

"I don't think that's possible," Bridget muttered.

Claire figured this wasn't the time to tell Bridget about the snake she killed earlier in the summer. She'd heard the telltale rattle coming from between the bales when she was feeding the horses and brought the pitchfork down on it without pausing to be afraid. Claire had been awfully proud of herself after she stopped shaking, but she doubted Bridget would see it that way.

They reached a gorgeous spot on the river where the water sparkled in the shallows and darkened in deeper pools. A cloud of gnats hovered over the water and the aspen trees on the far bank shivered in the breeze.

"I'm sorry about Frannie." Bridget slapped at a mosquito. "Dad was at his wits' end."

He must have been. Claire couldn't imagine him alone in that big house, all his girls far away. Bridget had made a quick telephone call to let him know they'd arrived safely, and Claire could tell from how he kept her on the phone that he was already lonely. "How long does he want her to stay?"

"The rest of the summer," Bridget said with an apologetic face.

A month? That was a long time if Frannie was going to keep pouting. Claire bent down to the wet pebbles along the water, choosing a rock with a jagged vein of quartz. "What am I supposed to do with her?"

"Dad wants her to help you. I'm sure you could use it." She waved a hand back to the house.

"What does that mean?" Claire couldn't help the defensive tone in her voice. Here it was, Bridget's judgement on her life.

"Nothing, Claire," Bridget said, as if she was overreacting. "It's just that it's got to be hard. You're in the middle of nowhere, and alone."

"I'm not alone," Claire said, throwing the stone into the rippling river. "I have Red."

"You know what I mean." Bridget frowned. "We're just worried."

"We?" Was Claire right in her suspicions? Was this some kind of scheme of Dad's?

Bridget met Claire's suspicious gaze. "Yes, we," she answered. "Claire, you stopped calling, your letters barely said anything. You didn't even let me come out when Jenny was born. We were both worried." Her eyes locked on Claire, demanding an explanation.

"As you can see, we're fine." Claire waved a hand at the river, the sky, the mountains.

"Are you really?" Bridget asked the question kindly, but it rankled. "This is a far cry from how you grew up."

Claire clamped her teeth together. Didn't Bridget understand that was exactly the point? She'd married Red to start a new life—a life utterly unlike the one she left behind. "I'm fine," Claire snapped. "We're fine. You and Dad can stop worrying."

Bridget's eyes widened and Claire saw a flash of hurt on her sister's face and felt terrible. Everything she'd done—sacrificing Marigold and cleaning and cooking and making Red miserable—it was all to show Bridget how happy she was. To show Dad how happy she was. Now here she was, picking a fight.

"I'm sorry," Claire said, crossing her arms over her chest as the wind chilled her skin. "Let's just enjoy our time together."

"I'm sorry, too," Bridget said, like Claire knew she would. "It's been a long day and that kid sister of ours got on my last nerve." She turned toward the house. "Forget I even said anything."

Claire decided she would. It was what the Reilly family did. Pretend everything was fine, even when it wasn't.

chapter 10

BRIDGET

Bridget eyed Red as they sat behind a line of cars waiting to get into Yellowstone National Park. He tapped impatient fingers on the steering wheel in a way that made it clear he didn't want to be in the hot cab of the truck, showing his sisters-in-law the sights. Claire sat beside her with Jenny on her lap and acted like nothing was wrong.

Dad was right to be worried about Claire. It wasn't just that they lived in that run-down house in the middle of nowhere and were barely making ends meet. Claire wasn't herself, and Red . . . well, he clearly wasn't an easy man to live with.

"Is it always this crowded?" Bridget asked, craning her neck to count how many cars were in front of them.

"It's a Saturday in August," Claire answered. "But don't worry, it's worth the wait."

Bridget wasn't so sure. She'd read plenty about Yellowstone National Park and it sounded like somewhere to avoid, not wait in line to visit. Hot springs, geysers, and wild animals, not to mention snakes. Her hands tightened on the first aid kit in her lap.

Claire had laughed when Bridget had taken it from her suitcase. "We're not going into a disaster zone."

"Best to be prepared," Bridget answered. She hadn't been prepared for the heat and was already perspiring in her linen shirtwaist. How did Claire manage to look as cool as a movie star in slim Bermuda shorts and a bright cotton boatneck? Bridget was sure Claire wasn't even wearing a girdle.

Bridget checked her wristwatch. It was almost nine thirty, an hour later than they'd planned to leave, thanks to Frannie. She'd refused to wake up for breakfast, and when Bridget had finally told her they were going to leave without her, she spent half an hour in the bathroom. When she finally came out to the truck in hot pink pedal pushers and a top that showed an inch of her tummy, she jumped in the back with the ice chest and fishing gear. "Wake me up if we see anything interesting."

Bridget wished her first aid kit included some kind of cure for Frannie's rude behavior.

It was finally their turn at the entrance, and Red dug in his pocket for the fee.

"Let me," Bridget said, opening her purse.

"Absolutely not." Claire stopped her. "You are our guests."

"Thank you so much, Red," Bridget said with a forced smile. He frowned in answer and Bridget's smile slipped. She'd just been trying to be polite.

The ranger recited his cheerful instructions: don't feed the bears, prevent forest fires, please don't litter, and "Enjoy Yellowstone, folks."

"Wagons ho!" Frannie called out from the back as they pulled forward.

Bridget decided to try one more time to make nice with Claire's husband. "Where is the ranch you work at when you're not squiring us around?"

Red didn't answer.

Claire jumped in, her voice overly bright. "Sunnyslope is just a few miles up the Madison from us," she said. "Red is marvelous with horses," she added with a smile toward her silent husband.

Bridget shuddered at the thought of horses. "Remember when that awful horse threw Luke and he broke his collarbone?" She wouldn't get on one of those unpredictable beasts to save her life.

Claire didn't answer, and Bridget saw her glance go to Red. Surely Red wasn't still jealous of Luke? No one was more surprised than Bridget when Claire broke up with the man all of Willmar thought she was going to marry. Then Red showed up with a ring and Claire was suddenly marrying a complete stranger. She hoped today's trip would prove to her what Claire saw in Red but so far, no joy there.

Red stepped on the gas and the truck jerked forward behind the line of paneled station wagons and pastel convertibles going into the park.

Claire showed Bridget the map of Yellowstone. "We'll turn south here," Claire told her, "and make a stop at the Lower Geyser Basin. Then you have to see the Grand Prismatic." Claire pointed to a spot on something called the Lower Loop. "Then Old Faithful," Claire went on. "We'll have lunch at the Firehole River and a swim. Frannie will like that."

Bridget wasn't sure about Frannie, or touring a hot spring—and anything called the Firehole seemed risky for a swim—but she expressed as much excitement as she could manage. She played peekaboo and patty-cake with Jenny until they pulled off the road and into a jam-packed parking lot.

"What is that awful smell?" Frannie's wail came through the small window in the back of the cab. "It smells like rotten eggs."

Claire laughed at Frannie. "You'll get used to it."

They scooted out of the truck and into the searing midmorning sun. Bridget's eyes stung and the handkerchief she held over her nose did little to alleviate the terrible odor. They followed a boardwalk with Claire reading aloud from her Haynes Guide like the schoolteacher she was. She told them about the geothermal activity in the area that made the hot springs and geysers, and the bubbling iron-red and mustard-yellow mud that belched acrid steam.

Frannie peered into the paint pots. "Looks like plain old mud to me."

"The least you could do is take an interest," Bridget reprimanded. Why did Frannie have to be such a pill?

Back in the truck, Jenny started to fuss and Bridget took her from Claire. She had plenty of experience with fussing babies and this was one way she knew how to help. Not more than ten minutes later, they pulled over again.

"You'll love this," Claire said as they found a parking spot. "The colors are fantastic."

As they got out of the truck and Claire gave Jenny to Red, Bridget saw them exchange a smile. Red leaned down and kissed Claire. For a moment, they looked like a perfect family.

Claire turned and caught her watching them. "We went here on our third date," she explained. "It's always been my favorite."

Red carried Jenny—happily kicking and cooing now, as if she were just as pleased to show off the wonders of Yellowstone as her mother—with Claire, Bridget, and Frannie following him over the boardwalk. Steam billowed toward them in hot waves. Bridget kept well back from the pool as Claire explained how the bright rings of azure, yellow, and emerald green were made by different kinds of bacteria that lived in the water. "It's hottest at the center," she said. "And deeper than a ten-story building."

Frannie stepped up to the edge of the boardwalk. "I heard the tour guide over there say that a couple years ago somebody fell into one of these pools and had their skin boiled off them before they could get pulled out."

Bridget's stomach went queasy. "Frannie, that's horrible."

Frannie blew out a frustrated breath. "First I'm not taking an interest, then I'm horrible. Jeepers, I can't do anything right."

Bridget looked at Claire. "Did that really happen?"

Red chose that moment to loosen his tongue. "Not to people who stay on the boardwalk."

If that was Red's idea of a joke, it wasn't funny.

Back in the truck, Bridget tried to forget the horrible image of someone falling into the boiling water. Hopefully, she'd never see that kind of injury when she was working at Mammoth. The truck slowed as they reached some sort of traffic jam. Red steered around a camper on the shoulder, trying to get past the slowdown. Suddenly the truck jerked to a halt, Red threw his arm out to stop Claire and Jenny as they slid forward. Bridget braced herself on the dash. A tourist with a camera slung around his neck looked over the hood in surprise, then hurried across the road.

"Idiot," Red ground out.

"It's a bear jam," Claire said, seemingly unperturbed that they'd almost run someone over.

"A bear what?" Bridget's pulse—already elevated from the almost-accident—went even higher. Red eased the truck forward, and Bridget saw a bear and two cubs in the ditch on the side of the road. A cluster of tourists took pictures of the frolicking cubs while the mother helped herself to the scraps of food the tourists tossed her way. The man with the camera was holding a hunk of bread out to the mother bear, urging her closer.

Were those people trying to get killed? Suddenly Bridget saw a flash of hot pink dart toward the bears. "Frannie!"

"Stay here." Red threw the truck into park and opened his door.

A wave of weakness rushed over Bridget as Red walked calmly toward Frannie. She stood a few feet away from one of the cubs, her hand extended toward the bear. She saw Red's lips move, his words too low to hear.

Bridget clutched at Claire's arm as the big bear lurched toward Frannie. Red darted forward and grabbed Frannie's arm, yanking her backwards. Frannie yelped in surprise and dropped—what was that? A sandwich?

Red dragged Frannie back to the truck and pushed her inside. Bridget caught a glimpse of the bear herding the cubs down the embankment and into the trees.

As the pounding of blood in her ears abated, she heard Frannie laughing hysterically. "Did you see that? Did you get a picture?"

Bridget's whole body flushed. "Of all the stupid things!" She turned on her little sister. "Frances Marie Reilly, what is wrong with you?"

Frannie didn't look a bit sorry. "A lot, according to you and Dad." She wiped her eyes with the back of her hand. "That was the coolest."

Red jerked the truck into gear and pulled back onto the road. He didn't say a word, but his face was as hard as stone.

"Frannie, that was really stupid," Claire said as she adjusted Jenny on her lap.

"Stupid doesn't begin to describe it," Bridget snapped.

Was she going to have to babysit her little sister in a place where there seemed to be a thousand ways to get killed? And Claire . . . for goodness' sake, couldn't she see this was no place to raise a child? Frannie deserved a spanking, and Claire needed to see sense. Dad was right. Claire needed to come home with Jenny, even if it meant leaving her ill-natured husband behind.

chapter 11

CLAIRE

Claire was absolutely mortified. What would Red think of the way her sisters were acting? She wouldn't blame him if he turned the truck around this minute and headed home.

That stunt Frannie pulled. And Bridget. Since they stepped off the bus, Bridget hadn't had a kind word for their little sister. Now, Bridget was threatening to lock her in the truck for the rest of the day like a naughty dog.

How quickly Claire had forgotten that her family was a far cry from *Father Knows Best.* In fact, what was going on right now in the truck was the reason she'd escaped to Yellowstone in the first place. The winter Frannie turned sixteen, their once-peaceful house became a war zone with Frannie and Dad in open combat. By the time spring came, Claire was sick and tired of being the peacemaker. When Millie told her of her plan to work at Old Faithful for the summer, Claire grabbed on to the idea like a lifeboat on a sinking ship.

Her job at the Old Faithful Inn laundry was hot and sweaty work, but Claire spent her free time falling in love with Yellowstone—and not worrying about her rebellious teenage sister pitted against her overprotective father. The summer of freedom was glorious . . . and then she met Red.

Claire tried to catch Red's eye and let him know she appreciated how his quick thinking averted disaster between her sister and the bear. He kept his attention on the road as if World War III wasn't going on around them.

She'd tried to smooth things over with Red this morning. Before anyone else was awake, she'd left the house and walked barefoot through the dew-wet grass to where Red was sleeping outside.

He'd been awake—watching the sun rise over the mountains—and lifted his bedroll so she could slip in. The lilt of birdsong accompanied the rippling music of the river as she curled into his warmth and tucked her head under his chin. "I missed you," she told him. He pulled her close, and in the beauty of the sunrise, all was well. If only it could stay that way.

Now, the road wound past Morning Glory Pool and Castle Geyser. She'd love to show both wonders to her sisters, but the mood in the cab was mutinous and Jenny was starting to fuss. "Let's go straight to Old Faithful," she murmured to Red. He nodded once, his jaw tight.

Red followed the line of cars into the parking lot and found a space among the station wagons and convertibles. Claire gratefully unstuck her hot legs from the seat and scooted out of the truck with a fussy, wet, and hungry Jenny.

"Do I need to hold your hand or are you going to act your age?" Bridget griped to Frannie as they clambered out.

"I'm not a child." Frannie sulked.

"Then stop acting like one."

Frannie stuck out her tongue at Bridget.

Red held out his hands for Jenny. "I'll take care of her."

Claire passed Jenny to him with dismay. Red would rather change a diaper than listen to her sisters quarrel, and she didn't blame him. Five minutes later, Claire sat between fuming Bridget and unrepentant Frannie on a bench facing the famous geyser.

A ranger with a megaphone gave his spiel. "Ten thousand gallons of water heated by volcanic magma has kept Old Faithful spouting about once an hour for as long as we've known her."

By the time the ranger finished, Red joined them with Jenny. He cradled her in his arms and gave her the bottle Claire had packed in the ice chest. Claire watched him, a sudden surge of love for him. He hadn't grown up with family. All this was new to him, and he was being patient with her difficult sisters. Red looked up from feeding Jenny and caught her gaze, his expression softening. Maybe they could salvage the day.

"There she blows, folks," the ranger said.

The spouting began and the crowd leaned forward, oohing and aahing over the column of boiling hot water arcing into the clear blue sky. Bridget took a dozen pictures and even Frannie said, "Pretty cool, I guess."

As the crowd dispersed, Claire led her sisters toward the Old Faithful Inn, Jenny happily babbling in Red's arms. Claire showed her sisters the laundry building hidden behind the imposing hotel. "The laundry maids were called bubble queens," she told them. "And we all lived together in the dorms over there." She pointed to the building next to the laundry. "That window up there in the top row, second from the end, was mine and Millie's."

"And when you didn't work, you got to do whatever you wanted?" Frannie asked, suddenly taking an interest.

"Did we ever!" Claire thought of the fun times she and Millie had as savages—the name for seasonal park employees. "We saw everything, went hiking and camping, and to dances."

"That sounds pretty neat." Frannie looked impressed.

Claire's spirits rose as she caught a flash of the little sister she remembered. Next, Claire led the way through the big red doors of the castle-like Old Faithful Inn. "This is the place for the tourists with money," she explained. Bridget and Frannie both looked up in wonder. It's what all the tourists did when they first saw the soaring height of the lobby. Staircases and walkways made of peeled lodgepole pines crisscrossed the outer walls, and high windows showed glimpses of sky and wisps of clouds.

"It's one of the largest log structures in the world," Claire told them as they crossed the lobby strewn with bentwood chairs and wrought iron candelabras. The three-story stone fireplace was cold in the summer months but still impressive. Red held Jenny where she could see the swinging pendulum of the enormous clock that counted off the minutes between Old Faithful's performances.

Bridget edged closer to Claire. "Now do you see what you left me to deal with?" she whispered, jerking her head toward Frannie, who was peeking into the dining room full of well-dressed tourists.

Claire pressed her lips together as guilt stung her. When she'd told Bridget she was going to Yellowstone for the summer, Bridget had moaned that she was deserting her to deal with Dad and Frannie on her own. Even after she married Red, Bridget hadn't let up on the guilt trip. "She's not so bad."

"Hey, you guys," Frannie interrupted, practically yelling across the lobby as she pointed to the dining room menu posted on the wall. "I could murder a hamburger and fries."

Claire joined Frannie at the double doors that led into the dining room. "We have sandwiches and pop in the cooler," she told Frannie.

"Which you'd know if you got up in time to help her make them," Bridget chimed in.

Frannie's brow wrinkled. "You mean the sandwiches that were in the ice chest?"

Claire frowned. "What do you mean *were*?"

Frannie shrugged. "I didn't have any breakfast. And the last one went to the bear."

Claire stared at her sister in dismay. How could she not know that was their lunch?

"Frannie, you are the living end," Bridget said with her familiar outrage.

Claire looked to Red, joining them with Jenny. They were hours from home and there wasn't another restaurant for twenty miles.

"What's the big deal? Let's just eat here," Frannie said, as if it was obvious.

Claire couldn't very well tell her sister that lunch at the Old Faithful Inn would cost more than she spent on groceries for a week. She glanced at Red and then back at the dining room. He passed Jenny to her, then dug in his pocket and frowned at four crumpled one-dollar bills. Not enough.

"You didn't take any money from the cookie tin?" It was the wrong thing to say. The money in the cookie tin was what they had left from Marigold, and Red's expression hardened. Heat crept up her neck and Jenny began to fuss in her arms. She glanced toward Bridget, hoping she hadn't heard their embarrassing dilemma or noticed Red's flare of temper.

No such luck.

Bridget was watching with a sharp gaze, but suddenly smiled brightly. "Goodness, Claire, I completely forgot." She opened her purse and pulled out her wallet, then a crisp twenty-dollar bill. "It's from Dad. He told me to take you out for a nice meal on him."

"Hallelujah, we're saved," Frannie crowed.

Claire's heart dropped as Red's face went flint hard. "We don't need your father's money," Red answered, his voice like stone grating on stone.

"Don't be ridiculous," Bridget snapped in her no-nonsense voice. "It's obvious you do."

Claire squeezed her eyes shut. Bridget couldn't have said anything worse if she tried.

"Wowsa." Now even Frannie had noticed Red's furious expression.

"Red"—Bridget tried to backpedal—"I didn't mean anything by it."

But it was too late.

"I know exactly what you meant," Red ground out. He took Jenny from Claire's arms. "Jenny and I will wait in the truck. I'd rather be hungry than eat on your father's dime."

chapter 12

BRIDGET

"Why can't you drive me to Mammoth?" Bridget asked Claire on Sunday morning. Bridget didn't want to be a pain, but an hour and a half in the truck alone with Red wasn't a pleasant prospect.

Red hadn't said a word to her since yesterday. Honestly, she hadn't meant to offend him.

And what was so terrible about letting Dad buy them lunch?

It hadn't helped that Jenny had been fussy during the night and Claire was up walking her back and forth in the tiny hallway. Bridget offered to help but Claire wouldn't hear of it.

They'd gone to church this morning in West Yellowstone and of course Frannie spent the entire Mass fidgeting. When the last hymn was announced, Claire shot Bridget a smile. "Amazing Grace." It was Claire's favorite, and one they'd all sung together in the choir at St. Malachy's. Those had been good days, before Frannie started acting up and Claire left them. Bridget had nudged Frannie. "Sing." Frannie had stubbornly kept her mouth closed.

Now, Claire held the fretful Jenny against her shoulder and bounced gently. "I don't want to leave Jenny or take her in the truck all that way," she said in response to Bridget's question. "I don't know what's wrong. She's been sleeping through the night for weeks."

Bridget was tempted to give Claire a well-deserved *I told you so*. If Claire had taken her advice about breastfeeding . . . but poor Claire looked at the end of her rope. "Try putting a warm hot water bottle under her tummy," Bridget suggested. "If she's still fussy tomorrow, call me at the hospital."

Claire picked up Jenny and rocked her in her arms. "Do you mind terribly having Red drive you?"

"Of course not." Bridget forced a pleasant expression onto her face. What else could she say? She had to get to her first shift at Mammoth Hospital, and she couldn't very well hitchhike.

After a lunch of cold cuts and potato salad, Bridget repacked her bags and changed into an appropriate outfit of a navy pencil skirt and white blouse, just right for meeting her new supervisor. She came into the kitchen to find Red walking Jenny back and forth while Claire warmed a bottle on the stove.

"Frannie," Claire called out, "do you remember how I told you to make the formula for Jenny yesterday? Could you make another batch, please?"

Frannie shrugged and slumped into the kitchen. "Sure, it's not rocket science."

Bridget watched Claire worry over Jenny. Dad was right, it was too hard to raise a baby without family. Claire should come home, where she would have help. If only her sister wasn't so stubborn and her husband wasn't so . . . hostile.

Claire sat down on the couch and Bridget watched Red settle the baby in her lap. Still, she admitted that Red was better with the baby than most fathers. He even changed diapers. Red didn't like her—that was obvious—but he loved Claire and Jenny. Maybe she could make him see the sense of moving his family back to Willmar for their sake.

She said goodbye to Claire with a firm hug, kissed Jenny, and told Frannie to behave herself. "You're sure you're okay?" Bridget asked her sister while Red started the truck.

"I'm fine, Bridget. Red and I are fine. Everything is fine," Claire said with a sharp note in her voice and weariness in her face.

Bridget didn't believe it for a minute, and she was going to help her sister, even if Claire insisted she didn't need help.

Red pulled the truck off the gravel road and onto the highway in silence.

Bridget smoothed her skirt and rolled up her window so as not to mess her hair. "I appreciate you driving me, Red."

He gave her a curt nod and they drove in silence for what seemed like a very long time.

"It was good to see Claire," Bridget tried again. "She looks wonderful."

He nodded again.

The National Park Service ranger at the West Entrance waved them through when Red explained that he was driving Bridget up to her job in Mammoth. Then, there was nothing but the rumble of the road for over ten minutes.

Red wasn't going to make this easy. But this was for Claire, so Bridget took a deep breath and turned to her brother-in-law. "Red, I feel like we got off on the wrong foot."

He glanced sideways.

"I just want Claire to be happy," she said. That was the absolute truth.

"You don't think she is?" Red said without taking his eyes off the road.

Bridget said the words she'd rehearsed in her head. "It's hard to have a baby and not have family around. She doesn't even have any friends, even though she's lived here for over a year."

Bridget saw Red's knuckles go pale on the steering wheel. "She has me."

"That's not enough." Bridget regretted that reply immediately and tried to backpedal. "I mean—"

"I know what you meant," he interrupted, his voice hard. "I'm not enough. The house we live in isn't enough. The life I've given her isn't enough."

The intensity of his words shouldn't have surprised her after yesterday. "You're putting words in my mouth."

"Your father is putting words in your mouth," Red spit back.

That sparked her temper. Was it so wrong that Dad worried about his daughter marrying an utter stranger and flouncing off without a backwards glance to her family? "What exactly do you mean by that?"

Red shrugged, his eyes on the road. They came up behind a pink and chrome sedan pulling a long bullet-shaped trailer and followed it closely around a series of curves. Bridget's mouth went dry. On one side of the road was a sharp drop-off down to a river, and a steep slope of shale-covered rock rose on the other side. Red edged the truck over the center line to look for oncoming cars.

Bridget gripped the edge of the seat.

Red pulled out into the left lane and the truck surged past the trailer. Bridget's heart skipped a beat when she saw an oncoming car in the distance.

"Your father," Red said, as if he wasn't rushing headlong into a collision, "can't bear to let go of his daughters, or—God forbid—let them love a man other than him."

Bridget's heart rate rose at the unfair accusation and their imminent death. They passed the sedan, and Red calmly steered back into their lane. "That's ridiculous," she said when she could breathe again. "Dad made us the center of his life." She didn't say *after Mother left*. Bridget wasn't going to open that can of worms.

"Did he?" Red asked her now.

"Did he what?" Bridget wished she'd never started this conversation. Red was impossible to talk to, and with him carrying on like this they were going to end up dead in an accident.

"Did he make you and Claire and Frannie the center of his life?" Red stepped on the brakes as the car in front of him turned left. "Or did he make *himself* the center of *your* lives?"

Bridget snapped her gaze toward him. "I don't like what you're implying." Bridget looked out the window at the scenery. Trees, a picnic area, a small waterfall with a cluster of parked cars. She was done trying to reason with Red.

The truck surged to a higher speed, as if he wanted to get to Mammoth as fast as he could. Well, she did too. Red's accusations rankled—about her, and about Dad. Was it selfish of Dad to want to keep his daughters close, or was it love? She supposed—although she wasn't admitting Red was right—that it could be both. And even if there was a grain of truth in what Red said, it didn't change the fact that Claire needed her family.

Bridget steeled herself against Red's hostility and went on to her second point—one that she knew he couldn't refute. "Jenny would have so much more if you moved back to Willmar."

Red looked over at her with disbelief. "Dresses and pretty shoes, you mean."

"Family," she shot back. "Not that you'd understand." She felt a little bad saying that—it wasn't Red's fault he'd been left in an orphanage—but he had to see her point.

"She has a family," he ground out. "Claire and me. And brothers and sisters someday."

"She needs more than that." How could Red not see they both needed more than what he was giving them? "Jenny needs her grandfather, her aunts who love her." Bridget was wound up now and knew she should stop. But she didn't. "Not to mention a decent place to live. You don't even have a doctor within an hour." She turned and looked at him. "I've seen terrible things happen to children. What if Jenny got hurt or sick? What if she died because you insist on living in this godforsaken wilderness?"

He shot her a look and she saw a flash of fear before the shutters came down. He stared straight ahead at the road. "This is her home, with Claire and me. You and Daniel Reilly are not getting your hands on my family."

chapter 13

FRANNIE

Claire slammed the saucepan down on the stovetop. "It's not rocket science, Frannie. Isn't that what you said?" Her voice was almost as loud as Jenny's screams.

Frannie's heart squeezed and her eyes prickled with tears. "Geez Louise," she said, "it's not the end of the world." She hadn't meant to mess up so bad. She swallowed hard and stuck her hands in her pockets.

Claire turned to her and Frannie felt even more terrible. Her sister sure looked pooped. If this was what having a baby did to you, she was never going to have kids. The door slammed and Red came in.

He took one look at Claire and went to her, taking the crying baby from her arms. "What happened?"

Jenny's howls dwindled to soft whimpers.

Claire's voice was all shaky. "Frannie mixed the formula yesterday. I told her three tablespoons of formula per cup. *Tablespoons.*" She shot a murderous glare at Frannie. "She put in three teaspoons. Poor Jenny has been hungry—that's why she didn't sleep last night and why she's been crying all day."

Frannie crossed her arms in front of her. "I didn't know." Tablespoons, teaspoons, how was she supposed to know the difference?

"I told you." Claire screwed a nipple on the hot bottle. "Now I have to wait for this to cool so she can get some nourishment." Claire's eyes were shiny as she put the hot bottle in the refrigerator.

Red walked Jenny across the kitchen, patting her back. He paced back to Claire, bending to kiss her cheek. "You go get some rest. After she has her bottle I'll put her down for her nap."

Frannie watched Red with surprise. He sure was sweet to Claire, even when she was being such a pain. And he seemed like he didn't mind taking care of the baby at all. Except for Dad, she'd never heard of a man taking care of a baby.

Half an hour later, Jenny and Claire were asleep in the bedroom. "Let's go outside," Red said. He grabbed a fishing pole and tackle box and led Frannie out the back door.

"I swear, I didn't know," Frannie said when they reached the river. "I thought she said teaspoons."

Red selected a fly and tied it on the end of his line.

Frannie sat down on a rock, her shoulders slumped. "Will Jenny be okay?"

Red gave her a look that might have been sympathetic. "No harm done other than a sleepless night for your sister."

"I told her I was sorry."

"Did you?" Red asked as he threw out his line.

Frannie watched the fly on Red's line land on the far side of the river and scowled. Maybe she hadn't exactly apologized, but Claire knew she was sorry. She picked up a rock and tossed it into the rippling shallows. "Claire and Bridget treat me like I'm still a kid and I'm not."

Red gave her a sideways glance like he wasn't buying it. "Why do you want to grow up so fast, anyway?"

Frannie watched Red flip his fishing rod, the fly whizzing back and forth over their heads. She knew Red had been raised in an orphanage. She'd overheard Claire telling Bridget that he'd run away when he was just a kid and had been on his own ever since. That sounded kind of cool to her, and it didn't seem to have hurt Red any to not have a family telling him what to do every second. She threw another rock in the river. "Because I want to do what I want."

Red let out a bark of a laugh like she'd said something funny. "I hate to break it to you, little sister, but growing up is mostly about doing things you don't want to do."

"That doesn't sound like very much fun."

"Sometimes it isn't." Red turned back to his fishing, but not before Frannie saw a troubled look on his face. She didn't get a chance to ask him, because a man was making his way down the riverbank toward them. He was tall and skinny and had white-blond hair and a tanned face that made it hard to tell his age. His jeans were dirty and he wore a cowboy hat that looked about a million years old.

Red nodded to him, then to Frannie. "Bucky, this is Claire's sister, Frannie."

Frannie forgot all about Claire then. "You mean, *the* Bucky?" she squealed, jumping to her feet. "The one who was Claire's date to the dance?"

Bucky froze and looked from her to Red.

"You are," Frannie crowed. This was terrific. "Millie told me all about it. She said she called dibs on Red but Red only had eyes for Claire." Frannie had pestered Millie until she spilled the whole story about how Red and Claire met. Millie told her how she'd literally run into Red on the sidewalk of West Yellowstone that summer Claire had worked at Old Faithful. He'd apologized and set her back on her feet, but Millie had taken one look at him and finagled a double date for the West Yellowstone Grange dance. She'd told him she and her friend were only in Yellowstone for another two weeks. "We have to go to a cowboy dance with real cowboys," she'd pleaded. By the end of the night Claire had stolen Red's heart. It was a dreamy story, and Frannie could understand why Claire had fallen for Red like a ton of bricks. He really was handsome with that red hair and blue eyes, like a cowboy out of the movies.

Bucky's ears were pink and he looked back up the river where he'd come from like he was going to make a run for it. Then Red asked him what kind of fly he was using and Bucky started talking about boring fishing. Frannie lay back on the grassy bank and closed her eyes, soaking in the sunshine. "Wait until I tell Millie I met *the* Bucky," she said. At least this day hadn't been a total disaster.

chapter 14

BRIDGET

Bridget stood outside the Mammoth Hot Springs hospital with her suitcases stacked beside her and the odor of rotten eggs making her eyes water. Red had driven her past a white-and-yellow hotel, a post office, and the park information center. He parked the truck in front of a three-story hospital, unloaded her cases, and left her at the curb without a word of goodbye.

She was just as glad to be done with him.

Bridget was determined to put Red and Claire from her mind for the moment. She needed to make a good first impression on the head nurse, who would—she hoped and prayed—write her a glowing letter of recommendation to the Mayo Clinic at the end of September.

She was ready to put her best foot forward.

There was only one problem. Lying on the grass—right next to the sidewalk that led to the double doors of the hospital—was an immense animal with extremely dangerous-looking horns. Her legs refused to move one step closer to the beast.

"It's a Roosevelt elk," a friendly male voice said behind her.

She didn't take her eyes off the animal. "Is it dangerous?"

"As long as you don't make eye contact, he'll leave you alone."

She quickly averted her eyes and took in the shorts-clad stranger with a collarless shirt, overlong hair, and suntanned face. The man gestured to her suitcases. "Do you need some help, Miss . . . ?"

"No, thank you," she answered quickly. Bridget didn't want Nurse Larkin's first impression of her to be sullied by her walking in with someone so . . . unpresentable. She walked past the elk, keeping her eyes averted as she opened the door and traded the acrid stench of sulfur for the satisfying scents of antiseptic and floor polish. She stepped smartly through a cramped waiting room to the front desk, where she met the flint-gray gaze of an older nurse. A junior nurse sat behind a desk and smiled at her in a friendly way. "Good afternoon," Bridget said. "I'm Nurse Reilly."

The matronly nurse took in her appearance with a frown.

Bridget knew her windblown curls were a mess, her skirt and blouse were wrinkled, and she'd perspired through her dress shields. She'd just have to comport herself in a way that overcame those defects. The nurse glanced past Bridget and her frown deepened. Bridget looked over her shoulder and irritation flashed through her. Putting her best foot forward would be easier if she wasn't being followed by a long-haired beatnik who had appointed himself her porter.

"I'm Larkin," the nurse said crisply. "And you are late."

Bridget bristled. "I beg your pardon. I was told to report at four o'clock. It is"—she glanced at her wristwatch—"three fifty-five."

The junior nurse, a cute redhead with wide blue eyes and freckled face, gaped at Bridget.

Bridget realized her error instantly. To contradict a supervisor was a sin only slightly less egregious than affronting a doctor. What was wrong with her?

It was the fault of this man—this no-goodnik—standing at her elbow with her luggage. He was making her nervous and she needed to send him on his way. She pulled out her coin purse and handed him two quarters. "Thank you for your assistance, you can leave now."

The man accepted the quarters with a quirk of his mouth. Bridget noticed the junior nurse had a hand over her mouth, unsuccessfully suppressing what sounded like a giggle. Bridget was nonplussed. What on earth had she done wrong?

"Dr. Sampson." Larkin addressed the man with an unmistakable note of disdain. "Don't you have better things to do with your time off?"

Doctor? Bridget's cheeks burned and she wished the earth would open up and swallow her. The man was certainly not . . . doctorly. Those shorts and that hair—how was she to know? Now she'd gone and insulted him with a fifty-cent tip.

The man didn't seem the least chagrined. He pocketed the two quarters and shrugged. "Not really."

A muscle in Larkin's cheek twitched. "Leave your luggage," she ordered Bridget. "I'll get the janitor to bring it up to your room. Beckett," she barked at the junior nurse, "take Reilly upstairs. Her shift starts in five minutes."

Bridget bristled at the injustice. She had a good mind to take out the letter that stated in black and white that she was to *report* at four, not *start* at four, but that wouldn't do at all.

She'd never get the recommendation she needed at this rate.

"Don't mind the old crow," Beckett told her as she bounced down the hall. "We changed all the shift times last week because we're so shorthanded." Beckett gave Bridget a quick tour of the first floor and briefed her on the workings of the hospital. It was all quite standard, Bridget was glad to note, with modern equipment and the latest procedures. On the second floor, Beckett stopped at a nursing station staffed by a dark-haired nurse with a Jayne Mansfield figure. "This is Rita Finch," she introduced the woman. "She's second in seniority after Larkin."

"A pleasure to meet you," Bridget said.

Finch flashed a Colgate smile. "You have no idea how happy we are to see you."

At Bridget's raised brows, Beckett explained, "We've been down two nurses since . . ." She hesitated. "Well, for almost a month."

"We've been simply worked off our feet." Finch nodded.

Beckett pointed to the roster on the wall. "The other nurses are Ruth Bateman and Madge Jennings. Our senior doctor is Dr. Luek. You'll meet him tomorrow."

"Did she meet Dr. Sampson yet?" Finch asked breathlessly.

"Did she ever," Beckett said with a grin.

"Isn't he a dish?" Finch gave Bridget a once-over. "I called dibs on him, but now that you're here I don't have a chance."

Bridget didn't respond to that ridiculous comment. She had no interest in romance with doctors, especially one who had made her look like a fool.

Beckett brought her up another set of stairs to the third floor. The walls were drab green and the linoleum floor was cracked and peeling. "The washroom is at the end of the hall." She waved at a telephone on the wall. "Larkin is a stickler about the phone. Short conversations only, and no long distance." She rolled her eyes, then opened a door halfway down the hall and stepped back. "Home sweet home."

Bridget stepped into her room for the next month. It was perfectly adequate . . . for a nun. A narrow bed, a window, and a small chest of drawers. Her suitcases took up most of the floor space. She reminded herself if all went well, she'd have her own apartment in Rochester by September. She thanked Beckett and quickly changed her clothes, pulling her white uniform over her girdle and nylons and pinning on her nurse's cap. She'd need to impress Nurse Larkin to make up for her blunders.

Ten minutes later she endured Larkin's decidedly unimpressed gaze.

"I'll have you shadow me, Reilly," she said. "Until I am sure you're capable."

Bridget bit her tongue. She had graduated at the top of her nursing class at St. Cloud Nursing Academy and had seven years of experience. She certainly didn't appreciate being treated like a candy striper.

She got right to work, following Larkin as she made her rounds. "One very important rule," Larkin said, handing her the clipboard after they changed the dressing on a severe burn. "Under no circumstances are you to go on a callout after dark without a park ranger. Not here in Mammoth or if you are riding along in the ambulance. Do you understand?"

"Of course." Bridget nodded, wondering at the head nurse's severity. But she had no time to ask questions as Larkin moved rapidly from one patient to another. By the time Bridget's shift ended at midnight, she was satisfied she'd made up for her poor start. As she signed off the floor, she fully expected a positive word from the supervising nurse. "Make sure you aren't late tomorrow, Reilly," was all Larkin said.

She trudged up the two flights of stairs with Beckett. "Don't let it bug you," Beckett said, covering a yawn with her hand.

It most certainly did bug her. Bridget said goodnight to Beckett. "Oh," Bridget said before she shut the door to her room, "I just remembered something I wanted to ask you."

"Sure, what?" the younger nurse said.

"Larkin told me to always have a park ranger along when we go on calls after dark, and she was quite adamant. Why?"

Beckett's face fell and she looked away. "Oh, that."

"What?" Bridget felt a tremor of unease.

"That's because of Patsy and Sylvia."

"The nurses that left?" She'd seen their names on some of the records from last month. Bridget was surprised that Beckett used their first names, since it was common practice for nurses to use last names both on and off the floor.

"They didn't leave," Beckett said. "But . . . well, it's maybe not something you want to hear on your first day."

"What?" Bridget folded her arms. If it was about the job, she needed to know.

Beckett looked down at the cracked floor. "The thing is, they got called out to the cabins over by the camping area—I mean, Sylvia did. One of the guests had a sprained ankle and needed a compression wrap. Sylvia took the kit and said she'd just run it over, quick as a wink. By herself." Beckett's voice dropped.

Bridget felt a chill travel up her neck and prickle over her scalp. She suddenly didn't want to know about Sylvia and Patsy.

"When she didn't come back, Patsy went to look for her." Beckett's voice was choked with emotion. "We didn't think anything of it." She sniffled and dabbed at her eyes. "They were such sweet girls. Patsy was engaged to be married."

Bridget's legs went wobbly and she put a hand on the doorframe to steady herself. "What happened?"

"It was a grizzly." Beckett looked up, and Bridget saw the younger nurse's eyes were full of tears. "Some campers left their garbage out and Sylvia must have surprised the bear in the dark." She swiped at her cheek. "Sylvia was dead when the rangers got there. We got Patsy back to the hospital, but we couldn't save her."

"Oh, no." Bridget felt as if the room was tilting sideways. How awful. "I'm so sorry, Beckett."

Beckett nodded her head, accepting Bridget's woefully inadequate sympathy. "Goodnight, Reilly. See you tomorrow."

Bridget shut her door, stomach churning. A simple call for a sprained ankle and two nurses dead in a horrible way. Here she'd thought it a stroke of luck she got the job at Mammoth in the middle of the summer, but it wasn't luck, it was tragedy. A terrible tragedy in this dreadful place.

She looked at her suitcases, yet to be unpacked. She could go home—back to the civilized world where bears didn't lurk in the dark. Where there weren't boiling pools and sharp-horned animals around every corner.

She sat down on the hard bed. She couldn't leave. If she left now, she'd never get hired at the Mayo. And what about Claire? She had to convince Claire to come home, where she and Jenny would be safe. She knelt down on the hard floor and made the sign of the cross. She prayed reluctantly for Frannie, and more fervently for Claire. She added a final prayer for the families of Sylvia and Patsy, even though she had never met them.

Then she prayed for herself. *Dear Lord, help me to keep my promise to Dad. Help me to get Claire and Jenny home, with or without Red.*

chapter 15

CLAIRE

Claire woke from her nap to Jenny babbling happily in her crib and Red frying up a dinner of trout and potatoes.

She was still annoyed at Frannie, and how she'd made poor Jenny miserable, but she felt terrible about blowing up the way she did. She'd wanted Bridget to see how happy she was here with Red. Instead, her visit had been one disaster after another. She hated to think what Bridget would report back to Dad. When she came out of the bedroom with Jenny in her arms, she gave Frannie a side hug and told her she was sorry.

Frannie actually mumbled a return apology.

Red was quiet, but after the dishes were done he gave her a serious look. "Let's take a walk to the river."

Was he going to apologize for being such a bear to her sisters? Not that she blamed him when it came to Bridget. How could she have forgotten how snippy her sister could be?

Frannie sprawled on the couch where Jenny was propped with a rattle. "I'll play with the little whippersnapper while you two lovebirds take a walk."

Claire looked doubtfully at Frannie. She hadn't proven herself terribly trustworthy with the baby. "I'll just be down the trail if you need me."

Red took Claire's hand as they walked to the river. The setting sun turned the water of the Madison to gold and silver. On the far side of the river, a red-tailed hawk circled the grassy meadow, landing high on a dead branch like a star on a Christmas tree. Claire felt a lifting of her spirits that had weighed her down since she got Bridget's letter—or even before that, when she'd heard about Dell. The beauty of the out-of-doors always did that for her. She just had to remember to open her eyes and see it.

With Red's rough, calloused hand in hers, she felt closer to him. Close enough to ask him about Dell, and what he was hiding from her. Then she could tell him again how sorry she was about Marigold.

They stopped at the edge of the river and Red turned to her. His eyes were shadowed and his forehead creased. "I got fired, Claire," Red got out. "After the fight at the Otter."

Her questions about Dell fled from her mind, but his words took a moment to sink in. The fight at the Otter had been days ago. Her mouth dried and she pulled her hand from his grip. He'd lied to her.

"I'm sorry." His eyes darted to hers. "I just—I didn't want you to worry."

Claire crossed her arms over her chest as anxiety crept up her throat.

Red turned her toward him, his touch gentle. "Claire, I've got a job lined up already. It pays more than Wormsbecker's place—a lot more."

She should have been relieved, but his assurance did nothing to assuage her rioting feelings. It wasn't about the money, or how they would pay the rent. How could he not know that? It was about trust and not keeping secrets.

"I'm going tomorrow," Red said.

She didn't understand his meaning. "Going where?"

"To Libby," Red answered, his voice firm. "To work in the mine."

Her pulse pounded in her ears as she looked at his earnest face. Where was Libby, and why was he telling her like he'd already decided?

"It's up near the Canadian border," Red rushed on at her confused expression. "The pay is twenty dollars a day. Bucky told me about it. In a month—maybe two—we can save up enough to get us through the winter."

Claire shivered as the breeze from the river turned icy. Her numb mind grasped only one thought. Red was leaving. "No." She worked her dry mouth as she struggled for words that could change his mind. "We have the money I got for Marigold." There was more than twenty dollars left in the cookie tin. She could make it last. "You can find a job here."

"I've looked," Red retorted. "Nobody's hiring. And winter is coming. You know how tough it is to get work here after the snow falls."

Claire remembered last winter when money had been tight. After the November hunts, Wormsbecker had cut Red's working days to only two a week. Even when Red started working full-time again, they had yet to catch up on the overdue bills.

None of that mattered because Claire couldn't breathe.

"You've been alone before," Red said, finally registering her panic. His brows came together and he squeezed her hands. "And you have Frannie to help."

"Why are you doing this?" Claire asked, her voice rising. Was it because of Marigold? Was he still angry?

"Claire." Red looked away. "I have to."

He didn't have to. Claire's stomach pitted and her chest felt as if it were being squeezed by a giant fist. Even when Red put his arms around her and pulled her close, she felt no comfort in his warmth.

Red walked with her back to the house as if it was all decided.

Claire put Jenny to bed and made up the couch for Frannie, her mind whirling. In their bedroom, Red shoved clothing in his pack as she tried one more time to change his mind. "Red," she said, "please don't go."

Red didn't turn around. "Bucky will help with Rosie and Bess, and anything else you need."

His mind was made up, and Claire couldn't change it. A cold

hopelessness rose like a flood, chilling her to the bone. Claire got into bed and when Red joined her and reached for her, she pulled away.

"Frannie is just outside." She felt the hurt and disappointment in his silence, but she turned her back to him so he couldn't see the tears on her face.

Before the sun was even up, Claire held sleeping Jenny in her arms as Red drove to the Depot and parked. The bus that would take Red three hundred miles north idled on the curb.

They'd been in this same spot almost two years earlier.

That time, Claire had been the one leaving, after her summer as a savage at Old Faithful. She'd made no promises to Red that day. In fact, she'd been determined never to see him again. Red Wilder was nothing more than a summer romance, one she'd look upon fondly once the pain of separation faded. Claire was going home to her family and students at Tara School. Red's Montana-sky eyes were filled with anguish. "Please don't go," he'd said.

Now, Claire said those same words to him, a painful pressure just above her collarbone making every word difficult to get out.

"I have to," he answered.

Claire closed her eyes and tried to pray. *Please, Lord, change his mind.* But in the dark with the stink of diesel fuel in the air and the gray light, it didn't feel like the Lord heard her.

The bus driver honked a warning.

Red got out of the truck and grabbed his pack from the back. Claire followed with Jenny, holding her close.

"Take good care of her." Red kissed the top of Jenny's head, his expression determined. It felt to Claire that he was already miles away. Red bent to kiss her goodbye but just like last night, she turned away. She couldn't accept his kiss when everything inside her was crumbling.

"Go," she said, dredging up words from a place that was raw and painful. "We don't need you." Even as the words left her lips she knew they were cruel and untrue. She saw the flash of pain on his face and wanted to take the words back, but something—a deep hurt she couldn't name—wouldn't let her.

The bus blared a final warning.

Claire didn't watch Red walk away. She held Jenny close and squeezed her eyes shut. If Red looked back before he stepped on the bus she didn't see it.

chapter 16

FRANNIE

Frannie stuck out her thumb.

A truck with a towering load of hay bales came toward her. The brakes screeched as it passed by and she watched it slow down and stop twenty feet ahead.

Boy howdy, a ride on her first try.

She'd woken up to find Claire and Red gone and a note on the kitchen table that read *Back soon, help yourself to breakfast.* "Don't mind if I do," she said to the empty house. She ate the last of the Jell-O salad, threw on her wrinkled capri pants and a blouse, packed her suitcase, and walked out the door.

It didn't take a psychoanalyst to see that things were wonky between Claire and Red, and she knew why. They'd gone down to the river last night after dinner, and when Claire came back her eyes were all weepy.

They'd been fighting about her, obviously.

Red didn't want her around. She could take a hint. She ran to the passenger door of the hay truck and pulled it open.

"Where you headin'?" an old cowboy with a lip of chew and a stained straw hat asked as she scrambled up the running board and into the passenger seat.

"Canyon Lodge," she said, shoving her suitcase under her feet.

"I can get you as far as Madison Junction." He put the truck in gear and spit gravel behind them.

She'd heard about the job at Canyon Lodge on the train while Bridget was reading her dumb old book. "Canyon is looking for help," a kid who looked like Pat Boone had told her. He was sitting in the last car with a gang of outdoorsy-looking teenagers. They passed her a flask and she'd started cooking up a plan to get back at Dad and Bridget.

The ranger at the West Entrance waved the hay truck through, and she watched the flash of the river along the road. By now, Claire would know she was gone, and she'd call Bridget right away. Then Bridget would call Dad. Holy smokes, what she'd give to be a fly on the wall when Dad got wind of what she'd done.

She laughed out loud and the old guy gave her a funny look.

Her next ride was with a businessman type who asked a lot of questions and tried to put his hand on her knee. Then she crammed in with a family of six in a loaded station wagon. "This is the place," the dorky dad said as he came to a stop. "Canyon Lodge."

She grabbed her suitcase, and watched the station wagon disappear in a cloud of dust. The place looked like something out of *Gunsmoke* or *The Rifleman*. Tall pines surrounded the rustic building and a sign over the door said *Cabins*. A sudden rush of doubt made her swallow hard. What if the redheaded kid was wrong and she didn't get a job? She'd die before she went back to Claire's with her hands in her pockets.

Frannie hefted her suitcase and squared her shoulders. "Here goes nothing."

Ten minutes later, Frannie sat in a hot-as-a-frying-pan office with a middle-aged beatnik named Twig. He asked her name, address, and age, and wrote them on a yellow card. She didn't give him her real address—she wasn't stupid—in case he decided to call and talk to her dad. "We don't usually hire in the middle of the summer," Twig said, "but Sherry got sent home with an appendicitis." Twig plodded to the door and called out, "Jerrylynn!" A girl a couple years older than Frannie bounced into the office in a skirt and sneakers, a blonde ponytail, and cat-eye glasses with little rhinestones on the corners. "Tell Frannie about working at the Grand Canyon of the Yellowstone River Lodge."

Jerrylynn gave a theatrical bow and put her hands together as if reciting a poem. "The hours are long, the pay stinks, the beds are hard and the mosquitoes are mean, but it's the best darn job you've ever seen."

Twig raised his bushy brows at her. "Still interested?"

Frannie's earlier attack of doubt went the way of the dodo. This was so much cooler than taking care of a baby in the middle of nowhere. "Abso-poso-lutely."

"Then you're officially a savage." Twig nodded to Jerrylynn. "Take her around, show her the bunkhouse and then start your shift."

Frannie followed the bobbing ponytail out of the office. Man-oh-man, this was neat. She was a grown-up now, with no party-pooper sisters or her dad to tell her what to do. Maybe she'd be escorting guests to their rooms, or working as a waitress or even telling tourists about the sights on one of the buses. Wouldn't Jonny and her friends back in Willmar be green when she told them about her job in Yellowstone National Park?

They walked by the front desk where three boys were goofing off. Two had crew cuts and looked college age, the other had a side part and glasses. "This is Frannie." Jerrylynn didn't slow down as she flicked a hand at the boys. "This is Ernie, Sam, and that kid there is Paul." Frannie gave what she hoped was an uninterested wave.

Next, Jerrylynn brought her through a spacious room with tree-trunk pillars and antler chandeliers. "Where is everybody?" Frannie took in the almost-empty room.

"Out seeing the sights," Jerrylynn said. "They'll be back at dinnertime, and they'll be hungry. Through there is the cafeteria." Jerrylynn motioned to closed double doors. "We don't have our own eating area, so meals for savages are served here before it opens to the dudes."

"Dudes?" Frannie asked.

Jerrylynn flashed a cute dimple. "You're a savage, the guests are dudes."

"Cool," Frannie said, eyeing the cafeteria and thinking that she could use something to eat. That Jell-O had been hours ago. But Jerrylynn was already heading to the great outdoors. Frannie skipped to keep up with her guide as they went down a hill to a ramshackle cabin. A clothesline stretched alongside it draped with shirts, pants, and girls' underwear.

"This," Jerrylynn said with a flourish of her hand, "is the rat trap." Frannie's face must have looked funny, because Jerrylynn laughed. "The boys' dorm is called the dungeon, and it's even worse."

Inside the screen door a row of cots lined one wall and open storage shelves the other, messy with piles of bright clothing. Jerrylynn showed Frannie to a bed in the corner and pushed aside a pile of clothes to make an open spot on the shelves.

Frannie dropped her suitcase and lay down on the bed. A nap would be divine.

"Oh, no, you don't." Jerrylynn poked her. "We have work to do."

"What's my job?" she asked, pushing herself up to stand again.

"You're a pillow puncher like me," Jerrylynn said. "That's what we call cabin maids."

Pillow puncher didn't sound so bad. Frannie followed Jerrylynn down a dusty trail to a line of log cabins. There were dozens—maybe hundreds—of them. Towels were draped over the railings, lawn chairs, ice chests, and children's toys were strewn all over.

"This is the low rent district," Jerrylynn explained as she stopped in front of a wheeled cart stacked with buckets, bottles, and the kind of cleaning brushes Frannie had seen Flo use. "Not fancy like the big hotel on the other side of the river, but not as rough as the sagebrushers have it."

"Sagebrushers?" Frannie didn't know that word either.

"The tenters over in the auto camp." Jerrylynn pushed open the screen door of the first cabin. "We need to get through all these, and then help out on the south side."

There were more? Frannie's high spirits took a nosedive. How long was she supposed to work? When did they get to relax and do all the fun things Claire had talked about? What about lunch?

The cabin wasn't big—just one room about the size of Frannie's bedroom at home—but it looked like the atom bomb had gone off in it. Sheets and blankets were tangled on two sets of bunk beds. Clothes and suitcases littered the plank floor. Beside an iron stove was a small table with a water pitcher and crumpled towels and on a shelf below, a white clay pot.

Frannie took it in. "People pay money to stay here?"

"And we clean up after them." Jerrylynn grabbed a broom. "We have a lot of traditions around here," she explained. "You'll get to know them. But one of them is the newbies get to empty the ducks."

"What's a duck?"

Jerrylynn pointed to the clay pot. Frannie lifted the lid and almost retched right there. She slammed the lid back down. "It's . . ." She couldn't even say it.

"Yep." Jerrylynn nodded. "Dudes don't want to walk to the outhouse in the middle of the night, you know, because of the bears." She started sweeping. "You have to take it to the outhouse, dump it, and rinse it good with that garden hose out there."

Frannie stared at the bucket. She'd never done anything so . . . disgusting. She wouldn't touch it. It was too icky.

"Get a move on," Jerrylynn prompted.

Frannie took a step back toward the door. Maybe she could go to Twig, ask for a different job. But that was a no-go. She'd been lucky to get this one. She could bug out and look like a dummy. A wimp. Go back to Claire and take her lumps. Get a lecture from Bridget, and Dad would hear how she'd come back with her tail between her legs.

No. Nope. No way.

She took a deep breath, held it, and did what she had to do.

chapter 17

CLAIRE

Claire sat down hard on the kitchen chair and read the note again. *Thanks for everything, sis. Don't worry about me, F.*

She'd driven home from the Depot, taking deep breaths and telling herself she couldn't fall apart. Lots of men went away to work. They went to logging camps and mines, and even to Oregon to work on the fishing boats. Red would be back. She was fine. But what would she tell Frannie? She'd have to give some explanation to both her sisters eventually—and that would get to Dad. Would he call her, frantic again? Would he tell her *I told you so*? She knew for certain that his opinion of Red would go even lower.

But when she walked into the house with Jenny in her arms, Frannie wasn't asleep on the couch. Claire's stomach did a somersault. Then she saw the note on the kitchen table in Frannie's messy cursive. *Don't worry about me.* Worry? She was furious. Where could she possibly have gone? Wasn't it enough Red had left, now Frannie pulled a vanishing act?

Jenny let out a hungry cry. Claire went back to the kitchen and started to prepare her bottle. Should she call Dad? Or maybe the sheriff?

She called Bridget.

"I'm going to wring her scrawny little neck." Bridget's voice was rough with sleep.

Claire's thoughts exactly. She cradled the telephone receiver against her shoulder as she fed Jenny her bottle. "Should we tell Dad?"

"Good grief, no." Bridget groaned. "We have to find her."

Claire hung up a few minutes later and finished feeding Jenny. Bridget didn't have a car and her shift started in an hour. "You go look for her," Bridget had commanded. "Maybe she's just pulling a trick on you."

If she was, Claire would give her a piece of her mind.

By the time Jenny was burped, changed, and dressed, Claire had a plan. She drove to Eagle's and ran in to ask Helen about Frannie. "She's eighteen, short blonde hair."

Helen's forehead creased with concern but her eyes lit with interest. "I haven't seen her, dear." Helen assured her that youngsters did that kind of thing all the time. "She'll turn up," she said with a smile.

Helen Eagle's assurances didn't ease Claire's mind.

Claire got back in the truck and drove the short distance to the Depot, which had gone from deserted when she dropped off Red early that morning to thronged with buses and motor coaches, all waiting to bring tourists into Yellowstone. Had Frannie taken a bus into the park—or one of the trains that went east to Idaho and California? Alarm raced through her as she parked. At this point, Claire wouldn't put anything past her idiotic kid sister.

"I don't remember a girl like that buying a ticket this morning," the young woman behind the glass answered when Claire described Frannie. "But you could check the dining lodge. We haven't boarded the buses yet."

The Union Pacific Dining Lodge was in the midst of the breakfast rush, with an army of waitresses carrying coffee pots and breakfast platters. Claire walked through the dining room with Jenny on her shoulder, looking for Frannie's petite frame and short hair. She was losing hope and wondering what to do next, when she caught sight of a familiar face at a corner table.

"Beth," Claire said in surprise. She hadn't seen Beth since that terrible day when she'd gone to the Henshaws'. Beth looked even worse than she had a week ago. She was wearing a dress that hadn't seen an iron, and her light-brown hair was falling out of a ponytail. A cup of coffee sat on the table in front of her, an oily film on its surface. "Mrs. Wilder." Beth blinked at her as her eyes welled with tears.

Claire couldn't very well walk away when the poor girl looked so distraught.

"May I?" Claire motioned to the chair opposite Beth's.

Beth nodded, her hands clutched around the handle of a small suitcase on her knees.

"Where are you going?" Claire asked gently.

"Home," Beth answered in a small voice.

The admission pulled at Claire's heart. She knew about wishing for the comfort of family. Wasn't that why she'd packed her suitcase the other night? She reached across the table and took Beth's hand, remembering what Grace Miller had said about Beth's parents. "Your parents will be glad to see you," she reassured the girl. What kind of parents wouldn't take back a grieving child?

The waitress put a cup of coffee in front of her. Jenny wiggled in her lap, reaching for the cup. Claire let go of Beth's hand and gave Jenny the spoon to play with. If Beth was leaving, Claire might never see her again. This might be her only chance to find out what Beth knew about Dell and Red. "Beth," Claire said, hoping that talking about Dell wouldn't be too much for the fragile girl. "What did you mean, when you said you were sorry about Red and Dell?"

Beth's pale brows notched. "Don't you know?"

Claire didn't relish confessing that Red had kept something from her that was obviously important. "Red told me he and Dell had a falling-out."

Beth fiddled with her coffee cup but didn't take a drink. "It was after you left to go back to Minnesota." She glanced up and the corners of her mouth lifted. "Red was miserable. We all knew why."

Claire had been miserable, too, after that beautiful summer in

Yellowstone. With Bridget working long hours, it was up to her to play peacemaker again between Dad and Frannie while she tried to forget Red and fit back into a life she didn't want anymore—a life without Red.

"My uncle Walt fired Dell when we got engaged. My dad was so angry. He told me he . . ." her voice broke.

"Beth, you don't have to talk about it." Claire felt terrible making Beth relive something so painful. Dad hadn't been happy when Claire married Red, but at least he hadn't disowned her.

"No, I want to tell you." She straightened her shoulders and met Claire's eyes. "It was a couple days before our wedding, Dell told me—"

"There you are, Beth." The harsh voice made Beth jerk in surprise, upsetting her coffee cup. Pete Henshaw suddenly loomed over them both. "Iris and I have been worried."

"Mr. Henshaw," Claire said, her heart tripping up a notch and her grip on Jenny tightening.

Pete Henshaw ignored her and took Beth's suitcase from her lap. "Come on home, Beth."

Beth pressed her lips together, her glance flitting from her father-in-law to Claire, her face pale. Was she asking for Claire's help? It almost seemed like it, with the look in her eyes.

If Beth didn't want to go with Pete Henshaw, she shouldn't have to do so. "Mr. Henshaw," Claire spoke up, straightening in her chair. "Beth tells me she's going home to her parents."

Pete Henshaw's jaw clenched but his voice remained reasonable. "Beth's not well, Mrs. Wilder." He put a hand under Beth's elbow and helped her to her feet. "She needs to come home with me."

Something wasn't right about Pete Henshaw's possessive grip on Beth or the defeated look on Beth's face. Claire's pulse pounded in her throat. She glanced around the dining room, but the waitresses were paying no attention and the patrons were busy with their meals. No one seemed to see anything amiss between Pete Henshaw and his daughter-in-law.

Jenny let out a stuttering cry and Claire adjusted her in her arms. It was past time for Jenny's nap, but she had to try to help the young woman. "Beth," she said as if Pete Henshaw wasn't glaring at her. "Would you like me to call your parents for you? Let them know you're on your way?"

"Mind your own business, Mrs. Wilder." Pete Henshaw's voice rose. "Iris and I are taking good care of Beth."

Jenny's cries escalated to a rhythmic bawl. An older couple at the nearest table looked up from their breakfast with irritated expressions. Claire patted Jenny's back.

Beth's shoulders drooped and she glanced at Jenny's reddening face. "Don't worry about me, Mrs. Wilder. You take care of your baby."

Claire watched Pete Henshaw walk Beth through the crowded restaurant. Was she really unwell, like Pete said? Despite Beth's assurance, Claire was worried about her—she just didn't know what to do. Claire put a dime on the table for her coffee and stood with her crying baby.

As Beth and Pete reached the door, Beth looked over her shoulder and Claire could have sworn she saw tears in the young woman's eyes.

chapter 18

FRANNIE

Frannie wanted to lay down and D-I-E, die.

She'd cleaned cabins for four hours. She swept the plank floors, took garbage to the bear-proof cans, and scrubbed out the ducks while holding her breath. It was beyond disgusting.

"Okay, let's get cleaned up before we miss dinner." Jerrylynn poked her in the ribs. "Race you to the rat trap!"

Frannie watched Jerrylynn dart up the trail. Her feet were killing her and she could barely move, how was Jerrylynn still as perky as a cheerleader?

When she got to the cabin, it was teeming with girls, most of them in their underwear and all of them talking. Jerrylynn saw her and shouted over the racket. "Girls, this is Frannie, she's the new Sherry." The girls around her said exuberant hellos. Somebody turned up the radio and everybody started singing along to "Teenager in Love."

Frannie looked down at her own clothes, sweat-stained and spattered with who-knows-what. Then at the girls dressing and undressing, nobody taking notice of anybody. Okey dokey. If everybody else was doing it she would, too.

Ten minutes later, the pack of girls was trooping out of the rat trap and down the trail toward the lodge. That's when a gang of boys joined them, all of them whooping it up. She'd hoped to see Sam, the cute one who looked like he was in college, but it was Paul—the one with glasses—who fell into step beside her. "How was your first day?"

"Cool," she said. She wasn't about to admit that she'd gagged a dozen times while emptying the ducks. "What's your job?"

"I'm a pack rat."

"A what-rat?"

"A porter." He laughed. "I help the dudes carry luggage and gear to their cabins, get the camp stoves working, stuff like that. Last year, I was a pearl diver." He answered her questioning glance, "A dishwasher. So this is a step up."

"You were here last year?" Frannie wasn't sure if she'd last another day.

"It's my third season," he answered. "I'll come every summer until they don't let me anymore." He leaned closer and whispered, "Honestly, they wouldn't even have to pay me."

Maybe Paul was a couple cards short of a full deck but she was too tired to figure it out. She just wanted something to eat and to go to sleep for a year.

She followed the whole gang through the lobby, now busy with families coming in from sightseeing, past the souvenir shop on one side and the Haynes photo shop on the other. The cafeteria was like the one at her high school, and all the kids lined up with trays to get servings of hamburgers, green beans, and mashed potatoes.

She filled her tray, then looked at the tables with a sick lurch in her middle that had nothing to do with hunger. All the kids were sitting in groups and laughing together. What if she had to sit by herself, like when she first went to high school and didn't have any friends? It had taken two years and plenty of pranks to get in with Jonny and his gang.

"Hey, Frannie!" Jerrylynn waved at her from a table by the windows. "I saved you a seat."

Frannie felt a rush of relief and sat down with Jerrylynn and a couple other girls. Paul sat across the table with Sam, the cute one, and the other boy she'd met but couldn't remember his name. "Thanks," she said to Jerrylynn, trying not to sound as relieved as she felt. They all dug in like they hadn't seen food in days. The boys goofed off, keeping everybody in stitches, competing to see how many cartons of milk they could guzzle.

"I have to scoot," Jerrylynn said as they shoved their empty trays through an opening to the kitchen. "I'm in the show tonight."

"What's the show?" Frannie asked.

Jerrylynn pointed to the stage on one side of the dining lodge. "It's different every night. Sometimes it's a song and dance number, or skits. Last night of the season, the guys borrow the girls' dresses and try to win a beauty pageant. It's a riot. Last year, Sam took home first prize."

Frannie wasn't surprised. Sam was a cutie patootie.

An old lady with white hair and glasses snagged Frannie's elbow. "You're the new girl?" she asked, and without waiting for an answer, "Can you sing?"

"I was in the church choir," Frannie said, then realized how lame that sounded. Before she could say wait-a-minute, she was on stage with a mimeographed sheet titled "The Dinner Bell Song," singing to the guests as they filed into the cafeteria.

After the dudes sat down to eat, Jerrylynn and some boys put on a skit about an unlucky tourist and a bear encounter. Sam played the bear and had everyone roaring. Then a five-piece band came onstage and everybody—savages and dudes—started dancing.

"Come on, new girl." Sam pulled her out on the floor to do the bunny hop. Suddenly Frannie's feet didn't hurt and she was having a blast. She jumped into one dance after another until everybody had their arms around each other's shoulders, singing the last song. She didn't know the words but managed the chorus of, "Yellowstone, Yellowstone, best place I've ever known."

Then they were walking back to the rat trap, with the stars and the mosquitoes out in full force. The boys shouted goodbyes as they veered onto the trail to the dungeon. Jerrylynn linked her arm with

Frannie's, and a girl named Vicky did the same on her other side. "So, Frannie," Jerrylynn said, "What did you think of your first day at Canyon?"

Frannie looked at her new supercool friends—one on each side. "I think I died and went to heaven."

"Up and at 'em!"

It was still dark when Frannie came awake, her nose cold from the bite of the morning air. A mosquito whined near her ear and she pulled the blanket over her head. Just a few more minutes of blessed sleep. The singing and dancing after dinner were terrific, but the thought of another day emptying ducks wasn't thrilling.

The girls around her began to stir. She rubbed her eyes and put her feet on the cold floor. How could it be so hot during the day and so cold in the morning?

Vicky was wiggling out of her pajamas and into a pair of pedal pushers. "Remember, Frannie-pants, we're going up to Mount Washburn after our shifts."

"What for?" Frannie asked. She kept her blanket wrapped around her shoulders as she sorted through her clothing for something kind of clean.

"Initiation."

Frannie gave Vicky one raised brow. She'd perfected the look in front of the mirror at home and was pretty proud of it. "What's that?"

"Just something everybody in our gang does." Vicky pulled a sweater over her head. "The boys are coming," she added.

"I'll be there." Frannie had been wanting a reason to wear her new short shorts and Sam was it. He was the best-looking boy of the whole bunch.

After cleaning a million cabins, Frannie and Vicky raced back to the rat trap that afternoon. "We have time for a shower if we hurry." Vicky grabbed a towel from the clothesline.

"I was going to call my sister," Frannie said. Claire was probably worried sick. Twig had told her she could use the telephone in the lodge office, but she had to be there before he locked up at five.

Vicky was already heading out the door. "Suit yourself," Vicky said over her shoulder. Frannie hesitated. A shower would be divine, and she wanted to look her best for Sam. "Wait for me." She grabbed her shorts and a shirt and ran to catch up. She followed Vicky to a concrete-block building set off from the west-side cabins. A strong odor of mildew came from the row of showers with flimsy plastic curtains.

"It's freezing!" Frannie yelped when she stepped into the spray of water.

"Then make it quick," Vicky said unhelpfully.

"You're late," Sam said when they met the boys in the parking lot. "But whoo-whee." He took a look at Frannie. "Worth waiting for."

Frannie's cheeks warmed. She'd bought the short shorts at the beginning of the summer and wore them for all of ten minutes before Dad went stark raving mad. Now, she could wear whatever she wanted and be friends with whoever she liked. Sweet freedom.

Frannie's stomach growled. "What about dinner?" Lunch was a long time ago. "And where's Jerrylynn?"

Ernie held up a sack. "Got sandwiches from the kitchen. And some bottles of soda. Plus a little something from Hamilton's." He grinned. Hamilton's was the tourist store across the canyon that had everything from batteries to beer.

"Jerrylynn didn't want to play hooky from the show tonight." Vicky hopped in the back seat of a cherry-red Chevy convertible. "She's such a dweeb."

Ernie and Sam crowded into the front seat, and Paul—Frannie saw with surprise—slid into the driver's seat.

"So where are we going?" She slid in next to Vicky. She didn't want to ask too many questions and sound like a nervous Nellie.

Vicky smirked and exchanged a look with Sam. "That's for us to know and you to find out."

Frannie wished Vicky had stayed at the lodge instead of Jerrylynn.

Sam passed around a bottle of beer and they approached a concrete bridge that crossed the Yellowstone River. The bridge was narrow—too narrow for two cars to pass—and Frannie looked across the span, wondering what they'd do if a car came from the opposite direction.

"Come on, Paul," Ernie said, taking a swig of beer. "Put the pedal to the metal."

Paul ignored Ernie's jibe and slowed to check for cars before driving across the bridge. Frannie knew who the square was then. "Hey, give me a taste of that." She held out her hand for the beer.

"See," Vicky said to Ernie. "I told you she was cool."

Frannie took a swig. It tasted terrible, but she smacked her lips like it was good. They drove for at least an hour, singing along to the staticky radio. Paul pulled the car over on a wide lookout where a sign said Lava Creek. "Come on, kids," Sam said. "We're wastin' daylight."

They hiked for what seemed like forever. While they walked through woods and over a rickety footbridge, they passed the beer and kidded around. Sam and Ernie were a panic and a half, but Paul was something else. "See this ridge of rock up here?" he asked, pointing to the dun-colored rock cliffs that rose above the dense blue-green forested slopes. "That's dolomite."

"Okay, nerd," Vicky said, and the boys laughed.

Paul was nerdy, but Vicky rubbed Frannie the wrong way.

Paul didn't seem to care about the jabs. "The dolomite shows that this whole area was made by volcanoes. And that volcano is still down there. Waiting. If it goes, this whole place—" He waved his hands to take in all of Yellowstone, then made an explosion sound. "It would make the A-bomb look like a firecracker."

"Thanks for the geology lesson," Sam said. "But it's summer and we're not in school."

Frannie hadn't known about the volcano under Yellowstone and thought it was pretty interesting, but what was Paul doing with this group of ultracool kids when Sam and Vicky didn't even seem to like him?

The sun was lowering when they reached a shallow creek trickling through huge boulders. They trooped over a smooth slab of rock and Ernie came to a stop at a steaming egg-shaped pool about five feet across and who knew how deep. "This is what they call Dead Savage Spring," Ernie announced. "You don't have to be Einstein to figure out why."

Frannie's heart tripped up a bit. "Is it dangerous?"

Ernie looked at her with a grin. "That's the point, Sherlock."

Frannie tried to look unimpressed, but a twinge of unease vibrated through her chest.

"You get to jump in," Vicky said. "That's the initiation."

Frannie remembered about the kid who'd fallen in hot springs at that place Claire took them to. She looked at Sam and Vicky—and wished Jerrylynn had come along. She shot a glance at Paul and felt a little better. Paul was smart. If he did it, it must be safe.

"We're going to count, and you jump," Sam said with a slur to his voice.

"In my clothes?" Frannie said.

"Unless you want to skinny-dip." Sam leered and Ernie laughed.

"Don't be such a jerk, Sam." Paul spoke up. "She doesn't have to do it if she doesn't want to."

"Shut up, egghead," Sam said. "You wouldn't even take the plunge."

"Wait," Frannie said, stepping back from the steaming water. "Then how did he get in the gang?" Maybe there was another way.

"Because he has the car, of course," Ernie said.

Frannie didn't have a choice. Unless she wanted to sit by herself at lunch and not have anybody to dance with after dinner.

"Don't be a chicken," Vicky prompted. She started to cluck and Ernie and Sam joined in, flapping their elbows.

Frannie couldn't back down now. She toed off her sneakers. "Okey dokey," she said, trying to pretend her heart wasn't beating like a drum. "Dead Savage Spring, here I come."

chapter 19

BRIDGET

Beckett hung up the telephone at the nurse's station. "Emergency coming in on the ambulance."

"What is it?" Bridget asked. She'd fumed all day about her idiotic little sister. Where could Frannie be? And what was she supposed to tell Dad? She'd put off calling him for days and felt terrible about it, but what was she supposed to tell him—that she was failing to keep her promises to him about both Claire and Frannie?

Beckett wrote down the call time on a clipboard. "The connection was terrible. All I got was *young woman picked up in the North Loop*. Do you have any idea where Dr. Sampson could be?"

"I'll find him," Bridget grumbled. Her feet were killing her and her head was pounding as she trudged up the stairs to the patient rooms. Why couldn't Dr. Sampson stay in his office like a normal physician? Instead, he wandered among the patient rooms—playing cards, pushing wheelchairs through the halls at breakneck speeds, fooling around like he was a kid. She'd walked into a patient's room one day to find him juggling bandage rolls. Of all the things. It wasn't how doctors should conduct themselves.

Not to mention, he'd played that terrible prank on her with the elk.

"What are you doing?" Beckett asked her yesterday afternoon when they'd gone outside to get a breath of fresh air.

"I'm avoiding eye contact so he doesn't charge," Bridget answered, her head angled carefully away from the elk that insisted on lying outside the doors of the hospital. Beckett broke into a fit of laughter, hardly able to catch her breath as Bridget's face burned with humiliation.

If Dr. Sampson wasn't a doctor, she'd tell him just what she thought of him. She found him reading aloud to the broken tibia in room six. "Incoming ambulance, Dr. Sampson." She checked her wristwatch. "If you don't mind."

He raised his brows at her tart tone. "Thank you, Reilly," he answered, then smiled at the little boy in the bed. "We'll have to wait until next time to find out what happens to Tom Sawyer."

Bridget didn't wait for him, but hurried downstairs to stock the supply cart before the ambulance arrived. She looked up to find Larkin watching her put the thermometers in their alcohol cups and braced herself for a caustic remark. Since she'd arrived, she'd had nothing but corrections from the senior nurse.

"Excellent work," Larkin said this time.

Would wonders never cease? The supervising nurse's expression remained severe. "Unlike some of these nurses who don't know the meaning of the word *professionalism*." She cut her eyes toward Finch, who was flirting with Dr. Sampson in the hallway as they waited for the ambulance.

"Thank you, Nurse Larkin," Bridget said, standing up and straightening her shoulders. "That means a lot to me." Since she was suddenly on Larkin's good side, she took the opportunity. "I'm hoping to get a position at Mayo Clinic this fall," she said. "I do hope I can count on a good recommendation."

Larkin's thin brows went toward her widow's peak. "If you continue to do your job at the high level I've observed." Her gaze sharpened on Bridget. "Have you ever considered working as a traveling nurse?" Larkin asked. "It is quite prestigious and the pay is first-rate."

Bridget wasn't about to tell Larkin that her favorite novels were about traveling nurses having adventures in exotic places. Larkin would think her as bad as Finch. Not to mention, even if she wanted to gad about the world, Dad would never stand for it. "It's something to consider," she replied evasively.

The wail of the ambulance siren sounded, then abruptly cut off. The ambulance driver and his assistant came through the back doors with a gurney.

"What do we have, Jim?" Dr. Sampson was at the patient's side.

"Young woman," the ambulance driver said. "She was picked up by a family and fainted in the car. They found a ranger and called it in. She's been in and out since we got her."

Bridget helped the ambulance driver transfer the woman to the table. She had matted sandy hair and a childlike face. A faded floral dress hung on her slim frame.

Dr. Sampson began an examination. "Reilly, get her vitals."

Bridget felt her forehead. "Skin pale and clammy. Breathing rapid."

Dr. Sampson held the girl's hand. "What's your name, dear?"

"Beth," the girl answered in a weak voice. "Beth Henshaw."

"We'll take good care of you, Miss Henshaw," Bridget said briskly. "Tell me, can you see me clearly?"

She squinted. "You're a little blurry."

Bridget nodded. "Are you experiencing any pain?"

"My head hurts." She looked like she might lose consciousness.

Dr. Sampson listened to her heart with his stethoscope and Bridget took her pulse, watching the second hand of her wristwatch as she counted. "Slightly elevated," she reported. She noted the patient's pallid skin and sunken eyes. Possible dehydration. "Is there someone we can call, Miss Henshaw?" Bridget asked. "Your family?"

"No," the question seemed to alarm the young woman, and she clamped her hand on Bridget's wrist. "It's not *miss*," she corrected. "It's *missus*, and it's my baby I'm worried about. Please." Her voice gained in strength as did her grip on Bridget's wrist. "Is my baby going to be okay?"

chapter 20

CLAIRE

Frannie was going to be the death of Claire.

"I'm in the Christmas in August show today," Frannie crowed when she finally called three days after running off. "You have to come watch."

Claire sat down hard on the kitchen chair, relief flooding through her. "Do you realize how worried we were about you, Frannie? What were you—"

"I'm fine, sis," Frannie interrupted without a shred of remorse. "See ya soon!" And the line went dead.

Claire stared at the receiver, her relief turning to outrage. Claire had been ready to call the sheriff to track down her sister—almost ready to call Dad—and here Frannie had been fine and dandy the whole time, working as a savage all the way over in Canyon. Claire rubbed a hand down her face and let out a long breath.

She dialed Mammoth Hospital to let Bridget know Frannie wasn't dead in a ditch. "She wants us to see her in a show this afternoon at Canyon Lodge," she told Bridget. "But I'm not—"

"I have this afternoon off," Bridget interrupted. "I'll give her a piece of my mind and make her go home with you to help with Jenny."

The last thing Claire wanted to do was drive all the way across the park at the height of the tourist season. She was in the middle of sterilizing bottles, had a mountain of laundry to get to . . . and she hadn't heard from Red since he left on Monday.

If she left, she might miss his call.

Claire twisted the coiled telephone cord around her fingers. If Frannie came home with her, she'd have to explain why Red was five hundred miles away and she didn't want to do that—not to Frannie and not to Bridget. "I have so much to do," she finally said. "And Jenny needs her nap. Anyway, Frannie is more of a hindrance than a help."

"I promised Dad," Bridget said as if it were all decided. "And I need to get back to work. Pick me up at noon." She said goodbye and hung up.

Frustration welled in Claire's throat. Why did Bridget have to be so bossy?

Claire lined up the piping hot bottles on the counter and carefully poured hot formula in each one as her stomach knotted. Three days. Why hadn't Red called? Was he angry about what she'd said at the Depot? But no, Red wasn't one to hold a grudge . . . or was he?

You don't even know him.

Dad was wrong. She did know her husband. She knew him enough to know he was keeping something from her—something Beth Henshaw tried to tell her before her father-in-law dragged her away.

Claire had tried calling Beth but Pete Henshaw had answered and told her Beth couldn't be disturbed. She'd driven by the house, but it had been shuttered tight and she was afraid to knock on the door again. She'd even considered going to Sheriff Eagle with her concerns, but what would she say? That Beth Henshaw was distraught? She'd just lost her husband. That her father-in-law was rude and overbearing? That wasn't a crime. Claire screwed the clean nipples on the bottles and put each one in the refrigerator with no idea of how to help Beth—or if she even needed her help.

Half an hour later, the truck was packed for a daylong excursion into the park, Jenny was fed and changed, and Claire stood in front of the mirror in the little bathroom, examining her pale face and the shadows under her eyes. Bridget would see in one glance that she hadn't been sleeping. She patted on some powder and put a bright red lipstick over her pale lips. That would have to do.

She propped Jenny on one hip and was just going through the door when the telephone rang. Two shorts and a long—their signal on the party line.

Her heart jumped. It had to be Red.

She snatched the receiver on the second ring. "Hello, Wilder residence."

"Mrs. Wilder." The voice on the line wasn't familiar and her hope deflated. "This is Lem Garrison, the superintendent."

Lem Garrison. Claire suddenly remembered the business card left in her door. "Oh, Mr. Garrison," Claire said. "You left your card last week." With Marigold and Bridget and all that had happened, it had completely slipped her mind. "I forgot to give it to Red, I'm so sorry," Claire admitted. Jenny started to squirm, reaching for the telephone cord with a squeal.

"Don't give it another thought, Mrs. Wilder." His voice was perfectly polite. "Is he there now?"

She hesitated. Why was the Yellowstone superintendent looking for Red? "He's not in at the moment," she said carefully. It was the truth, but not the whole truth.

"He's a hard man to track down," Mr. Garrison replied.

Claire rescued the cord from Jenny's mouth as alarm prickled up her neck.

"If you would, ask him to call me back. I have some questions for him about Dell Henshaw. Do you still have my card?"

Claire's grip on the telephone tightened. Questions about Dell? The superintendent looked into deaths in the park, but what would Red know about Dell drowning all the way up at the northern border of Yellowstone?

"Mrs. Wilder?" Mr. Garrison prompted.

Claire pulled open the drawer and there it was, with the official National Park Service emblem. She wet her dry mouth. "I have it right here, Mr. Garrison," she answered in what came out as an overly cheerful voice. "I promise to let him know."

Claire hung up and stood for a moment, looking at the telephone as if it held a clue to why Lem Garrison wanted to talk to Red. *Heard he and Dell got into it at the Slippery Otter.* If Grace Miller knew that, of course others did. Was that why Lem Garrison was looking for Red?

Claire walked slowly out to the truck. She settled Jenny on the seat but didn't turn the key. Another thought—startling and unwelcome—chilled her in the hot cab. Could this be why Red had been in such a hurry to go to Libby? To avoid the superintendent's questions about Dell? Was he hiding something not only from her, but from the authorities?

chapter 21

BRIDGET

Bridget was so mad she could spit.

She tugged off her uniform and threw it on her bed. She and Claire had been worried sick, and this whole time Frannie was safe and sound, working someplace in Yellowstone as a maid, of all things. She checked her wristwatch. Twenty minutes until Claire picked her up. Then, Bridget would give her little sister the telling-off she deserved.

But first, she had to do something she'd been dreading for days. She had to call Dad.

She knotted the belt of her dressing gown and went down the hall to the bathroom. The little room was hot and stuffy, thanks to a tiny window that didn't open. She turned on the taps and splashed cold water on her face.

Dad would want to know about Claire.

What was she supposed to say? That Red was rude and Claire looked exhausted? That Bridget had failed her father in every way?

By the time she had brushed her hair and dressed, she had five minutes to spare. She went to the hall telephone and dialed the operator. She'd be quick—too quick for him to weasel the truth out of her—and be done before the Crow knew she was using the telephone without permission. "I'd like to make a collect call, please."

"Bridget, thank the Lord," Dad said after he accepted the call. "I've been worried sick." His voice, so familiar, made her throat constrict.

"I'm sorry," she said in a rush. "I should have called sooner, but with the job and all, I just didn't have a moment."

"Well, you've called now, and I'm glad." He let out a long breath. "How is the job?"

Bridget leaned a shoulder against the wall beside the telephone, hearing the distance between them in the crackling silence. All of Willmar might consider her father a hard man, but when it came to his daughters, he was devoted. He was also a terrible worrywart. Bridget certainly couldn't tell him about the nurses who died. Neither could she tell him about the letter of reference she hoped to get for the Mayo. What could she tell him? "We're worked off our feet but I'm getting good experience."

"And your sister? How is she?"

Bridget launched into her rehearsed lines. "She's wonderful, Dad. Jenny is the picture of Claire and the sweetest baby." All true, and nothing for him to worry about. "Claire and Red took us all over the park the first day." She didn't mention the bear or Frannie eating the sandwiches or Red's boorish behavior. "We went to Mass on Sunday at a beautiful little church and the priest was very friendly."

"Have you talked to her yet, Bridget?" Dad asked. "About coming home?"

She put a hand to her waist to quell a ripple of unease. "You know how Claire is," she said carefully.

"Bridget," Dad said. "Something is wrong, isn't it?"

How did he do that? "Dad, it's nothing."

His voice rose in concern. "Is she sick? Is Red mistreating her?"

"No, Dad," she said quickly. Of course not.

"Then what is it?"

Oh, what could she say now? If she told him about Claire's real situation—how she and Red didn't have two dimes to rub together and lived in the middle of nowhere and something was definitely wrong between them—her sister would never forgive her. The line crackled and she hoped maybe they would lose the connection.

No such luck.

"Bridget?" Her dad's voice held the tone that had always pulled the truth from her. Her sisters had called her a tattletale, but it was only because she couldn't defy Dad like they could.

"It's Frannie," she blurted. "She ran off and got a job. She's working in the park and living in some campground." It wasn't tattling. He deserved to know what Frannie was up to and it was better than telling him about Claire.

He was silent for a moment and she could imagine him rubbing his eyes. "Do I have to come out there?"

"No." Heavens, no. The last thing they needed was Dad coming out, seeing Claire's situation and demanding she return home with the baby. Then Claire would really be furious with her. "Dad, I have to go," she said. "This is costing you a fortune. I'll write you a long letter soon, and I'll take care of Frannie."

Dad wasn't going to let her go that easily. "Tell Frannie I want her back at her sister's house or she'll have me to answer to." After giving his love to all of them, Dad said goodbye and hung up.

Bridget stood in the hallway, looking at the telephone as if it were the cause of her problems. Was Dad right that Claire and Jenny would be better off at home? What about her vows to Red?

Bridget walked down the stairs to the first floor. Dad's threat of coming out sounded serious. He hated leaving the store, especially with the fall season coming up. But like he always said—nothing was more important than his girls.

He might do it, and that would be a disaster.

She'd give talking to Claire another try. Her sister should at least give the idea of going home some consideration. Bridget pushed through the hospital doors and out into the bright August sun. She and Claire had all day together. Plenty of time for Bridget to talk some sense into her big sister.

chapter 22

CLAIRE

Claire fought lookie-loo tourists for an hour and a half before she finally reached Mammoth. She pulled up at the hospital, feeling like a frazzled mess from the hot drive and her spinning thoughts on Red, Dell, and Lem Garrison.

Bridget waited for her, looking as cool as a cucumber in a light-green dress. She climbed into the truck, throwing a glare at an elk lying in the shade next to the hospital doors. "I don't know why they let those beasts lounge wherever they wish."

"Hello to you, too," Claire said, putting the truck in gear and pulling away from the hospital. "And they were here before we were."

Bridget waved her comment away and propped Jenny on her lap. "Aren't you beautiful?" Jenny rewarded her with a gummy grin. "And your mommy is a knockout."

Claire rolled her eyes but was relieved to see her sister in good spirits. She was determined not to veer into any sensitive topics with Bridget. She'd get them to Canyon for the program, then Claire would calmly tell Bridget that she didn't need Frannie to come home with her. Frannie would be thrilled, and Claire wouldn't have to tell anyone about Red.

She turned out of Mammoth toward the east side of the park. "How is the new job?" Work was always a safe topic where Bridget was concerned.

"Full of surprises," she answered sourly. "Did you know about the nurses who died?"

Not as safe a topic as Claire had thought. "Yes," she said carefully. It was all anybody had talked about for weeks.

"Why didn't you tell me?"

"You didn't exactly give me time to write back," Claire reminded her with raised brows and a sidelong look. "And then when you got here, I didn't want to scare you."

"Thanks for that," she said sarcastically. Bridget spent the next stretch of road talking about the head nurse she called the Crow, and a sweet junior nurse named Beckett. "The senior physician is on the ball, but the seasonal doctor . . ." Her grimace said it all.

Claire suppressed a smile. "Is he good-looking?" The doctors who annoyed Bridget almost always were.

"Beckett calls him Dr. California. He's from San Francisco."

"Sounds like you're living in one of those books you're always reading," Claire said, her grip on the steering wheel relaxing. "Daring nurse finds adventure and love in Yellowstone National Park."

"I'm not looking for love or adventure," Bridget answered back. "But it is good experience. Yesterday, we had a broken tibia and a rattlesnake bite."

Claire listened to Bridget talk about her patients until they took the turn south toward Tower Falls. She pointed to the east. "That's the way to the Lamar Valley, where Red and I camped last summer." Her voice was cheerful, but a pang of longing pierced her remembering that blissful two weeks, her riding Marigold and Red on Rosie, their camping gear loaded on Bess. It had been heaven on earth.

"I can't believe you slept outside," Bridget said as if they'd slept on the moon. "I mean, how did you go to the bathroom?"

"Of course you'd worry about that." Bridget was a stickler for sanitation.

"It's a legitimate question," she answered back. "And horses." Bridget shuddered.

A prickling heat crept up Claire's neck that had nothing to do with the hot wind coming through the open windows. Why did it seem like she had to defend her life at every turn?

Bridget adjusted Jenny in her lap and twisted toward Claire, her expression serious. "Is everything okay, Claire? Really?"

Claire gave her a frown. Couldn't they just have a pleasant day together without bringing up how her sister didn't approve of her marriage or anything else in her life?

When Claire didn't answer, Bridget went on. "I mean, it's got to be hard. You come across as this strong pioneer woman, but . . ." She hesitated. "You deserve better."

"What?" Claire slowed as they approached a series of hairpin turns and glanced over at her sister. It suddenly felt like Dad was sitting right between them. "Did Dad put you up to this?"

"Up to what?" Bridget's voice went up in surprise, but she didn't look at Claire.

"You know what," Claire snapped, glancing back at the road. She should have known. "This is where Red belongs. Not selling menswear in Willmar." Claire clenched her hands around the steering wheel and concentrated on the last turn.

"What about Jenny?" Bridget straightened Jenny's dress. "You both would be happier at home. I told Red that and—"

"You what?" Claire took her eyes off the road to stare at her sister.

Bridget clamped her lips together and looked guilty.

Claire pushed harder on the gas pedal and the truck surged forward. "What exactly did you tell Red?" Claire kept her voice under control, but her stomach quivered with anger. Had Bridget said something terrible to Red on that trip to Mammoth?

Bridget nervously wet her lips. "We talked, that's all."

Claire couldn't believe her sister's nerve. "And you told him he wasn't—what?—taking good care of his family?" Claire's face went hot. "That's why he left, because you told him—"

"Red left?" Bridget jerked around to regard her with wide eyes.

Claire could have kicked herself. She concentrated on the road. "He went up north for a job, that's all," she snapped. "But he wouldn't have, if you hadn't stuck your nose in it."

"Claire," Bridget said, her tone urgent. "You have to come home. You can't raise a baby on your own. You know how hard it was on Dad when—"

Taillights flashed in front of her and Claire stomped on the brakes. Bridget slid forward, one hand catching her against the dashboard, the other arm wrapped around Jenny. The truck lurched to a stop behind a camper.

Claire was pushing her foot on the brake so hard it felt like it would go through the floorboards. Her words rushed out, like a flood over a broken dam. "I'm not on my own, Bridget. Red didn't leave us like Mother did." Even as Claire spit out the words, the shock of them hit her. The horrible fear she hadn't been able to name—that fear that had gripped her since she said goodbye to Red—became mercilessly clear: Red *had* left her. He'd left her just like Mother had left her family . . . and despite her vehement protest to the contrary, she was deathly, horribly afraid that her husband wasn't coming back.

chapter 23

BRIDGET

Bridget stared at her sister in shock, Claire's words ringing in her ears.

Red didn't leave us. The way Claire said it, the denial and hurt in her voice . . . Claire wasn't trying to convince Bridget.

She was trying to convince herself.

Bridget reached out to touch her sister's trembling arm. "Claire, I didn't mean to imply—"

Claire jerked away. "Just leave it, Bridget."

Bridget didn't say another word for the rest of the drive. Her throat was thick with unsaid words, her distress for Claire like a vice around her chest. Had Red really left her? And was it Bridget's fault? How had she messed things up so badly? The last thing she wanted was to hurt Claire.

What had happened between her and her sister? Claire was right beside her, but it felt like there was a vast distance between them.

She went over the conversation—if that's what she could call it—with Red on the way to Mammoth, and cringed at how heartless she'd been. She hadn't meant to imply he wasn't doing enough for his family—or had she?

Claire parked the truck in front of a log cabin structure swarming with tourists. She took Jenny from Bridget with a jerk and got out of the truck. Bridget hurried after her sister, the cheerful birdsong in the towering pines underscoring the cold silence between them.

"Let's find Frannie and get this over with," Claire said, pushing through double doors into a cavernous lobby of polished wood and antlers—and crowded elbow to eyelashes with tourists. A sparkling Christmas tree stood beside a massive stone fireplace and a troupe of teenagers in cowboy hats strolled through the crowd with a guitar singing "Let it Snow" at the top of their voices.

Bridget scanned the crowd for Frannie. She was going to get her little sister back to Riverside no matter what it took. Claire needed help even more now that Red was gone. There—she spotted Frannie weaving toward them wearing an outlandish costume and a grin like the Cheshire cat.

Frannie stopped in front of them, looking from Claire's stony face to Bridget's flushed one with raised brows. "What?"

"What on earth are you wearing?" Bridget asked.

Frannie did a twirl to show off a costume of green tights, a shockingly short skirt, and a man's white dress shirt. A string of plastic holly around her neck and a striped stocking hat completed the ridiculous ensemble. "Goody, you brought the kid." Frannie scooped Jenny from Claire's arms. "I want to show her to my friends."

"What—don't—" Claire sputtered, but Frannie was gone. Claire took off through the crowd, pursuing Frannie as if she were a kidnapper.

Bridget followed, not as concerned about Jenny as she was about Claire. Her sister looked as white as a ghost. She caught up to Claire, hovering on the fringes of a group of Christmas elves and a Santa wearing dark-framed glasses. Frannie was showing off a wide-eyed Jenny.

The girls exclaimed over her pretty dress. Claire reached for Jenny, but Frannie dumped the baby in Santa's arms. "Let's get a picture of her," Frannie said nudging Claire out of the way as one of the girls held up a Brownie camera. "Paul, turn her this way," she said. "Say cheese!"

The girl, a blonde with a bouncing ponytail and cat-eye glasses grinned at Claire. "She's a real doll."

Claire grabbed Jenny back from the Santa with a jerk. "Don't ever do that again," Claire said to Frannie, fury in her voice. Frannie's eyes widened.

Bridget looked at her sister with a furrowed brow. "Claire, are you—"

"I'm fine," Claire answered.

"Okey dokey, if you say so." Frannie punched Santa's shoulder. "We have to get ready for our number."

"Wait, Frannie." Bridget stopped her little sister. She had to get it through Frannie's thick skull that she was coming home with them. Today. "We need to talk."

"No time, sis!" Frannie pushed past her and was gone.

Claire pressed her lips together and Jenny started to fuss. "We might as well sit down and I can feed her." Claire led them to some empty chairs in front of the stage.

"Let me help," Bridget said as Claire opened the diaper bag and took out a bottle. Claire ignored her. Bridget felt the beginnings of a headache. Could this day get any worse?

"Reilly, I thought that was you."

Bridget recognized the voice and a flush crept up her neck. *Please, no.*

Dr. Sampson sat down in the empty chair beside her. He was dressed in shorts and a glaringly bright short-sleeved shirt, looking every bit the Californian with his tanned legs and sockless loafers. Bridget managed a tight smile, reminding herself he was a doctor even if he didn't look like one. She introduced him to Claire.

Claire said a distracted hello and concentrated on Jenny. Thank goodness the talent show started and Bridget didn't have to talk to her furious sister on one side, or the annoying doctor on the other.

They watched two boys act out a skit, dressed like park rangers. Everybody laughed, including Dr. Sampson, but Bridget didn't hear a word, replaying the terrible conversation with Claire in her mind. If only she could apologize and start over. She snuck a glance at Claire. Her sister's posture was stiff and her face tight.

Frannie was next on stage in her elf costume and sang a surprisingly good rendition of "Jingle Bell Rock," with the Santa in glasses accompanying her on the piano. Frannie ended up with third prize in the talent show and breezed back to Bridget and Claire after the final bows. Bridget was forced to introduce her to Dr. Sampson or appear rude.

"Wowsa," Frannie said, looking from his golden hair to his loafers. "You're a doctor? I'm feeling a bit feverish."

"Frannie Marie Reilly." Bridget was mortified. This was the absolute last straw. "Get your things. You're coming home with us. And don't put up a fuss."

"Whoa, sister," Frannie said, not at all concerned. "I'm not going anywhere."

"Claire needs you to help with the baby." Bridget looked to Claire for confirmation. "Tell her."

"I don't need any help," Claire said, putting Jenny up to her shoulder. "And working as a savage will be good for Frannie."

"See?" Frannie stuck her tongue out at Bridget like she was a five-year-old.

Bridget could feel her blood pressure rising. Why did both of her sisters have to be so stubborn? And why did she have to have this conversation with Dr. Sampson looking on? "Claire," she said, lowering her voice, "with Red gone, you're all alone in the middle of nowhere—"

"What?" Frannie interrupted. "Why is Red gone?"

Claire glared at Bridget.

"Holy moly," Frannie said when no one answered her. "First Bridget's sneaking around and renting an apartment in Rochester, now something's hinky with you and Red. The Reilly sisters have as much drama as *Guiding Light*."

Claire frowned at Bridget. "Rochester?"

"How do you even know about that?" Bridget narrowed her eyes at Frannie. "Were you snooping in my room?"

Frannie shrugged. "I didn't tell Dad, if that's what's worrying you."

"You're moving out?" Claire asked.

Bridget glanced at Dr. Sampson. He didn't even pretend he wasn't listening in on their private conversation. "I don't even know if I have the job yet."

Claire's eyes narrowed and her brows notched down. "Is this why you want me to move home—so you can leave Dad without feeling guilty?"

Bridget shook her head. That wasn't it at all. Oh, why had this turned into such a mess? "Claire, I—"

"Why can't you just mind your own business, Bridget?" Claire's voice broke in a tearful gulp.

Bridget felt her sister's words like a stab in the heart, not just because they hurt her—and they did—but because Claire was hurting, too. She would never lash out at Bridget unless she was feeling horrible herself. And it was all Bridget's fault.

"Doctor." Claire turned suddenly to Sampson with a wobbly smile that didn't fool anyone. "I need to get Jenny home. Would you mind terribly giving my sister a ride back to Mammoth?"

Bridget's mouth dropped open. Claire couldn't leave. Bridget needed to explain herself—cross the divide that had opened up between her and her sister. And what about Frannie? She had to go home with Claire.

Dr. Sampson's answer was immediate. "It would be my pleasure."

Claire hefted the diaper bag and choked out her thanks. She didn't even say goodbye to Bridget or Frannie.

Frannie looked at Bridget. "What was that all about?"

Bridget's throat ached and her eyes stung. "Nothing."

"It sure as shooting wasn't nothing," Frannie objected. "Is Claire okay?"

"She's fine," Bridget answered. Claire wasn't fine, and Bridget still had to do something about Frannie. "What am I supposed to tell Dad about you?" The question came out snappish, but she couldn't help herself. She was failing at everything Dad had asked of her.

Frannie's questioning gaze rested on her, and seemed to take in more than Bridget wanted her little sister to see. "Just tell him I'm fine," she said. "I'm fine, Claire's fine, we're all fine. Isn't that what we always say, no matter if it's the truth or not?"

chapter 24

CLAIRE

Claire got halfway home before she had to pull over, tears blurring her vision and her breath searing her chest. She turned into the parking area at Beryl Spring, jammed the truck into park, and stared out the windshield into the cloudless blue sky. Jenny began to fuss, and Claire picked her up, holding her close to her aching heart.

At the Canyon Lodge, she'd been dimly aware of the laughter and music around her, but her mind had been numb with shock. *Red didn't leave us like Mother did. He'll come back.* As she'd said those desperate words, she'd seen her own disbelief mirrored on Bridget's face.

Red would come home to them. Of course he would come home.

Jenny snuffled against her neck, fussing as the afternoon sun heated the cab. Claire pushed open the door and followed the boardwalk toward the cloud of steam rising from the hot spring. The wind dried her sweat-dampened blouse as she walked, blind to the blackened trees, the barren landscape where no vegetation grew in the sulfur-filled soil. At the spring, the acrid scent stung her nose. Claire gazed, unseeing, at the brilliant blue water bubbling up from deep under the earth.

She held Jenny close, rocking her and fighting against the memories she'd thought were buried forever. Bridget's hand in hers, Dad's anguished voice. The smell of Mother's perfume and the sticky touch of her lipstick on Claire's cheek. The pain in her chest like she was drowning.

We don't need her, Dad said that cold spring day. *We're fine without her.*

But mothers didn't leave their children, and Claire hadn't stopped hoping that her mother would come back.

Every day when Claire came home from school with Bridget, she hoped Mother would be waiting for them. Claire imagined how Mother would hug them both and say she was sorry, then everything would go back to how it had been. Spring went by, and then summer. Claire kept hoping, even when Dad hired Flo to take care of Frannie and the house. In September, Claire hoped Mother would be home for her birthday, then for Bridget's birthday in December. When Frannie turned one year old, Flo made a cake, and Dad brought home presents from Reilly's. Mother didn't come back.

Finally, Claire stopped hoping, because hoping hurt too much.

We're fine without her.

Dad was wrong. The Reilly girls were far from fine.

Bridget had cried herself to sleep for months after Mother left. When she got older she buried her nose in books with happy endings, worked impossibly long hours, and pushed away anyone who got close. Claire—she knew, because Bridget often told her—refused to be helped. She could do whatever she set her mind to on her own, thank you very much. And Frannie . . . well, nobody could say that Frannie was fine. Even when Frannie started to blow up at Dad and get in trouble, they kept up the charade that all was well in the Reilly household, even when it wasn't.

When Millie came up with the plan to work in Yellowstone, Claire leapt at the chance to leave Claire Reilly behind for a summer. Then Claire married Red and left that hurt little girl behind in Willmar for good.

Or so she thought.

Claire stood in the billowing steam, the pain hot and caustic and very real. That young Claire Reilly was still with her. The little girl begging her mother not to leave. The desperate child, clinging to her mother's legs had been with her all along.

Red, please don't go.

Claire's eyes stung from the sulfur-filled air billowing from the hot springs. She laid her cheek against Jenny's soft head. Red wouldn't leave. He loved them.

When he told her he was leaving, she wanted to pull him closer but something inside her pushed him away. *We don't need you. We're fine without you.*

Those caustic words had scalded her throat even as she said them. Was it too late to cross that distance between them? The distance not only between Riverside and Libby, but the rift between Red's heart and her own? She gazed at the brilliant turquoise water, the steam billowing into the azure sky. *Lord, let it not be too late.*

Jenny was almost asleep. Claire rocked gently. Red had kept secrets from her, but she kept one from him as well. A painful secret buried so deep it had never healed. He'd asked about her mother when they started dating. "She's not with us anymore," Claire had said. "I'm sorry," Red had answered, like people do when you tell them someone has died. She didn't correct him. It didn't seem like a lie then, but now that deeply buried wound had broken open and the pain of it was hurting them both.

Claire's breath came easier as a conviction grew in her mind. She had to tell him about Mother. She'd tell him Bridget was wrong, too. That Claire didn't care if they didn't have a dollar to their name, or what her Dad thought of their home or their life together. Red was all she wanted, with Jenny and the sky and the river.

Claire walked back to the truck and drove home with a certainty thrumming through her veins. She'd fix this. She would write Red a letter. She'd tell him the truth about her mother. She'd ask him to come home, and tell him she loved him. She needed him.

She wasn't fine without him.

chapter 25

BRIDGET

"Reilly, why aren't these follow-up calls completed?"

Bridget startled at Larkin's sharp tone. Her eyes were gritty and her head ached. She'd tossed and turned for three solid nights—sick about Claire and furious with Frannie, not to mention the insults she'd been forced to endure from Dr. Sampson.

He drove her back to Mammoth in his mint-green Thunderbird and refused to mind his own business. First, he asked about her sisters. "What was going on back there?" He jerked his thumb behind them as he tore around a curve at an alarming speed.

"Nothing to concern you," she'd snapped. "Can we talk about something else?"

"Sure," he'd said, as if he were going to be a gentleman and make pleasant small talk. "So you want to work at the Mayo Clinic?" Another subject that was none of his business. "I'm sure you'll get an excellent recommendation from the Crow."

She frowned at his tone. He didn't sound like he was giving her a compliment. "What do you mean by that?"

He veered around a truck camper parked on the side of the road. "She's impressed with you, is all I'm saying."

She bristled. "You don't like her, I presume?"

He shrugged.

"Larkin is a superb nurse," Bridget pointed out. And so was she. In fact, she'd wanted to be a nurse since she was eight years old, but she wasn't going to tell that to this arrogant doctor.

He blew out a sharp sound of disagreement. "She takes care of the patients," he said. "But she doesn't care for them."

Bridget felt her temperature rise. "I have no idea what you mean."

The engine of the convertible rumbled as the infuriating man sped up on a straight stretch. "You ever hear the old saw that a caring heart is the best medicine?"

Just who did Dr. Sampson think he was? "Just because Larkin doesn't appreciate you clowning around, doesn't mean she doesn't care about the patients." Why did her defense of the Crow feel like she was defending herself?

Sampson came alarmingly close to the tailgate of the truck in front of them before he put on the brakes. "I'm just saying if you want to be a good nurse, don't take notes from Larkin."

"If I wanted advice, Doctor, I'd write to Ann Landers, thank you very much." It was a terribly disrespectful thing to say to a doctor, but Bridget couldn't help it. The rest of the drive was accomplished in absolute silence and at terrifying speed.

When she got back to Mammoth with her heart in her throat, Bridget tried calling Claire. No answer. She tried again on Friday after working a double shift. Claire picked up, but claimed she was busy with Jenny and couldn't talk. Saturday was the same story. Bridget wasn't going to give up. She just couldn't stand Claire being angry at her.

When she saw Dr. Sampson on her shifts, she treated him just like any other doctor—with a professional coolness—but she didn't stop thinking about his unwelcome advice.

On Sunday, Bridget got up early to go to Mass—at a campground, no less. The outdoor amphitheater smelled of campfire smoke and rotten eggs, but the Mass was the same as at home. She asked forgiveness for her argument with Claire, her simmering anger toward Frannie, and even the outrage she'd directed at Dr. Sampson.

A caring heart is the best medicine.

She looked at Jesus on the cross above the altar. She hadn't told Dr. Sampson the real reason she wanted to become a nurse. As a child, she'd loved the Bible stories about Jesus healing the sick—the paralyzed man picking up his mat and walking, the blind man given his sight. Every time she heard about Jesus healing someone who was hurting, she felt a tug at her heart. She wanted to heal people, to ease people's pain like Jesus.

That didn't sound like someone who didn't care, did it?

It was easy enough for a doctor to spout platitudes. Doctors breezed in and out of the exam rooms, gave their opinions and wrote prescriptions. It was nurses that did the hard work. Nurses watched their patients suffer. They gave the families the bad news and watched the tears flow. Bridget had seen more than one softhearted nurse give up her career because she'd let herself get too close. A professional distance was absolutely necessary if she wanted to keep doing her job—and didn't God want her to help people?

"Reilly?" Larkin's voice rose as did her dark brows. "The follow-up calls?"

Bridget jerked her gaze to receive the full brunt of Larkin's glare. "Of course," she said, reaching for the stack of charts. "I'll get to that immediately."

Larkin stubbed out her cigarette. "See that you do." The green glass ashtray showed evidence of at least half a pack of the menthol cigarettes Larkin favored. After the supervising nurse signed off on the roster and left the floor, Bridget dumped the stubs in the trash can. Bridget could see her recommendation going straight in the same trash can if she didn't snap to it.

Half an hour later, she had only one call left to make. She dialed the number on Beth Henshaw's chart, noting that it was identical to Claire's except for the last digit. She held the receiver to her ear, imagining the party line ringing in Claire's little kitchen. "May I speak with Mrs. Henshaw?" she asked when a gruff male voice answered. "Mrs. Beth Henshaw?"

"She can't come to the phone," the man growled. "Who is this?"

Goodness, there was no need to be rude. "This is the nurse calling from Mammoth," she answered. "Mrs. Henshaw needs to make a follow-up appointment."

With a decisive click, the line went dead. "Of all the nerve!" she said, looking at the telephone receiver as if it was the culprit.

"What was that?" Dr. Sampson appeared at the desk. Today, he wore an electric-blue tie that set off his eyes and his California tan.

"Remember the pregnancy last week?"

"You mean Beth Henshaw?"

She nodded. "Livingston doesn't have her in their records, and just now when I called to talk to her about setting up a prenatal appointment, that—that so-and-so father-in-law," she sputtered, "he hung up on me!"

Dr. Sampson leaned a hip on the desk and frowned. "That poor girl has been through a lot, and so have her in-laws."

"What do you mean?" Bridget sat down and looked at the chart again, but nothing struck her as unusual. First trimester. Heat, anemia, dehydration resulting in a fainting spell. Mrs. Henshaw had been discharged into the care of her in-laws—a bulky man with a gruff manner and his wife, a frail-looking older woman with a white streak in her hair.

"Did you speak to her when she was here last week?" Dr. Sampson asked.

"Of course I did." Bridget talked to her about prenatal vitamins and drinking more water, and she'd very clearly told her to make an appointment in Livingston.

"Then you know that Beth's husband died two weeks ago."

Bridget hadn't known. She met Dr. Sampson's eyes, then looked away in annoyance. Was this his little lesson to her after their talk in the car? "I'm sorry for her," she said, and she honestly was, "but she needs an examination."

Dr. Sampson held out his hand for the telephone receiver. "Dial her again and let me talk."

Just after lunch, Beth Henshaw walked into the hospital with the brawny older man on one side, and the gaunt woman on the other. "Mrs. Henshaw," Bridget said, keeping her gaze upon the young woman, who looked pale and shaky. "Dr. Sampson will see you now."

"Iris will go with her," the older man ordered.

"That won't be necessary, Mr. Henshaw," Bridget said crisply. "You and your wife will be quite comfortable in the waiting room."

In the examination room, she shut the door firmly behind them. "Let's change you into a gown." She directed Beth to sit on the table.

Beth Henshaw remained standing, her arms crossed over her body.

Bridget had expected this. Many young women resisted such an intimate examination. "Don't fret," she said. "Dr. Sampson is a wonderful doctor, and I'll be right here."

Beth Henshaw's face crumpled and she began to sob.

Bridget guided her to sit on the examination table and offered the girl a paper tissue. Beth covered her face with her hands and sobbed harder. Bridget sat down beside her, glancing at her wristwatch. What was keeping Dr. Sampson? She patted Beth's hand. "There, there," Bridget said. "What's all this about?"

"I—I—" Beth took a great gulping breath. "Want to go home."

Bridget nodded with relief. "Of course you can, when we've finished your examination."

"No," the girl said with a violent shake of her head. "Home to my folks in Coeur d'Alene."

Bridget began to help Beth into the gown as she reassured her. "As long as you take care of yourself, there's no medical reason you can't travel up until the seventh month of your pregnancy."

Beth's tears started again, this time running silently down her face. "Pete and Iris—they say my parents don't want me."

Bridget tied the gown at Beth's neck and back, noting her trembling. She'd mention the patient's anxiety to Dr. Sampson. Hysterics weren't at all uncommon in newly pregnant women, and he most likely would prescribe a sedative. "Sit tight," she directed. "I'll go see what's keeping the doctor."

"Please"—Beth grabbed Bridget's wrist—"don't tell them I told you."

Alarm prickled through Bridget at the urgency of the girl's grip. "Of course not," she reassured the girl. Beth was surely overreacting, and anyway, it wasn't any of Bridget's business. Bridget left the room with a frown and ran straight into Nurse Larkin.

"Is there a problem, Reilly?"

"Not at all," Bridget answered. Nothing she couldn't handle on her own.

Larkin looked at her watch. "Don't dillydally, you have other duties to attend to."

Bridget watched Larkin walk briskly down the hall with a prickle of unease. Was she really as uncaring as Larkin? She checked the front desk, guessing that Dr. Sampson would be lounging there, trading jokes with Beckett or flirting with Finch. The desk was empty and she clenched her teeth. Could he be speaking to the Henshaws? Her rubber-soled shoes were silent as she approached the door to the waiting room.

"Iris, she's not going to stop trying to run away."

Bridget froze. That was Mr. Henshaw's gruff voice.

"Please, Pete. Let's take her to my brother's old place." The older woman's voice was pleading. "Nobody would find us there."

Bridget stepped out of the Henshaws' sight. Were they talking about Beth?

At that moment, Dr. Sampson came out of the second exam room and opened his mouth to speak to her. Bridget put her finger to her lips with an urgent look.

"I've lost both my boys, Pete." The woman's voice rose and was choked with emotion. "I can't lose my grandchild."

Dr. Sampson's brows came together. Bridget peeked around the doorframe to see Mr. Henshaw put his arms around his wife. "That's what we'll do then," he said, his voice surprisingly gentle. "We'll take her to Wyoming until the baby is born."

Bridget met Dr. Sampson's surprised gaze.

"But we'll keep the baby, Pete, won't we?" Mrs. Henshaw choked out.

"Yes, Iris," Mr. Henshaw said. "I just want you to be happy."

Bridget's gaze met Dr. Sampson's. Beth Henshaw hadn't been hysterical at all. Bridget hurried back toward the examination room, motioning for Dr. Sampson to follow. Outside the door, she gave him a whispered explanation of what Beth had told her.

They entered the examination room. "Beth, you remember Dr. Sampson?"

Dr. Sampson sat beside Beth and took her hand. "Tell me what's troubling you, Beth."

Beth swallowed and looked unsure. "Pete and Iris—they say my parents don't—that they won't want me. They say I have to stay with them or I won't have anywhere to go. I don't have any money and—with Dell gone—" She gulped a sob. "I don't have anyone else."

"Last week, when you came in," Dr. Sampson asked gently, "were you trying to get home?"

She nodded. "I used the last of my pin money to get a train ticket. But Pete found me. Then I tried to hitchhike and that's when I—" She gulped. "That's when I fainted. Since then they haven't let me out of their sight."

Bridget gave Beth a tissue. From what they'd heard in the waiting room, the Henshaws had every intention of keeping her child.

"Have you tried to contact your parents?" Dr. Sampson asked.

Beth wiped her eyes and went on in a choked voice. "My mom and dad don't have a telephone, but I wrote to them after Dell died." She shook her head and clasped her hands together. "They didn't write back, but if I talk to them . . . if they know about the baby . . ." She put her hand protectively over her flat stomach. "I think they'll take me back."

Dr. Sampson nodded. "I think so, too, Beth. And if you want to go home, we'll help you." Dr. Sampson looked at Bridget. "Won't we?"

Bridget looked from the questioning gaze of the doctor to the miserable girl. This was certainly not Bridget's business. And not the job of a physician, either. And yet, how could she refuse?

"Certainly." Bridget nodded. "Is there someone we could call to help you get there? A friend?"

Beth shook her head and looked down at her locked hands. "I only know friends of Pete and Iris."

A sharp rap made Bridget jump. Nurse Larkin pushed open the door and took one step in. "Dr. Sampson," she said with a disapproving look. "The couple in the waiting room has asked how much longer you will be. Please do finish up here and allow them to take this young woman home."

Dr. Sampson's usual good humor was nonexistent. His jaw went hard and he responded in a firm voice. "I'll be finished when I'm finished, Larkin."

Larkins brows flew up and a muscle in her cheek twitched. "Of course, Doctor."

The door closed behind Larkin and Dr. Sampson flipped the lock. Bridget glanced apprehensively at the door. Larkin wouldn't be put off for long, and neither would Beth's in-laws.

"Beth," Dr. Sampson said, crouching down in front of her to meet her eyes. "Think hard. Is there anyone—anyone at all—who could help you get to your parents?"

Beth bit at her lip and looked up, her pale face unsure. "There is one person," she said slowly. "I don't know her very well, but she said to—to let her know if I needed anything."

"Who?" Bridget asked hopefully. Beth needed a friend, and someone who was strong enough to stand up to Pete Henshaw.

"Her name is Claire Wilder."

chapter 26

CLAIRE

The telephone rang as Claire was settling Jenny down for her afternoon nap. It was their party line ring, and Claire rushed to the phone.

She'd sent the letter to Red, and by Saturday she was on pins and needles. She didn't even go out to hang the clothes on the line in case she missed him, but only Bridget called and Claire wasn't ready to talk to her yet. Claire went to Mass on Sunday and came straight home, hoping against hope that he would be sitting at the kitchen table, waiting for her. He wasn't, and the telephone remained silent all day.

How could he read what she wrote and not come straight home?

Claire grabbed the receiver before the second ring. *Please, Lord, let it be Red.*

But it was Bridget . . . again.

"Claire," Bridget said in a whisper. "I need you to come up to the hospital."

Claire took a sharp breath at her sister's desperate tone. "Is it Frannie?"

"No," Bridget said quickly. "I can't explain but please, Claire, come now." Claire heard a man's angry voice in the background. "And park behind the hospital, where the ambulance comes in." She hung up.

Claire sat down heavily on the kitchen chair. What on earth? It was Jenny's nap time, not to mention Red could call—or walk in the door—any minute. But her sister had sounded so . . . un-Bridget-like. And she needed Claire's help.

What else could Claire do but pack up Jenny and head to Mammoth?

It took Claire more than an hour to get there, thanks to a busload of tourists stopped in the middle of the road to take pictures with a bison. Claire parked behind the hospital, and as she juggled Jenny and the diaper bag, Bridget opened the back door and pulled her inside.

"What took you so long?" She hurried Claire down the hallway and pushed her into an examination room, before Claire could even ask for an explanation.

"Beth?" Claire gaped at the young woman sitting on the table with the tanned doctor she'd met at Canyon sitting beside her.

"I'm sorry," Beth said in a small voice. "I couldn't think of anyone else, and on the card you gave me . . ."

Claire remembered. *If there's ever anything I can do, anything at all.* The poor girl looked pale and young and scared. Claire shot a questioning glance at Bridget. "Is someone going to tell me what's going on?"

"They won't let her leave," Bridget said bluntly. "Her in-laws want to keep the baby." Claire didn't comprehend that outlandish statement before Bridget was talking again. "She's scared out of her wits. That horrible father-in-law of hers is going to hide her away somewhere in Wyoming until the baby is born, and he's getting very impatient out in the waiting room."

"Wait." Claire tried to catch up. A baby? Beth was pregnant? Claire began to put it together. Beth at the train station saying she was going home. Pete Henshaw claiming she was unwell. Her defeated look as he took her away.

"Did you call the sheriff?" It seemed like the logical solution if Beth was being mistreated.

Dr. Sampson frowned. "We talked about it, but it doesn't seem like they've done anything illegal. At least not yet."

Beth bit at her lip. "And Pete is good friends with Tom Eagle."

Claire nodded in understanding. The sheriff was Tom Eagle's oldest son. "What about your uncle?"

Beth shook her head and blinked hard. "He didn't even come to the funeral. You know how he is." Beth wrung her hands in her lap. "Mrs. Wilder, if you could just get me to the Depot, I can—"

A violent pounding on the door made Claire jump and Jenny startle. Pete Henshaw's face appeared in the small window. "I'm taking Beth home," he said. His gaze landed on Claire and his eyes narrowed. "What is she doing here?"

Claire backed away from the door.

"As I said," Dr. Sampson replied in a commanding tone, "I'm doing some tests. I must insist you stay in the waiting room."

Pete Henshaw's scowl made Claire's neck prickle in alarm. She should have stood up to him that day at the Depot. She'd been right when she suspected that Beth was afraid. She thought fast, and turned to Beth. "You could take the northbound bus from the Depot tomorrow morning, but . . ." She paused, considering.

"Pete will be there waiting for me," Beth finished miserably.

Claire nodded, putting down the diaper bag and walking Jenny back and forth across the small room as she thought of their options. She couldn't drive Beth all the way to Coeur d'Alene, it was at least five hundred miles. But she could get her to a bus. "Beth." Claire took her hand. It was ice cold and trembling. "I can drive you to Ennis tomorrow, and you can take the bus from there." Ennis wasn't far from West Yellowstone. Pete wouldn't look for Beth there . . . she hoped. "You can be home by tomorrow night."

Beth's eyes widened at the idea, but then her expression fell. "It's too much to ask, Mrs. Wilder. I couldn't —"

But Bridget was helping her down from the table and dictating instructions to Claire. "Make sure she eats and drinks plenty of water. Have her rest if she gets dizzy or nauseous."

Claire peeked out the window of the examination room. "How are we going to get her past Pete?" The man wasn't going to let Beth just walk away.

"Leave that to me," Bridget said. "You just be ready to go."

Three minutes later, the hospital fire alarm went off.

chapter 27

CLAIRE

"Do you think Pete will come after us?" Beth asked, twisting to peer out the back window of the truck. She was holding Jenny, who had started to wail when the fire alarm had shattered through the hospital.

Claire's hands slipped on the steering wheel, wet with perspiration. Pete would definitely come after them. As they sped away from Mammoth Hospital, the Yellowstone fire engine and at least three National Park Service trucks pulled up to the building, blocking every car into the hospital parking lot, including the Henshaws' red Ford.

That would give them some time, at least.

Claire's heart was still pounding. What had got into Bridget? It wasn't like her sister to break the rules, and pulling the fire alarm? She would be in trouble for that and maybe even lose her job.

Beth adjusted Jenny in her lap as the baby continued to cry. "What do I do?"

"She's probably hungry." Claire took a sharp right toward Madison Junction. Then with a sudden sinking of her heart, she remembered the diaper bag, sitting in the examination room at the hospital. She checked the rearview mirror and weighed her choices. They wouldn't be able to stay in Riverside tonight, not with Pete after them. But they needed food and diapers for Jenny, and money. "We have to stop at my house, then we'll go straight to Ennis." Beth needed bus fare and they'd have to stay the night somewhere in Ennis. Thank the Lord she still had some cash in the cookie tin.

Beth had managed to settle Jenny, patting her gently and rocking her.

"You're good with her," Claire said.

Beth smiled softly. "Dell was so happy about the baby." Her voice quivered. "We'd just told his parents the day before he—before he died. Iris and Pete were thrilled."

So thrilled that they wouldn't let Beth go. Yes, they'd lost Dell—and their older son, too—but that didn't excuse Pete and Iris Henshaw.

"Claire?" Beth said. "What I was trying to tell you before, about Red and Dell . . ." She hesitated. "You really don't know what happened between them?"

Claire's stomach twisted and she shook her head, her eyes on the road. She should know. Red should have told her.

Beth went on. "That fall, before Dell and I got married. Dell was stashing sheds." She said it like Claire would know what she was talking about.

Claire wasn't sure she did. "You mean elk antlers?" Elk shed their antlers, she'd seen them when she'd gone hiking and camping with Red.

"Yes, they're worth a lot of money," Beth answered.

"But isn't that illegal?" Claire asked. Taking anything out of the park wasn't permitted—not even wildflowers—Red had told her that the first summer she was here.

Beth nodded. "But Dell had a stash—a cache that he'd gathered and hidden—at Winter Creek, but he needed a way to get them to Helena. So he asked Red to drive him up there, then to Helena."

She hesitated, and Claire wanted to object that Red wouldn't do anything illegal—least of all in the park. He followed every rule and regulation to a T.

Beth went on. "They got pulled over by a ranger."

Claire glanced over at her. "So, Dell got a ticket?"

"Well, no." Beth's voice was hesitant. "It was Red who got in trouble, not Dell."

Claire wasn't following. "Why Red?"

Beth looked at her with surprise. "It's the Lacey Act."

Claire shook her head.

"It's a law saying you can't take animals or anything related to them out of the park, but it's all about who is doing the transporting—and it was Red's truck."

"So Red got the ticket?" Claire asked, starting to understand and looking over at Beth. "And what—a fine?" Had he been too ashamed to tell her about it?

Beth stared at her. "It's a federal crime, Claire. Red went to jail in Bozeman."

Claire took her foot off the gas and turned to look at Beth in shock, and then outrage. "What happened to Dell?"

Beth looked out the window and her face contorted. "That's the thing," she got out. "He put it all on Red, said he didn't know anything about the sheds in the back of the truck."

"And the ranger believed him?"

Beth nodded miserably. "I told him to tell the truth, but Dell said that would just get him thrown in jail, too. We were getting married that Saturday. Red was supposed to be the best man."

Claire dragged her attention back to the road in front of her. Red went to jail? This was the "falling-out" Red had with Dell? Why hadn't he told her?

"I know it was a horrible thing for Dell to do," Beth went on. "His parents let him do it, and they spread some awful rumors about Red having a whole setup with people smuggling sheds out of the Yellowstone for him to sell in Bozeman. You know how people here don't trust outsiders."

Claire knew all too well. Helen and Tom Eagle had made that crystal clear. But Red doing something like that? He couldn't. Then she had another thought, about Lem Garrison looking for Red, and her stomach soured.

"Was Dell doing that again—smuggling sheds—when he died?" Claire asked.

Beth nodded, and swiped away tears and took a deep breath. "I'm sorry, I just cry all the time."

Claire reached out a hand to touch her arm. "You don't have to tell me, Beth. It's okay." As much as she wanted to know, the poor girl had been through enough.

"No, I want to," she said quickly. "Dell told me the day before he died that he was going to get us a lot of money quick—to get a place of our own." Beth adjusted Jenny on her lap. "He said he was going to raft the sheds out of the park into Gardiner. He said someone was helping him, someone he trusted . . ." Beth's voice failed her.

Someone like Red? Claire wished she hadn't had the thought.

Beth took a trembling breath. "The park superintendent talked to Pete a few days later. I was upstairs, but I could hear them through the floor vent."

Claire put on the brakes for a slow-moving trailer, worry knotting in her chest at the mention of Lem Garrison. "What did they talk about?"

Jenny started to fuss again and Beth moved her back to her shoulder. "Pete said it was Red's fault Dell drowned," she said simply.

Claire jerked the wheel and then righted the truck between the white lines. "Why?"

"He said Red and Dell met up at the Slippery Otter the night before. He had witnesses—Tom Eagle, he said—who saw them talking."

So Red had been at the Slippery Otter, like Grace Miller had said. The knot of worry tightened.

Beth switched Jenny to her other shoulder. "Pete swore it was Red who made Dell do it. Red was up to his old tricks, he said."

Claire's foot pushed down on the accelerator as Jenny's cries increased. Claire thought about Red lying to her that night when he'd talked to Dell, and again about losing his job. How he'd left for Libby so suddenly. Lem Garrison looking for him. *He's a hard man to track down.*

Was she certain Red wasn't involved with selling sheds, and had nothing to do with Dell's death? He'd left for Libby and hadn't called her, hadn't returned even after she wrote that letter. Her stomach turned over with a sickening thought. Maybe Red hadn't left because of Bridget's meddling. Maybe Red left to avoid Lem Garrison's questions and the investigation into Dell's death.

And maybe, Red wasn't coming back.

Her heartbeat pounded in her ears. *Don't make the biggest mistake of your life, Claire.* Had she? Had she married someone she didn't know at all?

chapter 28

RED

Red stuck out his thumb for a ride when he saw the Buick coupe racing his way. The brakes squealed and the car swerved to the shoulder.

"Where you headed?" The driver was a businessman type in a sharp suit and a perfectly creased fedora. His eyes were red rimmed and he had a coffee cup balanced on the seat beside him with a liquid in it that sure wasn't coffee.

"Home," Red said, climbing in.

"Name's Chester," the driver jerked back on the road. "Heading to Butte."

"That'll do," Red said. He'd be home by tonight. His insides churned at the thought of facing Claire.

We don't need you. Claire's words the morning he left had cut him to the bone.

She hadn't kissed him goodbye, hadn't even waved when he got on the bus. He'd almost chucked the whole plan right then. Then he'd remembered the empty bank account. All the places he'd gone to looking for jobs. Bridget's accusations.

And Lem Garrison looking for him.

He'd been a fool to run. He'd get home and tell Claire everything. Hope she would take him back.

The boozy businessman took a swig from the coffee cup and the car drifted over the center line. He glanced at Red. "You a family man?"

The man was just making conversation, but the question was like a punch in Red's gut. A family man. At the orphanage the word *family* was spoken with the same reverence reserved for words like *heaven.*

Yes, he was a family man. But he hadn't done right by his family.

The kids at the orphanage called him *dummy* and *blockhead*, and he was. He felt the burn of shame in his chest as if he were still that boy, standing in front of the class with the words of his primer blurring in front of his eyes. As a kid, he spent most of his days in the corner, and the rest of the time looking out the window, wishing he was outside. After he ran away from the orphanage, he got good at a few things—fighting, stealing cars, and getting thrown in juvenile detention. A month short of his sixteenth birthday, a sympathetic judge gave him some advice: get out of Chicago before he ended up in a prison. He jumped a train west. When he found Montana and horses, he thought he had put the shame of the orphanage classroom behind him.

Wasn't the joke on him when he fell in love with a schoolteacher?

"Got a picture?" Chester said, taking another swig from his cup.

Sure, Red had a picture. His hand went to his jacket pocket but he didn't retrieve the black-and-white photo he'd taken of Claire on their first real date—the one without Bucky and Millie tagging along. They had gone to the Lower Falls, his favorite spot in the park. It was late in the afternoon, when the sun was just at the angle that made everything look like burnished gold.

They stepped out on the viewing platform and Red got up the courage to take Claire's hand. She let him, and his chest swelled with something like pride as they gazed together at the bright column of water thundering over the falls and down three hundred feet to the river below. Mist rose from the churning base, throwing up rainbows and making the canyon walls sparkle like diamonds.

She glanced at him, then back at the falls. "It makes you wonder, doesn't it?"

It sure did. Red wondered how a beautiful woman like Claire Reilly was standing beside him. "What do you wonder about?" He wanted to know more than anything what she was thinking.

She didn't answer right away, but stared at the marvel of the Grand Canyon of the Yellowstone. "Do you go to church, Red?"

He wasn't sure how to answer. "Is that important?" If it was, he'd be at church in West Yellowstone on Sunday.

She turned her gaze back to the rainbow mist. "It seems important to know what you believe."

He suddenly wanted to be honest about what he'd felt since he met her, even if it sounded sappy. "If you'd asked me three days ago if I thought God knew my name or cared a whit about me, I might have said no. But now," he met her eyes and his heart thudded with the truth of what he was saying. "Now, I might think different."

She looked down at their clasped hands and a smile tugged at her beautiful mouth. "Nobody ever told me that I made them think God might love them."

He swallowed the lump in his throat and looked back out at the falls, everything in him melting. "What do you believe, Claire?"

She looked reflective, like she was putting some thought into her words and he was glad. He wanted to know her heart—like he had shared his.

"I believe," she said slowly, "that God created this—the falls and Old Faithful and the sunrise and the mountains—to show us how much he loves us. When I look at something like this, I feel like God is here, and he loves us. He loves Claire Reilly. And he loves Red Wilder." She raised her brows at him as if challenging him to disagree.

He wasn't about to argue. "He sounds like somebody I might like to get to know."

She smiled at him then in that bright, sure way she had. "Maybe you should."

She'd asked him to take her picture then, with the falls behind her and that luminous smile. She'd had the photo developed and given it to him, writing Claire Reilly on the back. Not Claire. Claire *Reilly*. As if he'd ever forget who she was.

The picture was in his pocket, along with the letter from Claire that had come on Friday in care of the Zonolite Mining Company. The letter he hadn't read.

It could be Claire telling him to come home. Or it could be her goodbye to him. Either way, there was no reason for him to stay in Libby, mining Zonolite and dying a little each day from heartache. It wasn't something he could talk to her about on the telephone. He had to see her, and beg her to forgive him. For leaving. For Dell. For keeping secrets.

chapter 29

FRANNIE

Three more cabins and Frannie was done for the day.

"Your sisters are sure pretty," Vicky said as she stripped the bunk bed of the dirty sheets. "It was nice of them to come see you sing."

Nice? She wouldn't call what happened between Claire and Bridget nice. The usual Bridget-and-Claire-against-Frannie had looked a lot more like Claire-against-Bridget. She felt kind of sick thinking about it.

Frannie threw the wad of dirty sheets on the cart outside the door. Claire and Bridget could solve their own problems, she had better things to think about. Miracle of miracles, the whole gang had finagled two days off from Twig, and as soon as their shift was over they were going to blow this popsicle stand.

She peeked under the lid of the ceramic pot and choked back a gag. "When do I stop being the newbie and somebody else has to do these?" Frannie asked with a groan as she gingerly picked up the enamel pot and carried it to the door.

"Do what I do," Vicky said. "Pitch it over the rim of the canyon. No sweat."

Frannie stared at her. Could you really do that?

Vicky tossed a pillow in place. "There's a place between the upper and lower falls we call Duck Point, goes right down into the ravine. Get a clean one from the supply shed and nobody's the wiser."

"News to me." Frannie carried the duck down the trail to the narrow strip of trees bordering the canyon rim. Sure enough, there was a drop-off. She peered over but couldn't see all the way down. She thought of all the cabins and all the years the lodge had been there. There could be hundreds of these pots piled up down there. Maybe thousands.

One more wouldn't make a bit of difference, would it?

Frannie held the duck over the edge but couldn't make herself let go. She thought about how Claire was always talking about how gorgeous everything was in Yellowstone and how they had to keep it that way for future generations and all that junk. Frannie let out a sigh and trudged to the outhouse. She kicked herself as she held her breath and emptied the disgusting contents into the disgusting pit toilet.

Back at the cabin, she put the cleaned duck in its spot under the water basin.

"Did you find the place?" Vicky asked, sweeping a pile of dust under the carpet.

"Sure did," Frannie said. "Thanks for the tip."

Frannie had been one of the gang since the silly initiation at Dead Savage Spring. That night, Paul drove them back to Canyon with everybody goofing off. When they got back after midnight, everybody piled out of the car. "Race you to the dungeon," Sam said, and he and Ernie tore down the trail.

"I'm hitting the privy," Vicky announced, leaving Paul and Frannie to walk down the dark trail together.

At the turnoff for the dungeon, Paul stopped. "You know," he said, kicking at the dirt path with his toe, "I wouldn't have let you get hurt, in the hot pot."

She shrugged. "I figured you wouldn't." Nobody—but nobody—was going to know how scared she'd been.

"Anyway," he said, the moonlight lit his face and she noticed that his eyes were really nice, hazel with gold flecks. "The gang's a lot more fun now that you're in it."

"Thanks, Paul," she said. He turned to go but she stopped him. "Why do you put up with them?" she asked. Sam and Ernie were always mean to Paul, calling him *egghead* and *nerd* and making fun of him.

She made out the movement of Paul's shoulders as he shrugged. "I don't know," he said. "I guess having them as friends is better than not having friends at all."

Frannie felt the pang of recognition. She knew about that.

When their shift finally ended, Frannie and the girls met the boys in the parking lot where Paul was putting the top down on the convertible. He took her bag, stowing it in the trunk. "Me and Jerrylynn get shotgun," she said and vaulted into the front seat.

Sam scowled, but it was too late. "Hey, why don't you let me drive?" Sam said to Paul. "Nope," Paul answered. Frannie was glad—it was about time he stood up to Sam.

"Where are we going, anyway?" Ernie asked as they pulled away from the lodge.

"It's a surprise," Paul said with a glance sideways at Frannie.

Frannie gave him a wink. She and Paul had met up after dinner the night before, when the rest of the crew trekked across the bridge to Whittaker's for beer and supplies. Yellowstone was packed to the gills, and the chances of getting a campsite in any of the popular places were slim to none. Paul suggested a place outside the park that sounded cool, and they'd decided to keep it a secret from the others, just to make Sam crazy.

"Hey, nerd," Sam said. "That's not fair."

"Don't call him that, birdbrain," Frannie threw over her shoulder.

Jerrylynn played the peacemaker. "We'll know when we know, Sam. I just want to get away from the crowds."

"Fasten your seat belts," Vicky said in her Bette Davis voice. "It's going to be a bumpy night."

Paul pointed the convertible toward the lowering sun, and Frannie turned on the radio. This was the life. The wind in her hair, the top down, and the radio blasting. She could die right now and be happy.

"Hey," Sam said as they passed by the West Entrance and the girls waved and threw kisses to the ranger in the window of the station. "You never said we were leaving the park."

"We're leaving the park," Paul said, and Ernie and the girls erupted in laughter. Sam didn't laugh.

"Aw, don't be sore," Paul relented. "Listen, I know a guy over on Hebgen Lake who works at the fire tower. We're going to camp there and then go up the lookout tomorrow. He's got a telescope and everything."

"Cool," Jerrylynn said.

"Climbing the fire tower?" Vicky asked. "That will be a blast."

Even Ernie looked impressed.

Paul had more to say. "This guy says he's felt some tremors up in the lookout for a couple weeks now, and there's a fault line north of the lake."

"What's a fault line?" Jerrylynn asked.

"Kinda like a crack in the earth," Paul said.

"Sounds neat," Frannie said. It really did. She liked hearing about all the stuff Paul knew.

"Sounds lame," Sam griped. "Bunch of bookworms talking about rocks."

"If you don't like it, you can get out any time," Frannie said. She wished he would. Whatever she'd seen in Sam, she didn't see it anymore. "How much farther, Paul?"

Paul passed her the road map and she unfolded it over her lap. She traced the road from Madison to the West Entrance, and then north to a road that wrapped around Hebgen Lake. She saw Riverside on the map, a tiny dot beside the Madison River, but didn't say a word about them going right past her sister's house.

Frannie did a quick measure with her fingertip. "One mile to West Yellowstone, then head north on 191. If we hurry, we can find a campground before dark."

Paul turned up the radio and Jerry Lee Lewis sang, "Shake, baby, shake." Frannie laid her head back on the seat, threw an arm around Jerrylynn's shoulders and sang at the top of her voice, "Shake, baby, shake. I said, shake, baby, shake."

This was going to be the best night ever.

chapter 30

CLAIRE

By the time Claire got to Riverside, Jenny was red-faced and howling.

She parked the truck and hurried Beth inside. "Do you know how to change a diaper?" Beth nodded and Claire gave her a clean diaper, a washcloth, and the powder. "Change her on the couch. I'll get her bottle ready."

Claire put a pan of water on the stove and started warming a bottle from the refrigerator. Jenny's cries gained in momentum as Beth pinned on the dry diaper and pulled on Jenny's plastic pants.

Suddenly, a violent pounding shook the house. "Mrs. Wilder, I know you're in there." It wasn't hard to recognize Pete Henshaw's rusty growl.

Claire locked eyes with Beth. What were they to do? He was a big man, and if he wanted to, he could carry Beth out of the house. "Go," Claire whispered. "Into the bathroom and lock the door."

Pete banged on the door again. Claire heard the bathroom door shut and the lock click.

Claire took a deep breath and opened the door.

"Where is she, Mrs. Wilder?" Pete Henshaw looked past her, his determined gaze searching the room.

"Are you looking for Beth?" Claire asked with all the composure she could muster considering she was holding a screaming baby. Iris appeared behind him and Claire felt a moment's relief. Surely the woman could see how absurd this whole situation was?

"I know she's in there, Pete." Iris's desperate tone doused any hope of her as an ally.

Claire patted Jenny, glad Pete couldn't hear the pounding of her heart. "I brought her to the Depot," she lied.

"I don't believe you." Pete Henshaw put his boot on the threshold, like a salesman who didn't want the door shut in his face.

Claire looked down. "For heaven's sake, Mr. Henshaw." She marshaled her teacher voice and squared her shoulders. "What would you like to do, search my house?" Claire bounced Jenny on her shoulder, her heart hammering as she hoped he wouldn't call her bluff.

He hesitated.

"If you'll excuse me," Claire continued, "I have a hungry baby to tend to." She marched to the kitchen, leaving the door wide open. Her legs were quaking, as she rescued the bottle from the hot water and tested the temperature, hoping Pete Henshaw couldn't see her hand shake. She risked a glance at the door.

The big man remained on the threshold.

Jenny was frantic for her bottle. Claire sat down and settled Jenny on her lap. When Jenny latched on to the nipple, the room suddenly went quiet. Claire glanced back at Pete with a raised eyebrow as if asking if he was going to violate the rules of common decency.

"Pete," Iris said. She nudged him forward.

Pete scowled as he looked from his wife to Claire. "Come on, Iris." He put a firm hand on his wife's arm and guided her down the steps. "Don't worry," he said. "We'll find her." Outside, the Henshaws' truck started up. Claire sagged with relief when she heard the grind of gravel under tires.

When Jenny finished her bottle, Claire knocked on the bathroom door.

"I think they'll be back," Beth said as she came out and peered out the front window. "After they check the Depot."

"We'll be gone by then." Claire handed Jenny to Beth. "You burp her. I'm going to pack up some things for us."

Claire put five bottles of formula in an ice chest, threw in some sandwich meat and a half block of cheese. The can of powdered formula and the rest of a loaf of bread went in a paper bag. When Claire pulled the cookie tin from the top shelf to get money for their hotel in Ennis and the bus ticket, she found nothing but a scrawled note. *I borrowed some money. I'll pay you back, I promise. Frannie.*

Oh, the nerve of her! Claire crumpled the note and threw it in the garbage. She could just wring Frannie's little neck.

In the bedroom, Claire grabbed her suitcase and packed a set of clothes for herself and Jenny, and then considered Beth. "You can't show up at your parents' with just the clothes on your back." Claire pulled out a couple of summer dresses from hangers. "These should fit you for a couple months at least."

Beth touched the fabric of a soft pink shirtwaist. "I've never worn anything so pretty."

Claire looked at the closet full of dresses, all gifts from Dad and reminders of her life before Red. Was her life still here with Red? Or would she have to go home with Jenny and tell Dad that he'd been right all along? Her throat tightened at the thought. She pulled the rest of the dresses from their hangers. "You can have them all. After the baby is born you'll have something nice to wear." She forced herself to keep a spark of hope. Hope that she hadn't made a mistake. That Red would come back.

Finally, they were in the truck heading north out of Riverside on 191. "Watch for Pete's truck," she told Beth. They'd be in Ennis in an hour, and God willing, Pete Henshaw wouldn't look for them there.

That's when the truck engine sputtered and the speedometer dipped.

Claire pushed on the gas pedal. The engine died.

"What is it?" Beth asked, alarm in her voice.

Claire steered to the side of the road. The truck coasted to a stop and Claire had a sinking realization. She'd driven to Mammoth and back without once looking at the gas gauge. The needle was firmly on E.

Of all the stupid things.

Beth looked out the cab's back window. "There's a car coming," she said, her voice strained. "Maybe it's someone who can help."

Panic jolted through Claire at the flash of red in the rearview mirror. It could be a good Samaritan . . . or it could be Pete and Iris Henshaw.

chapter 31

FRANNIE

Paul pumped the brakes. "Hey, what's that?"

Frannie ignored him and kept singing at the top of her lungs. They had turned up highway 191 and blew past the turnoff to Claire's house. Frannie hadn't felt a bit bad about not stopping to say hello to her sister. This night was going to be abso-poso-lutely perfect. Friends, fun, and no sisters to answer to.

Paul dialed down the volume of the radio and slowed the convertible. "Somebody's having car trouble."

"Aw, don't," Sam complained. "Let some other Goody Two-shoes help them."

Paul pulled onto the shoulder and stopped the car.

Frannie took one look at the dusty blue Chevy truck and the woman getting out of the driver's side and groaned. What terrible luck. Here she was having the time of her life and all of a sudden Claire is in the picture? This had to be God punishing her. Paul got out of the car and walked toward the truck. Frannie figured she better go with him. She climbed out and jogged to catch up.

Claire caught sight of Frannie and her eyes went all big and surprised. "Oh, Frannie," Claire choked out, and then—of all things—she threw her arms around Frannie and squeezed her hard. "I've never been so glad to see you in all my life."

Frannie could barely breathe—it actually felt nice that Claire was glad to see her—but why was her sister out in the middle of nowhere all teary-eyed? Then, everything happened fast. Claire asked Paul for a ride and threw a suitcase and ice chest in Paul's trunk, and she and some girl holding Jenny squeezed into the back seat with Sam and Ernie and Vicky.

"Where to?" Paul asked.

Frannie was about to tell him to turn around and take her back to the turnoff they just passed, when Claire blurted out, "Anywhere you're going."

"Huh?" Frannie twisted around in the seat to see her sister.

"I'll explain later," Claire said, turning to look behind them at the road like somebody was coming after her.

Frannie gave her sister a frown over the seat back. Something was hinky here. Was Claire running away and leaving Red? Her heart sank. And what was the story with the girl who looked kind of pale and not too steady on her feet? Just then Jenny opened her eyes and saw Frannie peering at her. She let out a squeal. "Hey." Frannie got a warm kind of glow. "The little ankle biter remembered me."

"This isn't cool," Sam complained. "Last I checked we were going camping, not starting a nursery."

Frannie suddenly had just about enough of Sam. Claire was her sister and nobody got to complain about her except for Frannie. "You don't have to stick around." Frannie gave him a narrow-eyed stare.

Paul put on the brakes and looked in the rearview mirror at Sam, his expression as serious as a heart attack. "What she said."

Sam's face went from handsome to ugly. "Is that so?"

"Sure is," Frannie said. If Sam was going to be like that, he could thumb it back to Canyon in the dark.

Sam pushed open the door and jerked himself out of the car. "Come on," he said, looking at Ernie and Vicky and Jerrylynn. "We don't need to hang out with these squares."

There was a moment of silence and nobody moved.

Jerrylynn gave Vicky a look. "We'll stick with Frannie and Paul." Vicky didn't seem happy about that, but she didn't disagree.

"Come on, Ernie," Sam huffed. "We don't need these nerds."

"Wait," Ernie said. "Where are we going to—"

"Are you coming or not?" Sam barked. Ernie looked mulish, but slid out of the open door and slammed it behind him. Paul put the car in park and jumped out. He popped open the trunk and tossed two duffle bags on the gravel.

As they left Sam and Ernie in the dust, Frannie raised herself up on the seat and shouted back at them. "Goodbye and goo-ood riddance!"

chapter 32

CLAIRE

"You're not going to just leave them there, are you?" Claire asked the young man who had miraculously appeared with Frannie, of all people.

"Don't worry, they'll be fine." He waved one hand at the rearview mirror. "I'm Paul."

Claire recognized him now as the Santa Claus from the Christmas party. The blonde with the ponytail and glasses introduced herself. "I'm Jerrylynn, and this is Vicky." She waved a hand at a dark-haired girl who didn't look quite as friendly.

"I'm Claire, Frannie's sister. This is Jenny, and this is my friend Beth."

"Now that we all know each other, where are you headed?" Paul asked.

"Yeah, sis," Frannie demanded. "What the heck is going on?"

"We're going to Ennis," Claire said. No need to mention they were being chased by an angry man and his wife. "To catch the bus into Idaho in the morning."

"Why are you going there?" Frannie asked with narrowed eyes.

It was none of Frannie's business, and Claire didn't want to get into Beth's personal life in front of strangers. "None of your business, but you can pay me back the money you borrowed." She held out her hand, palm up, to Frannie.

Frannie screwed up her face in what might have been an apology. "No can do. That moolah is long gone."

Claire glared at Frannie.

"We can drive you to Ennis," Paul said into the rearview mirror.

Vicky crinkled the map in the back seat. "Ennis is fifty miles from here," she said with a note of annoyance. "By the time we get up there and back, it will be too dark to set up camp."

Beth's brows notched and she glanced at Claire. "We don't want to be a bother."

"You're no bother," Paul said. "But you know it's the busiest time of the year, and even in Ennis you might have trouble finding a vacancy at a motel."

He was right. The middle of August was always packed within the park, and all around it. And anyway, they didn't have any money for a hotel, thanks to Frannie. She had just enough to buy Beth a bus ticket.

"You could camp with us," Paul suggested. "We have a big tent and some extra sleeping bags since we kicked those blockheads out. I can drive you to Ennis in the morning to catch the bus."

"What about the fire tower? And the telescope?" Frannie said quickly. Claire could tell she didn't like the idea.

Paul shot Frannie a smile. "I'll be back in time for breakfast."

"That's very kind of you," Claire answered.

Frannie groaned. "The last thing I need is my big sister being a wet blanket."

"Don't mind her," Jerrylynn said, shoving Frannie. "We'd love to have you."

Claire considered Paul's offer. They were driving past Hebgen Lake now, and the lowering sun cast a shimmer of gold on the smooth surface of the water. It was going to be a beautiful night. Beth could get some rest and in the morning they would go to Ennis and get her a bus ticket. "Beth," Claire said. "What do you think about camping out tonight?"

Beth looked unsure. "What about Jenny?"

"She's slept in a tent before, with Red and me," Claire answered. Jenny had slept as snug as if she was in her crib at home.

"It's all decided then," Paul said and grinned when Frannie stuck out her lower lip in a pout.

They drove past Hebgen Dam at the west end of the lake, and the winding road dropped into the canyon. A few minutes later Paul turned into a campground at Beaver Creek. "Full up here," the Forest Service ranger told them. "You might find some space downriver at Rock Creek." Paul thanked him and went back to the highway.

The river where Red and Claire had fished a dozen times glinted darkly in the shadows of the canyon. Claire's heart squeezed at the thought of Red. Where was he tonight? In Libby, or somewhere else? Was he missing her and Jenny? The road followed the Madison farther downstream, where rocky buttresses loomed on the opposite side of the canyon and dark drifts of trees shadowed the hillsides.

"This must be the place," Paul said, slowing at a sign with the symbol of a tent and an arrow pointing to a gravel road. They turned down the road that ran between the highway and a ridge. The campsites on either side were spacious—each with a picnic table and a fire pit—and all occupied with tents, trailers and parked cars.

"Gee, it's crowded here, too," Paul said.

A hairpin turn around the ridge led to more camping sites. The sites on the ridge side were surrounded by trees. The spots on the other side stretched along the fast-flowing Madison.

"What about over there?" Frannie pointed to a grassy area next to the river. A yellow Pontiac and small silver trailer were parked close to the bank, and a couple sat beside the river in lawn chairs. It wasn't a designated camping site—no picnic table or fire ring—but there was plenty of room for a tent, and the river close by for water.

Paul pulled over and called to the couple. "You mind if we take this spot?"

The man waved him in. "Welcome to the neighborhood."

"Let's get set up." Paul pulled over on the grass and killed the engine.

The young couple were the friendly sort. "Ooh, a baby," the woman cooed when she saw Jenny in Beth's arms. "Can I hold her?"

Claire nodded her consent. They introduced themselves as Jeffrey and Dottie Gardner.

"Are you two newlyweds?" Claire asked Dottie.

The young woman's cheeks went a little pink in the fading light as she nodded. "My uncle gave us the trailer for our honeymoon. We're heading into the park tomorrow."

Paul and Frannie, along with their other two friends, pulled a canvas tent and a set of tent poles out of a green canvas bag. With Jenny settled in Dottie's arms, Claire asked Paul for some matches. She set up a circle of rocks close to the riverbank, then went to find dry wood.

The surface of the Madison glittered as the sun went down, clouds of gnats like a mist over the running water. Across the river, the mountain sloped sharply upward, thick with trees. Claire stood for a moment, her gaze drawn to the massive dolomite ridge jutting heavenward like a cathedral carved of rock. The beauty of the sunset and scenery was a balm after the tense flight from Mammoth and she whispered a thankful prayer that Beth was safe now. When Claire returned to the river with an armful of kindling it was to find Frannie waiting for her. Claire prepared to get an earful about how she'd ruined her sister's fun.

Frannie crouched down close to her and whispered. "What's going on, Claire?"

Why was she whispering? Claire laid a handful of kindling on a bed of dry grass. "Just what I said."

"Claire." Frannie's voice was serious. "Are you leaving Red?"

Claire frowned. Frannie had it all wrong. "Of all the things, Frannie. Why would you think that?"

Frannie raised her brows. "You're acting weird. You and Red were having it out the other night at your house. Then he went away and now here you are with a suitcase and the baby."

Claire didn't want to get into the whole business with the Henshaws, and she certainly didn't want to tell Frannie about Red and how awful everything was. Claire arranged the larger pieces of firewood in a teepee shape and dug in her pocket for the matches. "Beth has a family emergency. I'm just helping her. Everything is fine." Claire struck a match on a stone. The tip flared but the wind blew it out.

"Was it my fault?" Frannie blinked and in the dim light looked like she might be fending off tears. "Did you guys fight about me, and then he left?"

Claire stared at her sister. "Of course not." Was that really what Frannie thought? She let out a huff of breath. "We had a disagreement the other night, but it wasn't about you. I wrote him a letter and cleared everything up. He's probably on his way home right now." She hoped he was. Claire struck another match, shielding the flame from the breeze, and held it to the dry grass.

"You wrote him a letter?" Frannie looked at Claire as if she'd sent Red smoke signals. "That was sure dumb."

Claire glanced up at her as the dry grass turned black, the tiny flame licking at the kindling. "Why is writing a letter dumb?"

Frannie frowned. "Red's a swell guy and all, I'm not saying anything against him, but what good will a letter do when he can't read?"

What? Claire forgot the fire and turned on her sister. "That's a terrible thing to say, Frannie." If Frannie thought this was a joke, it wasn't funny.

"You're a bigger dope than I thought, Claire." Frannie was looking at Claire with wide eyes. "I watched him when Dad gave him the newspaper back home, he looked at it but his eyes didn't move."

That didn't prove Frannie's outlandish claim. Red would have told Claire if he couldn't read. "That's ridiculous." The dry grass was burning in a bright flare, the small kindling catching fire and starting to crackle and pop.

She shrugged. "Have you seen him read?"

Claire struggled for a rebuttal. He read the *Better Homes & Gardens Baby Book*. And the hymnal at church on Sundays. Then Claire remembered she was the one who had read the baby book aloud to him, and in church he didn't sing anything but the choruses. Claire remembered his letters the winter after she left Yellowstone. Shiny rocks and flowers. A hawk's feather. She'd thought it terribly romantic, but could Frannie be right? But what about the letters Claire wrote him that whole winter—had he not read them?

The campfire was sputtering out. "I'm a teacher," Claire argued. "I'd know if my own husband couldn't read."

But would she? Or was this something else he'd been keeping from her?

Frannie had to be wrong. Because if Red couldn't read . . . then he didn't read the letter that Claire sent to Libby. And if he didn't read the letter, he wouldn't know how much she needed him to come home to her.

chapter 33

RED

Red got lucky in Butte and caught a ride on a tanker truck heading to Yellowstone. "They don't like us making gasoline deliveries during the day, on account of the tourist traffic," the burly truck driver said as Red climbed up into the cab. "I'm scheduled to be at Madison Junction by ten p.m."

That meant Red would wake up next to Claire tomorrow morning. If she hadn't given up on him. On them.

Claire, don't give up on us.

He'd known from those first dates that Claire Reilly was too good for a luckless orphan like him. Still, even after she left him at the end of that summer—and took his heart with her—he couldn't let go of the hope he had for them.

He'd spent his last dollar on Marigold because of that hope. And that same hope sent him driving one thousand miles to Willmar as soon as the snow melted the following spring, when he finally got smart and knew he couldn't live without her.

Even now, with the rumble of the tanker truck jarring his bones, his heart surged at the remembrance of standing outside that little schoolhouse with his hat in his hands. He'd taken a chance—a desperate chance—and if Claire turned him down again he didn't know what he'd do. Then, Claire opened the door of the schoolhouse and she wasn't the Claire he knew. She stood looking at him, a woman with a job and a life and a family. A beautiful stranger.

His hope had flickered and died. He'd been stupid to think she loved him. An idiot. He couldn't do anything but stand and stare. But then . . .

But then . . .

Claire Reilly crossed the space between them in one glorious moment. Her face was buried in his chest, and she made a sound like a sob or maybe a laugh. Then, she kissed him and that kiss gave him the courage to ask her to marry him one more time.

She'd said yes. And he figured he was the luckiest man in the world.

But after that, she took him to meet her family and he realized just how out of his league Claire Reilly really was. It wasn't just the big house in the middle of town, or the shiny Coupe de Ville in the driveway, or the housekeeper who took his jacket at the door and looked at him like he might steal the silver.

It was Daniel Reilly.

The man took one look at Red and knew he wasn't worthy of Claire. Daniel Reilly . . . who wouldn't shake Red's hand or walk his daughter down the aisle.

"You hungry?" The driver of the tanker truck was slowing down, then pulling over at a diner just outside of Ennis.

Red shook his head. He had a pocketful of cash from a week of working in the mine, but he couldn't have swallowed a bite. He jumped out of the cab and walked across the parking lot to where the Madison River ran under a railroad bridge. The water he was looking at now had streamed past Riverside on its way north to Hebgen Lake, then passed the Hebgen dam and rushed through Madison Canyon before widening and slowing as it meandered toward Ennis. This water had passed by his sanctuary—his home with Claire and

Jenny. Was Claire still there, or had she realized that her father was right and she'd made a terrible mistake?

Back in the rumbling cab of the tanker, his face burned with the truth of it. What Bridget said was right. He wasn't doing enough for his family. It was time to change that, even if it meant giving up Montana. He'd give up anything for Claire and Jenny.

It was full dark when the tanker reached West Yellowstone. Red hopped out of the cab and thanked the driver. He shouldered his pack and started walking the three miles to Riverside.

He'd tell Claire he was sorry right off. Then he'd come clean with all the business about Dell. He'd go talk to Lem Garrison, and after that, he'd take Claire back to Willmar. Nothing mattered except taking care of his family—for better or worse.

He didn't see a single car between West Yellowstone and Riverside and by the time he came in sight of the house, his bones ached from walking on the hard road. As he came round the bend, the sanctuary that was his and Claire's was finally in sight. He stopped dead in his tracks.

Where was the truck?

Red's stomach pitted and he dropped his pack. His legs were like concrete blocks, stumbling toward the house. When he pushed open the front door, the echo of the empty rooms hit him like a punch in the gut.

Claire was gone.

More than that, the house looked wrong. An empty baby bottle sat on the table, a puddle of dried formula on the floor. The cupboard door was open. Claire never left the house without tidying up. And where was Frannie?

Could Jenny be sick? His mouth went dry. Even as he told himself there could be a dozen reasons why she wasn't home at this time of night, his steps—slow like he was wading through deep water—took him to the bedroom.

Standing in front of the closet, his legs went weak.

Claire's dresses were gone. Her suitcase was missing. He ran back to the kitchen and pulled out the cookie tin where they kept their extra cash. It was empty. He sat down hard. He'd been right about the letter.

It was Claire's goodbye to him.

Red put his head down on the kitchen table. He shouldn't have run. He should have faced Lem Garrison's questions and Claire's disappointment and Bridget's judgement. Bridget. She'd come waltzing into their life, telling Claire it wasn't enough—that he wasn't enough.

Bridget would know where she was now.

He jumped up, grabbed the telephone, and dialed the operator. "Mammoth Hospital," he demanded. He waited, shifting restlessly from one foot to the other as the ringing sounded in his ear. It might not be too late to change Claire's mind.

The call was answered by a curt voice. "Mammoth Hospital."

"Bridget Reilly, please," he said quickly.

"Nurse Reilly is with a patient," was the snappish reply. "Is this a personal call?"

"It's an urgent call," Red barked. "Tell her to call Red Wilder as soon as possible." He hung up and stared at the phone. How long would it take for her to get back to him? Or would she not get back to him at all? He paced to the bedroom and looked at the empty closet again. He stalked to the kitchen. He sat down on the couch, then stood up again.

As much as he wanted to blame Bridget for all of it, he knew it was his fault. He'd been a heel to Claire since she sold Marigold. He went to the kitchen window and looked out at the pasture and the shadowed forms of Rosie and Bess.

That night, when he'd come home to find Marigold gone and the house scrubbed and shining, new furniture and a refrigerator full of Coca-Cola, he'd run from Claire and his storm of mixed-up emotions. He knew why Claire had sold Marigold and was bending over backwards to prove to her sister that they were better off than they were.

She was ashamed of him. Ashamed of their life together.

Red had been so sure Claire was as content as he was—not just content, ecstatic—with their life. When they had Jenny, everything was perfect. Him and Claire. Jenny. Rosie and Marigold. Elk in the freezer and fish in the river. The sky and the mountains out their door. Everything they needed. He'd thought Claire felt the same.

But she didn't.

How had he not seen it?

Claire wanted her life to look like the one she'd left—with a pretty house and nice clothes and fancy dinners. That's what she wanted to show her sister. Not a shack with ancient appliances and a leaking roof. Not a broken-down truck and a husband who couldn't provide for his family.

The telephone rang. Two shorts and a long. He grabbed the receiver.

"Bridget?" His heart was at a full gallop.

"Red, what are you doing home?"

He pushed down the surge of ire when he heard her imperative tone of voice. "Do you know where Claire is?" He heard the telltale click of the party line being picked up but he didn't even care if the neighbors knew his business. All that mattered was finding Claire.

The silence was a beat too long and he realized . . . Bridget was keeping something from him.

"Red," she said, her voice careful. "I—I can't say."

"Can't?" he ground out in reply. "Or won't?" She'd come here intent on getting Claire home. Well, her plan had worked. "Bridget"—he hated the desperation in his voice—"did she leave me?" It was out and he couldn't take it back. The ugly words. The fear that had haunted him since the moment she said "I do" in front of the altar at St. Malachy's.

Bridget said quickly, "Red, it's not what you think."

What else could it be? Her dresses and her suitcase were gone.

"We have to talk in person," she rushed on. "Tomorrow morning."

"I'm not waiting until tomorrow." He couldn't wait another second.

Bridget hesitated. "Come up to Mammoth—"

"Claire took the truck," Red interrupted, "but I'll steal a car and go look for her if I have to."

There was a long pause. Red could hear the tinny sound of an open line and wondered if it was Helen Eagle listening in on their conversation in order to spread gossip all over town. "Okay," Bridget said finally. "I'll come to you."

"When?" he demanded.

"I'll leave right now," she said. "Just stay put."

He hung up without responding. Red wasn't about to stay put. It would take Bridget over an hour to get to Riverside—if she even was coming. By then, it would be almost eleven o'clock. He grabbed his jacket and left by the back door. He stopped at the pasture fence. Rosie came to him and he laid his hand on her sleek neck.

He took a breath. Then another. He felt his heartbeat slowing. It wasn't Bridget's fault Claire was gone. It was his. He deserved all the names he'd ever been called at the orphanage—an idiot. A dummy. His vows in front of God were to love and honor Claire. Keeping the truth from her was not honoring her. He'd thought if he told her how dumb he really was—if she really knew him—she would stop loving him.

He lay his head against Rosie's warm neck.

"I'll find them," he told Rosie. "I won't come home until I do."

chapter 34

FRANNIE

How could Claire not know about Red? When you loved somebody and were married to them, weren't you supposed to know everything about them?

"Frannie," Paul yelled from where he and Vicky were putting the tent poles together. "We need a hammer for the stakes. Could you ask around and borrow one?"

"Sure thing," Frannie called, but she wasn't done with her sister. "Claire, are you really okay?" Frannie didn't believe the lame story about Claire taking Beth to Idaho.

"I'm fine," Claire said.

That old line. She let out a long breath and stood up. "I'm going to find a hammer and when I get back you're going to tell me the truth, the whole truth, and nothing but the truth."

She headed down the gravel road toward a campsite with a tent set up next to a red-and-white trailer. A mom and dad sat at the picnic table with a girl who looked about sixteen. Playing cards were scattered on the table between them. Frannie remembered her manners, introduced herself, and said, "Do you have a hammer we could borrow? Just for a couple minutes."

The dad put down his hand of cards. "Sure do, young lady. It's in the trunk of the car." He disappeared toward a wood-paneled station wagon.

"I'm Mildred Wilson," the mom said with a friendly smile. "And this is Connie." The girl nodded shyly at Frannie. She had long hair in barrettes like Frannie used to wear and a pimply chin.

Two girls ran up from the river and Frannie did a double take. The girls were carbon copies of each other, including the mud splatters on their bare legs and grass stains on their matching short sets.

"Mom, Mom," one of the girls said, "we asked the ranger about the bear—"

"—and he said it was because of the full moon," the other girl finished.

"Girls, say hello to Frannie," Mrs. Wilson said. "Frannie, this is Jean, and this is Jan."

"Hiya," Frannie said. She expected the mother to scold her daughters for being such a mess, but she didn't. The girls said hello, then began to chatter about a bear and a forest ranger.

Frannie felt a wet nose on her leg.

"It's just Sadie," Connie said when Frannie made a start of surprise. "She's friendly."

"She's so cute." Frannie ran a hand over the dog's silky ears with a pang of envy. "I wish my dad would let us have a dog." She'd begged him for years, but he'd always said three girls were enough.

Connie dropped her voice with a glance toward the car, where they could hear her father rummaging. "Dad says it was a moment of weakness when he brought her home, but he really has a marshmallow heart."

Frannie felt a pang of envy. A dad with a marshmallow heart would be nice.

The man came back with a hammer in his hand. "Strangest thing about that bear," he said. "He barreled through here like he was being chased by the devil himself. Never seen anything like it." He gave Frannie the hammer. "Where are you from, Frannie?"

Frannie figured since he was doing her a favor, it was only polite to talk for a while and actually she didn't mind. They were a nice bunch. She told him she was from Minnesota and was working as a savage at Canyon.

"We're from Livingston, but my Mildred here isn't too keen on Yellowstone." He smiled fondly at his wife.

Mildred Wilson shuddered. "It sets my teeth on edge, to be honest, with those mud pots and hot pools. Doesn't feel right."

"She likes to fret," Mr. Wilson said. "She told me she wanted to get out of the park before the whole thing blew up." He gave his wife an indulgent smile. "I'd rather fish, so fine by me."

"Thanks for this," Frannie said hefting the hammer. "I'll bring it back in a minute." As she headed back toward their spot on the river, her shoulders drooped and her steps were slow. That family had it all. A sweet mom, a nice dad, and even a dog. Why couldn't she have a family like that? She searched her memory for the last time her family had fun together. It had to be before Claire married Red. Maybe before Claire went to Yellowstone that first summer. She guessed it was about the time she'd started dating Jonny and hanging around his friends. That's when Dad had started harping on her, and she'd taken to staying in her room and listening to her record player.

Her insides squirmed in an unpleasant way as she remembered Claire asking her to come downstairs one winter night. "We're going to make hot chocolate, your favorite," Claire had called through her bedroom door.

"Leave me alone," she'd shouted, annoyed that Claire thought she was still such a baby. Frannie stopped for a minute at the river. There had been a time when she and Dad got along. They'd play cards, or go to the Chatterbox for ice cream. She could talk to him without fighting.

She picked up a rock and threw it in the dark water. He really seemed to love her back then.

One time, when she was about fourteen, she'd asked him about Mother. Bridget was in nursing school and Claire had gone on a date with Luke. She and Dad were playing crazy eights at the kitchen table.

"We've done fine without her," Dad said curtly. She wanted to tell him then that she wasn't fine. She wanted a mother, like all her friends had, but it seemed like a mean thing to say. Like Dad wasn't enough.

"I heard you tell people she passed away," she said, even though her dad's face and voice said he was done talking about it. "You tell me not to lie."

"I say she's not with us anymore," he said. "It's not a lie." He looked tired, and maybe sad. He put away the cards in the middle of the game and told her to go to bed. Was that why Bridget and Claire never talked about Mother? Because it made Dad sad?

Frannie looked toward their camping spot and saw Vicky and Jerrylynn roasting hot dogs over the fire. Claire and her friend Beth were sitting with the neighbors, eating sandwiches. Frannie had been pretty terrible to Claire since she got to Yellowstone. Just thinking about it felt like a big river rock was sitting in her stomach. She headed toward the campsite. Maybe she should tell Claire she was sorry for being a brat, and then Claire might tell her what was really going on with Red.

Paul was almost done getting the tent up. She gave him the hammer, and Jerrylynn handed her a stick with a hot dog on it. "I saved you one."

"Thanks." Frannie was hungry enough to eat a horse. She glanced toward Claire again. Maybe now wasn't a good time to talk to her sister with all those people around.

Frannie stuck the hot dog into the flames. Vicky passed her a can of beer and started singing "Yes, We Have No Bananas." Frannie joined in. She would talk to Claire and tell her she was sorry, but not tonight.

Tomorrow was soon enough for all that junk.

chapter 35

BRIDGET

Bridget hung up the telephone and wanted to scream.

Red had it all wrong and it was her fault. Her fault he'd left for a job who-knows-where, and her fault Claire had to rescue Beth Henshaw. Now Red thought Claire had left him when that was nothing close to the truth. She hadn't been able to explain it all to Red after she heard that click on the party line. She'd bet her bottom dollar it was Pete Henshaw listening in.

Now she had to get to Riverside before Red did something stupid.

She checked the duty roster, then called the upstairs extension. Beckett answered in a sleepy voice. After some begging and promises, Beckett said she'd be down in a few minutes. "Don't tell Larkin," Bridget warned. "She's on the warpath after that fire alarm fiasco."

If Larkin knew she was leaving the floor without permission, Bridget could kiss her recommendation—and the job at Mayo Clinic—goodbye.

Bridget hung up and pulled open the closet where the nurses and doctors stowed their personal items. Dr. Sampson's jacket hung on the hanger where he'd exchanged it for his white doctor's coat. She slipped her hand in the pocket and fished out his keys. His shift wasn't over for hours, and by that time she'd be back.

She was almost to the front door when a voice as sharp as broken glass stopped her in her tracks. "Reilly, where do you think you're going?"

Bridget turned around slowly to face Larkin, who stood in the waiting room with a thunderous expression. "I have a family emergency."

"And you may go when your shift is over, in"—Larkin looked at her watch—"one hour and fifty minutes."

"Beckett is covering for me," Bridget offered without much hope.

Larkin stared at Bridget as if daring her to walk out that door.

Bridget wavered, the job at Mayo and her apartment in Rochester teetering on the precipice of Larkin's disfavor. But Claire . . . her sister. Her best friend. Bridget had made such a hash of things. Claire had been heartbroken about Red . . . and what she said about Mother proved just how distraught her sister was. Bridget had to fix this mess. She let out a long breath, turned on her heel, and walked out the door.

The light-green Thunderbird was the only car in the parking lot. She slid into the driver's seat and stared at the steering wheel for a long moment. She'd seen people drive plenty of times. It couldn't be that hard. Then why was her heart hammering like she was about to take off in a space rocket?

The key went into the ignition, and she turned it. The engine roared to life. "So far, so good," she said, putting her trembling hands on the steering wheel. She moved the gearshift into drive and tapped one of the pedals. The car shot forward. She panicked and jammed her foot on the other pedal. The car jerked to a stop. This would work. She'd drive to Riverside, talk to Red, and drive back. She just hoped she wouldn't meet any other cars on the road.

Five minutes later, the Thunderbird crept out of Mammoth Hot Springs toward Madison Junction. The speedometer said she was going twenty-five miles per hour. That seemed fast, so she let off on the gas a little. The road was—thankfully—almost empty this late at night. The full moon had risen, and the river gleamed in a bright ribbon beside the road as she concentrated on staying in her lane and considered what she would say to Red.

Claire wasn't leaving him. Whatever was going on between them, they could work it out. She just knew it. Not because of the novels she read where the happy ending was guaranteed, but because she knew Claire.

She pushed down on the gas pedal and the speedometer crept up to thirty.

Claire was the bravest person Bridget had ever known. She'd gone to teachers' college in Moorhead, then learned to drive so she could teach thirty miles away at Tara School, even though Dad already got a job for her at Willmar Consolidated. But no, she wanted to teach in a one-room schoolhouse and that's what she did. She braved snowstorms and ice and fought the school board tooth and nail to keep Tara open despite yearly threats to shut it down and bus students to Willmar. Claire Reilly had been a force to reckon with.

But Claire Wilder . . . Claire Wilder was a wonder.

Not only did she have a baby in this wilderness, she knew how to shoot a gun and fish and even cook wild animals. She rode a horse—a horse!—and did her own laundry and drove a truck.

And Red.

It was hard not to admire him at least a little. He was just as brave and capable as Claire—whether it was shooting an elk to feed his family or changing a diaper—and wasn't that about as romantic a hero as she'd ever read about in her books?

Bridget had always wondered what it would be like to be brave like Claire. To go on her own adventure like the nurses in her novels. The closest she'd come to making that a reality was the Mayo Clinic in Rochester but that grand plan had just gone up in smoke.

The full moon lit the road before her, as she took the road west toward Norris Junction and drove a tiny bit faster. She was going to have to apologize to Red. She never should have made that promise to Dad. And what Red had said about her father—that he'd made himself the center of their lives—she'd given that a lot of thought. Dad had spent the last twenty years taking care of his girls—protecting them—and maybe he didn't know how to stop.

As much as she hated to admit Red was right, maybe it was time for Dad to let go of his tight hold on Claire. And time for Red and Claire to hold on to each other with all their might. Because wasn't that what all the romance books were really about? That love—real love—was worth fighting for? Maybe it sounded a little corny, but that didn't make it any less true.

Bridget passed the deserted ranger station at the edge of the park and slowed to a crawl to make the right-hand turn up highway 191 toward Riverside. She was glad the intersection was deserted, because she couldn't find the turn signal.

She was picking up speed again when the Thunderbird's headlights illuminated a lone figure on the side of the road. She knew that cowboy hat and the lanky silhouette. She stomped on the brakes and came to a screeching halt. "I told you to stay put," she said.

"Where did you . . . ?" He stared at the Thunderbird.

"Doesn't matter right now." Bridget fumbled, then remembered how to put the car in park. "Get in. I have to talk to you."

Red opened the passenger door and sat down heavily on the leather seat. "Where is she, Bridget? I went to the Depot and to all the motels in West."

"Listen, Red. It's not what you think." She filled him in about Beth Henshaw, shivering in the cool night air. She'd left the hospital in her uniform and without even a sweater. "Claire isn't leaving you. She's getting Beth to her parents in Idaho and then she'll come right back."

There. That should settle things. She might be able to patch things up with Larkin if she got back quick. In the light of the dashboard, she saw Red's clenched jaw and stony expression. What was wrong now? Red should be relieved. Claire was helping out a friend and then she'd be back, and they could iron out their differences. She slapped at a mosquito. "I couldn't tell you on the phone because of the party line. For all I knew, the Henshaws were listening in and I didn't want them to know where Beth was going."

Red twisted in his seat to face her. "Why should I believe you?"

Bridget's brows came down. Of all the nerve. Here she'd kissed her recommendation goodbye and he was accusing her of lying to him? Before she could summon an indignant reply, he opened his door and walked around the car to the driver's side. "Move over."

"What?" She scooted over as he got in. He put the car in gear and was driving before she'd even settled in the passenger seat. "Where are we going?"

"To Ennis. To find Claire and Jenny," he said. "I'm not going home without them."

chapter 36

RED

Red didn't believe Bridget's story.

She'd been looking down her nose at him since she'd handed him her purse at the Depot. Why would she change now? And either way—if Claire was leaving him or if she was helping Beth—he needed to find her. Pete wasn't somebody to cross.

"This isn't my car," Bridget sputtered. "How far is it to Ennis? I have to get it back before—"

"Not far," he said. He pushed the car over the speed limit and the cool night air whipped past them.

Bridget crossed her bare arms. Red juggled the wheel and shrugged out of his jacket. She put it on with a grateful look and shoved her hands in the pockets.

Immediately, he realized what he'd done.

Bridget pulled the letter from Claire out of the jacket pocket. "What's this?"

He gritted his teeth and didn't answer.

"It's from Claire," she said, peering at the envelope in the moonlight. "What does it say?"

He shrugged. It might say she was leaving him. Or it might not. He couldn't bear to know. He tapped the brakes as a coyote appeared out of the darkness and dashed across the road.

She turned it over and frowned. "You haven't even opened it. Why on earth not?"

Red clenched his jaw. It wasn't her business.

"Red?" she asked again in that huffy way she had.

He pushed down on the accelerator, the headlights eating up the road in front of him. He might as well tell her. If—when—he got Claire back and brought her to Willmar, everyone would know his shameful secret, including Daniel Reilly. And anyway, what did his pride matter now? "I can't," he rasped, the words sticking in his throat.

"Can't what?" she asked.

He threw her a glare. Was she really going to make him say it? But her expression was truly bewildered.

"Can't read." A wave of shame rushed up his neck and into his face as he waited for her scorn. For the mocking like the kids at school. Stupid Red Wilder.

"That can't be," she said in disbelief.

Did she think he'd make something like that up?

"You wrote letters—you and Claire—that winter after you met."

He jerked his chin. "I didn't write." Not really. After she left him to go home to Minnesota, Red couldn't eat. He hardly slept. Everything he saw reminded him of Claire. She'd left him her address, and he mailed her bits and pieces he picked up on the trail or at the river. A blossom of pink bitterroot just the color of her cheeks when she blushed. A hawk's feather. A sprig of fragrant sage. He even bought a cheap Brownie and took a picture of the place they'd fished on the Madison the day she caught her first trout. He put an X on the spot and sent it to her. He carefully copied her address onto the envelopes, but he didn't write any words of his own.

"But she wrote to you," Bridget continued to object. "Didn't you read her letters?"

Red remembered the day he got that first letter from Claire. He'd put it in his pocket and walked the streets of West Yellowstone for an hour until he found himself standing at the back of Our Lady of the Pines Catholic Church. The church was small, with peeled pine benches and a single stained-glass window behind the altar. Nothing fancy, but Red felt something expand in his chest—the same feeling he got when he saw the colors of the Grand Prismatic or a sky full of stars. Or Claire Reilly. It was something he couldn't put into words, but in the silence of that little church he felt a measure of peace he hadn't had since she left.

"Father Donahue read them to me," he admitted to Bridget.

The old priest hadn't asked his name or what Red was doing in his church. He walked right past Red and disappeared out a side door, came back a minute later with two bottles of root beer. Red thanked him and they sat in silence on the front step of the church, soaking in the last of the September afternoon. Red took the unopened letter from Claire out of his pocket and looked again at the neat address, her perfect handwriting.

"What's that you have?" the priest asked.

"A letter from a girl." He wanted to say *his* girl, but he didn't think she was that. "She came out for the summer."

"Afraid to read it?" the priest asked.

Red nodded. That was part of it. Maybe Claire would tell him to stop mailing her reminders of Montana. Or that she was getting married to that Luke fellow he'd heard Millie tease her about.

"I'll do the honors," the priest said, holding out his hand. "Sometimes it's easier that way." Claire's letter wasn't very personal, but she didn't tell him to stop sending her gifts. And she didn't say anything about marrying Luke Charpentier. Red thanked the priest and left the church feeling twenty pounds lighter. He wasn't going to tell Bridget that the next time he saw Father Donahue, it was in the county jail. He spent three months up in Bozeman after the conviction on the Lacey Act. The priest brought him his mail every week and read Claire's letters to him.

He glanced over at Bridget and she wasn't eyeing him with the disgust he'd expected. "Can I read it to you?" she asked.

Humiliation swamped him at her gentle tone and he wished she'd stay bossy and aggravating. Anything was better than her pity. He didn't want to hear through Bridget that Claire had given up on him. But . . . what if Bridget was telling the truth and Claire wasn't leaving him? He jerked a nod, cursing that flame of hope that refused to die.

Bridget stuck a finger under the seal and popped it open.

He steeled himself for whatever would come.

"Dear Red," she began, then her voice halted. "Oh, no," Bridget said softly. "Oh, Claire."

An iron band clamped around his chest. "Out loud," he said, his voice rough. He watched the road but he didn't see the white lines or the dark trees flashing past.

"Dear Red," Bridget said again, her voice quivering, *"I've always thought it didn't help to dig up the past, that it was better to keep it buried. I think now I was wrong. I should have told you about my mother."*

Red sent a sideways glance at Bridget. Her mother? What did their mother have to do with Claire leaving him?

Bridget cleared her throat and continued.

"Mother left us when I was eight years old. I didn't understand at first. I hoped that she would come back. For years, I hoped. I hoped for me—and for Bridget and Frannie and Dad. She didn't come back (not even once). I stopped hoping, because hoping hurt too much."

Bridget's voice broke and she took a gulping breath.

Red gripped the steering wheel hard. Claire had let him believe her mother had died. Why hadn't she told him what really happened?

"Then I met you, and Red, you have so much hope. You hope every time you go fishing (even if they aren't biting), every time you deal out the cards for solitaire (which you always lose). You hoped every time you asked me to marry you (even when I always said no).

"I'm not good at hope, Red. I gave up on us at the end of that summer. Putting you out of my mind and out of my heart felt safer than hoping. But you didn't give up. You hoped so much that you bought me a horse and showed up at Tara with a ring.

"Red Wilder, you had enough hope for us both.

"On our wedding day, when my dad refused to walk me down the aisle, I decided Claire Wilder would be a new person. One who was stronger. One who left her past behind. You know what happened then."

Bridget paused, and Red remembered that moment in the church, and what it had meant to him.

She went on. *"But I couldn't leave Claire Reilly behind, Red, even though I wanted to. That little girl is still a part of me."*

Bridget let out a little sob and opened her handbag for her handkerchief. "I'm sorry, Red," she said. "I can't."

"Keep reading," he ordered, then softened his tone when he saw the tears glinting on Bridget's cheeks. "Please, Bridget."

She blew her nose, then started again with a ragged voice. *"When I sold Marigold, you were so angry. Is that why you left? Or did it have something to do with Dell? All I knew was that you had turned into a stranger. You were so far away from me, even as we slept beside each other that last night. It was all so terrible and when you left for Libby, I was afraid you were leaving me forever, just like Mother.*

"I didn't know how to talk to you or even if I could trust you."

Red's hands tightened on the steering wheel as the words hit him like arrows in his heart. She didn't trust him. She couldn't tell him.

Bridget sniffed and swiped at her eyes. *"It felt safer to push you away. I told you I didn't need you—that we didn't need you—but Red, nothing could be further from the truth. I need you. I'm not fine without you. I want to trust you with my secrets, and I need you to trust me with yours. Please come back, Red. Don't give up hope for us. All my love, Claire."*

Claire wanted him back. She wasn't leaving him. He blinked hard, the road in front of him blurring. He slowed down to bump over the bridge across the Madison. He'd kept secrets from her, and she'd hidden things from him. But they could fix it.

"There's a postscript," Bridget said. *"I'm sorry about Marigold. It was the only way to prove to my sister (and Dad) that we were happy."*

Red pressed down on the gas pedal. Marigold didn't matter anymore. They were almost to the turnoff to Hebgen Lake and the road that would take them to Ennis. He'd find her there and tell her everything.

The headlights illuminated a vehicle on the side of the road and Red jammed on the brakes. "What—?"

Bridget put her hands on the dash to stop herself from lurching forward. "Is that your truck?"

Red was already out the door, running to the truck, hope briefly flaring to life. Claire and Jenny. He wrenched open the driver's side door but even as he did so, he already knew.

The truck was empty. His wife and child were gone.

chapter 37

CLAIRE

Beth was not looking well.

Claire made her eat a sandwich and drink water, like Bridget had ordered. What she needed now was sleep. Unfortunately, it looked like Frannie and her friends were going to be staying up late.

Paul had taken forever to set up the tent, then the two girls—Vicky and Jerrylynn—hauled a downed tree trunk to the campfire to sit on. Now, they were burning hot dogs black and drinking beer, singing goofy campfire songs Claire recognized from her days as a savage. Claire couldn't blame them for enjoying the beautiful night. The full moon shone on the river, and a light breeze was keeping the mosquitoes at bay. If it wasn't for Beth's situation and her troubling thoughts about Red, Claire would be enjoying herself, too.

Jenny started to wiggle and fuss in Dottie's lap. "She wants her bottle," Claire told the young woman. When Claire came back from Paul's car with the bottle of formula, Dottie took it from her hands. "I've got a hot plate in the trailer to warm it. Be back in a jiffy."

Jeffrey watched his wife walk away. "She's from a big family and can't wait for us to have kids."

Claire missed Red even more, looking at this couple. By the time Claire had Jenny's diaper changed and put her into her pajamas, Dottie was back with the warmed bottle.

She gave Beth a concerned look. "Are you feeling okay?"

Beth attempted a smile. "Just tired."

"Let's get to bed as soon as Jenny is asleep." Claire looked at the tent, then at the four teenagers making a ruckus at the fire. "I'll ask them to quiet down."

"Jeffrey," Dottie said, reaching to take her husband's hand and looking up at him with pleading eyes. "Let's sleep in the car tonight."

Jeffrey looked at her like she was crazy. "Why?"

Dottie gave him a meaningful look. "So we can see the moon. It's so gorgeous and romantic."

Jeffrey opened his mouth.

"And"—she stopped him from speaking—"we could let Claire and the baby and Beth sleep in the trailer."

"Oh, no," Claire objected. That was too much. She couldn't put them out of their beds.

"We couldn't possibly," Beth said firmly.

"We insist," Dottie said, although Jeffrey didn't look like he agreed. "We'll be up for ages yet, and babies need their bedtime." She gave Beth a kind smile. "And you look tuckered out."

As much as Claire hated to impose, it was what Beth needed. "You're so kind," Claire said, relief in her voice. "That would be wonderful."

After Jenny had her bottle and was back asleep, Dottie led them to the trailer. It was a kidney-shaped four-wheeler, the kind Claire saw every day going in and out of the park. Dottie pulled open the aluminum door. "It's nothing fancy," she said.

Claire went up the two steps. Inside was a tiny kitchenette with a table attached to the wall and two upholstered benches in sunshine yellow. A small countertop with a sink and a one-burner stovetop was in the center, and the rear was a double bed made up with a quilt and pillows. Outside the small back window, the river sparkled in the moonlight.

"Are you sure, Dottie?" Claire asked a last time, hoping she wouldn't change her mind.

"Absolutely." Dottie gathered a few blankets and an extra pillow from a storage cupboard. "Sleep tight."

Claire settled Jenny in the middle of the double bed while Beth sat down at the dinette. When Claire came back, Beth was dabbing at her tears with a kitchen towel. "It's been so horrible since Dell. With Pete and Iris. But you and your sister, and now this—" She nodded to the snug little trailer. "I can't help it, but I'm still afraid something terrible will happen."

Claire reached out and took Beth's hand. It was ice cold. With everything that had happened to her, of course she was fearful. "We're safe," Claire said. The Henshaws would never find Beth here, and in the morning Claire would get her home to her parents. "Let's get some sleep." Claire squeezed her hand. "I promise you, things always look brighter in the morning."

chapter 38

FRANNIE

Frannie squirmed down in her sleeping bag.

She had stayed up late, drinking beer with her friends and gabbing with Dottie and Jeff. Frannie told them goodnight as Vicky and Jerrylynn stumbled off to the tent.

"We're going to go for a walk downstream," Dottie said, holding Jeffrey's hand. "It's such a beautiful moon I want to enjoy it a little longer."

Frannie helped Paul douse the fire with river water. He spread his sleeping bag down a couple yards away from the tent and said, "Sleep tight."

"Don't let the mosquitoes bite," Frannie answered.

But Frannie couldn't sleep. She lay awake with her thoughts swirling like a tornado. Was Claire leaving Red? Did Paul like her as more than a friend? Was anyone going to do something about the dog barking at the Wilsons' campsite? She thought about Dad, and how terrible she'd been to him. It gave her a queasy feeling, thinking of him home alone and probably worrying about her.

Frannie gave up trying to get any shut-eye. She slipped out of her sleeping bag and quietly undid the tent flaps. She'd just go see if Claire was awake. As she walked toward the trailer, a movement down by the river caught her eye. It was Paul standing by the water. She walked between the clumps of silvery grass and whispered, "Is that dog keeping you awake?"

"Nah." He stuck his hands in his pockets. "Just thinking."

Frannie looked over the sparkling water to the dark rise of the canyon wall above them. "You worried about Sam and Ernie?" She was proud that Paul had finally stood up for himself, but maybe they had been a little mean to dump Sam and Ernie in the middle of nowhere like they did.

"Heck no," he said. "I bet they're sleeping like rocks in a motel."

He was probably right. "Thanks for being so good about my sister and her kid," she said, nodding toward the trailer.

"She's swell," Paul said.

"She's a pain," Frannie retorted and Paul laughed.

"You look like Claire," Paul said. "I could see the resemblance right away."

Frannie was glad the dark hid the heat on her cheeks. Claire was beautiful, everybody said so. "I can't see it."

Paul made a sound of disbelief. "Wish I had a sister."

Aw, that just made her feel even worse. She'd never doubted that Claire and Bridget loved her—Dad, too—and she'd been a brat to all of them. She glanced over at the trailer. The lights were out and Claire was probably asleep. She'd get up early and talk to her sister tomorrow, before they headed off to Ennis. Claire would forgive her—she was good that way. And maybe she'd even help her smooth things over with Bridget and Dad.

Frannie suddenly realized what a mess she was, with her hair all sticking up from tossing and turning. Her goofy pink pajamas. "I better get to—"

Suddenly the ground started to shake and she staggered. Paul reached out to her, and they were both thrown to their knees.

"Stay down—" she thought she heard Paul say as shouts and crashing filled the air.

She couldn't have stood up if she tried. She flattened herself to the grass while everything went topsy-turvy, the ground rolling like waves. It seemed to go on forever, then—as suddenly as it had started—the shaking stopped.

That's when she looked up and saw the mountain. Was it . . . moving?

How could a mountain move?

But it wasn't moving . . . it was falling. Time seemed to slow as the immense rock buttress above the canyon broke off and slid downward. Sparks flew, boulders that had to be as big as houses bounced like ping-pong balls down the canyon wall. She glimpsed Paul's gaze following the mountain down, his eyes wide with shock. Seconds behind the unbelievable sight came a roar like a freight train. Frannie raised her hands to cover her ears, but as she did the wind hit her.

Then she was flying.

She tumbled, her arms flailing, grabbing for anything to stop her wild careening. She landed among the rocks and felt a burst of pain in her shoulder as her body was pushed like a toy, crashing into rocks, scraped along the dirt. She was yelling, she knew it because her throat hurt, but she couldn't hear herself over the roaring. Her hands found a branch, bark, a tree. She grabbed at it, holding with all her might. A sleeping bag flew past her like a kite, and an ice chest tumbled upstream. A yellow car—was that Jeff and Dottie's car?—careened sideways up the riverbank. People—she could see people—tumbling along the ground, tossed like rag dolls.

How much longer could she hold on?

Suddenly the wind stopped. She blinked her gritty eyes, trying to see the campground. Paul. Her sister and Jenny. Her friends. No moon, no stars. Nothing but black. She let go of the tree, her hands cramped and burning.

Then . . . what was that?

A rushing, rumbling sound like a waterfall. Not the river, it was too loud. And it was coming from downstream, wasn't it? The fleeting question was followed by a ridiculous lightning-quick thought: *Paul would know.*

Then, a wave of water hit her like a brick wall and she couldn't think at all.

chapter 39

CLAIRE

Claire lay awake, looking out the back window of the trailer at the full moon reflected in the river, the slope of the canyon rising like a protective wall beyond, covered in a blanket of lodgepole pine and blue spruce. Jenny slept between her and Beth, the whisper of her breath joined by the distant ripple of water and the song of night insects.

Despite Claire's weariness, her thoughts would not let her sleep.

If Frannie was right, Red hadn't read her letter.

Could Frannie be right? Why would Red keep something like that from her—or his secrets about Dell and going to jail that winter? Even as Claire wondered, she turned the question on herself. Why hadn't she told her husband—the man she had promised to love and honor—about her mother? Was it the shame of it, or the hurt she didn't want to relive? Keeping that painful secret buried had—that morning at the Depot—hurt both Claire and Red.

Were Red's secrets as deeply buried? Claire's heart ached with the realization that neither of them had trusted the other with the pain of their pasts. Claire had tried to leave her past behind, determined that it wouldn't affect her future. Had Red wanted to do the same? Or was he running away from Lem Garrison and whatever had happened when Dell drowned in the Yellowstone?

Would he come home to Claire and Jenny, or had her father been right all along?

Claire curved her arm around Jenny and closed her eyes. She tried to pray—for faith in her husband. For the hope she lacked.

Claire didn't know she'd fallen asleep until she felt Beth shaking her. Claire tried to pry open her eyes, but she was so tired. Beth shook her again. Hard. Claire opened her eyes and tried to sit up.

It wasn't Beth. The trailer was shaking.

Moonlight poured into the back window. Beth braced herself against the back wall of the trailer as it rocked from side to side. "Claire!"

Was it a bear?

Claire pulled Jenny protectively into the curve of her body as cupboard doors flew open in the kitchenette and the contents crashed to the floor. The bed shifted underneath them. Jenny whimpered and began to cry. Claire looked out the window. Trees and rocks were falling across the river.

Not a bear, an earthquake.

The quaking stopped and all was suddenly silent.

"Is it over?" Beth asked in a breathless whisper.

Was it? The trailer was listing sideways. Claire and Beth had slid down to the foot of the bed.

"We need to get outside," Claire said. She gathered Jenny into her arms and stood carefully on the uneven floor. "Careful," she warned Beth, "there's glass." Claire started picking her way toward the door when a roar like a freight train ripped through the silence. The trailer jerked like it had been hit. Claire flew forward, clutching Jenny to her chest, as she hit the kitchenette with her shoulder. The trailer rolled as the sound rent the night and everything went black.

The deafening sound faded to an echo. "Claire," Beth moaned. "Is Jenny okay?"

Claire ran a hand over Jenny in the pitch dark—where had the moonlight gone? Jenny let out a furious wail. "I think so." *Lord, let her not be hurt.* Claire felt carefully in the dark with one hand, trying to determine where she was. She felt the wall, the handle of a cupboard door. The trailer moved again, not jerking but listing, as if it were teetering on a precipice.

"My arm," Beth said. "It hurts."

Claire was calm, her thoughts strangely clear. *Find the door. Get out.*

A shout from outside, "Are you okay in there?"

"Help us!" Claire yelled back, supporting herself with one arm, the other keeping Jenny tight to her body. She half crawled along the wall, groping for the door in the dark. She felt her way along the cupboards, the small sink, the dinette table. The door must be opposite. "Help us, please!" Claire called out again.

She reached up and found the door, now tipped to the sky like an escape hatch. She twisted the knob and pushed upward, flinging it open. The night sky was pitch black and dust choked the air. With Jenny in one arm, Claire found a foothold and pushed herself upward. *Get out. Get help for Beth.*

Claire's shoulders cleared the door and now she could smell the sharp scent of pine. Jenny's cries increased in volume.

"Where are you?" A man's voice, close by.

Claire raised her voice. "In the trailer! Help us, please. I have a baby."

"Climb down to me," he said. "The water is rising."

Water? Claire thought she must have heard wrong. She could see the dim form of a man, his arms reaching toward her. Claire wavered, then decided. "Take the baby," Claire said, leaning toward him. "My friend is stuck. I have to help her."

Claire groped for his hands, found them, made herself unclamp her grip on Jenny.

"I've got her," the voice said as Jenny's weight left her arms. "Hurry, I think the trailer's going."

Going where? Claire clambered back down into the dark trailer. She could hear other cries along with Jenny's now. Yells and shouts. Frannie and her friends? Or Dottie and Jeffrey? She prayed no one was hurt. "Where are you?" she called to Beth.

"Here." Beth's voice was strained with pain and fear.

Claire used both hands to stay upright, stepping over debris with her bare feet as she followed Beth's voice. A hand brushed against hers. Claire grabbed at it. "Come on," she pulled Beth back toward the door.

"We're coming," Claire yelled, her calm replaced now with a desperate urgency to have Jenny back in her arms. She could still hear her crying and it pulled her like a tether around her heart.

"Climb up," Claire told Beth, as they reached the spot below the open door.

Suddenly, the trailer rolled back with a sickening lurch, throwing them both into the opposite wall. Claire lost hold of Beth. "Beth," Claire choked out before the trailer bucked again. She groped for Beth, bracing them both until the violent movement ceased into sudden silence.

Claire couldn't hear Jenny.

"Jenny!" Claire cried out. Panicked, Claire let go of Beth and clambered toward the door. Claire grasped the frame but could see nothing but black beyond the confines of the trailer. "Jenny!" *Oh, God. Where is she?*

A new sound, that of rushing water, filled the air. Cold coming over the threshold of the door like a waterfall, covering her feet and ankles. Water? She didn't stop to wonder why and where the water was coming from. *Get out. Find Jenny.*

Beth was there, clutching at her arm.

The water was to her knees. How was it rising so fast?

"Climb up," Claire ordered. Claire boosted Beth upward toward the top of the trailer. By then, the water was at Claire's waist, glacier cold and thick with silt.

"Claire!" Beth called back. "Take my hand."

Claire climbed, Beth pulled, and Claire was up and out of the water, on the flat top of the swaying trailer. Claire lay for a moment, her breath coming in gasps. She lifted her head. No moon, nothing but black. Where was Jenny?

"Jenny!" Claire called out. Had she—was she in the water? Was she safe?

The sound of water was all around them, they were afloat, tipping to one side and then another like a cork, but she couldn't see farther than the edge of the trailer.

Claire pushed herself to standing. She'd gone to sleep in her clothing, and now her blouse and denim jeans were soaking wet and gritty with mud. She searched for any sign of Jenny in the dark. Her throat hurt and she realized she was calling out her daughter's name over and over.

Where was the campground? Where were Frannie and her friends? The cars and the trailers and tents? There had been dozens of people—maybe a hundred. Now she was surrounded by nothing but black water and choking dust.

"Frannie!" Claire called out. Then again, "Jenny!" Something knocked into the floating trailer, the impact throwing Claire back to her knees. *Lord, help us. Let someone hear us.*

Beth crawled closer, only her ghostly pale face visible. "Claire." She gasped out what Claire—in her panic over Jenny—hadn't yet realized. "Claire, I think we're sinking."

chapter 40

BRIDGET

"Who hitchhikes this late at night?" Bridget asked.

Red hadn't said a word since they found the empty truck and Bridget couldn't blame him. Her head was full of questions and her stomach roiled with worry. Had Pete Henshaw caught up with Claire and Beth? Where would he take them?

Red continued up the road in the direction they'd started, but they hadn't gone half a mile when they saw the two hitchhikers.

Red slowed down and pulled over on the shoulder.

Bridget twisted toward Red. "What are you doing?" They weren't going to pick up two strangers in the middle of the night. Not if she had anything to say about it.

The kids came up to Red's side of the car, breathing heavily. Both had crew cuts—one was tall and the other short and stocky—and both looked oddly familiar.

"Have you seen two women and a baby?" Red asked.

"What?" the tall kid said.

"Two women," he repeated slowly, and Bridget could tell Red was trying not to lose his temper, "and a baby. Their truck broke down back there."

The short one answered. "Sure," he said in an offended tone. "That's why we're stuck here."

"What do you mean?" Bridget asked.

"Where did they go?" Red demanded at the same time. He looked like he might leap out of the car and shake the answer out of the boys.

The tall kid took a step back. "Mister, I'm just looking for a ride to somewhere with a motel, that's all."

Bridget finally placed the face. "You're one of Frannie's friends."

They turned their attention on her. "Sure, Frannie's the one who dumped us here," the short one said.

"What about the women and the baby?" Red barked with impatience. "What happened to them?"

The big kid shrugged. "We were going camping, then Frannie made us pick up these ladies and a kid, and when I made a joke—I was kidding around—she said *get out* like she was in charge of us."

Thank the Lord. Bridget felt a weight lift from her shoulders. Claire and Beth were with Frannie, not Pete Henshaw.

"Where did they go?" Red growled.

The boy's eyes widened and he took a step back.

Bridget laid a hand on Red's arm. It was rock hard with tension. "We need to find them, boys," she said calmly. "It's very important. Do you know where they went?"

"Well, sure," the shorter boy said. He used that word a lot and it was beginning to irritate Bridget. He pointed into the dark with his thumb. "They were heading toward the dam to camp out, and then tomorrow they are going up to the lookout."

Red put the car in gear. "What kind of car?"

"A red converti—Hey! Are you just going to leave us here?" The short kid grabbed the side of the car as Red started to pull forward.

"You can come with us or stay," Red said, tapping the brakes. "Up to you."

The boys looked at each other.

Red inched forward. The boys threw their packs in the back seat and jumped in. Red accelerated so fast they tumbled backwards.

"I'm Miss Reilly, this is Red Wilder." Bridget said over the seat back. "And you are?"

They said their names as they righted themselves. "Neat car," the one named Ernie said, looking over the Thunderbird's back seat. "Where are we going?"

Bridget ignored the kid. "They aren't with Pete," she said to Red. He should be happy.

A muscle in his jaw twitched. "I still need to find them."

Bridget could understand how he wanted to talk to Claire after that letter. The campgrounds couldn't be far. They'd find Claire and Frannie, and if she was lucky she could still get the Thunderbird back to Mammoth before Dr. Sampson notified the park rangers of his stolen car.

The full moon shone on the mirror-smooth water of the lake as they sped along the shoreline. The mountain rose on her other side, dark with trees. It was a peaceful night, and the drive was beautiful, but Bridget could feel the tension coming off Red like a heat wave. He probably wasn't going to forgive her for what she'd done, meddling in their marriage. She really was sorry she'd ever agreed to Dad's—

Suddenly, the car began to shake.

Bridget bounced hard in her seat, then hit the door with her shoulder.

The boys yelped in back.

Red wrestled with the steering wheel.

Bridget braced herself against the dashboard as Red jammed on the brakes and the boys crashed into the back of her seat. The car veered sideways and there was a horrible crunching sound.

The car stopped, but . . . it was still shaking.

Bridget held on for dear life as the road buckled and swelled like ocean waves and a stand of trees on the hill fell with a terrific crash. Her body bounced like she was on a carnival ride. She caught a brief sight of the lake, choppy with white-tipped waves. Then . . . all was abruptly still.

A distant crash of stone against stone echoed in the dark.

Bridget tried to marshal her jumbled thoughts. What had just happened? An earthquake? She pushed herself upright, but the world was still tilted. Red slumped against the steering wheel. "Red!" She pulled him gently upright.

"What—" he groaned out. "Are you hurt?"

Bridget did a quick assessment. Her shoulder hurt where she'd hit the door, but apart from that she was uninjured. The boys pushed themselves up from the floor. "Are you both okay?" Bridget asked.

"I think so," Sam answered in a dazed voice. "What happened?"

"Earthquake," Red said. He pushed open the car door, climbed out of the car and up the bank to the road.

Bridget opened her door and followed. Now that they were safe and the world had stopped shaking, her legs began trembling on their own as she took in their surroundings. Trees lay like matches spilled from a box. The paved road where they'd just driven was buckled and cracked, the white lines zigzagging in a crazy pattern.

"Look." Red pointed.

Bridget walked forward. A cold shiver prickled up her back. Less than twenty feet in front of them, the road broke off and disappeared into the lake. If they had been just a little farther down the road . . . She looked back at the Thunderbird. She knew she should be concerned about the enormous dent in the front bumper from the boulder that had stopped them from careening down the bank, but she couldn't bring herself to worry about that just now.

"What is that?" Sam was turned toward the lake, a look of confusion on his face.

Bridget followed his gaze. What more could happen?

A giant wave rushed across the surface of the lake. They watched in silence as it gained in height and speed to pass them, the sound like a rushing wind, continuing on into the dark.

"That's got to be twenty feet high," Ernie said, his eyes still pinned to where the wave had disappeared into the dark.

"The dam," Red said, his voice had a tremble in it. "It's going to top the dam."

A tremor of apprehension went up Bridget's spine. "What's below the dam?" But suddenly, she knew.

"Campgrounds." Red was already turning back to the car. "Claire and Jenny. Frannie." He started to run. "Come on."

But where could they go? The road was gone.

Suddenly, another tremor shook the ground, throwing her to her knees. The boys yelled and Red shouted for everyone to stay down. The trees around them shuddered and the ground heaved. Bridget held on to the ground until the shaking stopped.

When it did, she stayed on her hands and knees.

"We have to warn them," Red said, pushing himself to standing. "There's fishing lodges and houses all along the canyon. And then Ennis. Hundreds of people. Maybe thousands." He came to her and reached down to help her up.

She didn't give him her hand.

"What are you doing?" He looked like he'd carry her to the car if he had to. But she had something more important to do.

"Praying," Bridget said, still kneeling. She'd never been so close to death, and she wasn't going one step farther before she asked God's forgiveness for her sins. "If I die tonight, I want to be ready."

chapter 41

FRANNIE

God, I don't want to die.

Gritty water filled Frannie's mouth. Her shoulder hit something hard. Panic surged in her chest as she held her breath.

God, please help me!

She tried to swim, but the water was coming at her from every direction. Her lungs burned. She gulped air and went under again. She floundered, then her feet scraped on rocks. Relief shot through her. But where was the shore? Her eyes could be closed, it was so black, or maybe she was blind.

God, I don't want to be blind.

She pushed herself to standing, but her knees buckled and she was crawling. Her heart knocked in her chest, pain making its way to her panicked brain now that she wasn't fighting for breath. Her hands hurt and her feet felt like they'd been cut with knives. Her fingers sunk into mud, the water now only inches deep. She felt rocks, and then grass. She let herself collapse on dry ground.

She was alive. It was over. *Please, God, let it be over.*

She strained to see. She wasn't blind, but it was so dark. The air was murky and thick with the scents of mud and pine and gasoline. Where was Paul? Claire and Jenny and Beth, what had happened to them? Jerrylynn and Vicky and all the campers?

Slowly, she became aware of voices around her. A man calling, "Verona!" Far-off, a woman crying out, "Help us!"

She shivered in the cold night air. Would someone come and find her?

Minutes went by. No one called her name. She moved her legs and then her arms. She pushed herself up to her hands and knees. She stood. The world spun a little, but she was standing. She wasn't dead.

"Miss?" A man's voice in the dark. "Miss, can you walk?"

"I think . . . so." Her voice was hoarse, and her mouth didn't work right. She took a step. Her feet sank into wet mud. "What happened?"

Before he could answer, it started again. The shaking. "No," she whispered. *Not again, please.* She clutched at the stranger.

"It's an aftershock," he said, releasing her when the world stopped trembling. "Get to higher ground. I've got to find my wife."

"Don't leave me." The words came out in a hoarse croak, but the man—whoever he was—was already gone, calling, "Verona!" into the dark. A coyote howled not far away and her wet skin prickled with goose bumps. She sat down and pulled her knees to her chest, curling up with despair and fear. She pushed her face into her knees. She would close her eyes and count to ten, then she'd wake up and find out this had all been a terrible nightmare.

She counted to ten. Lifted her head and opened her eyes.

It wasn't a dream. It was a dark and horrible reality.

Where were Claire and Jenny and Beth? She tried to remember. She'd been looking at the trailer when the earthquake started. And Paul. He was right beside her. Vicky and Jerrylynn were asleep in the tent. She tried to get her bearings, but nothing looked familiar. Then she realized she could see. The moon was back. Not full and bright as it had been, but weak and shrouded.

She saw trees thrown like pick-up sticks, and a picnic table sticking out of a muddy bank. Trailers and upside-down cars lay in a jumbled pile. She saw pale forms of people, walking and stumbling, and—where were their clothes? She looked down at herself and gasped. She wore only her brassiere and her underwear. Her skin was scraped and muddy. She dimly remembered the wind pulling at her pajamas, the water hitting her and tumbling her like a rag doll.

Water. *Get to higher ground.*

She made herself stand up and walk, her brain as slow moving as her body. She saw lights. Headlights. Was it the ridge that had divided the campground? She went toward the lights, climbing up the slope to an overturned car. She sat down beside it. She could hear voices crying out for help, calling names.

Nobody was calling for her. Where were her friends? Her sister? Was she the only one left?

A bubble of hysteria rose in her throat.

She wanted to run away. She wanted to cry her eyes out. Mostly, she wanted someone—Claire or Bridget or even Dad—to save her from this nightmare, to tell her that everything was going to be okay.

Somebody, please, come and take care of me.

chapter 42

CLAIRE

The trailer was sinking.

The water sloshed over the top of the trailer as it tipped and bobbed like a cork. Pure fear rushed through Claire's limbs. Where had the water come from? Could she and Beth swim to shore? But in what direction?

Claire pulled herself to her hands and knees. She strained to see through the dark but it was like trying to see through ink. The trailer was slowly turning in a circle, as if caught in a whirlpool. Claire felt Beth push herself to standing and stagger closer. Heard her small sound of pain. The trailer listed sideways, one end dipping deeper into the dark water. "We have to swim," Claire said.

Something hit the trailer, and Claire caught Beth just before she fell into the black water. Beth held her left arm close to her chest. "I think my arm is broken."

They couldn't swim. Not in this, and not with Beth hurt.

"What's that?" Beth looked toward dark shapes rising out of the water.

Claire followed her gaze. Black against black, dark fingers jutting out of the water. Trees. Lodgepole pines with thick trunks and evenly spaced branches. Why were the trees underwater? The trailer lurched again.

"Beth," Claire said, gathering a handful of Beth's shirt in one fist. "When we get close, I'm going to try to grab a branch. Stay with me."

Claire felt her nod. They had to reach the trees before the trailer sunk from underneath them. The biggest tree loomed in the dark, its branches reaching toward her. Claire leaned forward. *Just a little closer.*

The trailer dropped from under her feet and icy water rushed to her neck. She flailed, losing her grip on Beth. Water filled her mouth, tasting of dirt, then closed over her head. Claire held her breath and kicked hard, her legs encumbered by her clinging wet clothes. She broke the surface and gasped for air, groping blindly for the tree. Her fingers closed over a branch, the needles stabbing at her palm. She held tight. The branch bent with her weight, her hand slipped. "Beth!"

Then Beth was there, her pale face above water, one hand reaching out. Claire caught her arm. Beth coughed as Claire pulled her toward the branch. "Grab it," she ordered.

"My arm," she gasped. "I can't—"

The branch broke.

Beth disappeared under the black water.

Claire lunged for another branch, grabbing on with one hand while searching the water for Beth with the other. *Lord, no. I can't lose her.* She felt a cold hand grasp hers. Claire pulled, then got her arm around Beth's waist. The bark bit into her hand and the limb bent under their weight, but it didn't break.

Claire pulled Beth's good arm up to the branch. "Hold on."

Beth caught hold and clung, her breath rasping in Claire's ear.

Claire pulled in a lungful of air. They were safe for now.

But where were they? And how could they get to shore? Claire could see nothing past Beth's pale face and the tree they clung to. "Listen," Claire said to Beth. She held her breath and Beth did the same.

Over the lapping sound of the waves, she heard voices. People crying out for help, other voices answering. Echoing across the water from one direction and then the other.

"Are they close?" Beth breathed.

It was impossible to tell.

What had happened? Claire tried to piece together the moments after the earthquake, but it was a jumble of fear and panic. Shaking and an unearthly roar. Jenny.

Where was Jenny? *Please, God.*

Was she safe? Who was the man who had taken her in those awful moments? Had they been swept away in the water? Was her baby still alive?

"Help!" Claire croaked out in panic, her throat gritty. She had to get to shore, she had to find Jenny. "Help us!" She raised herself higher out of the water, desperately straining to hear a voice returning her call for help—her call for hope. No one called back.

Jenny was gone. Frannie. All the people who had gone to sleep under the full moon. Where were they? The tree swayed, and with a sickening realization, Claire felt the cold water splash at her chin, when it had just moments ago been at her neck.

Fear shuddered through her body in an icy torrent. She and Beth were alone in the dark. No one was coming to save them, and the water was rising.

chapter 43

RED

"On three," Red said to Bridget and the boys. "One . . . two . . ."

Bridget gunned the engine.

"Three!" He pushed hard. The boys groaned. The back tires found purchase on the dirt and the car jerked back onto the buckled road. The fancy convertible had a dented bumper, but the tires weren't flat, and the engine worked.

After the second quake, Red had knelt down with Bridget and prayed. The two boys mumbled along with them. After they said amen, he helped Bridget up. "We need to get to a telephone and get word downstream." He glanced to where the ominous wave of water had rushed toward the dam. He hoped it wasn't too late.

"Where are we going?" Bridget asked as they headed back the way they had come.

"Sunnyslope." Red hated driving the opposite direction from where Claire and Jenny might be, but he didn't have a choice with the road gone. He slowed to veer around a fallen spruce and a scattering of rock, then eased over a foot-wide crack in the road. He'd call the Forest Service. They'd be able to get word to the campgrounds about the dam.

"Do you think . . ." Bridget sounded tentative, as if she didn't want to ask the question. "Do you think Claire and Jenny and Frannie . . . ?"

Red didn't answer her unfinished question.

Just before the turnoff to Sunnyslope, the headlights ran out of road and he stomped on the brake. He got out of the car and walked to a sharp drop-off. At the bottom of the six-foot scarp, a car was wedged nose-down.

"Help me!" A desperate call came from inside the car.

Red stifled a curse. He didn't want to waste a minute, and certainly not for the man in the baby-blue Cadillac.

It took far too long to extract David Endicott from his car. When Red and the boys were finally able to pull him through the passenger-side window, he was blubbering like a baby and blood stained his expensive cowboy shirt.

"Get him up to the car," he told Sam and Ernie. Instead of following them, Red scrambled up the scarp to the back trunk of the Cadillac. It only took a minute to pry it open, and what he found inside was exactly what he'd expected. He had proof now, as much good as it would do him.

Red got back to the Thunderbird, where Bridget was examining the gash on David Endicott's arm. "He needs stitches."

"Hold on," Red said. He bumped the car around the scarp, ignoring David Endicott's groans of pain. He didn't have it in him to feel sorry for Endicott, being that the man was the cause of his troubles.

The last time he'd been to Sunnyslope was the morning he'd run away from Claire. He'd seen the empty closet, and shame burning him up had kept him from coming clean with her about Dell—and about getting fired. So he'd fled, catching a ride with Bucky and praying Wormsbecker would change his mind.

Wormsbecker needed him. When Red had signed on at Sunnyslope four years earlier, a lot of the horses had been in bad shape—overridden, untrained, lame. He'd turned the herd around. Between him and

Bucky, Wormsbecker's clients could count on good hunts and bringing home big game. But when Bucky turned into the ranch the morning after the fight, Red saw that his luck had run out. Wormsbecker sat on the front porch of the ranch house with David Endicott beside him. Red climbed the porch steps, took off his hat, and hid a swell of satisfaction at the sight of Endicott's black eye.

"You don't work here anymore, Wilder," Endicott said in a high-pitched wheeze.

Red ignored Endicott. "Sorry about last night," he said to his boss with as much regret as he could manage. "I was out of line. If you could see your way clear to—"

"Save your breath, Red," Wormsbecker spoke around the cigar in his mouth. "Lem Garrison was by this morning, bright and early. He was looking for you."

Now it was Red who felt like he'd been sucker punched. If the Yellowstone National Park commissioner was looking for him, it was about Dell.

Wormsbecker tapped his ash into his coffee cup and narrowed his eyes at Red. "I've heard you're behind the shed racket in Gallatin County."

Red's body tensed. "That's a lie." He'd bet his last dollar Pete Henshaw started that rumor.

"Then why is Garrison looking for you?" Wormsbecker growled back. "Get your horse and get off my property."

Red jammed his hat back on his head and walked away, the thought of Lem Garrison turning his stomach. He'd met the superintendent just once, the same summer he'd met Claire. He'd heard about a job in the park looking after the ranger's horses, and tried for it. He couldn't believe his luck when he got an interview. He and Garrison hit it off and talked for an hour about horses. Red had the job wrapped up and was about to give his notice at Sunnyslope when Dell's betrayal landed him in the Bozeman jail. Garrison wasn't going to hire someone who had violated the Lacey Act, but what felt even worse was Red had lost the respect of a man he admired.

Now, in the light of the full moon, Red turned the Thunderbird down the gravel road to Sunnyslope, but the road to the ranch looked nothing like it should. The once-straight split rail fence was a crazy serpentine, and a stand of lodgepole pines lay flattened in the meadow. The scents of rock dust and pine sap thickened the air as the Thunderbird's tires crunched into the ranch compound.

"Holy cow," Sam said in an awed voice.

Red took in the moonlit chaos.

A massive crack rent the earth down the center of the compound and the big ranch house was cracked open like an egg. Water spewed from broken pipes like miniature geysers and shattered glass glittered on the lawn. On the other side of the circular drive, the massive horse barn leaned to one side. The paddock fence lay on the ground and Queenie, a dappled mare, stood miserably with a length of barbed wire wrapped around her leg.

Bucky lay in the dirt in front of the off-kilter bunkhouse.

Red stopped the car with a jerk, clambered out, and sprinted to Bucky.

Bridget was right behind him.

"Bucky, you hurt?" Why was Bucky even here on a Monday night? Then he remembered poker night. Bucky usually sat in for a few hands, ended up broke and sleeping in the bunkhouse. Bucky mumbled something and opened his eyes, blinking as if to clear his vision.

Bridget nudged Red aside. "Let me check him."

Red looked toward the destroyed farmhouse. "Is anybody else in there?"

"Wormsbecker . . ." Bucky put his hand to his head.

Red ran toward the demolished farmhouse.

"Red, don't," Bucky called out. "The place is coming down."

He ignored Bucky. If Wormsbecker was alive in there, he had to try to get to him. Red heard a muffled shout and ran around the side of the house, dodging puddles of mud and streaming water. He slammed his shoulder against the jammed kitchen door. Wood splintered and the door opened enough for him to push through.

In the slivers of moonlight, the kitchen looked like it had been ransacked by a hungry bear. Open cupboard doors, spilled coffee and flour. A stream of water gushing from under the sink. And something smelled wrong. Red's pulse ratcheted as he recognized the scent.

Bucky pushed in behind Red, sniffed and caught Red's eye. "Propane leak."

"Walt, where are you?" Red called.

"Here." Wormsbecker's voice held a note of irritation. "In the pantry. My darn leg's pinned."

Following Wormsbecker's voice, they crunched over broken dishes to the back of the dark kitchen. The pantry was a narrow room lined with shelving. Broken bottles littered the floor, the scent of propane masked by the sharp odors of brandy and vinegar. Wormsbecker was wedged against a wall, trapped by an oak beam that had come down from the second floor.

"Get this thing off me," Wormsbecker growled as Red and Bucky picked their way through the debris. Red put his shoulder to the beam and lifted it enough for Bucky to pull Wormsbecker out. The house creaked as it settled another few degrees sideways.

"I was getting a bottle of brandy," Wormsbecker explained as if Red had asked what he'd been doing when the quake hit. "Everything came down on me. I yelled for Endicott, then I heard his car start up and him hightailing it out of here."

"He didn't get far." Red helped Bucky get the man to the kitchen. "Take him outside," he said. "I need to try the telephone."

In the front hall, a telephone lay on the floor amid crumbled ceiling plaster. He put the handset to his ear and punched at the receiver. No dial tone. Suddenly, the house started to creak. The wood floor buckled and another chunk of plaster fell from the ceiling. Outside, he heard Bucky shout his name. The building groaned and a window shattered. He pushed at the front door but it only opened a few inches.

Red's heartbeat pounded in his ears, but he kept calm. There was no way he was going to be buried in Walt Wormsbecker's ranch house. Not when he had to find Claire and Jenny. Red took a step back and kicked hard at the door. It flew open and he staggered across the porch.

As he reached the front step, Red heard the crackle of electricity, and a deep percussive boom sent him flying into the dark.

chapter 44

FRANNIE

Frannie sat in the cold beside the toppled car, staring into the dark. Her thoughts were fuzzy, like her head was full of static. She was alone, and nobody was coming to take care of her.

She became aware of the commotion around her. Pale shapes of people, climbing up from the water as she had done. Cries for help. Car doors slammed and an engine started. She watched a pair of headlights bump over grass and creep up the hill toward the highway. Were they leaving? Was everyone leaving her here alone? Didn't anybody care about her?

She tried not to cry. If Bridget was here, she'd tell her to think of somebody other than herself. If Claire was here, she'd be brave because Claire was always brave. Where were Claire and Jenny and Beth? What about Paul and her friends? She had to find them. But how could she find anyone in this pitch dark?

"Help!" A voice came from below her, down where the water had almost killed her. The voice sounded young and scared.

Frannie wasn't Claire and she wasn't Bridget. She was hurt and cold and scared, too. She couldn't help anybody.

"Help my mom, please!"

Frannie stood up. Her legs didn't want to hold her. She stumbled a few steps. "I'm coming," she shouted. "Where are you?"

Frannie made her way down the ridge, stabs of pain shooting through her bare feet. She made out two pale forms struggling toward her. It was a girl and a woman. The girl's face was covered with mud, the woman wasn't wearing a stitch of clothing. "Help," the girl whimpered. "She's bleeding so bad."

Frannie put one arm around the woman and supported her as they climbed up the slope.

"I was asleep in the car. Mom was in the water—" The girl choked on a sob.

They reached the overturned car. The headlights lit the woman's ghostly white face, and Frannie could see her mud-covered torso. The woman was naked and scraped and bleeding, but that wasn't what made Frannie's stomach turn over with a sickening lurch. Her arm was a mass of blood and flesh and the gleam of white bone. Frannie stepped back from the horrible sight. It was too awful. She wanted to run right into the dark and never look back.

"It hurts terrible." The woman's voice was a croak of pain.

"Mom." The girl knelt beside her. "Mom, you're going to be okay."

Through the mask of mud, Frannie recognized Connie—the one with the dog and the twin sisters and the marshmallow-hearted dad who loaned them the hammer that Frannie hadn't bothered to return. The woman was the sweet mom who didn't like Yellowstone. Frannie's chest squeezed and the panic she'd manage to push down crept up her throat again.

"What should we do?" The girl looked up at Frannie.

Why was she asking her? Frannie wasn't a nurse like Bridget. She hadn't even taken a first-aid class when it was offered at the high school. Frannie took another step back. There had to be someone—an adult—in charge here.

She looked into the dark. There were shouts and movement, calls for help. No one was coming to help Connie and her mother. There wasn't a doctor or a nurse or a telephone to call an ambulance.

"Stay here with her," Frannie said. They needed light, and something to wrap this poor woman in. "I'll be right back." She went to the upside-down station wagon and tried to open the side door but it was stuck. The back gate came open and she pulled out a cardboard box, her hands rummaging for something—anything—that might help.

She felt a long cylinder. A flashlight. Within a few moments, she found a sleeping bag. She ran back to Connie. She laid the sleeping bag on the ground and they helped the injured woman to lie down.

Almost immediately, a stain of blood darkened the fabric.

A man stumbled up the incline and into the beam of the headlights. He had gray hair and a bushy mustache and was dressed in striped pajamas and a pair of rubber boots. He stared at the upended car.

Frannie turned her flashlight beam on him. "Is that car yours?"

He nodded.

"Find me something to stop her bleeding," she ordered. "Towels or sheets or something." That was her voice, and it sounded calm and even like she knew what she was talking about.

The man disappeared in the dark, and she hoped he wasn't leaving them, too.

"Will she be alright?" Connie asked her.

"She'll be fine," Frannie said, hoping it was true more than she'd ever hoped for anything in her life. Her mind was working now. Bridget had talked nonstop at the dinner table about her patients at the hospital. Maybe some of it had sunk in.

The man in the pajamas came back with a pile of kitchen towels. She gently laid one where the bleeding was worst. She pressed carefully and the woman winced.

"I'm sorry," she said as her insides flip-flopped. The last thing she wanted was to hurt the woman, but if they didn't stop the bleeding—

"The twins." The mother groped for Connie with her good hand. "You have to find them."

Frannie remembered the girls with the grass stains, so excited about the bear. Where were they in this dark nightmare?

"I will," Connie said to her mother. "Please, will you help me?" she asked Frannie.

"Please," the mother said, locking eyes with Frannie. "Please find my girls."

Frannie couldn't say no to this poor lady. She looked at the man in the pajamas. "You stay with her," she ordered. "And keep pressure on the wound. Can you do that?" Frannie gave him a stern look, as if he were the kid and she was the adult.

He gulped and looked a little sick. "I'm not so good with blood."

Frannie wanted to say she wasn't so good with earthquakes, but they didn't have much choice.

"There's a suitcase in the back of my car," he said. "In case you want to . . ." he trailed off and averted his eyes as Frannie stood up.

"What?" Frannie asked, then she looked down at herself as she remembered she was only in her brassiere and panties. She felt no embarrassment, not with everything that had just happened. But she found the suitcase and pulled on a man's sweater that reached almost to her knees and a pair of slippers that were a little too tight. Then she led Connie down the slope to what was left of the campground.

Frannie waded in up to her shins. The water had risen in the short time they'd been on higher ground. She'd help Connie—because she'd promised—but as soon as she had found the little girls, she'd look for her friends and her sister.

"Jan!" Connie and Frannie both called out. "Jean!"

"My mom was here." Connie pointed to a boulder and a mound of broken trees. Frannie skimmed the flashlight over the water and illuminated a half-submerged trailer.

"Mom!" She heard the frantic voice of a young girl, then a second voice. "Mom, are you there?"

Connie splashed waist deep into the water and Frannie followed. In the light of the flashlight beam, a wet head popped up from underwater. It was one of the twins, gasping for air. Then the identical girls were splashing through the water to Connie. They threw their arms around their sister, hugging her like they would never let go. The first girl said through chattering teeth, "We were taking turns—"

"—diving under to find Mom," the second twin finished.

Frannie helped Connie get the twins up the hill. Connie's mom was right where they had left her. When she saw her three daughters, she reached out her good hand to clutch at Connie and whisper, "God has his arm around us."

Frannie directed her flashlight at the man in the pajamas. He looked green, and the kitchen towel he held over Mrs. Wilson's arm was soaked with blood.

God had his arm around them? How could she say that? The woman was terribly injured. People were hurt or looking for their friends and family in this horrible disaster. Calls for help echoed in the dark night and she had no idea where Claire and Jenny were, or Paul and her friends.

God didn't have his arms around anybody here.

In fact, it looked to her like God had deserted them all.

chapter 45

RED

Red came to in front of the ranch house.

Bucky was bending over him and he could see his friend's mouth move, but he couldn't hear anything but the ringing in his ears. He sat up, rubbing his face to get his senses back.

"—are you okay?" Red heard his friend's voice as if far away.

"Yeah." He made his mouth work. He remembered the telephone. Claire and Jenny. The dam. How was he going to get word into the canyon?

Wormsbecker stood over him, looking at the ranch house. It hadn't fared as well as Red had. The front half was gone, and fire lit the broken-out windows. "Spent a fortune getting ready for the A-bomb," Wormsbecker complained, "and here my place gets destroyed by a quake." He glanced over at Ernie and Sam, sitting on the top rail of the pasture fence as if they were watching a rodeo. "You two," he snarled, "get off my fence. Start bringing horses out of the barn before the whole thing comes down." He scowled at Endicott, who was holding Bridget's handkerchief over his wounded arm and looking green around the gills.

Red scrambled up to standing. "Do you have a radio in the bunker?"

Wormsbecker gave him a withering look. "'Course I do, what do you take me for, some kind of idiot?" He got up and limped through the compound. Red followed on his heels with Bridget coming after.

"I've got everything down here." Wormsbecker stopped at a steel door set in the ground. He pulled it up to reveal a set of stairs, then pulled a switch and lights came on. "Battery operated," he explained. "Got a generator, too." He leaned heavily on a steel railing as they went down the stairs.

Red had heard Wormsbecker talk about the bunker—his shelter in case of an attack by the Russians. He figured there were a lot of things to worry about in this world, but an atomic bomb dropped on western Montana didn't top his list. At the bottom of the steps, a room about fifteen by fifteen feet was lined with shelves of canned goods, books, and labeled boxes. On the wall opposite the stairs was an Army cot and a desk.

Wormsbecker pointed to a box labeled with a red cross. "Take care of Bucky and Endicott," he ordered Bridget. "Get out of my way," he barked at Red, before pulling the plastic dust cover off a shiny ham radio set. He sat down heavily at the desk and put on a set of earphones. "If anybody knows anything, they'll be relaying it here." He jabbed at a button and twisted a couple of knobs. A meter came to life, its gauge swinging wildly.

Red watched Wormsbecker fiddle, impatience flooding through him. "Can you get ahold of the Forest Service? Or anybody in the canyon? We have to warn them about the—"

Wormsbecker held up a hand to silence him.

Red heard a crackle and a tinny voice coming from the headphones, but he couldn't make out the words. "It's Warren Russell over in West," Wormsbecker said, then listened intently.

"Ask him about the dam," Red said.

Wormsbecker gave him an irritated look, but he spoke into the microphone. "Warren, any word on Hebgen Dam?" He was silent. "Warren?" He pulled off the headphones. "I lost him. But he said the fire department contacted Civil Defense in Helena, and Fish and Game will fly over at first light to see the damage."

First light? Red felt a surge of frustration. "That's six hours from now." By then the dam might be gone—or it could be already. He needed to get to Claire and Jenny, Beth and Frannie—not to mention all the campers in the canyon and the people farther downstream in Ennis.

A shudder rocked the room, shaking the shelves of food and sending a coffee cup skittering across the desk and shattering on the floor. Red grabbed the desk to keep from toppling over.

"Aftershocks," Wormsbecker said unnecessarily. "This is the safest place to stay the night."

Red wasn't staying the night anywhere. He examined the map of Gallatin County on the wall beside the desk, tracing Hebgen Lake Road along the northern edge of the lake. "Here's where the road fell in," he said, more to himself than to Wormsbecker.

He couldn't get to the canyon by that road. He considered the southern route—driving back to West Yellowstone and taking highway 20 along the south side of the lake, then looping up on highway 287. That route would take over an hour at the best of times. With the damage he'd seen, his chances of making a fifty-mile trip with no scarps or slides blocking the road were unlikely. He looked at the red pushpin that marked Sunnyslope Ranch. Did a quick measure of the distance to the canyon as the crow flew. He was so close. He squinted at the map. Despite what Wormsbecker said, there was a way to get to the canyon tonight.

Red took the stairs out of the bunker two at a time. He needed to talk to Bucky.

Smoke drifted over the ranch yard, and small fires crackled and popped in the remains of the house. Bridget was checking Bucky's pulse. Endicott was on the grass, his injured arm swathed in a gauze wrap. "That was a five-thousand-dollar Cadillac," he complained when he saw Red, as if Red was the one who ran it off the scarp.

Red ignored him.

"You're most likely concussed," Bridget was telling Bucky. "You'll need to take it easy for a few days."

"Bucky," Red said as he reached them. "I need a horse."

Bucky peered up at him. "You're going into the canyon." It wasn't a question.

Red gave a nod. "If the dam goes—or if it already went—"

"Wilder, don't be an idiot." Wormsbecker hobbled up. "You can't ride into the canyon in the dark—not with these aftershocks. And you're not risking my horses."

Red turned on Wormsbecker. "Beth is in the canyon."

The mention of his niece stopped Wormsbecker's bluster. "My Beth?"

Bridget answered. "She's with Claire. And she's pregnant."

Wormsbecker scowled.

"It might work," Bucky said. "If you take the trail around Mount Hebgen to Kirkwood ridge, then follow the creek downstream, that would get you pretty close to the dam."

"Even if you can get in there," Wormsbecker protested, "what help can you be?"

Red had already asked himself that. Claire might not be there, or maybe he wouldn't find her. But Red had failed Claire when he left her to go to Libby, and he wouldn't take a chance that he might fail her again. He gave Wormsbecker a hard stare. "I'm going. And I need a horse."

Bucky wobbled to his feet. "We could move pretty fast and get there in a few hours."

"Oh, no, you don't," Bridget said, pushing Bucky back down to sitting. "You're likely to fall right out of the saddle."

Red agreed with Bridget, Bucky didn't look up to par. "She's right, Buck. And you need to take care of Queenie." He jerked his head toward the gray mare.

Bucky wasn't easily dissuaded. "You can't go on your own. What if you get hurt out there?"

Red would take that chance. He had to.

"He won't be on his own," Bridget said, standing up. "I'm going with him."

Red thought maybe his hearing was going again, but Bridget was looking at him in a stubborn way that reminded him a lot of Claire. "No," he said. Absolutely not. He couldn't be slowed down by an inexperienced rider. Not with so much at stake. "You hate horses." He strode toward the pasture.

Bridget trotted after him and grabbed his arm, swinging him around and pinning him with a glare. "What if Claire needs me—if she or Jenny are hurt?"

Red gritted his teeth, but she had a point. Claire and Jenny—or others—might need medical help. "Pack some supplies and send them with me, but you are staying here."

Bucky walked a crooked line toward them.

"We need clean water, and whatever you can find for first aid," Bridget told him. She looked down at her nurse's uniform, smeared with dirt and Endicott's blood. "And I need some clothes."

"Wait a minute," Red sputtered. Hadn't Bridget heard what he just said?

Bucky was already following Bridget's orders and even Wormsbecker was going to find supplies. Red had lost the fight. He was stuck with an inexperienced rider tagging along on a trip even he wasn't sure was doable. If they made it—and that was a big *if*—he didn't know what they'd be facing. Maybe it would be a good idea to have someone with medical knowledge, but did it have to be Bridget?

He walked to the back pasture where the horses milled nervously. He'd need a good trail horse—one he could trust not to bolt at the first tremor. And a dependable mount for Bridget. As he approached the fence, his heart lifted. His first good luck of the night—and maybe a small nod from the Lord that he was doing the right thing. A horse was standing beside the fence as if waiting just for him, her golden coat shining in the moonlight.

Marigold whinnied. She sounded as glad to see him as he was to see her.

chapter 46

FRANNIE

"Help us!" The faint cry came from somewhere out in the dark.

Frannie and the man in the pajamas, who had introduced himself as Mel, stood at the edge of the brown water and listened.

"Us?" Frannie asked Mel. "How many people are out there?"

Mel shook his head and made a megaphone with his hands. "Where are you?" he called out.

Frannie listened hard, but heard only the lapping of the rising water.

The moonlight was still dim, but light enough for Frannie to make out what used to be Rock Creek Campground. It looked less like a campground, and more like a junkyard being slowly covered by water.

There were at least thirty people on the ridge now, most of them injured in some way. Some people had left—those whose cars hadn't been crushed into oblivion. But what about everyone else? How many were still down in the wreckage? Or out in the water?

Jan—or was it Jean?—ran down to her. "Someone's coming," she got out breathlessly, "on the road up there." She pointed to the highway where just hours earlier Frannie and her friends had taken the turnoff to the campground.

Frannie ran up the ridge, then climbed a steeper slope to reach the highway. Mel followed, and by the time a wood-paneled Jeep Wagon came to a stop, at least ten people had gathered around the newcomer. The man who stepped out of the car and introduced himself as Roberts was at least six feet tall with shoulders as wide as a door. He had a full beard and wore a flannel shirt and jeans. "They told me there was some kind of landslide down here."

Mel made a quick explanation of what they knew—the earthquake, then the mountain falling, the wind, and the rising water. "We could use some help," he finished.

Frannie jumped in. "Are they sending ambulances? Doctors?" *Somebody?*

The man frowned. "It's just me, miss."

Frannie's spirits fell to the muddy ground. They needed more than one man in a station wagon. But at least they could do something for Mrs. Wilson. "Do you think you can get to a hospital?" she asked.

Roberts rubbed his beard. "You say the road is blocked that way?" He nodded toward the slide. "We could go back east and try to get to the hospital in Bozeman." He jerked his thumb in the direction from which he'd come. "It's a long way, and the road is in rough shape, but I'll take as many as my car will hold."

Frannie looked at Mel and knew he was thinking the same thing she was. If Roberts was the only help coming, they needed to find all the people who needed medical help. "There's more people down there, probably hurt," she motioned to the wrecked campground. "Maybe a lot more."

Roberts took off his jacket and pushed up his sleeves. "Then let's go get 'em."

chapter 47

CLAIRE

"Help us!" Claire's throat was raw as she called into the black night.

She stopped to listen. The lapping of the waves, the howl of coyotes in the canyon. Was that a voice, calling back? From what direction? She strained to see through the inky blackness but could only make out Beth's pale face and the dark tree, rising above them.

The water was at her chin again.

She pulled herself and Beth to a higher branch. Beth was weakening, and Claire wrapped her legs around Beth's waist to keep her close. They clung together, the water rushing past them smelling of mud and gasoline, the air gritty with rock dust.

"Can they hear us?" Beth asked. "Will someone come?"

"They have to," Claire said, trying to quell her panic. She tightened her grip on the rough bark. Someone had to come. She couldn't hold on for much longer.

"Pray with me," Claire told Beth.

"I don't know how," Beth said. "I've never prayed before."

"I'll help you." Claire said the Lord's Prayer, slowly. She asked the Lord to take care of Jenny and Frannie and her friends. Everyone in the Canyon. "Send someone to us, Lord." Beth said amen and they waited. The water swirled around them and the tree swayed.

Fear rose into Claire's throat. *Please, Lord.*

"We have to keep trying," she told Beth. Claire shouted again for help. Listened. She prayed again, desperation thudding as she looked up into the dark sky. Her body shivered and her arms shook with the effort of supporting her own weight and Beth.

No one was coming.

Suddenly, the sound of crashing rock rumbled through the dark. The water heaved, the tree swayed, and an icy wave broke over Claire. Beth went under. Claire gasped and coughed, Beth pulling her down. "Beth!" Claire grabbed for her and somehow got her head above the water.

Beth struggled, one arm useless while the other groped for a hold on Claire. "What's happening?"

It was another earthquake—an aftershock—shaking the rising water.

Another swell hit them, gritty water filling Claire's mouth. "We have to climb higher." The tree bent, swaying like a reed in a current. Claire, blindly searching higher, found a thick branch, her palm burning from the scrape of bark on her waterlogged skin.

She pulled them both up. "Hold on," she ordered Beth.

"I can't." Beth's voice was choked with panic.

"You have to." Claire couldn't hold them both. Not for much longer. "You're stronger than you think." Beth had defied the Henshaws, tried twice to escape. She had it in her to fight for herself, and for her child.

Beth's breath was a gasp, a small whimper of pain, but she reached with her uninjured arm, found the branch Claire clung to. Her weight eased and Claire could breathe again. The echo of crashing rock faded across the canyon.

"That's what Dell said," Beth whispered, when she'd caught her breath. "He told me I'm stronger than I think, when we got married and my parents—they were so angry."

Claire adjusted her weight and pulled Beth closer. She had to keep Beth's spirits up. "He'd want you to be strong for the baby."

"Claire, I'm sorry." Beth's voice was small. "If it wasn't for me . . ."

Claire swallowed, her mouth tasting of dirt. "Don't, Beth." Claire stopped her from going on.

"You should swim for shore," Beth said, and Claire could tell she was trying to be strong. "I'll stay, and you can send someone back when you get help."

Claire had already considered the idea and discarded it, but now she weighed it again. She was a strong swimmer—Dad made sure all of his girls were—but Claire couldn't see farther than a few feet. What direction should she go? And the water was treacherous. She could be hit by an uprooted tree or tangled in branches or who-knows-what else. Not to mention the surge of waves if another aftershock hit.

Could Beth even hold on without Claire?

And if Claire did reach shore, what if no one was there to help Beth? Claire couldn't risk it. She'd lost Jenny, and she had no idea where Frannie was or if she was even alive. She couldn't abandon Beth. She tightened her grip on Beth. "We stay together."

"But . . . you have to think of Jenny."

Claire's stomach twisted. She was sick with the thought of Jenny. Claire couldn't lose Jenny—and Jenny couldn't lose her mother. The thought of Jenny growing up without a mother to tuck her into bed, without a mother to hear about her friends, and talk to her about boys, and see her get married . . . all the things Claire's own mother had given up. She wouldn't let that happen to Jenny.

"Claire." Beth's voice was little more than a whisper. "What are we going to do?"

"We hold on, Beth," Claire answered, trying to sound confident and failing as her own voice wavered and broke. "And we hope."

The words sounded heavy and impossible in the darkness. She was weakening, the cold water sapping her strength, the moonless night stealing her courage. The temptation to give up hope weighed on her, pulling her down toward the cold water. It had hurt too much to keep hoping for her mother to come back. It had hurt to hope for a life with Red. That same hopelessness had crushed her when Red left for Libby.

Claire wasn't good at hope. She'd told Red in her letter—the letter that had not brought him home. It was his hope that she had relied on, that had saved her. Now he was gone, and her own hope was dwindling.

Hope for rescue. Hope that she would see her baby and Red and Frannie again.

Claire's grip weakened and the dark water pulled at her.

Lord, give me hope. Give me the hope I need to hold on to.

chapter 48

BRIDGET

Bridget couldn't believe how far it was to the ground.

They rode through the dark, Red in front and Bridget clinging to the back of a long-legged mule. If she fell off, she'd break a bone, maybe even hit her head on a rock and sustain a concussion. She started to slip and jerked the reins. The mule sidestepped into the brush. She teetered and grabbed the saddle horn.

Red glanced back. "Loosen your hand on the reins and try to relax."

Try to relax? He had to be insane.

Red had saddled the pretty golden horse for himself while Bucky put a saddle on this mule he called Flick. It had long black ears and very large yellow teeth. "She'll take good care of you," Bucky said as he boosted her into the saddle.

Bridget didn't believe that for a minute.

If Frannie was here, she'd probably say something about how this was just like one of Bridget's hospital romance novels, where the intrepid nurse is thrown into an adventure and gets the handsome doctor in the end. Frannie would be wrong.

This was all too real.

Her bottom hurt, her hands were cold, and she didn't feel like a heroine. The only thing that kept her from turning this beast around and going back to the destroyed ranch was the thought of Claire and Jenny and Frannie and Beth. Also, she didn't actually know how to turn the mule around.

Red made his horse stop and waited for Bridget to catch up.

"It takes about half an hour for a horse's eyes to get accustomed to the dark," he said as she reached him. "When Marigold can see better, we'll move faster."

Faster? Weren't they already going fast? Then the other thing he said dawned on her. "That's Marigold?" Wasn't that the horse he'd given Claire for her wedding present—the one she said something about in the letter?

He ignored her question. "This trail goes around Mount Hebgen." He pointed to a dark hulk of mountain at their left. "Then we'll follow the creek to the lake. We should come out on the upper side of the dam in a couple hours."

Bridget forced herself to loosen her grip on the reins as Red clicked his tongue at his horse and moved into the dark. She'd stay on this animal all night if it meant she'd find Claire and Frannie.

The darkness closed around them, and Bridget began to breathe normally again. With only the clop of hooves breaking the silence, she considered Claire's letter to Red. How had she not known how Claire felt? They were sisters and best friends, at least until recently. But they never talked about their mother.

Bridget didn't remember very much about the day Mother had left. Claire had put her to bed that night, helping her brush her teeth and say prayers, even tucking her in just like Mother did. Claire had told her everything would be fine.

How did she not know how much Claire had been hurting?

As if Red could read her thoughts, he twisted in his saddle. "Why didn't Claire tell me about your mother?"

Bridget didn't know how to answer him. Why wouldn't Claire tell her husband about Mother leaving them? "Dad never wanted us to talk about it," she said.

That night after her mother left, Bridget hadn't been able to sleep. She'd snuck downstairs for a cookie, but when she got to the kitchen Dad was there.

He was crying.

That's when Bridget realized something terrible had happened. She'd run back upstairs and snuck into bed with Claire. It had scared her, seeing her strong dad bowed down in such pain. She never wanted to see her dad cry like that again, and so she didn't make him talk about Mother. But that didn't explain why Claire didn't talk to her husband about what happened.

Bridget gripped the saddle horn as Red's horse sped up and Flick followed.

"Maybe she was ashamed," she answered him, as she bounced on the saddle.

Red turned in his saddle, not even looking where they were going. "Ashamed?" he said, like he didn't believe her. "But she's so—" He seemed at a loss for words. "So confident and . . . perfect."

A lump rose in Bridget's throat. "She wants everyone to think that." Claire, model-beautiful and confident, getting married and moving to Montana, learning to ride a horse and shoot and cook. *I decided Claire Wilder would be a new person . . . I couldn't leave Claire Reilly behind, Red, even though I wanted to. That little girl is still a part of me.* Oh, Claire. Bridget's heart ached for her sister. "She always says she's fine—insists she's perfectly fine." Hadn't Claire told Bridget that a dozen times in the past few days? "So no one will know she's not."

"I'm fine," Red said thoughtfully. "Claire says that a lot."

In the dark, surrounded by trees and the light of the stars, Bridget felt like she could see the past more clearly. Her sisters, her father. Herself.

Bridget wasn't brave like Claire. She knew better than to put herself—or her heart—in danger. It was better to be alone than risk getting hurt like Dad had been that night she saw him crying. Better to break up with a suitor before she let herself care too much. Better to be hard-hearted—oh, how she hated that Dr. Sampson!—than brokenhearted. *A caring heart is the best medicine,* Sampson had said. But Bridget knew better.

A caring heart was an invitation to pain.

She took care of other people's pain—broken bones and abrasions, illnesses and disease—but did whatever it took to avoid any pain of her own. Physical or mental . . . or heartbreak. The worst pain of all. Bridget was doing just fine. But it didn't take a genius to see that Claire and Frannie weren't.

I'm the reason Mother left us. Did Frannie act out because she really thought it was her fault Mother left?

It would explain a lot.

Red's horse broke into a trot and Bridget clamped her hands on the saddle horn as Flick followed suit. Suddenly, the line of trees next to the trail swayed wildly and the ground bucked and heaved. Bridget shrieked as Flick staggered. She bent over the saddle horn, clutching the mule's short black mane for dear life. She closed her eyes—*Lord, make it stop.*

The quaking stopped.

Bridget stayed where she was as the crash of rocks and the crack of falling trees echoed in the dark. She was still on the mule. *Thank you, God.* She heard Red speaking in a low voice to his horse. Carefully, she opened her eyes.

"You okay?" Red asked.

No, she was certainly not. Her heart was galloping and her blood pressure was probably sky high. "I'm fine," she said, and could have bit her tongue.

Red reined his horse back toward the trail. "Let's go, then."

Bridget's legs quaked as they started out even faster than before. She was going to die on this trail. She'd be hit by falling rocks or get pinned under a tree. She'd be thrown from this mule and break her neck before she ever found her sisters.

This wasn't like one of her novels, no matter what Frannie would say.

This story had no guarantee of a happy ending.

chapter 49

FRANNIE

Frannie stood at the edge of the rising water.

She was freezing cold and soaking wet. They'd found five more survivors, but not Claire or Jenny or Jerrylynn or Paul. She wasn't giving up, she just didn't know where else to look.

Frannie had organized the search with Mel and Roberts. Four uninjured men from the ridge joined in, one of them about a hundred years old but they needed all the help they could get. Frannie grabbed a teenage boy named Lance and told him to look for supplies in the remaining cars and trailers. "We need clean water, clothes, and blankets," Frannie told him. "And anything else you can find before the water covers it all." A woman with an injured eye said she'd watch over Mildred Wilson, and Frannie put Jean and Jan to work building a couple campfires.

Down in the wreckage, Frannie and Mel found a boy named Phillip trapped in an upside-down trailer. Phillip's foot was crushed and bloody, but his only concern was for his mother, who was barely conscious in a tangle of rocks and debris twenty feet away. Next, Frannie found Vicky sobbing under a pile of branches, naked as a jaybird. She asked her about Jerrylynn as she helped her up the bank. "I was in the tent, and then the water—and—" Vicky hiccupped and started to cry again.

"Get her a blanket and put her by a campfire," she told Lance, then went back down. Jerrylynn had to be somewhere. She just had to be.

Roberts found the kindly Mr. Wilson pinned under a boulder not far from the slide. He and Mel carried Mr. Wilson up the hill to join his family, and the girls surrounded him, kissing his cheeks. Frannie was happy for them, until she saw Mr. Wilson's leg. It looked like it had been shredded by a grizzly and was bleeding so bad Frannie's stomach turned over.

"Do you think we should put a tourniquet on it?" she asked Mel, who was looking sick in the flickering campfire light.

"Do you know how?" he asked.

"Not unless seeing it on television counts."

She helped Connie wrap her father's leg in a bedsheet and headed back down the ridge, where she met Roberts coming up carrying a frail white-haired man in his arms, while another man dragged a wheelchair behind them. "Polio victim," Roberts said. "Found him stuck in the mud."

Now, Frannie picked her way back down the wreckage to the edge of the rockfall, looking for Jeff and Dottie's trailer or some sign of Jerrylynn. Her flashlight was growing dim and her spirits were plummeting. She hadn't heard the cry for help from across the water since Roberts showed up. Had whoever was out there given up—or worse?

A faint shout came from a tumble of debris out in the dark.

Frannie waded toward the voice. Mel followed, his flashlight sweeping the wreckage around them. She picked her way around the pile of downed trees. The beam of the flashlight skipped over the water and then—there—a blue plaid shirt, a pale face.

"Paul!" Relief rushing through her. Frannie splashed to him. He was sitting in the water with the thick end of a tree trunk over his lap, and another fallen tree against his back.

Mel caught up and bent over him. "Let's get you out from under there."

"I'm stuck pretty good," Paul said.

Frannie wedged her flashlight under her arm, then she and Mel got a grip on the underside of the trunk that pinned him. They strained together. It didn't budge. Frannie pushed at the huge tree trunk behind Paul's back. It was twice as thick as the one on his legs and not going anywhere.

"We need help," Frannie said after they tried again.

Mel said he'd be back and waded away. Frannie crouched down beside Paul. He was pale and he'd lost his glasses. She was so glad to see him she thought she might cry. "How did you manage to keep your clothes on?" Her voice cracked with emotion. "I woke up in my skivvies."

"Just lucky, I guess." Paul's lips turned up in a weak smile. "Are you okay? I mean, did you get hurt when it . . ." He moved his head to indicate the horrible mess they were in.

"I'm fine," she said. She'd almost died, but what else could she say?

Paul cleared his throat. "Have you—did you find anybody else? Jerrylynn or Vicky?"

"Vicky," she said, "but not Jerrylynn." Tears pricked at the backs of her eyes. "Not yet."

"Your sister and—"

"Not yet," she said again. Her chest was tight and she couldn't breathe when she thought about Claire and the baby. "I will," she said. "I'll find them just like I found you." She would. She had to.

Suddenly, another tremor hit. Frannie grabbed for Paul as the water around them turned into choppy waves. Cries came from the ridge as the crash of rocks reverberated through the canyon. Paul groaned and Frannie fell to her knees beside him. The crushed cars and trailers shifted and metal shrieked against metal.

It stopped as quickly as it had started.

Frannie shone the weak beam of her flashlight on Paul. "Are you okay?"

His face was pale, and his jaw clenched. "I think so."

Mel came splashing back with Roberts. "That was a big one."

"We have to get him out of here," Frannie answered sharply. Another quake like that, and Paul could be crushed. She and Mel and Roberts counted to three and strained to lift the tree. Frannie pulled with everything in her. Mel grunted with the effort and a vein on Roberts's forehead bulged. The tree didn't move an inch.

"Hold on," Frannie said. She ran the flashlight down the trunk, following it to where the root end was stuck under an upside-down Buick. She came back to Paul and followed the tree to its other end. "The top is jammed under this trailer."

Roberts and Mel joined her at the trailer. The water covered the wheels and lapped at the underside. "We're not going to get that to budge," Roberts said.

"Let's try," Frannie said. She gripped the axle and looked at the men. "One," she said with a glare. They each took a hold. "Two, three." She pulled with all her strength.

Nothing happened except her hands—already covered in scrapes—hurt worse.

Roberts grabbed her arm as she started to wade back to Paul. "Listen," he said, his voice low. "I don't want to worry the boy, but somebody up on the ridge was talking about the dam failing."

"What dam?" Frannie asked, peeved that Roberts had called Paul a boy.

"The one at the top of this canyon," Roberts said grimly. "They say it could go any minute."

"Didn't it already?" Mel appeared out of the dark. "Isn't that where all this water came from?"

"This isn't from the dam, it's from the river." Roberts looked grim. "If the dam goes, we'll have a real flood."

Frannie thought she'd heard him wrong. This could get worse? What would happen to Paul if they couldn't get him out from under that tree?

Roberts patted her shoulder. "You should get to higher ground, miss. Let us do what we can for him."

Frannie clamped her teeth together. Desert Paul? Fat chance of that. She turned the flashlight on Mr. Mountain Man, ready to give him a telling-off, and was stopped by the concern in his eyes. She let out a breath. Getting mad wasn't going to help Paul.

I'm not a child, she'd said to Bridget. *Then stop acting like one.* She hated it when Bridget was right. "He's my friend," she said to Roberts. "I won't leave him."

Roberts gave her a long look, then nodded. "I'll try to find a crowbar."

Frannie waded back, determination growing with every step. When her flashlight found Paul, she could see the relief in his face. Her spirits lifted for a split second, then she saw the water. It had been at Paul's waist when they found him, but now was halfway up his chest. She knelt beside him. "Don't worry," she said. "We're going to get you out of here."

Roberts showed up with a crowbar he found in a car trunk, but ten minutes later threw it down in frustration. "There's nothing to get any leverage against, it's all mud."

"Paul." Frannie had an idea. It wasn't a great idea, but they were running out of time. "Do your legs—I mean, are your legs broken, you think?" Paul was a smart guy, and she figured he knew what she was asking.

He met her eyes. "I can't feel them."

"Roberts," she called. "Mel. Come over here."

When the two men waded over, Frannie looked Paul in the eyes as serious as she had ever been. "We have to pull you out." The truth was, if they didn't get him out, he'd drown in front of their eyes.

Paul nodded grimly.

"Are you sure, son?" Roberts said. "If something's broken under there—"

"I'm sure," Paul said.

Frannie took his hand in hers. Paul's mouth firmed as Mel and Roberts each hooked their hands under Paul's arms.

Paul nodded. "Do it."

"Together, now," Roberts said. He and Mel heaved.

Paul's face contorted like he was trying not to scream.

"Keep pulling," Frannie ordered. Paul's grip on her hand was so hard she thought he might break a bone.

Roberts and Mel strained again. This time, Paul did scream.

"Stop!" Frannie finally cried out. Paul's face was bone white and his lips quivered, but he hadn't moved a bit. "I'm sorry," she said to Paul. Sorry her idea didn't work. Sorry she'd hurt him. Sorry he was going to drown here. Tears flooded her eyes, blurring her vision as panic crept over her.

Paul was stuck, and the water was rising fast.

chapter 50

RED

Red felt like Bridget was telling him what he should have known all along. Claire wasn't fine. The letter proved that. How could he not understand his wife, after a year of marriage?

Marigold stopped, and Red strained his eyes in the dark to see what had brought her to a halt. He threw his leg over the saddle, slid down, and pulled his pack saw from the leather scabbard. It was the third time he'd had to stop to clear a fallen tree from the trail. Bridget silently waited on Flick. His sister-in-law wouldn't win any prizes in a rodeo, but she was staying on and not complaining.

His ears strained for the sound of falling rock, and every muscle was tight with tension in anticipation of another tremor. They'd had two since they left Sunnyslope, but by the grace of God no trees or rockslides had come down on them.

The cold sweat chilling his back had little to do with the hard work of sawing through the Douglas fir and dragging the two halves of the tree out of the way. His gut told him they didn't have much time.

They had to move faster.

"Red?" Bridget said as he pulled himself back on Marigold and nudged her to a fast walk. "Can I ask you something?"

He would have preferred to ride in silence, thinking over Claire's letter to him and what Bridget had told him. He should have been honest. Should have brought everything out into the light instead of hiding in the dark.

Bridget didn't take the meaning of his silence. "Did you leave because of what I said to you, on the drive to Mammoth?"

His hands tightened on the reins and Marigold hesitated. He urged her forward. "Partly," he answered but the truth was, he couldn't blame Bridget.

The fault was all his own.

He'd been a heel when Claire's sisters showed up, and that day they toured the park. He'd snapped at Frannie and bit Bridget's head off when she offered to pay for lunch. Even now, his neck got hot with humiliation. Then, when he drove Bridget to Mammoth and she'd told him Claire needed more than he was providing for her, he'd believed every word. When Bucky told him about the job in Libby, he knew he was running away again—and for more reasons than money. Claire had begged him to stay, but he'd refused to hear her.

Bridget was quiet behind him, and he hoped she was done questioning him. No such luck. "Why did you come back?"

The answer to that question was easier. Being without Claire and Jenny was like trying to breathe underwater. The longer he was away, the more he realized he'd been wrong to leave them. He'd hit rock bottom and being without them had hurt more than admitting he'd failed. Then he got the letter. "Because you were right," he finally said.

He heard Flick let out a bray and turned in his saddle to see Bridget's open-mouthed surprise. "Don't pull on Flick's mouth like that," he told her.

Bridget loosened her grip on the reins. "I was . . . what?"

Had it just been this morning when he'd knelt beside the bed in Libby in the cold dawn and asked God to guide him? *Lord, let me do the right thing. Show me how to take care of them.*

He didn't get an answer.

When he was in jail, he'd asked Father Donahue how he was supposed to know what God wanted him to do—about Dell, about Claire Reilly who had left him heartbroken. "I ask him to tell me, but he doesn't answer." It was all fine and good for the priest to tell him to pray, but what was he supposed to *do*?

"Son," Father Donahue said, "that's not how it works. The important thing is to trust him." The priest pinned Red with his sharp gaze. "Then do your best. He'll work with what you give him."

The advice seemed backwards to Red, but now he thought maybe he understood a little better. Here, on a trail in the dark, on his way to a canyon that might be flooded, his wife and daughter missing. He'd do what he thought best, and trust that God would make it the right thing. And when he found Claire, he knew what he had to do for her—for their family.

He pulled Marigold to a halt and turned her sideways on the trail so he could look at Bridget. "You were right," he said again. "She needs more than I can give her. She needs her family, and so does Jenny. When I find Claire and Jenny, I'm taking them back to Willmar, like you said."

Bridget opened her mouth, then closed it. Red hadn't figured he could render Bridget speechless, but he'd take silence if he could get it. He touched his heel to Marigold and turned her down the trail, suddenly desperate to find his family. If something had happened to them . . . if he was too late . . . He wouldn't let his mind go there. He'd find them both. He wouldn't give up hope.

I'm not good at hope, Red . . . you had enough hope for us both. Claire's words beat into his brain to the rhythm of Marigold's hooves on the trail.

Lord, wherever Claire is, whatever she might be facing, give her my hope. Give her the hope she needs to hold on.

chapter 51

FRANNIE

Frannie knelt next to Paul.

The water was at his chin.

She couldn't breathe and there was a sharp pain in her chest, like she'd just run ten laps around the school track. She pushed desperately at the tree trunk on top of his legs. Her hands scrabbled against the rough bark, her breathing coming in ragged gasps. They couldn't just sit here and let Paul drown in front of their eyes.

Mel and Roberts stood beside her, doing nothing. Had they given up? They couldn't give up.

"Frannie." Paul's voice reached through her frantic efforts. "Frannie, it's okay. The Lord must want to take me home."

"No. He. Doesn't." She pushed on the tree with every word. Paul was only nineteen. He had his whole life ahead of him. He was smart and funny and kind and no way would God take him this early. But a small voice—a voice she hated—whispered that people died young all the time. God didn't save them.

Paul grabbed her hand and squeezed. "Would you do something for me, Frannie?"

"Anything." An ache in her throat made it hard to get the words out.

"Would you pray with me?" His voice was soft and he wouldn't meet her eyes, as if he'd asked too much.

The ache turned into agony. She didn't want to. God didn't like her. And he didn't help her. She'd prayed for her mother to come back. She'd asked God to help her be good, like Dad wanted. She'd even said a prayer at the top of the water tower—that she wouldn't get caught—but the police were waiting for her as soon as her foot touched the ground. God hadn't answered her, not ever. Paul should ask somebody else to pray with him. And anyway, she didn't know how to pray. What was she supposed to say?

Paul was looking at her, the flecks of gold in his hazel eyes shining in the light of the flashlight. "Please, Frannie?" He was trying to be brave, and she figured she better try to be, too.

Maybe this time—like the desperate prayer she'd offered when she was drowning—maybe this time, God would hear her. "Okay."

But what was she supposed to say?

Out of nowhere, she remembered the twenty-third Psalm. Something from the Bible had to be good. "The Lord is my shepherd," she said. "I shall not want." It seemed completely wrong. They wanted so much—for the tremors to stop, for Paul to live. For help to come for the Wilsons and everyone around them in the dark.

Paul said it with her. "He maketh me to lie down in green pastures."

Mel and Roberts joined in. "He leadeth me beside the still waters."

Frannie could hardly keep going. Frustration choked her. None of that was true. These were horrible rocks Paul lay on, and the waters were anything but still.

Paul tipped his head back to keep his mouth and nose out of the water. "Though I walk through the valley of the shadow of death, I will fear no evil."

Please, Lord, she begged. *Don't let him die.* Frannie wished she hadn't been so stupid. She'd thought being brave was about climbing the water tower, or teasing a bear, any of the other stupid things she'd done. When Paul was really the brave one. She could barely whisper the rest of it past the knot in her throat. "And I will dwell in the house of the Lord forever."

The three of them sat in silence as the water rose.

God wasn't answering.

And why would he? She only prayed when she was desperate. *I'm sorry, Lord. I don't deserve anything from you. But this isn't for me. This is for Paul.* She clutched Paul's hand under the water. *Save him, please. Save him.* Tears slipped out of Paul's eyes and ran down his wet cheek.

The trailer behind them creaked.

Frannie straightened. Had she imagined that? She swiped her wet sleeve over her eyes and turned the flashlight beam on the trailer, blinking hard to see better. The trailer creaked again and . . . looked for all the world like it moved.

Frannie waited, afraid to even breathe.

Then, it definitely moved.

Frannie jumped up. "Mel!" she cried, sloshing around behind Paul. "Help me."

Mel stayed where he was. "But we just—"

"Do it," Frannie demanded. She didn't have time to explain. If what she thought was happening was really happening, maybe he had a chance. Paul's eyes were frantic as the waves splashed over his nose. "Both of you, pull him up."

Mel took one arm and Roberts took the other. Frannie went to the trailer where the treetop was jammed under the axle. "Pull!" she yelled. She grabbed the axel as Roberts and Mel pulled on Paul. She lifted up on the trailer. It moved. Not much, but some.

She looked back. Paul's nose and mouth were above water.

"The water," Paul croaked. "It's lifting the trailer."

"Pull again!" Frannie shouted. The rising water buoyed the trailer and the axel moved up a few more inches.

Roberts and Mel pulled . . . and Paul was out.

He lurched to standing, Mel and Roberts on each side, breathing hard. Frannie splashed through the water and threw her arms around

Paul and Mel and Roberts—all of them—squeezed in a big muddy bear hug. When Mel stepped back, Frannie saw he was crying. They were all crying. Well, not Roberts, but he looked a little misty-eyed.

Thank you, thank you, thank you. Frannie's legs were wobbly, but she'd never felt better. Better than climbing the water tower or hot-potting or riding in a fast car. God had heard her. He'd heard her prayer. Maybe it wasn't all mumbo jumbo. Maybe God really did love her like Bridget said.

"Can you walk?" Mel asked Paul.

He tested his legs and winced. "I think so." They were still cold and alone. They had badly injured people waiting for help, the water was rising, and Frannie hadn't found Claire and Jenny or Jerrylynn. Despite it all, she felt a surge of satisfaction and of something else. Something warm and solid.

Was this what faith felt like?

If this was faith, she'd take all God had to give her, because they needed it tonight. They all needed it.

Frannie stood at the campfire with Paul, Mel, and Roberts. Mel and Roberts had helped Paul up the hill, and Frannie found a camp chair to put him in while he warmed up beside the fire. He figured he had a sprained ankle—or maybe broken—but other than that, he was alive and well. It was a genuine miracle.

But not everyone was well.

"We have to get the Wilsons to a hospital," she told Roberts. They couldn't wait any longer.

"What about us?" Vicky's voice came from where she was huddled in her blanket by the fire. "Are you leaving us here to die?"

"Stop being dramatic," Frannie said. "There's not enough room for everybody and you're not hurt." Jeepers, couldn't Vicky think of anyone other than herself?

"I'll get them loaded in the wagon and head out," Roberts said, "but you need to get the rest of these people to higher ground." The water had risen halfway up the ridge, covering most of the cars and trailers in the campground below. "If the dam goes, this whole place will be underwater."

Frannie and Mel helped Roberts transfer the most severely injured to the back of the wagon. They folded down the seats and made a bed for Mr. and Mrs. Wilson, and put Phillip and his mother beside them. Roberts had room for Connie and the twins in the front seat.

As Frannie hugged the girls goodbye, a cheer went up and a set of headlights could be seen weaving through the dark from upriver.

Help was here. *Thank the Lord.*

A dark green vehicle the size of a tank pulled up. Everybody clustered around the new arrival, inundating the driver with questions about the earthquake, the dam, and—most desperately—"Can you get us out?"

"Listen, folks," the newcomer said, raising his voice. "I have good news and bad." He looked like a military type, and introduced himself as Frank.

Everybody quieted down.

"The dam is holding for now," he said. "But the road is out right past it. The whole thing just broke off and fell in the water. Even my Suburban can't navigate that."

Frannie's hopes plummeted. How could they get to the hospital if both sides of the canyon were cut off?

Vicky stumbled forward, clutching her blanket around herself. "We're trapped here?" Her voice was high and she pulled in shuddering breaths like she couldn't get enough air.

Frank ignored her. "There's a camp set up at a high point over the dam. They've got some food there, and supplies. Maybe a hundred people already there. That's your best bet for rescue when the sun comes up. I can take as many people up as can fit in this Suburban."

Vicky shoved her way to the passenger door. "I'm not staying here one second longer."

Good riddance, Frannie thought. Vicky wasn't alone in wanting out of the destroyed campground. Frank was able to get almost everyone left on the ridge into the roomy vehicle. The woman with the injured eye, the teenage boy named Lance, and the polio victim, along with those who weren't hurt at all.

Mel tied the wheelchair to the top of the Suburban, then looked at Frannie. "Maybe we should all go?" he asked, as if she was the one in charge. "There's some room left in the back."

Frannie wasn't going anywhere until she'd found Claire and Jenny and Jerrylynn. "There are still people out there," she said. "I'm not leaving until I find them."

"I'm sticking with Frannie," Paul said. She gave him a grateful look.

Mel nodded. "Me too, then."

Frannie could have kissed Mel right there, except that would be embarrassing for them both.

"I'll come back to help if I can," Roberts said. "In the meantime, move yourselves up to the road."

"We will," Frannie said. "And Roberts"—she leaned into his driver's side window—"we need a boat. And quick. We have to get to whoever is out there in the water. It might be my sister." Whoever it was, she had to help them.

She prayed she wouldn't be too late.

chapter 52

BRIDGET

"What's wrong with the lake?" Bridget asked Red.

Flick followed Red's horse up from the rocky creek bed and to the edge of the dark lake. The half-obscured moon lit the scene like a black-and-white movie, but it didn't look at all like the lake they'd driven beside moments before the earthquake.

After Red's shocking words on the trail, Bridget hadn't had the heart to ask him any more questions and so the ride over the past two hours had been silent. Bridget took the time to pray. She asked the Lord to watch over Claire and Jenny, Frannie and her friends. Beth. With every tremor, she'd prayed she and Red wouldn't be crushed by falling rocks and trees. *Thank you, Lord.* It was a miracle they weren't dead.

But they still had to find her sisters.

Red urged Marigold closer to a crumbling precipice that overlooked the lake. Bridget wished she could stop Flick from following, but the mule had a mind of her own. As they drew closer, she could see that the once mirror-smooth lake was choppy with waves and floating deadwood. Her breath caught as she peered over the edge of the broken-off bank and saw that the water had receded dramatically. Bridget's pulse tripled. "Did the dam . . . ?" Were they too late? Had the lake emptied down into the canyon?

Red slid off Marigold's back and walked closer to the edge to look down on the muddy lake bottom. "I don't know."

The clouds parted and sudden moonlight lit the lake. "What's that?" Bridget asked. She watched in astonishment as a large house floated toward them, carried on an invisible current.

Red called out. "Hello?" His voice echoed over the water with no response. He walked back to Marigold and pulled himself into the saddle. From his higher vantage point he called again, with no response. "Looks like Grace Miller's place. She has a fishing lodge on the other side of the lake."

Bridget added Grace Miller—whoever she was—to her prayers.

"The dam should be a mile or so up this way."

Marigold, as if sensing Red's urgency, picked up her pace. Flick followed and all Bridget's attention went into keeping her seat and not letting her teeth clack together as she bounced behind Red.

Red pulled Marigold to a stop. "This is it."

The dam wasn't much to look at. Just a concrete barrier stretching along the narrow end of the lake. Hundreds of floating logs were jammed against it, as if they were waiting to go over the top.

"Seems to be holding, at least for now," Red said.

Thank you, Lord. If the dam held, maybe her sisters and Jenny were safe. Cold and scared and waiting for rescue, but safe.

"Look." Red pointed to a constellation of lights that seemed to hang in the dark sky above the dam. "Headlights. And campfires."

Red turned Marigold toward the points of light, and leaned low over her neck. The horse shot up the hillside. Flick followed and Bridget held on, her heart swelling with hope. Claire had to be here. Safe with Jenny and Beth and Frannie. *Please, Lord, let them be here.*

At the top of the ridge, dozens of cars and campers were parked haphazardly on a large flat meadow, their headlights blazing. As Red and Bridget reined their mounts to a stop, flashlight beams swarmed toward them like fireflies. Men, women, and children—some in pajamas and bathrobes—surrounded them, buzzing with questions.

"Is the road open?"

"Have you heard anything from outside?"

"Is help on the way?"

Red raised his voice to be heard above the barrage. "Has anyone seen a woman and a baby? I'm looking for my wife."

A chorus of voices answered as Bridget scanned the faces in the flickering lights. She didn't see Claire or Beth or Frannie. And no baby's cry met her ears. Red dismounted and glanced back at her. "I'm going to look for them."

He disappeared, leaving Marigold and Flick and Bridget on their own.

A woman pushed through the throng of people. She was wearing a bathrobe and had curlers in her hair. "Are you a nurse?"

Bridget reached up to touch her nurse's cap that had miraculously stayed pinned to her hair during the jarring ride. "Yes. Is anyone injured?"

"Thank the Lord," the woman said with both relief and urgency in her voice. "Follow me."

Bridget carefully slid off of Flick's back, her legs aching and wobbly. "Stay," Bridget said to Flick, and followed the woman up the ridge.

They reached the flat meadow where two lines of cars faced each other. "I'm Peggy Greer," she introduced herself. "I've done what I can, but I only had a first aid course a few years ago."

Bridget tried to make sense of what she was seeing.

The headlights illuminated at least a dozen people lying on an assortment of sleeping bags and blankets. At first glance, they looked covered in mud, but then Bridget saw the blood, the makeshift bandages, and realized many of them weren't even wearing clothes. "What on earth happened to them?"

"They're from downriver," the woman said. "At the slide."

Bridget didn't know what she meant by that, but it didn't sound good. She searched the faces of the injured, looking for Claire's wide eyes or Frannie's pixie haircut, for Beth or little Jenny. "Have you seen a woman with a baby? Or a young girl, about eighteen with short hair?"

Mrs. Greer shook her head. "I've been here all night. Please." She tugged Bridget toward a station wagon. "These people just came in, I don't know what to do for them." Bridget followed Mrs. Greer to the open tailgate of a station wagon. "This is Mildred and Roy Wilson," Mrs. Greer said. Three young girls moved aside for her to see the couple. The woman was pallid but conscious, with blood-soaked kitchen towels wrapped around her arm. Her husband was covered in mud, his leg wrapped in a dirty bedsheet.

"She's a nurse," Mrs. Greer said to the woman. "She's going to help."

The woman nodded weakly. "Thank the Lord for you, dear."

Bridget's throat tightened, but she reminded herself to remain professional. Mrs. Greer pointed the flashlight. Bridget gently removed the bloody towels and looked at the wound. The woman's arm was almost completely severed at the elbow. Bridget replaced the bandages. The pain this woman was suffering must be unbearable. Next, she looked at the husband's leg. The twelve-inch gash on his thigh went all the way to the bone. He was pale and looked to be in shock.

"He's lost a lot of blood," Mrs. Greer said and Bridget covered both the patients again with the sleeping bag, her mind spinning. These injuries were life-threatening even in a hospital setting.

"Will my mom and dad be alright?" the girl asked. Tear tracks lined her face and two mud-covered younger girls clung to her.

"It's going to be okay," Mrs. Greer answered for her. "We have a nurse now, and she'll be able to help them."

Bridget didn't have the heart to correct the woman.

Next, she examined a boy named Phillip with a crushed foot. "Help my mother," the boy begged Bridget. "She's hurt bad." Bridget checked the mother, who almost surely had a broken collarbone, but it was her rapid pulse and clammy skin that concerned her most.

"Nurse Reilly will take good care of her," Mrs. Greer assured Phillip.

Mrs. Greer had far more confidence in Bridget's abilities than she had a right to. The mother's injuries were severe, and she might have internal bleeding.

Mrs. Greer continued along the line of station wagons, each holding several injured victims. Bridget caught fragments of the night's events—an avalanche, a flood, a horrific wind. Hard to believe, but the injuries spoke for themselves. They returned to the first station wagon, with the critical older couple and Phillip and his mother. "What should we do for them?" Mrs. Greer asked.

Before Bridget could answer—if she had an answer—headlights bounced up the hill and came to a stop. "More injured here," a man called out from the open window of a Suburban with a wheelchair tied to the roof.

"I'll be there in a moment," Mrs. Greer said to the driver. A girl of about twelve appeared out of the dark with an armful of towels. "Linda." Mrs. Greer beckoned her nearer. "This is Nurse Reilly, get her whatever she needs."

Bridget faltered, but Mrs. Greer was already gone. She looked at the line of station wagons, the wounded lying on the ground. The dark, the dirt. The sheer magnitude of the injuries she'd already seen, with more coming in. She had no plasma or morphine, no penicillin or doctor to consult or X-ray machine. Not even sterile solution to clean the dirt-covered wounds.

Linda stood at her elbow, awaiting orders. What about Claire and Jenny and Frannie? Were they among the wounded—or worse—were they hurt and waiting for help?

Phillip's hopeful face was visible in the light of Linda's flashlight. His hand clutched hers. She felt that tug on her heart, that pull to heal those who were hurting. "Linda," she said briskly, "bring me the pack from that mule I came in on."

Linda jumped to comply.

When Linda came running back, Bridget took an inventory of their supplies. A gallon of clean water in a plastic bottle, a first aid kit with several rolls of sterile gauze, ten gauze pads, and twenty

Band-Aids, along with a large bottle of iodine and a tube of surgical dressing. Bucky had thrown in a tin of aspirin and—"Bless you, Bucky," she whispered—a pint of brandy.

Mrs. Greer was back, and Bridget turned to her. "What else do we have to work with?"

"We're using sheets and towels for bandages, we found some canteens of water, and there's ice left in a few cold chests." Mrs. Greer looked to Linda.

Linda spoke up. "I found five blankets and a tin of instant hot chocolate."

It wasn't much. But it was all they had. Bridget straightened her nurse's cap and smoothed her hair. "Mrs. Greer," she said with a nod, "let's take care of our patients."

chapter 53

CLAIRE

"Beth," Claire croaked, her throat parched and rough. How could she be so thirsty when she was up to her neck in water? "Beth, we have to climb."

Beth didn't answer.

Beth's body was limp against hers, her hand—clutched around the branch—as white as bone. She'd stopped shivering, and Claire knew that was a bad sign. Claire tried not to think of the baby. Beth couldn't lose the baby, not after losing Dell.

Two more tremors had shaken the waters and sent waves crashing over them. Claire had pulled herself and Beth up another ten feet of tree, and the branches were thinning. Every muscle ached with the effort of holding on. Claire's legs were numb with cold and heavy as lead.

Her thoughts were as numb as her body. She'd told Beth they had to keep hoping . . . but could Claire hope when everything inside her was slipping into the cold depths?

Jenny was gone. Frannie was gone.

She was losing Beth to the pull of the water.

No one knew they were there. No one was coming to save them.

Beth would have been better off with Iris and Pete. At least she and her baby would have lived. Beth would never get to Ennis now, never see her parents.

And Red. He would never see his wife or child again. Red, who had so much hope for them. If she hadn't sold Marigold, would they be at home tonight—Jenny in her crib, Red playing solitaire and Claire listening to the radio—safe and warm in their sanctuary?

Bridget. Her sister and her best friend. Where was she? In Mammoth, not knowing that both her sisters were lost in the dark and devastation? If Claire and Frannie both . . . she couldn't bear to think of Bridget's sorrow. Of Dad's broken heart.

I can't hold on.

Claire's arms were trembling and useless. She couldn't pull them to the next branch. She couldn't rouse Beth or make herself care that the water was lapping at her chin, wetting her lips. Claire had stopped calling for help. Her cries were nothing but rasps in her parched throat, swallowed by the darkness. She couldn't even pray, with prayers she'd known since childhood just jumbled and meaningless words.

Beth sputtered and struggled.

Claire closed her eyes, tipped her head back, the hot tears escaping from the corners of her eyes and burning down her cold face.

She had to give up. She had to let go.

As despair swamped her, she opened her eyes one last time. And saw the stars.

Claire had seen the Montana sky at night a hundred times. The milky array of stars, the flood of brilliant points of light. But tonight, she saw them anew.

The beauty of them. The brilliance. So clear they seemed to pierce her heart.

For a moment, the cold and fear burned away, replaced with wonder. *It makes you wonder, doesn't it?* Claire's memory was as lucid as a film as she blinked into the night sky.

Red standing on the viewing platform of the Lower Falls, his russet hair glowing in the late afternoon sun. His calloused hand holding hers, his blue eyes taking her in like she was the marvel. *What do you believe, Claire?*

She could see the rainbows on the canyon walls, feel the sun on her shoulders. She believed that beauty spoke of God. *God is here, and he loves us. He loves Claire Reilly. And he loves Red Wilder.* She saw Red's Montana-sky eyes. The light of hope in them that he always carried for her. For them both.

Red. He loved her.

Red loved her, and he loved Jenny.

She hadn't made a mistake—far from it. The day her father refused to walk her down the aisle she'd made the best decision of her life. Whatever had happened with Dell—whatever had driven Red to go to Libby, it had been because he loved them, she knew that now. And he would come back.

The cold crept back through her heavy limbs. The gritty water swirled around her neck. Her arms trembled with the strain of holding Beth, and the tree swayed. A veil of clouds moved over the sky like smoke, obscuring the moon.

The stars vanished, but the light of hope remained, as if one of the crystal stars had fallen from the sky and now burned brilliant and hot in her heart. *What do you believe, Claire?* Did she only believe that God was to be found in a beautiful waterfall or a sunset or the love in Red's eyes? Or was he there even in the dark and devastation of the night? He was with her now. In the water, in her fear and weakness. He was still with her, like the stars behind the veil of clouds.

He never left her. And he had given her hope of her own.

"Beth," Claire said, as that hope gave her strength to do the impossible. "We have to climb." Claire pulled Beth upwards, out of the cold water. The tree swayed as they reached the uppermost branches.

Claire called out, over the water, pushing the air past her aching throat. Calling for help.

I won't give up hope, Lord. I'll keep holding on.

chapter 54

FRANNIE

The cry for help carried across the canyon.

Frannie stood at the edge of the water. It was definitely a woman. It could be Claire. If it was—or even if it wasn't—she had to do something.

"I'm going out there," Frannie told Paul.

"How?" Paul stood beside her, looking out into the dark. She'd wrapped Paul's ankle in a torn-up bedsheet and he was able to hobble around, but he wouldn't be running any races. The moon shed a thin light on the remains of the campground. The river—or lake or whatever it was now—had crept farther up the bank, almost covering the ridge and creeping close to the road where they had set up camp. "You don't even know where they are and that water has all kinds of stuff in it."

Frannie didn't want to hear his reasoning. "I'm a good swimmer."

"That's not it, Frannie," Paul explained patiently. "Listen." He turned to her and met her eyes. "You have to assume that whoever is out there, if they could swim to shore, they would have. Maybe they can't swim, or are hurt, or whatever. But you gotta have some way to get them back. Like a boat."

They didn't have a boat, and Frannie was starting to find Paul's logic annoying.

Mel came back with an armful of wood. "And the clouds are moving in. You won't be able to see a thing."

"I'm going to find a way," Frannie grumbled.

Lance had salvaged an assortment of camping boxes, ice chests, and suitcases from the cars and trailers before they were covered with water. Frannie dug through them, looking for anything that might help.

She came back as Mel was getting the campfire blazing and dumped her discoveries on the ground. One life vest, several lengths of rope, and a blow-up air mattress.

Frannie explained her plan.

"Absolutely not." Mel's voice went firm. Since when did Mel start sounding like her dad?

"Frannie," Paul said, "that sounds dangerous."

"I can't just sit here," Frannie argued back. In truth, the thought of going into that dark water scared her. A lot. Who knew what was under the surface? But hadn't Red told her that growing up was mostly about doing things you didn't want to do? She was going to save her sister and that was that.

Paul grabbed her hand, and whispered, "Frannie, I don't want to lose you."

The look on Paul's face made Frannie falter. He'd almost died tonight. She'd held his hand and prayed with him and now there was something between them. She didn't know what it was, but it wasn't like Jonny. It was something real. "It might be my sister out there," she argued weakly, her eyes burning.

"All the more reason," Paul said. "If something happens to you . . ." He didn't have to explain. Her Dad . . . what if he lost two of his daughters? But how could she *not* try to save whoever was in the water?

"I'll go," Mel said. "You hold the rope."

Frannie looked at Mel with her raised eyebrow. He didn't look like he could do a lap in a kiddie pool.

"I used to be a lifeguard," he said. "I can do it."

Frannie wasn't convinced, but Paul blew up the air mattress while Mel spliced together the nylon ropes.

"You think it's long enough?" Frannie asked.

Mel frowned. "It's all we've got. And I'm not going out there without a way to get back."

The clouds had continued to gather and it was pitch black when Mel tied the rope around his waist and put the life vest over his pajamas. The canvas straps barely reached around his chest.

Paul handed him the air mattress. "This should hold whoever is out there and we'll pull you all back."

Frannie called into the dark. "Hello! Are you out there?"

Was that an answering call? She couldn't tell.

Mel waded into the water with grim determination. Frannie fed the rope out as he disappeared into the dark.

Frannie started praying again. *Lord, help us save them. Claire and Jenny . . . or whoever it is.* She had faith now. This would work just like it had worked with Paul. She fed out the last of the rope. That had to be enough. They listened. Her hope rose when she felt the rope go taut. "He's got them!" The tension loosened, then the rope jerked like she had a fish on a line.

She pulled, her hope soaring. Until Mel came out of the dark, stumbling and wading up the bank, gasping for breath.

Alone.

Frannie's hope drained away, leaving her weak.

"What happened to the air mattress?" Paul asked.

"Got hit by a branch twenty feet out, put a hole in it," Mel gasped out. His pajamas dripped muddy brown water. "There's too much out there, branches and trees and debris." He was breathing hard. "Rope kept getting hung up. Just about pulled me under."

"How close did you get?" Frannie said.

He shook his head, his teeth chattering. "No idea where they were."

Mel and Paul climbed back up the ridge to the fire. Frannie stayed by the water, looking out in the dark. If Mel was this cold after ten minutes in the water, how was whoever was out there surviving? And how much longer could they wait? She tried not to think about Jenny. The kid was so cute . . . so tiny. Tears pricked the backs of her eyes and despair hit her like an ice-cold dunk in the water. What had happened to that warm glow of faith she'd had? Frannie looked up at the sky. *Lord, why did you give me faith just to fail me again?*

Lightning flashed through the darkness like a flashbulb, illuminating for an instant the devastation of the fallen mountain, the destroyed campground, the dark water. Her spirit plunged to a new depth. Weren't an earthquake and a slam-bash wind and a flood enough? What more was God going to do to them? A plague of locusts? As if in answer, a crack of thunder shattered the night and—like a curtain dropping over the canyon—the rain poured down.

chapter 55

RED

It was a teenage boy named Lance who renewed Red's hope.

The pressure in Red's chest built as he searched the length and breadth of the camp above Hebgen Dam, asking at every crackling campfire, every car filled with trapped campers fiddling with their radios to try to get a station.

"Have you seen a woman and a baby?" he asked. "Two women, or a girl around eighteen with short hair? A red convertible?"

No one gave him any hope.

As he searched, he heard bits and pieces of what had happened in the canyon. Rumors and stories—an avalanche, wind, some kind of flood. Every new calamity he heard sent a shot of urgency through his veins. They had to be safe. *Lord, keep them safe. Let me find them.*

When Red had checked every square foot of the camp, he tracked down Bridget in what looked like a field hospital. She was bent over the open tailgate of a station wagon, the shirt and trousers Bucky had given her at Sunnyslope streaked with dirt and blood. A woman in a bathrobe and curlers stood beside her, holding a flashlight on a boy's foot. Red's dread ratcheted up another notch—the foot looked like it had been through a meat grinder. An older woman lay beside him, barely breathing. "They're not here," he told Bridget. "I'm going to check the campgrounds downriver."

"Who are you looking for?" A teenage kid with an armful of blankets came into the puddle of light. "I've talked to just about everybody in camp."

"A woman named Claire and a baby," Red answered, his hope dim. "And a girl named Frannie."

The boy jerked his gaze to Red. "There's a Frannie down at Rock Creek."

Every muscle in Red's body was suddenly alert, and his blood raced in his veins. "Is a woman named Claire with her, and a baby?"

"Is she hurt?" Bridget asked.

Lance looked back and forth between them, as if he didn't know which question to answer first. "Frannie's not hurt," he said to Bridget. "I don't know about anybody named Claire or a baby. They sent everybody up here, but she and a kid named Paul stayed."

Rock Creek was at the bottom of the canyon. "I need to get there," Red said.

"There's a guy named Roberts," Lance said helpfully. "I heard he was heading back downriver. I'll get him for you." He dropped the blankets and disappeared.

Bridget covered the injured boy with one of the blankets. "I'm going with you, Red."

Red was fine with that, as long as they could leave right now.

But the boy reached up and grabbed Bridget's arm. "Don't go," he begged. "Please, my mom needs you."

The woman in the bathrobe didn't like the idea either. "Please, Nurse Reilly," she said, turning the flashlight on the line of station wagons. "I can't do this without you. There are so many hurt."

Red could see the indecision on Bridget's face. Claire might be hurt at Rock Creek. Or Jenny. But there were wounded here who needed her, too.

The woman in the bathrobe didn't mince words. "The Wilsons

won't make it without your help, Nurse. And there's more injured coming in every time I turn around."

Bridget looked to the boy and his mother, the line of station wagons, and the hurting people lying on the ground. She closed her eyes for a moment, then opened them and turned to him. "I have to stay here, Red."

He swallowed and nodded. "I'll bring them back," he promised.

"Let me send some supplies with you." She put two blankets and a canteen of water in a plastic garbage bag and shoved it in his arms. "I wish I could give you more, but we don't have anything left."

He nodded, his throat tight.

Bridget stepped closer. "Red, what I said that day . . . on the way to Mammoth." She looked like she was having trouble getting the words out.

Red remembered every word. *What if Jenny got hurt . . . what if she died because you insist on living in this godforsaken wilderness?*

"I was wrong." She met his gaze.

He shook his head with a jerk to disagree, not trusting his voice. She wasn't wrong. He never should have brought Claire to Montana. They could be in Willmar right now, safe. What did it matter if he had to endure Daniel Reilly's disapproval? He met Bridget's eyes. Something had changed between him and his critical sister-in-law on the long ride into the canyon. He wouldn't say they were friends—but they weren't enemies. "I'll find them," he told her, shouldering the garbage bag. Claire and Jenny, Frannie, and Beth.

He'd find them or die trying.

Ten minutes later, he and a big man named Roberts were bumping across the camp and down the hill. "Lance said you're looking for Frannie?" Roberts asked as the boxy Jeep Wagon tipped dangerously to the side.

Red jerked his chin. "And my wife and daughter," Red said. "She's Frannie's sister."

Roberts got a look on his face that made Red feel sick.

"What?" Red needed to know what the big man didn't want to say.

"There's somebody out in the water at Rock Creek," Roberts said. The heavy car tipped dangerously to the side. "Frannie thinks it might be her sister."

Red's stomach contracted and a wave of nausea went through him. "What do you mean, out in the water?" He'd fished the Madison a hundred times and couldn't envision anything more than a fast-flowing river, perfect for fly fishing.

Roberts reached Hebgen Lake Road and turned toward the canyon. "There's a slide at the mouth of the canyon, from what I can tell. The Madison is backing up and the water is coming over the road. To tell you the truth"—he flashed Red a frown—"I'm not sure we can even make it back to Rock Creek, but I'll get you as close as I can."

Red knew the winding road between Hebgen Dam and the mouth of the canyon like a map in his head, but now it might as well be the landscape of the moon. Lightning traced a path across the dark sky, the bright flash illuminating the cracked road, the flattened trees on the northern ridge, rockfalls around every turn.

Red tried to imagine what kind of landslide could stop a river. What would he find when they got there—if they got there? Rain started to patter on the windshield and Roberts switched on the wipers. They made a steady thrumming that only increased Red's anxiety, like a clock counting down the time he had to save his family.

"Frannie told me to come back with a boat," Roberts said as he crept around a boulder the size of an outhouse in the middle of the road. "I asked all over the camp, that's what was taking me so long to head back." He glanced apologetically over at Red. "No boat, but Lance found a life vest in somebody's trunk. Not much, but I figured who knows? It might help."

A life vest when they needed a boat? Father Donahue's guidance came back to him. *God will work with what you give him.* He closed his eyes. He couldn't have come through this dark night—the explosion at Sunnyslope, the ride through the canyon—to not be able to save his wife. *Lord, I'm trying to trust. Help me.*

The rain had gone from a sprinkle to a downpour, beating on the windshield like the pounding of horses' hooves. Red leaned forward, willing Roberts to move faster. What if God had given him his heart's desire—a family—just to take it away? *I'll take them to Willmar, Lord. I'll wear a suit and tie and work for Daniel Reilly. Whatever you want of me. Just let me find them.*

Finally, Roberts brought the station wagon to a stop. Red stepped into the pouring rain and walked with Roberts to where the road disappeared under a dark expanse of water.

Roberts scowled. "Can you swim?"

"Some," Red lied. Swimming lessons weren't part of his education at the orphanage.

Roberts looked at Red with a doubtful expression. "I don't suppose you'd listen if I told you not to chance it?"

Red grabbed the garbage bag Bridget had sent with him.

Roberts handed over the life vest and a silver flashlight. "Good luck."

Red watched as the wagon made a three-point turn and the red taillights disappeared. The dark night closed around him. Red took off his boots and socks and put them in the garbage bag. He fastened the life vest around his chest and clicked on the flashlight, roaming the beam over the water's oily surface. How deep was it, and what was underneath?

He stepped into the water. The shock of cold went up his spine and rocks bit into his bare feet. He forged onward as the water rose around him.

Hold on, Claire. Hold on and keep hoping. I won't give up on us.

chapter 56

FRANNIE

It was raining cats and dogs and horses and cows.

Frannie couldn't hear a thing across the water with the rain beating down on the plastic tarp she and Paul and Mel held over their pitiful selves and their pitiful campfire. Cold needles of water trickled down the neck of her sweater and a shiver wracked through her.

It had to be Claire out there. It just had to be.

Hold on Claire, she said silently to her sister. *If you die out there, I'll kill you. And so will Bridget and Dad.*

Frannie stared into the red coals of the fire. "I should have told her I was sorry," she said to Paul. She'd been horrible to Claire. She figured there would be plenty of time to make it up to her. Now, she might never see her sister and little Jenny again.

Another aftershock rocked the hillside. Frannie crouched down and braced herself. Stone scraped on stone, and the crack of trees falling broke through the beat of the rain. "When is it going to stop?" She didn't want to sound like a baby, but she was sick and tired of the ground shaking her around like a maraca.

Paul poked another wet log into the campfire. "The aftershocks could go on for days."

Frannie left the shelter of the tarp and walked to the edge of the ridge. No headlights coming out of the dark. No Roberts coming with a boat.

"Water has to be over the road by now," Mel said dolefully. "He's not coming."

Paul put his arm around her. "It'll be okay."

She swallowed against the egg-sized lump in her throat. Paul was being sweet, but if Claire and Jenny were . . . gone . . . nothing was ever going to be okay again. She peered through the veil of rain toward the rising water. "I wish I could do something," she choked out. "Anything."

Mel put another piece of wet wood on the fire.

"Let's sing," Paul said.

"Sing?" Was the cold getting to Paul's brain? This wasn't Canyon dinner hour.

"You know, like the *Titanic*."

How was the mess they were in like a ship going down in the Atlantic?

"They sang hymns in the lifeboats while the ship was sinking, to keep calm maybe," Paul explained. "And some survivors heard them and were able to swim to them in the dark."

"Are we the lifeboat in this scenario?" Frannie asked. It did kind of feel like they were alone in an ocean.

Paul shrugged.

"It can't hurt," Mel said.

It wasn't going to help. And anyway, what could they sing? "Tutti Frutti"? "Blue Suede Shoes"? That didn't seem right when people were miserable. Suddenly, she had a spark of an idea.

No, it was too stupid.

But . . . it was a song everybody knew. And it was Claire's favorite.

"Okay," she said. "Here goes nothing." She took a deep breath and started to sing as loud as she could. "Amazing grace, how sweet the sound . . ." She felt a sob coming up her chest. She should have sung with Claire at church. Why had she been such a brat? She faltered and stopped.

Paul took her hand in his. "That saved a wretch like me," he sang in a pretty nice voice that reminded her of all the fun they'd had at dinner hour.

"I once was lost but now am found." Mel's voice was good—like he was part of a barbershop quartet or something. "Was blind but now I see."

When she'd sung this song at St. Malachy's, she hated it. Now, the words meant so much more. She'd been lost and found her way. Paul had been saved from a horrible death. She'd been blind, too. Blind to what a horrible sister she was.

They started the second verse together. Then the third, growing in volume. It was something to do, and that helped. She put her whole heart into it. "The Lord has promised good to me, his word my hope secures—"

"Did you hear that?" Paul said, holding up a hand for quiet.

They went silent. The rain was letting up and the clatter on the tarp died to a gentle rustle. Mel directed the beam of his flashlight toward the washed-out road. "Someone's coming."

Frannie's hope soared. Help? A boat to get to Claire?

A flashlight beam bounced toward the campfire. She squinted. It was a man wearing a cowboy hat and something around his neck. He got closer, into the light of the campfire and the weak beam of light, and . . . it couldn't be. Frannie wondered if she was finally losing her marbles. "Red?"

"Frannie." He dropped something and ran to her, pulling her into a hug. "Thank God," he said, squeezing her so tight she could barely breathe. He was dripping wet, too, but Frannie had never been so glad to see anybody in all her life.

Then she remembered about Claire and Jenny. Oh, no. She buried her face in his jacket. She couldn't tell him. She couldn't even look at him. Not with how much he loved Claire, what a good dad he was to Jenny. Tears choked her throat. She should have tried harder, kept at it even with no light and the rain coming down. "Claire," she choked out, "I think she might be—I think she's . . ."

It was too terrible to say.

He stepped away. "Roberts told me." His voice was tight, as if he was fighting not to cry himself.

Frannie brought him to the campfire and introduced him to Paul and Mel.

Red nodded at them but said to Frannie, "Tell me what happened."

Frannie skipped all the stuff about the camping trip and finding Claire and Jenny and Beth in the broken-down truck. And the part about how it looked like Claire was leaving Red. She told him about the trailer, and the water and the wind. How she'd searched everywhere. And how they'd heard shouts from out in the water but couldn't reach whoever it was. "I think there's more than one person out there." She hoped it was three. Claire and Beth and Jenny.

"Now with the rain coming down," Paul put in, "we can't hear a thing."

"And the water is treacherous," Mel added. He eyed the life vest in Red's hand. "Is that the boat we asked for?"

Frannie's hopes sank.

"Show me where you heard them," Red said.

Frannie grabbed the other life vest and the rope they'd used with Mel, and the four of them went down the slope. The rain had lightened to a drizzle.

"They're out that way somewhere." Mel pointed into the dark.

Red lifted his flashlight, but the beam was swallowed in the veil of misty darkness. He shouted, "Claire!" The desperation in his voice was unmistakable.

No answer.

Red waded into the water. With a sudden sickening lurch, Frannie remembered something from that day they went to Yellowstone. Something really important. She splashed toward Red, and grabbed him by the arm. "You're not going out there, Red," she told him.

"I have to," Red said, holding out his hand for the vest Frannie carried. "I'll bring her back."

Frannie waded out of his reach, holding the vest behind her back. "Nope."

"Frannie!" His voice was sharp, like a dad threatening a naughty child.

This time, Frannie wasn't being a brat just for kicks. She couldn't let him go out there. No way, no how. It had to be her.

"Frannie, give it to me." Red waded toward her.

"No," she snapped.

In the past six hours, she'd survived an earthquake, that horrid wind, and a flood. She'd rescued a dozen people, learned to pray, and witnessed a miracle. Now, she was going to save her sister—and her brother-in-law. But she wasn't going to swim in this bulky sweater. "Turn around unless you want to see me in my underwear."

That stopped Red for a moment.

She pulled the sweater over her head and threw it to Paul.

He caught it and sputtered, "Frannie, what are you doing?"

She tied the vest around her neck, and the length of rope to her waist. It would help her on the way back. "Give me the other vest, Red."

He came closer and his voice held an edge of anger. "I'm not going to let you go out there, Frannie."

She was going to have to lay it out for him.

"Red." She stopped him with an upraised hand. "I know you want to be the one to save them, but I'm the only one that can get out there *and*"—she emphasized the word with a glare—"get them back."

Red's jaw went tight. "How do you figure that?"

She gave him an exasperated look. "What happens when you get to them?" she demanded. "There are at least two people out there. And we figure they aren't able to swim, right?" She looked at Paul for confirmation. He nodded reluctantly. "And we have two life vests."

Red grimaced, and she could see he was beginning to understand.

"I can swim back without a vest . . . and you can't."

His shoulders sagged and she knew she was right. Red couldn't swim. She'd remembered when she saw him wade into the water, how they had gone to the Firehole River that first day touring the park.

They'd all taken a dip to cool down except for Red. He hadn't gone in any farther than knee-deep. "Claire will kill me if I let you drown."

Red rubbed a hand over his face. "Frannie . . . if something happens to you . . ." He didn't have to finish.

"I know," she said. Her dad would hate Red even more. She'd just have to make it back alive with Claire and whoever was with her. "Trust me, Red." She held out her hand for the other vest.

He hesitated, then untied the vest and gave it to her, his jaw tight. "Be careful."

Frannie hugged it to her chest, and a shiver that had nothing to do with the cold went clear up her scalp. She was really going to do this. She tried not to think about the dark water, and what was floating in it. Or if she could find Claire. Or if she could make it back.

"Frannie," Paul said from the bank. It was too dark to see his face but she could tell by his voice he was trying to be brave for her. "Go get 'em."

She threw him a kiss as if this was just another prank. "Abso-posolutely," she said, and was glad that her voice didn't sound as scared as she felt.

Then she plunged into the icy water and started swimming into the dark.

chapter 57

BRIDGET

Bridget had nothing left to give.

If help didn't come soon, her patients were going to die.

She and Mrs. Greer had depleted the gauze and iodine within minutes. They used what clean water they had to cleanse wounds and bandaged them with strips of towels. Between patients, Bridget sanitized her hands with the brandy, and gave a dose of the spirit to a girl named Vicky who was nearly hysterical. Linda and Lance had scoured the camp for ice to pack around wounds, clean water, blankets, and food.

When Red had left, Bridget felt like her heart was being torn in two. What if Claire and Frannie needed her? What about Jenny?

And yet, the pull of her duty to the injured here was undeniable. Phillip and his mother. The Wilsons. She couldn't leave such critical patients. And Red . . . if she'd learned one thing about her brother-in-law on that dreadful ride into the canyon it was that Red Wilder didn't give up. If her sisters were out there, he would find them.

As she treated the injured and tremors continued to shudder over the ridge, Bridget prayed for Claire and Jenny and Beth. For Frannie.

For Red. *Lord, help them.* Bridget saw families kneel in prayer as the earth trembled. She saw husbands and wives, hands clasped and heads bowed. Hundreds of prayers, spiraling to heaven like sparks from the myriad campfires. Was Claire praying? And Red? Would this night bring even Frannie to her knees?

When the rain started, Bridget ordered the critically injured to be moved to the backs of station wagons or into trailers. The rest of the refugees huddled in cars or around campfires. Now, with the rain easing, Refuge Point—as they were calling this place—was a muddy mess.

Bridget found Lance at the campfire. "Is there any more hot chocolate?"

Lance held up a tin cup. "This is the last of it, Nurse."

"Give it to Phillip with these." She shook the last two aspirin from the bottle Bucky had sent. It wouldn't touch the pain the boy was experiencing, but it was all she had. "Small sips," she ordered Lance as he headed toward the trailer where they'd transferred the injured boy and his mother.

Linda was at her side. "The stones are heated."

"Wrap them in a blanket and come with me." Bridget followed her flashlight beam to the station wagon where Mrs. Greer was holding vigil over the Wilsons. "Tuck these stones up next to them," she instructed Mrs. Greer. "Not too close, just enough to warm them up." The Wilsons' temperatures were dropping as their bodies began to shut down.

"Is there anything more we can do for them?" Mrs. Greer whispered, out of earshot of Connie and the twins.

Bridget was asking herself the same question. She gazed around the makeshift hospital, her flashlight taking in injuries from severe to minor. Sprains and scrapes, cold and shock. A woman with an injured eye, a little boy who needed stitches. Phillip would most likely lose his foot, and his mother—it might be too late to save her.

She could only shake her head in answer to Mrs. Greer's question. She had nothing left. No medicine, no bandages. Nothing to administer or chart. No more she could do to alleviate the terrible suffering all around her.

"Will my mom and dad get better?" It was one of the Wilson girls, her twin beside her.

Bridget didn't have an answer, at least not one she could voice. Mrs. Wilson's pulse was increasingly weak. Mr. Wilson's wounds were still seeping blood, and his skin had a gray tinge. The truth was these poor girls would most likely be orphans before dawn. Bridget admonished herself as she swiped at the tears blurring her eyes. Getting weepy wouldn't help anyone. She needed to remain professional. Wasn't that what her training demanded?

The thing was, she hadn't been trained for this.

Bridget had none of her usual protections—no medicine to administer, no bandages or needles or doctor to consult. No charts or protocols, and no way to clock out at the end of her shift. She looked down at her dirty clothing, smeared with mud and who-knows-what. She didn't even have a uniform to hide behind.

But what more could she give her patients? How could she help in this nightmare?

A caring heart is the best medicine.

Darn that Dr. Sampson. She'd dismissed his sentimental maxim. And anyway, a caring heart wouldn't heal anyone or stop them from dying . . . would it? Bridget looked at the suffering around her, and thought again about how Jesus had healed the sick. He hadn't done it from some lofty perch in the sky. He'd been beside them, in the dirt and dust. He'd held their hands, touched them, and treated them with love. He'd wept with them. She'd felt the call on her heart to heal since she was a little girl . . . but could she risk the heartbreak of really caring?

The Wilson girls huddled close to their parents, their muddy faces streaked with tears.

She had to. Her own heart was all she had left to give. She could offer hope. Shore up courage. Administer kindness.

Bridget held out her hand to one of the twins. "Are you Jean or Jan?" she asked.

"Jan."

"I'm Jean," the other girl said. They looked so cold and alone.

Bridget pulled Jan and Jean to her and wrapped her arms around them. They were covered in dirt and smelled of river water and campfire smoke. Connie came close, and Bridget took the girl's hand in hers so that they were all holding on together. "Girls, let's pray for your parents."

As she prayed the Lord's Prayer with the girls clasped close to her, tears welled in Bridget's eyes and this time she didn't try to keep them from falling. When—if—Roy and Mildred Wilson died, she would grieve with these children. If Phillip lost his foot or his mother, it would break her heart.

She kept the girls in her embrace long after they said amen, her head bent in silent supplication. *Lord, I beg you. Send help. We're barely holding on.*

chapter 58

CLAIRE

"You have to let me go." Beth's voice was a whisper.

Claire clutched at Beth as she slipped farther into the water. "No," Claire said. Her frigid lips didn't form words like they should. "Keep holding on."

But Beth's eyes closed and she went limp. Her weight sagged against Claire, pulling her downward. Claire couldn't breathe, her grip on the branch failing as her frozen hands cramped with her weight and Beth's. *Lord, help me. Help me hold on.*

Then she heard it.

Singing.

"Amazing grace, how sweet the sound."

Was it her mind playing tricks on her? Was the memory of Bridget and Frannie and Claire singing together at St. Malachy's going to be her last thought before she lost her grip and slipped under the water? Dad, in the pew below, looking up at his girls, the pride and happiness in his eyes.

"That saved a wretch like me."

She wasn't imagining it. "Beth," she said sharply, jostling her. "Do you hear that?" *Please tell me you hear it. Please wake up.*

"I once was lost, but now am found." It was stronger now, voices joining in. "Was blind but now I see."

Beth's eyes flickered. "I hear it," Beth whispered.

"Beth," Claire begged, "stay with me. Sing with me."

"He will my shield and portion be."

Beth reached up, her thin white hand grasped at the branch. Her fingers closed around it. The weight on Claire eased, and she could breathe again.

Beth's lips mouthed the words and Claire whispered them with her. "As long as life endures."

The singing stopped, but Beth stayed with her.

The rain turned from a clatter to a rustle. The water was at Claire's chin. The tree bent with their weight. There was nowhere left to go. No more branches to save them.

But the singing . . . people were out there, close enough that she could hear them. Close enough to help them. She waited, hope giving her strength she knew wasn't her own.

Then, a sound. A shout. A calling over the water. "Where are you?"

Claire didn't move. It sounded like . . .

"Where are you?"

It was . . . could it be? "Frannie," she croaked. With a surge, she stretched upwards and shouted with everything in her, pushing the single word past her dust-dry throat and parched lips. "Frannie!"

Splashes. Coming closer.

Then Frannie was there. Reaching out. Her hand gripping Claire impossibly warm and solid. "I knew it was you," she said, breathless. "I just knew it."

Claire couldn't speak. Frannie was alive. She had come. She wore an orange life vest around her neck, her fair hair plastered against her head. Frannie put her arms around Claire as best she could, bumping into her as the water swirled around them.

"Beth, thank God," Frannie said. Frannie floated back, her eyes meeting Claire's in the dim moonlight. "But where is . . . ?"

Jenny.

Claire blinked against her blurred vision and shook her head. Beth was slipping. "Help her," Claire gasped.

Frannie grabbed at the tree branch with one hand and Beth with the other. The tree bent with their weight. She shoved a life vest at Claire. "Help me get this on Beth."

"Her arm," Claire warned as Beth moaned. "It might be broken."

Frannie nodded in acknowledgement but didn't waste breath on an answer. Between them, they strapped the vest on Beth, tying the canvas straps tight. As the vest buoyed Beth, her weight on Claire eased and she breathed with relief.

Frannie unfastened the knots in her own vest and it took a moment for Claire's numb mind to understand what she was doing. "Take this." Frannie shoved the vest at her. "Put it on." She held on to the branch above them to keep from going under.

"No," Claire said, understanding dawning. "You can't—"

"Do it," Frannie snapped. The branch cracked. Frannie's feet pumped under the water to keep herself afloat. "You have to hang on to Beth," she said. "I'm going to tie this rope to you and tow you to shore, but there's junk in the water so we have to—"

"No." Claire was still holding the life vest in one hand, the branch in the other. She couldn't let Frannie swim in this treacherous water without the life vest. It was too dangerous.

"For Pete's sake, Claire," Frannie sputtered out, "just let me save you."

Claire heard the determination in Frannie's voice, and saw that stubborn expression she knew from eighteen years of taking care of her little sister.

"It's not far," Frannie panted. "I can do this. But you have to do what I say. Please."

As much as everything in her wanted to protect Frannie, she couldn't. Not if she wanted to live. Not if she wanted to give Beth and her baby a chance. Claire put the water-soaked vest over her head and tied the straps with frozen fingers. Frannie knotted the end of a rope through the loop on the vest.

"Let's go," Frannie said. "Lay on your back, and hold on to Beth. Don't let her go."

Claire swallowed. She wouldn't let go. Not when they were so close to being saved. Then, they were moving. The tree that had been her and Beth's salvation receded into the darkness. Frannie's strokes were strong, each one a tug that pulled them through the dark water.

"Watch out," Frannie warned with a splutter.

Something—a floating log—hit Claire's legs and then disappeared in the dark. Beth groaned in pain. Frannie's strokes slowed. She changed direction once, then a few strokes later, veered again. Claire could hear her breath rasping in her throat. Claire tried to kick her legs but they were leaden weights.

Frannie stopped once, treading water. "I'm coming back," she yelled into the dark. "Where are you?"

Claire heard shouts. Men's voices. Frannie adjusted her direction and set out, her strokes sure and strong again.

"Almost there," Frannie gasped.

Then, Frannie was slowing . . . standing . . . her shoulders coming out of the water. Claire's cold-deadened feet knocked against something. Solid ground. Claire closed her eyes, the world shifting and spinning. Were they saved? Were they safe?

Shouts and splashing sounded around her.

"Mel, help me with Beth." Frannie's voice was distant and echoey. Claire felt Frannie pull Beth away from her.

Claire tried to turn herself from her back to her front, to get her legs under her, but her body wouldn't obey.

Strong arms—impossibly warm—went around her and she heard her name. "Claire." The voice sounded far off and blurred, but so much like Red's gentle voice in her ear, just like when they woke in the morning, the sun dawning outside their bedroom window.

Claire let herself believe for a moment that it was Red. That she was safe at home, in his arms. *I need you. I'm not fine without you.* If only she could say those words to him. She felt herself lifted out of the water. Carried. Gently lowered to solid ground. She pried open her eyes with effort. Golden light brightened the sky—when had the sun risen?—and Red was there.

Red. Somehow. A surge of relief and joy and—

"Claire?" Red's voice was urgent and his face—his eyes—anxious and questioning.

Her chest collapsed, her heart buckling and fracturing. The pain so intense she couldn't breathe. The agony. How could she tell him? How could she break his heart, as hers was shattered?

"Where is Jenny?" His voice cracked.

Red, I'm so sorry. Claire tried to speak, her mouth dry and her throat silt-coated and aching. Her husband's face went out of focus. Claire felt herself falling into an empty void. *I'm sorry, Red. I lost our little girl.*

Then the golden light dimmed, darkened, and turned to black.

chapter 59

BRIDGET

When the sun rose, Mildred and Roy Wilson were still alive.

After Bridget prayed with Connie and the twins, she'd gone to Phillip. "Tell me about your mother," she asked him. He'd told her how his mother made the best pies in all of Ohio and won ribbons at the state fair.

"It's just her and me," he'd whispered. "I can't lose her."

Bridget smoothed a hand over his brow, his skin was cool and damp. She wanted to assure him he wouldn't lose his mother, but it would be a hollow promise. "I don't even know your mother's name," she said.

"It's Dolores," he said.

"That's a beautiful name," Bridget told him with a lump in her throat.

"Will help come now?" Phillip asked her as the sun rose over the refugee camp. Bridget tucked the blanket closer around him and wished she knew the answer.

Red hadn't come back to Refuge Point. Roberts had returned just before dawn and told Bridget where he'd left Red. "I've never seen a man more determined," he told her. "If his wife is anywhere to be found, he'll get to her."

Bridget assumed he was trying to be kind, but his words sent a chill of apprehension up her spine. She'd heard about Rock Creek as she'd worked through the night. It's where the Wilsons and Phillip had been camping when the earthquake hit. She could only pray Claire and Jenny hadn't been close to the terrible rockslide, or caught in the wind and water that followed.

"Look!" Lance's shout carried over the camp. The high-pitched whine of a small motor cut through the air as an orange and white airplane flew above the ridge. "It's dropping something!"

A red parachute opened against the pink-and-blue sky. Lance ran across the ridge, dodging one way, then another as the missive changed direction on the invisible breeze. He caught it and ran back to Bridget.

"It's a message." Bridget opened the metal cylinder as a crowd gathered around. She took out a rolled paper and smoothed it against the hood of a car. "Help is coming," she read out loud.

*Thank the Lord*s and *hallelujah*s went through the crowd.

Bridget sat down, her legs weakening with relief. How long would it take? *Soon, Lord. Please make it soon.*

As the sky brightened, it filled with aircraft. Big planes at high elevations and little planes buzzing lower. One small aircraft flew so low she could see a camera pointed at them behind one of the windows. If they were able to fly over, why weren't they landing to help her patients? Bridget glared at the flying aircraft. She would be giving someone an earful when she got out of here.

Bridget walked to the verge of the ridge and looked down at Hebgen Lake. The dam was still holding, thank the Lord, but the entire lake seemed to have shifted in its bowl. On the north side—where she and Red had ridden—the water receded a dozen feet, as if it were low tide. She squinted at the deadwood floating on the surface like great rafts.

"Somebody said they were waterlogged trees sitting at the bottom of the lake." Lance stood beside her. "The quake must have shook them up to the top."

The quake had done more than disturb the logs on the bottom of the lake. Bridget knew she would never be the same. The Wilsons. Phillip and his mother. Everyone trapped in this canyon. So many lives shaken by one catastrophic event.

"Is that a boat?" Lance shielded his eyes from the rising sun.

She followed his gaze. A boat—with what looked like several people aboard—was navigating a crazy path over the log-strewn lake.

"Someone's coming!" The shout went up behind her.

Lance ran down toward the dam. Bridget watched from her vantage point as the boat veered around the logjam. The whine of the motor cut out as it reached the muddy shoreline. Lance was there to meet them, wading into the water to pull the boat closer. He helped two people climb out of the boat into the knee-deep water. Bridget squinted, not believing her eyes.

It couldn't be. She took a step closer to the slope. No, her eyes weren't deceiving her. A bubble of hysterical laughter rose in her throat as Dr. Kevin Sampson strode up the hill like a heroic doctor out of one of her novels, coming to save the day.

chapter 60

RED

Red held Claire in his arms as the rising sun revealed the devastation of the night.

Rock Creek Campground was gone, covered by a mountain of rubble. Downed trees blanketed the slopes on either side of the canyon, and where the Madison River had flowed clean and sparkling, a dark lake continued to rise.

When Claire had collapsed in his arms, he'd thought his heart would stop beating. Where was their little girl? The most likely answer—in the water that had almost taken Claire—he couldn't make himself consider. He carried Claire up to the campfire. Mel and Frannie carried Beth and they built up the fire to warm the unconscious women and Frannie.

With the warmth of the fire and the blankets Bridget sent, Claire and Beth both roused. Claire told him about Jenny. "I gave her to a man, outside the trailer," she told him between hiccuping sobs. "I'm sorry, Red."

The iron band around Red's chest loosened. There was still hope. "You did the right thing." Thank God she had, or Jenny would have been in the nightmare Claire and Beth had barely survived.

If she'd given Jenny to someone at Rock Creek, where was she now? Had he missed her at Refuge Point? Or had whoever saved Jenny somehow got out of the canyon? He refused to consider the other possibility—the one that sat like a cold chunk of ice in his gut. "We'll find her."

Claire buried her head in his chest.

"I wish I'd been the one to save you." Shame laced his voice, but he didn't care if Claire heard it—or anybody else. It had just about killed him to let Frannie go out into the water after Claire. Frannie didn't admit it, but he'd seen her exhausted face when she got the two women back. He knew he wouldn't have made it, just like she'd said.

"You brought the life vest," Frannie piped up as she huddled close to the blazing fire. "We couldn't have got them without it."

He gave Claire another sip from the canteen. They had more to talk about—Dell and Red's past, their future back in Willmar—but those things could wait. There was only one thing he had to make sure she understood. "I ran away," he said, his gaze on her beautiful face. "But I was always going to come back."

Claire met his eyes. "I know—I knew, but . . ."

He waited as she caught her breath and found the words.

"You can know something in your head, and still not believe it all the way through—all the way to your heart."

He nodded. She'd been abandoned by someone she loved, by someone she desperately needed. "For better or worse." He'd made a mess of that vow, but he'd learned his lesson. He'd never leave her again.

She nodded. "'Til death do us part."

Her words hit him in the heart and he pulled her tight against him. In a few minutes, Claire fell into an exhausted sleep.

When the sun was well over the horizon, a small orange-and-silver plane droned overhead. Frannie jumped up and waved. The plane dipped its wings in acknowledgement, then continued upriver.

"They'll need a helicopter to get us out," Mel said. He licked his finger and held it up to test the wind. "And even then it'll be tricky."

An hour later, a helicopter with a high-pitched whine appeared in the sky over the slide. Red watched as the small craft landed like a hummingbird on the edge of the ridge, its landing skids jutting off one side into thin air.

Frannie cheered and ran to meet the pilot.

She came back with a message. "He can take two people out," she said.

Red didn't like putting Claire in that flimsy helicopter, but she and Beth needed medical care. "Where are you taking them?" he asked the pilot, after he got the women settled into the passenger seats.

"I'm setting down on the other side of the slide," the pilot yelled over the thrum of the blades. He pointed toward the mouth of the canyon. "There's a line of volunteers and ambulances going to Ennis with the survivors."

Survivors. The word twisted in his gut. He kissed Claire, wishing he didn't have to let her out of his sight again. "I'll see you in Ennis."

She nodded, her eyes shining with tears and unsaid worry.

"I'll find her," he said as they parted. He'd find their little girl.

They stood back as the helicopter lifted off the ridge. Red held his breath as the little craft hovered, then wobbled in the wind. Finally, it buzzed westward and the clatter of blades faded away.

Red went back to the campfire with a war going on inside him. An urgency to do what he'd promised Claire, and a paralyzing dread of what he might find. He stared into the campfire, then rubbed his hand over his face and stood up. "I'm walking out over the slide," he announced.

Mel frowned. "The helicopter is coming back for us, it'll just be a while."

"I'm going to stay with Paul," Frannie said. "I want to go in the helicopter."

Red nodded. It would be better to go alone, just in case. He shook Mel's hand. "Thanks for watching out for Frannie." He did the same to Paul. Frannie threw her arms around him and hugged him. "Meet us in Ennis," he told her gruffly, his eyes stinging.

Red walked toward the slide, dread weighing him down. He'd promised Claire he'd find Jenny. Now, he prayed with everything he had that he wouldn't.

Not here. *Please Lord, not here.*

Not amid the rubble covering Rock Creek Campground . . . the last place his daughter was seen alive.

chapter 61

BRIDGET

Bridget rushed down the hill toward Dr. Sampson and Beckett. Help had come. For the Wilsons and Phillip and his mother. For everyone waiting for deliverance from this nightmare. *Thank you, Lord.*

She didn't even care that Dr. Sampson looked clean and pressed and perfect, while she . . . she stopped suddenly and looked down at herself. She was a mess—covered in mud and blood and smelling like a mule. She took a deep breath and straightened her shoulders. She would maintain her dignity at the very least.

Beckett reached her first. "Oh, Bridget."

Emotion welled up in her chest and—oh, why was this happening?—a sob broke through. Tears prickled at her eyes and it looked very much like Beckett was going to hug her. That would surely be her undoing. Bridget pressed her trembling lips together and lifted her chin. She refused to crumble and cry like some silly heroine from a novel. She had patients that needed care. "Beckett," she said crisply, sidestepping the embrace. She directed her attention to Dr. Sampson. "Doctor, I do hope you've brought supplies." She managed it without even a tremble in her voice. "We have severely wounded patients that need your attention." She turned toward the camp. "If you'll follow me."

An hour later, Bridget had shown Dr. Sampson the most seriously injured. He administered morphine and blood plasma to Mildred and Roy Wilson. Phillip's foot was stabilized and he was given pain medication and penicillin. "He'll need surgery," Dr. Sampson said, "but with luck, he won't lose it." Dr. Sampson confirmed her suspicion that Phillip's mother was in serious danger. "Internal injuries," he said. "She'll need surgery as soon as possible." Beckett had brought clean water and coffee. One of the airplanes had parachuted a crate onto the ridge. It was filled with sweet rolls—of all things—and the junior nurse was distributing them to the refugees.

Dr. Sampson looked at the sky. "I was told air transport would be here soon."

"They're certainly taking their sweet time," Bridget complained.

As if in response, a thrumming beat filled the air and a massive yellow helicopter appeared. Shouts and cheers went up. The helicopter hovered, then slowly descended to a clear spot on the meadow. The roar of the engine abruptly ceased and the double propellers slowed.

The Air Force pilot met them at the edge of the camp. He wore a flight suit and carried a helmet under his arm. "We can take four injured at a time," he told them. "They've got emergency triage set up at the West Yellowstone airport, and airplanes standing by to transport the seriously wounded to Bozeman."

"Only four?" Sampson's brows came down as he looked at the helicopter.

Bridget had bit back the same complaint. The helicopter looked big enough to hold twenty people.

"This whirlybird is made for high altitudes," the pilot answered, "but the wind is bad up here. I can't chance too much weight."

Bridget didn't know what that meant, but it didn't sound good. "Let's get the Wilsons loaded, and Phillip and Dolores," she said to Beckett. "We haven't a moment to lose." Beckett headed toward the makeshift hospital.

The pilot stopped Bridget. "We'll need a nurse to go with them in the 'copter and stay with them to Bozeman," he said. "We don't have any medical personnel with us."

Dr. Sampson looked at her. "Reilly?"

Bridget's eyes widened and she stepped back. "Absolutely not." Not on her life. "I'm not stepping foot on that—that —flying banana."

Dr. Sampson raised his brows. "I thought you'd want to stay with your patients."

She did. Of course she did, but . . . she gazed at the yellow helicopter. Not on that. And anyway, she couldn't leave. "My sisters are out here somewhere," she argued.

"We have rescue operations going all through the canyon," the pilot answered. "You'll be more likely to find survivors at the hangar in West Yellowstone or in Ennis where the Red Cross is setting up. They might be there already."

Beckett came back from the line of cars and trailers. "The Wilsons are ready to go, but Connie is asking for you, Reilly."

Roy and Mildred were on stretchers, Connie and the twins standing tearfully beside them. "You'll stay with Mom and Dad, won't you?" Connie asked Bridget. "Please, don't leave them."

Bridget glanced at Dr. Sampson. His somber gaze met hers and she realized with a sinking dread that she didn't have a choice. "Of course," she said. She'd been in an earthquake and ridden a mule through falling rock and crashing trees. She'd risked injury to both her body and her heart in the last twelve hours. She might as well keep it up. "I'll be with them every second." Bridget looked at the helicopter again and her stomach gave a lurch.

The pilot looked at the sky. "We have to get moving before the winds shift." He nodded to Beckett. "Get them on board."

"We'll get the girls to Bozeman as fast as we can," Dr. Sampson assured Mildred and Roy.

Every person on Refuge Point gathered in silence as the four victims were carried on stretchers to the waiting helicopter. Bridget saw lips moving and heads bowed in prayer. Bridget said a grateful goodbye to Lance and Linda, and then to Mrs. Greer, fighting back tears as the older woman insisted on hugging her.

"I'm praying for your sisters," Mrs. Greer said. "And I'll stay here until the last patient is rescued."

Bridget's pulse beat as hard as the helicopter rotors and her legs were quaking at the thought of flying in the huge yellow contraption, but she had one more task to complete. She turned to Dr. Sampson and steeled her nerve. She'd say it quick, and then get on board before he could get mad. "About your car, Dr. Sampson. I have a confession to make."

chapter 62

RED

When Red reached the top of the slide, he stopped to catch his breath and look back at the canyon. What had been the clear-running Madison and forested Rock Creek Campground was a mountain of debris and flattened timber. Drowning treetops jutted from the dark surface of the rapidly filling lake.

He had reached the summit without finding any evidence of Jenny, and the torturous pain in his chest subsided to a dull ache.

He could still hope.

The helicopter that had taken Claire and Beth buzzed over his head on another sortie into the canyon. He turned around, surveying the scene on the Madison Valley side of the disaster. At the bottom of the landslide, the highway to Ennis resumed abruptly out of the rubble. A half dozen cars were parked along what had been the Madison River, but was now a waterless, muddy ditch.

Suddenly, the boulders beneath his boots shifted and the landslide trembled. He crouched low as rubble dislodged and tumbled downward. Below, he could see trees shivering. The echo of rockfall died away as the earth steadied under him. The aftershocks were a little like riding an unbroken horse—made it tricky to stay in the saddle—and he'd be glad when the mountain stopped bucking.

He picked his way down the slope toward the waiting cars, his head pounding and his mouth dry as dust. He couldn't remember when he'd eaten last, or had a drink of water, but none of that mattered until he found Jenny.

When he got to the base of the slide the first person he saw was Lem Garrison.

Red didn't bother with niceties as he approached the superintendent of Yellowstone National Park standing next to a dark sedan. "I'm looking for my little girl." Red's voice cracked. "I need to get to Ennis."

Lem's brows went up, but he didn't hesitate. "Get in, Red."

Red slid into the sedan and Garrison pulled around to head west at a speed well above the limit. Without taking his eyes off the road, he passed Red a canteen. "You were in the canyon during the quake?"

Red drained the canteen, the tepid water soothing his tight throat. "Rode in from Sunnyslope," he answered. "My wife was—" His voice broke and he cleared his throat. "My wife and daughter were at Rock Creek."

Garrison glanced over. His grim expression showed he knew what happened at the campground. "I'm sorry, Red," he said. "Is she . . . ?"

"No," Red answered quickly. "Claire made it out on the first helicopter," he said. "But we didn't find Jenny." He blinked, his eyes suddenly stung with grit. "She's only four months old."

Garrison didn't respond with platitudes and Red appreciated that. They both knew the chances of a baby surviving where grown men and women had perished. Garrison navigated around a crevice in the road and let the silence stretch.

As they gained speed again, his brows came down. "You rode into Rock Creek from Sunnyslope? With those aftershocks?"

"I had a good horse." Red had left Marigold and Flick in the care of the kid, Lance. Told him they belonged to Wormsbecker and to see if he could get them back when—if—the roads opened up. "Claire was down there, and with the phones out, nobody knew if the dam was holding. I thought I could warn the campgrounds, but—" He swallowed the lump of regret. "I was too late for Rock Creek."

Garrison gave him a long, appraising look.

The water had revived Red, and now he had his own question. "Why aren't you in Yellowstone?" There had to have been some damage in the park and Lem Garrison was in charge of the whole two million acres.

Garrison grimaced. "We were visiting my in-laws in Ennis. I'm stuck here until I can get a helicopter. They're all tied up with the rescue operation." He went on the shoulder to get around a boulder sitting in the middle of the road. "Figured I might as well help out."

"Do you think people are hurt in the park?" Red asked. If the damage at Rock Creek was anything to go by, there could be hundreds—maybe thousands—of injured.

Garrison shook his head. "We got radio reports from my people there. Nobody was seriously injured that they know of, thank God. The dining room ceiling of Old Faithful collapsed, and the fireplace in the lobby sustained some damage." Garrison glanced over at him. "Plenty of tourists putting up a fuss, and a few of the geysers aren't so happy either, erupting all over the park. The scientists are going to be busy for months."

They rode in silence again and Red thought about how he'd dreaded talking to Garrison enough to take off to Libby, just to find him waiting when he got out of the canyon. Was it bad luck, or a nudge from God to come clean about Dell?

"Red," Garrison said before Red decided, "when you applied for the job at the park, I asked around about you."

Red felt a knot tighten in his gut.

"Grew up an orphan, petty crimes. Time spent in jail."

Red felt about two inches tall. Garrison was somebody he admired. After the lies Pete Henshaw spewed—and knowing Red's past—of course the superintendent pegged him as the crook smuggling sheds out of the park. Was it even worth it for Red to tell him who the real culprit was?

Garrison glanced over at him and Red couldn't figure out his expression. "When you came to talk to me about the job, I was impressed."

Red didn't let himself feel any satisfaction. After that interview, he'd fallen for Dell's scheme and his chances at the job had gone down the drain.

"The thing is," Garrison went on, "I couldn't figure out why you took the blame for Henshaw."

Red twisted around to stare at Garrison, surprise rendering him momentarily speechless.

"I've been around the block a few times," Garrison answered his surprised look. He gave his attention to the road as they hit a shredded stretch of asphalt, slowing down just enough to keep the car under control. "I figured it was Henshaw—and he probably was working with somebody—but didn't have any proof. And you didn't point your finger at him to save yourself." Garrison looked over at him, and he thought maybe he saw respect in the older man's gaze.

Red felt his neck heat. Respect from Lem Garrison wasn't what he'd expected.

"Then," Garrison went on in a somber voice, "the poor kid drowned in the Yellowstone, and a raft of sheds washed up downriver. I figured he'd tried it again and this time he didn't get so lucky."

Now Red wasn't following. "Then why were you looking for me?"

A wrinkle creased Garrison's forehead. "I was hoping you had an idea who put Dell up to it. There's a lot of illegal elk sheds being sold up in Bozeman, and I aim to figure out who was paying Dell for a raft of sheds that got him killed."

Red's breath loosened in his chest. Garrison wasn't looking to lock him up, and maybe he could get justice for Dell. "There's a blue Cadillac at the bottom of a scarp on Hebgen Lake Road," Red said. "The trunk is full of sheds." When Garrison checked the license plate, he'd find David Endicott's name and address and it wouldn't take much digging to figure out that Endicott had a side business in Bozeman selling elk antlers.

Garrison's brows went up and he nodded. "Red, after all this"—he lifted a hand to indicate the damage on the road—"you come talk to me."

"I told you all I know."

"I mean about that job," Garrison said. "I knew I was right about you—and a man with the guts and skill to ride into that canyon in the middle of a quake is somebody I want working for me."

Red didn't trust his voice to speak so he gave a nod in response. He should have been man enough to face Lem Garrison right after Dell's death, instead of running off to Libby. If he had, Jenny would be safe at home and Claire wouldn't have endured that night in the water. But what-ifs and should-haves didn't help with the right now.

Finally, Garrison pulled into the parking lot in front of a sprawling brick building with an American flag flying on a tall pole. Ambulances and police cars lined the curb. Nurses helped the injured through the door, and uniformed Army carted supplies. Red felt the urgency return to his limbs and had the door open before the car was fully stopped.

"Red?" Garrison said as Red climbed out. "I'll be praying for your little girl."

Red pushed through the doors of Ennis High School to find it wall-to-wall with anxious-eyed men, women, and children.

"Please, everyone." A woman wearing a light blue dress with a red cross on the pocket held up her hands in front of a set of double doors. "We understand you're looking for your loved ones. Please make an orderly line."

Red moved toward the line, then jerked to a stop.

Pete Henshaw, head and shoulders above the crowd, was just a few feet in front of him. Red sidestepped into a hallway before Pete spotted him. He didn't want any kind of altercation with Pete, not until he'd found Jenny. But Beth was here, and he didn't want Pete to find her—or Claire. Who knew what a man like Pete would do, even in the middle of a crowd.

He headed down a side hallway, looking into the open classroom doors for somebody to ask about a baby without Pete catching sight of him.

"Red."

He stopped and turned back at the sound of his name.

Father Donahue, dressed in black with his white clerical collar, poked his head through a doorway. "What are you doing here?"

Red ducked into the room. "I'm looking for Jenny." He explained in as few words as possible about Claire and Beth and how they ended up at Rock Creek and why he didn't want to run into Pete Henshaw. "Who would know if a baby came in on one of the transports out of the canyon?"

"The Red Cross supervising nurse is our best bet." Father Donahue grabbed Red by the elbow and steered him out the door and down the hallway. "Claire and Beth are probably in the gymnasium here." He stopped at a closed door. "You warn Beth. I'll track down the nurse and ask about Jenny."

Red nodded and opened the door.

The cavernous gymnasium was a clamor of noise. Rows of cots lined up on the basketball court held the injured. Doctors and nurses hurried between them. Two National Guard soldiers bumped past him with a man on a stretcher, his eyes closed and his face streaked with dried blood.

He found Claire and Beth underneath the basketball hoop. They were scrubbed clean and in fresh clothing. Beth lay on a cot with a needle in her arm and a glass bottle of clear liquid hanging on a stand beside her. Her other arm was in a sling. Claire sat on the cot next to her.

When she saw Red, Claire flew to him, alarm in her eyes. "I've been asking the nurses about Jenny, but it's so chaotic no one has been able to answer me."

He held her tight. He'd never have enough of holding her in his arms. "I ran into Father Donahue. He's asking the Red Cross." He hurried her back to Beth. "Is she okay?"

Claire nodded. "The doctor said Beth's fine, and so is the baby."

That was a relief, but he had to tell them the bad news. He lowered his voice. "Pete Henshaw is here."

Beth started with alarm.

"He can't do anything here," Red said. "You're safe." He hoped it was the truth. Pete Henshaw could bluster all he liked, but he couldn't take Beth against her will with so many people around.

"Red." Father Donahue veered through the cots with a frazzled-looking nurse in his wake. His brows were pulled down in a way Red didn't like. "Nurse Westly says she took in a baby early this morning, a little girl."

Red turned to the woman, his hope soaring.

"Where is she?" Claire rushed forward. "How was she—was she alright?"

"A Forest Service ranger brought her in this morning," the nurse answered quickly. "He said he'd been at Rock Creek and walked out over the slide during the night."

It had to be Jenny. There couldn't have been more than one baby brought out of the campground alone. Relief coursed through him and he took Claire's hand in his. *Thank you, Lord.*

The nurse looked uncertainly from Red to Claire. "She was in good health . . ."

Red's brows came down. He didn't like the way the nurse said *was.* From the look on Claire's face, she didn't like it either. "Where is she now?" he demanded.

The nurse swallowed and took a step back. "Like I told Father . . ." She stuttered a little. "I-I sent her home with her grandmother."

"With who?" Claire's voice rose and her grip on Red's hand tightened.

"Her grandmother," the nurse said again. "Just a few minutes ago."

"What did she look like?" Red ground out, his heart trying to hammer its way out of his chest.

"She was frail-looking, a streak of gray in her hair. She seemed perfectly harmless." She looked from Red to Claire, her face pale. "It wasn't more than five minutes ago."

Claire met his gaze and he could see the same emotions he was feeling flash across her face—disbelief, confusion . . . and fear.

The Henshaws had taken their little girl.

chapter 63

CLAIRE

Claire ran behind Red, veering through the makeshift hospital and into the crowded school hallway. Fear for Jenny pumped through her weak limbs. Red bulldozed through the crowd, and they burst through the front doors of the high school . . . just as the Henshaws' red truck roared out of the parking lot.

She stared at it, weakness flowing through her. The Henshaws were taking Jenny.

But no. There was Pete Henshaw staggering out the door behind them, his eyes on the truck. "Iris!" He pushed past Red, stumbling into the parking lot as the truck careened onto the highway.

Claire struggled to stay upright, emotion swamping her. If Pete didn't have Jenny . . . Claire had a flash of memory. Iris clutching Jenny close, her vacant expression. *Dell is such a good baby.*

Iris had her little girl.

Red grabbed Pete by the front of his shirt. "Where is she going?" he demanded.

What would Iris do with Jenny? Run away with her to Wyoming, like she'd wanted to do with Beth and her baby? Claire couldn't let that happen. She'd lost Jenny once. She wouldn't lose her again. A West Yellowstone police cruiser idled in front of the school doors. Claire was in the driver's seat before she knew what she was doing. Red was rounding the front of the car and pulling open the passenger door.

Claire put the car in drive, then stomped on the brake.

"What are you doing?" Red said.

"Get in," Claire yelled to Pete out the open window. Pete Henshaw was just as desperate to stop Iris as she and Red. They might need his help. Claire swung the wheel in the direction she'd seen Iris go—south, back toward the slide. She pushed her foot down on the accelerator and the police car bounced over the curb and onto the highway.

She looked in the rearview mirror and caught the surprised face of Father Donahue. God would forgive her for stealing a car, and they could deal with Sheriff Eagle when Jenny was back in her arms.

Red turned in his seat and growled at Pete. "What is Iris doing? Where is she going with our daughter?"

Pete kept his eyes on the road ahead. "She won't hurt her."

Dizzying fear thrummed through Claire's body. She strained to see further down the road, looking for the red Ford. "You were keeping Beth a prisoner," she accused. How could they trust his word now?

"I wasn't going to let Iris keep the baby," Pete said quickly. "You have to believe me."

Claire could see his stricken expression in the rearview mirror. She swerved around a boulder in the center of the road. "Look." Claire saw the red tailgate ahead. "That's the truck." Claire pushed down on the gas, the police car surging forward. The Henshaws' truck veered from one side of the damaged road to the other. Claire could barely breathe, thinking of Jenny with Iris, driving wildly on the rough road. Could Jenny have survived Rock Creek Campground just to die in a car crash with Iris Henshaw?

"You've got to understand," Pete went on, his voice breaking. "We lost both our boys. She's not herself."

Ahead of them, the truck slowed and turned off the main road.

"Where does that road go?" Claire asked Red.

"It's a Forest Service road," Red said. "Goes to the Hutchinson Bridge."

"She can't go too much farther," Pete said. "The bridge was damaged by the quake." Pete kept talking. "I didn't want to lose Iris, too. You've got to believe me."

Claire turned down the road, her racing heartbeat pounding against her ribs. She glanced at Red, taking her eyes off the road for a split second. He was leaning forward, determination in every line of his body.

The road curved, and she lost sight of the truck. She took the curve far too fast and they all slid sideways. The bridge came into sight and—there—the red truck—nose down on the edge of the riverbank, the passenger door gaping open. Claire jammed on the brakes, and the car shuddered to a halt.

Claire pushed out the door and ran to the truck. "Jenny," she gasped as she reached it. The cab of the truck was empty.

"Claire." Red was right behind her. His voice held a note of panic and Claire followed his gaze. The Hutchinson bridge listed sideways, its deck buckled and broken. The guardrails on one side hung loose and twisted, dangling over the waterless ravine of the Madison River twenty feet below.

Claire's breath lodged in her throat.

Iris Henshaw stood on the devastated bridge with Jenny in her arms.

chapter 64

RED

Pete was out of the car and running toward the bridge. "Iris," he called out. "What are you—?"

"Stay away from me." Iris took a step backwards, toward the twisted guardrail and the precarious drop to sharp rocks below. Jenny yelped a stuttering cry that made every muscle in Red's body tense.

Claire lunged toward the bridge and Red caught her arm. "Don't," he whispered.

She's not herself. Red looked at the woman on the bridge holding his daughter. Her cheeks were sunken and her eyes were shadowed. Iris wasn't in her right mind. What might she do to herself—and to Jenny?

"Slowly," he said to Claire. He took her hand. It was ice cold and he could feel her trembling. They reached the spot where Pete stood, just before the road met the plank decking of the bridge.

"Don't come any closer," Iris yelled, her eyes darting wildly from Pete to the drop-off.

Red felt Claire strain forward and tightened his grip on her hand. Claire gave him a look of pure anguish. "Easy," he whispered.

"It's your fault." Iris's voice was a choked sob. "It's your fault Dell is dead."

It took Red a moment to realize she was talking to Pete.

"Iris," Pete pleaded. "I tried to stop him. He was always headstrong."

"No," she spit out. Tears glinted on Iris's cheeks as she looked down at Jenny. "Dell is a good boy." She put Jenny on her shoulder and swayed back and forth. Jenny's cries stopped. "You stay away from me, Pete."

Pete's hand went over his heart like she'd pierced it with her words.

Claire let go of Red's hand and stepped forward. "Iris." Claire's voice was tight. "It's Claire Wilder. Do you remember me?"

Red figured it was a good idea for Claire to try to reach Iris. They were both mothers and didn't mothers understand each other?

"You took Beth away from me," Iris gazed down at Jenny, then raised her face to Claire with a look of distress. "You stole my grand-baby away from me."

The bridge creaked and shuddered as Iris rocked Jenny back and forth.

Red's knees went soft. He'd almost lost Jenny at Rock Creek, now she was in danger again—and just out of reach.

"Iris." Claire's voice was weak. "Please, don't do this."

Iris shook her head and stepped closer to the edge. "Stay back."

Red's heart pounded. Iris was like a pain-crazed horse. Pete couldn't reason with her and she didn't trust Claire. He could understand her pain some, after almost losing Claire and Jenny himself. She'd lost both her sons—and was trying to make some sense of Dell's death when there wasn't any sense to be made. But he didn't know how to get through to her.

Lord, tell me what to do.

He had to do something. Red took a deep breath. The answer wasn't going to come from the blue sky. *Lord, make it the right thing, I'm begging you.*

He sent a look to Claire, squeezed her hand . . . then dropped it.

He took one slow step onto the bridge. "Iris," he said. Softly. Carefully. Like he would to a spooked horse. "Dell was a good man."

Iris nodded and her shoulders drooped. Jenny's whimpers resumed.

Red didn't move any closer. "He was my friend. Remember?" He could see her eyes focus on him now. Good. "You had me over for dinner once. You made pork chops and mashed potatoes." It was the summer before he met Claire, and Dell had just started at Sunnyslope. "Best meal I had all month."

Iris looked down at Jenny. "I remember."

Red nodded. "Dell was happy with Beth, wasn't he?"

Iris swayed back and forth.

Red took another careful step forward. "He wanted to do right by his wife, and his baby—be a good husband and father." Red swallowed the lump coming up in his throat. "I know how he felt. A man would do anything to take care of his family. To be worthy of them."

Behind him, Red heard a soft intake of breath from Claire.

He met Iris's anguished eyes. "He just went about it the wrong way." Red had gone about it the wrong way himself, running off to Libby. Thinking that twenty dollars a day would make him a good husband, instead of sharing his past and his heart with his wife.

Iris seemed to deflate a little, her shoulders sagging and her grip on Jenny slackening. Red took another step. He'd covered half the distance between the edge of the bridge and Iris.

"You were his friend," Iris said, as if just now remembering Red. "And you went to jail, instead of him."

Now wasn't the time for Red to do any finger-pointing. "I didn't want him to miss his wedding day." He made his mouth curve into a small smile.

"If you were his friend, why didn't you stop him?" Iris asked, her voice filled with anguish.

Red swallowed hard. He should have stopped him. That was the awful truth.

He was just as much at fault as anybody.

That night before Dell died, Red had gone to check on a horse at Sunnyslope. Bucky was there, and he told him Dell wanted to talk to him. Red met up with Dell at the Slippery Otter, thinking maybe Dell was going to make things right between them. Instead, Dell asked Red to help him raft a load of sheds down the Yellowstone.

"How stupid do you think I am?" Red had asked.

Dell had argued, his voice rising and a few of the regulars at the Otter looking over at them. "They're just sitting in the park rotting. It's not like it hurts anybody."

Red had walked out of the Otter and washed his hands of Dell.

Jenny sputtered a cry. Red looked over his shoulder at Claire. Her gaze was pinned on Iris, her hands gripped together in anguish. He had to get the woman back to safety, and his daughter back in Claire's arms.

He turned back to Iris. If she wanted someone to blame for Dell's death, he was willing to take it. But what if that put her closer to the edge of the bridge with Jenny? *Lord, help me.* "I tried," Red said. "I should have tried harder and maybe I could have saved him." It was the truth. He wished more than anything that he'd stopped the kid. "I'm sorry, Iris."

Jenny began to cry in earnest. Iris rocked her back and forth, her gaunt cheeks glittering with tears. Her mouth opened, but no words came out.

Maybe Red was getting through to her. He stepped closer. "Iris," Red said, his hands out, palms up and pleading. "Can I have Jenny back now? She's hungry." He was close now, maybe four or five strides from Iris. The tipped bridge felt sturdy enough, but Iris was so close to the edge. Too close.

"I miss my boys." Iris's voice was a groan of agony. "I miss them so much."

"I know," Red said gently, his heart twisting for the poor woman. "But you can't keep Jenny."

"Jenny?" Iris looked down at the crying baby, then at Red. Her brow furrowed. "This is your little girl." She said it as if she were seeing Jenny for the first time. "Yours and Claire's baby."

"Yes," Red said carefully. "It's Jenny. And we love her very much. Just like you loved Sid and Dell."

Iris's gaze shifted to Claire, then back to Red, as if trying to decide if that was the truth. Jenny's cries became more insistent.

Red held his breath.

Iris frowned. "I saw her with the nurse. Pete was looking for Beth and I just wanted to hold her for a little while."

"I believe you," Red said. "I know you didn't want to worry us."

Iris's face cleared and she looked at the bridge, the river below and the broken guardrails as if taking them in for the first time. She took a step toward him.

Red moved to meet her, his hands outstretched for his little girl.

Then the world tilted. A shriek of steel and the crack of wood rent the air. Red staggered, trying to keep his feet under him. He shot a look over his shoulder. Claire and Pete were on the ground, rocks tumbling down the embankment.

An aftershock, and it was a big one.

Red staggered toward Iris as she floundered, reaching out for the guardrail that wasn't there. Jenny, slipping downward. The bridge heaved. The wood decking splintered under his feet. He kept his eyes on Jenny as he vaulted forward.

Iris crumpled sideways toward the tilting edge of the bridge.

He was there, one arm scooping up Jenny, the other shooting around Iris and stopping her headlong fall.

He had them both and he held on tight, riding out the shock waves.

The shaking stopped, but the bridge continued to shudder and tilt toward the riverbed below. He clamped Jenny to his chest and anchored Iris to his other side. Claire was on her knees at the edge of the bridge, reaching out to him, her eyes huge and panicked. *Hurry, hurry.* Her anguish pulled at him like a rope around his heart. Pete was watching the tilting bridge with a terrified expression.

Red didn't hesitate. He clutched his burdens—his daughter, and the woman who had taken her—and pounded over the buckled decking with long strides. *Lord, let the bridge hold.*

He staggered once, then caught his balance. Ten feet, then five. Then he was there, clearing the groaning bridge.

Iris fell into Pete's outstretched arms.

Red stumbled to his knees in front of Claire. She flung her arms around him, Jenny squeezed between them. Jenny wailed, and Claire shuddered with a sob. Red held his wife and daughter to his pounding heart. They were safe. His family was safely in his arms and he would never let them go.

chapter 65

CLAIRE

"Dad!" Claire waved as her father stepped off the bus at the Depot.

Red stood beside her, Jenny in his arms. He shifted from foot to foot like he did when he was nervous. "Don't worry." Claire kissed him quickly. "It's going to be fine."

The biggest earthquake in the history of the Rocky Mountains had happened four days ago and the county was in an uproar. As soon as the roads opened, West Yellowstone was filled with tourists trying to get out of Yellowstone National Park—and newspaper reporters, the Red Cross, and the National Guard trying to get in.

Unfortunately, the newspaper reports of the earthquake got to Dad before the telephone lines were back in service. When Claire was finally able to call out, Flo was overjoyed to hear they were all safe, but Dad was already on a train west. "He was beside himself," Flo said. "He'll be there at five o'clock."

"Today?" Claire said in disbelief, her eyes locking with Red's as he burped Jenny after her morning bottle. "Today," Claire said after telling Flo goodbye.

Now, Dad pushed through the crowd at the Depot and pulled Claire into his arms, squeezing her like he'd given her up for dead. "Say hello to your granddaughter," Claire told him when he finally let her go. Dad said all the right things about Jenny—that she was beautiful and looked just like her mother—but he didn't say one word to Red.

"He'll warm up," Claire whispered to Red as he loaded Dad's matching suitcases into the back of the truck. She hoped she was right.

They drove through West Yellowstone, with Dad asking for all the details about the earthquake and her ordeal in what was now being called Quake Lake. A journalist from Helena wrote a whole article about Beth and Claire and their night in the water. "They didn't stop knocking on our door," Claire told Dad. "We even got a telegram from Art Linkletter asking us to appear on his show." She'd told him she had no interest in being on television, much to Frannie's sorrow.

As they drove north on highway 191—where damage was still evident in stretches of buckled road and downed trees—Claire downplayed what had happened as much as she could. Dad was already aghast, he didn't need to know all the details.

Claire bounced Jenny on her lap and Jenny cooed and dimpled, showing off for her grandfather. Claire hadn't let Jenny out of her sight since they got back to Riverside, even sleeping with Jenny in the bed between her and Red. When she woke—as she did most nights—with the nightmare of cold water closing over her, Jenny's soft breathing and Red's warm presence consoled her.

Now she watched as Red drummed his fingers on the steering wheel as they got closer to Riverside. What on earth was Dad doing, acting as if Red wasn't sitting right beside her?

"Did you ever find out who brought her out of the canyon?" Dad asked.

"A Forest Service ranger." Claire let out a long breath. Thank goodness for Joseph Shields, who had been doing his last round at Rock Creek. "He heard me and got to the trailer just as the water started rising." Joseph had come to Riverside after the article came out. He and Jenny had ended up on the west end of the rising water after the trailer was swept away. He figured the best thing to do was get the baby to safety. He decided to hike out over the slide in the dark and was the first survivor to reach Ennis. "He said she was as good as gold." Claire touched Jenny's nose with one finger and her daughter broke into a grin.

"And you found her in Ennis?" Dad asked.

Claire glanced at Red. "Eventually." She wasn't about to tell Dad about the terrifying chase after Iris Henshaw. "Here we are," Claire said brightly as Red slowed the truck and pulled up in front of their house.

Dad's eyes went wide and his mouth fell open. "This is . . . where you live?"

Red cut Claire a sideways glance that said he'd been right to be worried.

Claire didn't care what her Dad had to say. Their home was wonderful. The house had come through the earthquake and its many aftershocks miraculously unscathed. A broken front window—repaired with cardboard for now—was the only damage. The paint was still peeling and the porch was cracked, but wildflowers added their color to the buffalo grass and the mountains provided a stunning backdrop. Stretching above it all was the immense blue sky. Who needed anything more?

"Come on," Claire said. "Bridget and Frannie will be here soon and I have dinner in the oven."

Claire climbed out of the truck with Jenny, but before she made it to the cracked front steps, Bridget roared up in a mint green Thunderbird convertible with a hefty dent in its front bumper. She jumped out of the car and ran to hug Dad.

"You drive now?" Dad threw a disbelieving look at the car.

Maybe Claire should have warned Dad that there were some surprises in store. Bridget sang out a hello to Red, who was getting the luggage out of the car. He gave her a nod.

"I thought you were bringing Frannie," Claire said as they trooped into the house. Claire had hardly seen Bridget since the earthquake, just a tearful reunion when she got back from transporting the injured to Livingston, and then she was needed at the Red Cross site in Ennis.

"Yes, where is your little sister?" Dad griped. "I have a thing or two to say to her." His tone said it wasn't going to be a happy reunion.

Bridget looked out the open front door. "Speak of the devil."

A car door slammed and a moment later Frannie came in, making a beeline for Dad. She threw her arms around him and burst into tears.

Dad's arms were pinned to his sides by Frannie's embrace, his face so shocked, Claire had to hide a laugh behind her hand. Bridget choked back a laugh of her own.

"Oh Dad," Frannie pressed her face on his white shirt. "I've been such a dummy. Can you forgive me?"

"What on earth?" Dad looked from Claire to Bridget as if they could explain to him the behavior of his youngest daughter.

"Frannie"—Claire handed Frannie the dish towel to dry her eyes—"you can tell Dad all about it at dinner. Introduce Paul and then wash up."

"Dad, Paul. Paul, Dad," Frannie said with her usual lack of manners. They sat down elbow-to-elbow at the little table and said grace.

"What do we have here?" Dad eyed his plate as Claire dished up.

"Elk stew," Claire said. Claire hadn't had any time to make something fancier and anyway, this was turning into her specialty.

Dad's brows went up, but he dipped his spoon and gave it a try. "You'll have to give Flo your recipe," he said politely.

Dad still hadn't said a word to Red and, in fact, he avoided looking his direction. Bridget caught her eye and frowned. Claire wasn't the only one who noticed.

During dinner, Frannie gave a dramatic account of the earthquake, the wind, and the flood, and by the end of her spiel Dad was looking queasy. Paul took over when Frannie ran out of steam. "I talked to my friend in the lookout tower, he was right at the epicenter."

"What's an epicenter?" Bridget asked.

Paul was more than happy to answer. "It's where the earthquake was strongest. He pinpointed it at the spot where highway 287 and 191 meet."

"You mean we kicked Sam and Ernie out at the epicenter?" Frannie slapped her knee. "Serves them right."

"All kinds of neat stuff is happening in the park," Paul went on. "Over two hundred springs are erupting all over the place and even Old Faithful has changed its schedule."

"Did anyone inside the park get hurt?" Dad asked with a frown.

Paul shook his head. "I heard one lady broke her wrist when she slipped on the stairs trying to get out of the Yellowstone Inn. The injuries and fatalities were almost all in the Madison Canyon."

Silence descended around the table. The search for survivors in Madison Canyon had gone on all week, and the fatality count was revised every day. So far there were sixteen known dead, fourteen of them at Rock Creek.

"I saw Jerrylynn's parents yesterday," Frannie said softly.

"I'm so sorry about your friend, Frannie," Claire said with a rush of sorrow for the sweet girl with the ponytail and the generous spirit.

Frannie's eyes got teary. Paul put his arm around her.

Dad's brows came down at that and he glared at Paul.

Bridget was just as somber. "Mildred Wilson's funeral is tomorrow." She looked to Frannie. "I'm driving up to Livingston for it. Do you want to come?"

"Yes," Frannie said. "And I have something for Connie and her dad." The way she said it sounded suspicious.

"What is it?" Bridget asked with a frown.

"That's for me to know and you to find out," Frannie said. Frannie had grown up a lot in the past week, but she was still Frannie.

Dad leaned back from the table. He pulled his pipe from the inside pocket of his suit coat. "Red," he suddenly said, as if he hadn't pretended Red didn't exist for the past hour. He had the serious look on his face Claire knew well. "I'd like a word with you." He glanced around the table. "In private."

Bridget's gaze met Claire's.

Frannie's eyes went from Dad to Red. "Uh oh."

Red's expression was unreadable as he pushed his chair away from the table and stood. "Let's talk outside."

chapter 66

RED

"Let's go to the river," Red said as he and Daniel Reilly went out the back door.

His father-in-law hadn't even looked at him—much less shaken his hand—since he stepped foot off the bus. Red had hoped that after the quake, with all that had happened to change him and Claire, Daniel Reilly might have changed, too.

No such luck.

Red led the older man past the horse shed and pasture where Rosie, Marigold, and Bess grazed, flicking their tails. Marigold shambled over to the fence. Red stopped to scratch her ears. Whatever Daniel Reilly had to say could wait while he said hello to his second-favorite horse.

Daniel Reilly eyed the horse as if it were another competition for his daughter's affections. "Is this the horse you gave my daughter for a wedding present?"

Red rubbed Marigold's soft nose. Bucky had shown up with her a couple days after the quake. "Wormsbecker's giving her back to me?" Red had asked with disbelief. His former boss didn't have a generous bone in his body, even for someone who saved his life. "Nope." Bucky slid down from the saddle. "To Claire. Said he owed her for Beth."

Red nodded now in answer to Daniel Reilly. He wasn't going to explain what Marigold meant to him—to both of them. If he hadn't had such a reliable horse, and if he and Bridget hadn't gotten to Refuge Point, and then to Rock Creek Campground with the sorry offering of one life vest . . . well, he'd thank God for this horse the rest of his days.

He led the way down the path to the river. They stopped at the bank and Red looked out over the water, the evening sun reflecting on the rippling current. He wasn't going to run from whatever Daniel Reilly had to say to him. In fact, he'd start the man out and get it over with. "Mr. Reilly," he began, "I know this isn't what you wanted for Claire."

"Red," his father-in-law growled, "let me say my piece. It's going to be hard enough."

Red braced for the worst. He was a failure, Claire deserved better. He hadn't lived up to his promise to take care of his family. All of the things he had once believed but didn't anymore.

Claire had changed all that.

She knew the worst about him, and she still loved him. When they got home—after that night of anguish when he thought he'd lost her and Jenny, and then chasing down Iris Henshaw—he told her about Dell and the sheds and going to jail. Turns out she knew most of it from Beth. "I've made mistakes, Claire." He didn't sugarcoat his past in Chicago, or how close he'd come to prison.

She didn't shrink back from him, even with all that. But then he told her his greatest shame.

Admitting he'd never learned to read was the hardest thing he'd ever done, and he couldn't even look at her for fear of what he'd see in her eyes. When he finally met her gaze, it was filled with love, and he thought his heart might burst with how that felt. She leaned in to kiss him. "Isn't it a happy coincidence you married a schoolteacher?"

A coincidence? He'd thought marrying a schoolteacher was a cruel joke on him, but it wasn't. It was part of God's plan all along. Red wanted to keep kissing Claire then, but he had one last confession to make. "I made God a promise, Claire, if I found you."

She frowned. "What kind of promise?"

"That I'd take you back home, to live in Willmar." He had more to say, about Claire needing her family and how he'd been selfish, but she put a finger on his lips to stop him. Her brows pulled together. "We *are* home, Red. And if you think we're going to live anywhere but right here in Riverside, you have another think coming."

He didn't argue with Claire when she used that tone. And after that, they didn't talk any more.

Now, Red fixed his gaze across the water, at the mountains purpling in the dusk, and braced himself for whatever Daniel Reilly had to say.

Daniel studied the rippling water at their feet. "On the train out here, when I didn't know if Claire was dead or alive—when I thought maybe all my girls might be gone—I had a lot of time to think."

Red felt a trace of sympathy for the man. He knew how it felt to be helpless, thinking the worst and unable to do a thing about it.

"Red"—he picked up a rock from the shallow water at their feet—"my daughters are everything to me." He rubbed the smooth stone in his hand, his voice dropping. "When you came along, I didn't want to let Claire go—I didn't know *how* to let her go." He kept his eyes on the rock. "I wanted to hold on to her. Was that such a bad thing?"

Red didn't figure the question was directed at him, so instead of answering he watched a hawk circle overhead and disappear into the dark shoulder of the mountain.

Daniel Reilly threw the rock into the river. "What I'm trying to say"—he finally turned to face Red—"is I didn't want to lose her."

Red thought about how much he loved Jenny, and how someday he'd face the same kind of heartache. It was right for Claire to separate from her father and make a family of her own, but that didn't make it any less painful. He met the older man's steel-gray eyes. "She's still your daughter."

Daniel Reilly grimaced and ran a hand through his shock of white hair, then met Red's gaze. "I hope you can forgive me for what I said, in the church."

Red remembered the humiliation burning through him as he stood at the front of the church waiting for Claire to walk down the aisle, hearing Daniel Reilly spit out in front of all the guests, "Don't make the biggest mistake of your life, Claire." Red's heart had plummeted, the flame of hope—hope for love and a family and Claire—flickering out, leaving a cold emptiness in his chest.

Now the man was waiting for his forgiveness. "Daniel," Red said, "I don't hold it against you." He couldn't, because what happened in the moment after Daniel Reilly's insult had relit Red's hope to a blaze, and sealed his heart to Claire's just as surely as the vows they would make: Claire, sure and confident and beautiful, her voice ringing out for everyone in the church to hear. "Dad, if you don't walk me down the aisle, I'll run down it without you." And she did, racing toward him, her blue eyes locked on his. Ready to become Claire Wilder—and leaving her father standing alone at the back of the church.

Daniel Reilly's steely eyes shone with tears in the fading light, and Red knew the man was remembering the same moment—the moment Claire had chosen Red. Then, one side of Daniel's mouth quirked, and he shook his head. "She really is something, isn't she?"

Red let out a breath. Something they could agree on. "She sure is."

Daniel stuck out his hand to Red. "Can we start again?"

Red looked at his father-in-law's outstretched hand. An offer of acceptance, and maybe even respect. It was a lot to live up to, but Red was ready to try. For Claire and for the family they would make together. He put his hand in Daniel's.

It was a beginning.

Daniel turned to go back to the house, but Red stopped him. "Can I say something, Daniel, before we go in to see what kind of Jell-O concoction Claire has for dessert?" It was maybe overstepping, but he wasn't going to run from what had to be said. For Claire, and for Bridget and Frannie.

"If you have to," Daniel answered gruffly.

Red met his father-in-law's eyes in the fading light. He'd seen how buried secrets hurt, how they festered in the dark. He knew now that talking about what was painful didn't worsen the wound, but allowed it to heal. It was time for the Reilly family to talk about the past . . . about their mother. "Talk to your daughters, Daniel. Don't let the past come between you."

chapter 67

BRIDGET

"Don't be such a worrywart." Bridget watched Claire twist the dishcloth into a knot as Red and Dad walked down the trail to the river. "Red can handle himself."

As usual, Frannie was shirking dish duty, sitting on the floor with Paul and playing with Jenny, but Bridget didn't mind. It was nice not to be fighting with her. And Paul seemed to be a decent young man.

Claire turned from the window, her brows raised. "You've changed your tune."

Bridget took the dish towel from Claire and began to dry the dishes. "You have no idea."

It wasn't just Bridget's opinion of Red that had altered. It was how everything she thought she knew had been turned over and shaken loose. She'd been in an earthquake, ridden a mule through the dark, and taken risks. Real risks—with her life, her career, and her heart. After the terrifying helicopter flight and the long journey to Bozeman, Mildred Wilson had died, and Bridget's heart had broken. The thing was, the pain had meant something—and that made it easier to bear. But not only that . . . she was still thinking on it, but it felt like since she sat beside Mildred and Phillip and Dolores—since she'd let herself care *about* them and not just take care of them—her own wounds had begun to heal. And she wondered . . . was that what that tug on her heart had been all along? Not a call to heal others like Jesus did, but an invitation to let him heal her own heart?

She didn't know, but she wasn't afraid anymore—not like she had been. Oh, she still never wanted to see a rattlesnake, and she wouldn't willingly get on a mule again, but she wanted to be brave—maybe even as brave as Claire—with her heart and with her future. She put the dish away in the cupboard and found Claire watching her with narrowed eyes.

"What's going on, Bridget?" Claire asked.

How did Claire do that? "Nothing at all," Bridget lied, then changed the subject. "Have you heard from Beth?"

Claire gave her a look that said she knew what Bridget was up to, but she answered anyway. "I got a letter today. Her parents are happy to have her back and she promised to come visit next summer with the baby. And before you ask"—Claire passed her another plate—"she's been to the doctor and is perfectly well."

"That's wonderful," Bridget said. "You don't think the Henshaws will bother her there, do you?"

"No." Claire shook her head. "Poor Iris."

"There are new treatments for depressive states like Iris's," Bridget said. "Sending her to the hospital was the right thing to do."

"I feel terrible for her, but I'm glad they're going to Wyoming after Iris is released. I don't want them anywhere near Jenny." Claire pulled the plug in the sink and watched the water go down the drain. "So what is it? Is it about Dr. California?"

Bridget should have known she couldn't put off Claire for long.

"Hey Paul," Frannie piped up. "Take the ankle biter for a minute, would you? I need to get in on this." She dumped Jenny in Paul's arms and skipped into the kitchen. "Spill the beans, Bridget."

"There's nothing to spill about Kevin Sampson," Bridget said.

Frannie and Claire exchanged doubtful looks.

"Is it the job in Rochester?" Frannie asked. "Did you get it?"

Bridget put her hands on her hips. "What is this? Twenty questions?"

Frannie let out a huff of impatience. "Tell us quick, before Dad comes back."

She wasn't going to be able to dissuade them. Her sisters knew when something was up, but they had no idea what a shock was in store.

"Bridget?" Claire was looking concerned. "Is something wrong?"

Bridget felt a smile tugging at the corners of her mouth. She might as well just come out with it. "Nothing's wrong. It's just . . . I'm not going to the Mayo Clinic." She really was terrible at keeping a secret. "At least not immediately."

Frannie and Claire exchanged a questioning look, then Frannie's eyes got big and she burst out with, "Are you getting married?"

Bridget swatted Frannie with the towel. "Of course not." Where did she get these ideas? "I think . . ." Now she couldn't deny the grin that broke free along with a rising bubble of excitement in her chest. "I think I might be going to . . . Hawaii."

Claire stared at her, and for once even Frannie was speechless.

"I did get the job at the Mayo Clinic," she explained in the silence. "The hiring committee saw the article in the *Chicago Tribune*. You know, the one about Red and me riding into the canyon." Bridget rolled her eyes. The article was titled "Heroine on Horseback." Partly true, but the reporter had exaggerated her role in the disaster. "They tracked me down at the Red Cross Center to offer me the position."

"Get to the part about Hawaii," Frannie demanded.

Claire looked out the window. "And hurry, before they come back."

Bridget relented. "It was the Crow—Nurse Larkin. She recommended me for the traveling nurse program. I didn't even know she did it—but they offered me a temporary position in Honolulu."

"Wait," Claire interrupted. "Was this before or after you pulled the fire alarm?"

"Before." Bridget still couldn't believe she'd done that. Maybe that was the start of her bravery.

"Hawaii," Claire said, her voice amazed, and Bridget felt a prickle of satisfaction at being the sister going on an adventure. "It's just like one of your books."

"Have you told Dad?" Frannie asked.

Bridget's bubble of excitement dissolved. "No, but . . ." She looked down to see herself wringing the dishcloth. Dad looked like he'd aged ten years since the earthquake, how could she add to his burden by going so far away? "Maybe I shouldn't take the job. Dad's been through a lot."

Claire took the towel out of her hand. "Bridget, this is something you want to do, I can tell."

Bridget nodded, unable to answer. She really did want to do it, but . . . poor Dad. She didn't want to see him sad.

"We'll help you break the news." Frannie tucked her arm through Bridget's elbow. "It's about time we started talking about things that are real in this family."

Bridget wasn't sure she was ready for that. It sounded hard. But if Claire and Frannie helped her . . . they'd had more practice with disappointing Dad.

Claire linked her arm on Bridget's other side. "He'll be fine."

"He'll have a conniption fit," Frannie contested. "But then he'll be fine."

Bridget blinked as her vision got cloudy. Maybe, with her sisters beside her, she could be brave, even with Dad.

Claire looked out the window. "Here they come. Are you ready?"

Bridget felt a rush of alarm. "Right now?"

"Right now," Claire said with an encouraging nod.

Frannie linked her arm through Bridget's. "You bet your sweet patootie, right now."

chapter 68

FRANNIE

Frannie had her own news to break to Dad, and she couldn't put it off any longer.

She'd taken pity on him and given him a day to recover from the whole dying-in-an-earthquake thing and Bridget's I'm-going-to-Hawaii thing. She still couldn't believe her big sister was going to the land of hula dresses and surfboarding.

What a lucky duck.

Frannie was in Dad's hotel room at The Nest. He was packing to catch the train home and thought Frannie was going with him. Poor Dad. Maybe she should have broken her news to him sooner.

Dad had taken the news about Bridget better than expected. He'd gone a little pale, and asked a boatload of questions, but in the end he'd agreed that it would be good for Bridget's career. Then Paul gave Dad a ride to The Nest in West Yellowstone, because—as much as Dad loved Claire—he wasn't going to sleep on a couch.

Frannie and Claire and Bridget stayed up late talking about the earthquake, and Hawaii and all sorts of stuff, then Bridget and Frannie tossed a coin for the couch. Frannie lost and had to sleep on the floor, but she didn't mind. Before they went to sleep, they all said their prayers together like they used to.

It was nice to pray again and really believe somebody could hear her.

Now Dad fastened the last clasp on his monogrammed luggage. "Where's your suitcase, Frannie?"

Frannie took a long breath. She'd rehearsed what she had to say—and was positive this wouldn't turn into the usual knock-down-drag-out. She was going to be an adult and stay reasonable.

She just hoped Dad would, too.

"Dad," she said carefully. "Don't take this the wrong way, but I'm not going home with you."

"Don't take it the wrong way?" he said, turning on her with his brows pulled down. "How exactly am I supposed to take it?"

This wasn't starting out well.

"They need my help at the Red Cross Center," she told him.

"You've done enough," Dad objected. "You've been at it for a week." He used the voice that said he was right and she was wrong, and she felt the aggravation that always came when she tried to talk to him about something important.

"Dad," she said now, sitting down on the bed so that they weren't facing each other like boxers ready to go a round. "I could have been one of those people under the mountain." She didn't like to remind him of how close she had come to dying, but it was the truth. "My friend died there. A lot of people died."

Dad's face softened and he sat down on the bed beside her.

Frannie mourned Jerrylynn, even though she'd only known her a week. That night had been terrible, but also the most important thing that had ever happened to her. For the first time in her life, she wasn't Claire and Bridget Reilly's kid sister. She wasn't Jonny's girlfriend or the school troublemaker. She'd done a lot of stupid things to try to show people she was an adult, but that night she'd really grown up.

"I want to help," she said simply. "I need to help."

Frannie didn't feel like she'd done enough—or that she ever would. She had survived and others had died. She didn't know if it was by the grace of God, like Bridget said—or stupid luck. But she knew she couldn't just walk away.

The days after the quake, she'd volunteered to be a slide walker. She and a bunch of others—kids and housewives and people from the Red Cross—walked all over the avalanche that covered Rock Creek Campground, searching for clues of who might be missing. They didn't find much—fishing gear and camping equipment, mostly. She'd found a single small child's shoe that had made her actually cry, thinking of how it could have been Jenny under that mountain of rock.

Then she'd found the dog. The poor thing was wandering the rocky slide area, matted and covered in mud. Frannie had forgotten all about Sadie. She gave the poor thing a bath and some food and brought her to see Paul, who was working in the Red Cross's makeshift office in West Yellowstone.

"She saved my life," she told him as Sadie sniffed his ankle cast. If Frannie had been able to sleep that night and stayed in the tent, who knew if she'd be alive today? She took Sadie to Livingston when she and Bridget went to Mrs. Wilson's funeral. Bridget wasn't happy about a dog in that fancy car, but Connie and the twins started crying when they saw Sadie, and Mr. Wilson got teary-eyed.

"What else is there for you to do?" Dad asked now. He was really trying, and she felt a rush of appreciation. Maybe this would work.

"The thing is," she explained, "nobody knows who was at the campground that night." The Red Cross had received thousands of calls and telegrams from people who thought maybe they had family or friends at Rock Creek. "They need me to help with making the list of possible missing persons."

"How do you do that?" Dad asked.

"I mostly follow up on telephone calls." Yesterday, she got a call from a woman in Iowa City. She said her son and his wife and kids had been in the area and she hadn't heard from them since the earthquake. Frannie did some detective work and found out that the family had registered as visitors at the museum in Virginia City on August 17, the day of the earthquake. She marked them on the list as possibly missing and said a prayer that they were somewhere else.

"And Dad"—Frannie couldn't disguise the excitement in her voice—"I met the director of operations for the Red Cross, and guess what?"

He raised his brows as if nothing would surprise him now.

"She's a woman!" Frannie couldn't believe it herself. "She's in charge of the whole operation and she travels all over the country wherever there's some kind of disaster." What a cool job.

Dad was quiet for a while, then he patted her hand. "I'd hoped you'd come home with me," he said, "but I can see this means a lot to you."

Wowsa. Was it really going to be this easy? "It'll just be a month, Dad. Two at the most. And maybe"—she wasn't sure about this, but he looked so dejected she had to tell him something good—"maybe when I get home we could talk about college." She figured if she *applied herself* like everybody told her to do in high school, she might be able to get a cool job with the Red Cross.

His brows went up and she could see that got his attention. "Will you at least stay with Claire? So I know you're safe?"

She'd done it. They'd gotten through a whole discussion without arguing. Boy howdy. She threw her arms around her dad and kissed his cheek. That surprised him even more than the stuff about college. "I've already got a neat place set up with the other volunteers," she said. "But I promise, I'll check in with Claire every day."

She'd try to remember to check in with Claire. She really would try.

"Let's go." Dad looked at his watch, and now that she'd said her piece, she noticed Dad was looking a little nervous. "We're meeting your sisters at the Depot before my train. There's something we need to talk about."

chapter 69

CLAIRE

Claire walked into the Depot with Bridget beside her.

She'd had a rock of worry sitting in the center of her chest since her father called her this morning.

"Meet me for lunch at the Depot with your sisters. We have to talk." Dad had refused to say more.

Claire had planned on seeing her father off this morning at the Depot, but the tone of his voice didn't bode well for a happy goodbye. Red said he'd keep Jenny, and told her not to worry when he kissed her goodbye.

"Do you know something I don't?" she asked him. He and Dad had talked a long time that first night. Red told her Dad had apologized to him about the wedding, and that made her worry even more. That was so unlike her father.

Now Red said, "I think it's a good thing he wants to talk to you all together."

"Do you think he's sick?" Bridget asked after she picked her up at the Red Cross headquarters in Ennis. "Maybe he has cancer, or TB."

"Maybe he is going to try to convince me to come home again," Claire said.

"You don't think he's going to get remarried, do you?" Bridget asked, turning to face Claire with horror. "To that lady from church that has had her eye on him?"

"Absolutely not." But Claire couldn't shake the feeling whatever he had to say wasn't good news.

The Depot was teeming with customers. Reporters with camera bags, Army National Guard and Red Cross workers, and tourists waiting for trains out of town.

Helen and Tom Eagle were at a table filled with locals. "Hello, Claire," Helen said with a friendly smile.

Claire. Not Mrs. Wilder. Would wonders never cease?

Helen's eyes lit with interest on Bridget. "This must be the sister we read so much about." Helen introduced herself to Bridget and told her how much she admired what she'd done with Red—"Isn't he a local hero?"—while Claire searched the tables for their father.

"There he is." She took Bridget's elbow and dragged her away from Helen Eagle.

"Isn't she the one you said didn't like you?" Bridget whispered as they veered through the room.

"Yes," Claire said. The earthquake had changed more than the landscape of Gallatin County, it had turned Red from an outsider to a hero. Red had a new job starting next week in the park, and Claire had an invitation to Helen Eagle's bridge club. Claire was glad about the job, but would rather go fishing than play bridge. She veered through the crowded room, stopping where a waitress blocked the aisle.

"I woke up and didn't know what was happening, but I knew I had to get out of the house." Grace Miller's rough voice cut through the rattle of cutlery and the clink of coffee cups. She sat among a bevy of reporters, all staring in rapt attention at the silver-haired woman. "I had to kick the door open, and Sandy, that's my dog"—she leaned down to pat a furry malamute at her feet—"Sandy was right with me. I got the door open and then I saw a big crevice opening up in front of me. I jumped, and so did Sandy and then the house dropped right into the lake."

"Excuse us," Claire said to the waitress.

As they moved away, she heard Grace Miller cackle. "I hope they find my house, because I left my teeth right beside the sink and I'd sure like to get them back."

They reached the corner booth where Dad and Frannie sat. She slid into the booth and raised her brows at Frannie. Her little sister shrugged to say she didn't know what was going on either.

"What is it, Dad?" Bridget said in her imperative tone. "Are you alright?"

"Yeah," Frannie said. "What's up?"

Dad picked up a paper napkin and folded it into a square. "I have some things that need to be said."

Claire felt like she might be starting to get sick. Could something really be wrong with Dad?

"About what?" Frannie said with a frown.

"You're scaring us," Bridget said, all her bluster gone.

Dad cleared his throat, looking down at the napkin that was now a crumpled ball in his hand. "It's about your mother."

Claire's mouth went dry. She glanced at Frannie, and then at Bridget. No one said a word. What on Earth had got into Dad?

"I realize—well, I mean—I know we don't talk about her." He cleared his throat. "And I'm sorry about that."

"Dad," Bridget said, "You don't have to—"

"Let me finish." He held up a hand. "I wasn't an easy man to live with," he said quickly. "When you girls were born, things were tough. The Depression was on, and I'd just started the store. I worked too much." His voice cracked. He leaned an elbow on the table and pinched the bridge of his nose like he did when he was tired.

Claire's heart twisted. Her father shouldn't have to go through this, but now that he'd started, she wanted to hear the rest. She needed to hear it.

Dad went on. "I thought making money was what I had to do—all I had to do—to be a good husband and a good father. It was hard work, keeping the store afloat in those early years."

Claire remembered. Dad would sometimes come home late at night, too tired to help her with her spelling list. He'd spread papers out on the kitchen table and tell Mother to turn the radio down. Dad went on. "Your mother told me—when she left—that I was married to the store, not to her."

Bridget's hand searched for Claire's and they locked fingers together. "But she's the one who left us," Bridget said, always the one to defend Dad.

Dad stared down at his coffee. "She made the decision to leave," he said. "But it's my fault she didn't come back."

Claire's throat suddenly felt thick and swollen. *I'll come back to visit.* But she never did. She'd hoped for so long, because of that promise. Until hoping hurt too much, and she gave up not only on Mother, but on hope itself. "What do you mean?" Claire managed to get the words out.

Dad let out a long breath. "I told her that if she left, it was for good. That if she walked out that door, not to come back."

The memory rose in Claire's mind. *Marie, I meant what I said.*

"I thought it was best for you girls," he said, raising his gaze with a pleading look. "A clean break. No coming in and out of your lives. Visits in the summer, passing you back and forth like a used car. It would be too hard on you. And," he looked down at his hands, "too hard on me."

Frannie's brows were pulled down. "So it wasn't my fault?"

Dad let out a breath that sounded like a sob. "No, sweetheart, it was mine."

"It would have been nice to know that," Frannie said, but without anger.

Claire reached across the table to Frannie. They had learned not to talk about Mother, because it hurt Dad. Frannie—growing up with no answers to her questions—had filled in the blanks herself, and got the answers wrong. She took Frannie's hand in hers, as she'd done for so many years.

Bridget let out a breath. "Did she try to come back?"

He nodded. "On each of your birthdays for a couple years." A tear leaked from the corner of his eye. "I did what I thought was best. But now, well"—he took a deep breath—"I see it was a mistake, and I'm sorry."

Claire wasn't sure how she felt. Relief, that their mother hadn't forgotten them. Sorrow that they could have known her. Hope that perhaps it wasn't too late to find her . . . to know their mother again. There was a hint of anger, too, even as she knew that what Dad had done, he'd done out of love for his daughters.

"You girls are everything to me," he said. "And now that you're grown, it's—" He reached out to Bridget and clasped his hand over hers. "It's so hard to let you go."

"Dad," Frannie said as if he was a child himself. "You can keep holding on." She gave him a stern look. "Just not so tight."

Frannie grabbed Dad's hand so that they were all linked together. Frannie and Dad and Bridget and Claire. The Reilly sisters and their father—broken apart, but by the grace of God brought back together.

Stronger and closer than they'd ever been.

epilogue

CLAIRE

One Year Later

"Are you sure you want to do this?" Red asked Claire.

Despite the blazing August sun, a chill prickled over Claire's skin. "I told Beth I'd be there."

Red helped Claire into the truck, and Jenny scrambled up the running board and climbed onto what remained of Claire's lap. As they drove out of Riverside and turned north on highway 191, Claire's heartbeat quickened. They passed the spot on the road where Beth and Claire ran out of gas, then crossed Duck Creek where a fault line ran close to the road, splitting the earth in a silent testimony to the seismic shift that broke open the earth and their lives.

Claire scooted nearer to Red's solid presence as they turned onto Hebgen Lake Road. She hadn't come this way since that night a year ago with Frannie and her friends. She pulled Jenny close. "We almost lost her," she said.

Red's eyes met hers, and she could see he was reliving that long night. "I almost lost you both."

They reached Hebgen Lake, mirror-smooth and reflecting the cloudless blue sky, then Hebgen Dam, reinforced now in case of another quake. Claire caught a glimpse of the high ground above the dam, the place they called Refuge Point, where Bridget had worked to save the critically injured.

They dropped down into the canyon, where landslides still scarred the slopes and downed trees marred the beauty of the mountain. Claire put her hand to her pounding heart as the hum of the truck wheels quieted on the newly surfaced road. They were getting close.

Red glanced at her with a worried frown. "We don't have to do this."

"I want to." It was time to revisit the place where she'd almost lost everything. The view widened and then . . . she could see it.

Earthquake Lake.

Claire struggled to swallow, her throat suddenly dry. In her memory the flooded canyon was a churning dark ocean, but today the narrow lake was a placid strip of blue water. The only hint of its deadly creation were the tips of lodgepole pines and Douglas firs reaching out of the water toward the blue sky.

As Red drove the six-mile length of the lake, memories rushed over Claire like the wind streaming through her open window. The icy water, the taste of mud and the grit of rock dust in the air. The rough bark of the branches biting into her skin. Holding on.

Red slowed and pulled the truck onto the shoulder where a dozen cars were already parked. Frannie and Paul waited beside Paul's red convertible, identical to the one he'd lost in the quake. Frannie hugged Claire, squeezing her despite the bump between them. "How's the littlest ankle biter?"

Claire held Frannie for a long moment, her emotions close to the surface. Her sister had saved her life—hers and Beth's. She stepped back and swiped her eyes, offering a watery smile. "Ready to meet his—or her—Aunt Frannie."

"You better get a move on," Frannie said, blinking back tears of her own, but her voice was lighthearted as she spoke to Claire's tummy.

"Aunt Frannie only has another two weeks before it's bye-bye savage and hello co-ed."

Claire said hello to Paul, and Red shook his hand, then they all looked up at the massive rockslide, its steep slope blotting out the blue of the sky.

"Can you climb up there in your condition?" Frannie asked, eyeing the trail to the top.

Claire rolled her eyes. "I'm pregnant, not an invalid."

"Good, because I don't want you to miss out on my surprise." Frannie gave Paul a knowing grin.

Claire frowned at her. "Frannie, this is supposed to be a memorial, not some—"

"Don't worry." Frannie poked her in the arm. "You'll like it."

Red led the way with Jenny riding on his shoulders. The trail wound upwards, cutting through the slide of dirt, boulders, and splintered trees. Frannie stopped to catch her breath. "It's terrible that Bridget is missing this. Can you believe she's in Alaska now?"

Claire was glad to take a rest. "At least she's coming in a few weeks to help me with this little one." She patted her stomach and got a sharp kick in her ribs. Bridget had insisted, and this time, Claire was glad to accept the help.

They reached the top, where an area of the slide had been leveled as a viewing platform and the memorial site. "Nice turnout," Frannie said.

Claire searched the familiar faces in the solemn crowd. Friends from West Yellowstone—Grace Miller, Bucky, and Father Donahue. Mel, giving Frannie a bear hug. Then—there she was—walking toward Claire with a baby in her arms, her expression somber but her soft gray eyes alight with friendship.

"Beth!" Claire reached out and they embraced with Beth's baby and Claire's pregnant belly between them, and Claire felt Beth's shuddering intake of breath. She pulled back and met her friend's tearful gaze.

Claire understood. They had survived that deadly night, but so many had not.

"This must be DJ." Claire touched the baby's dark blond hair—just like his father's—and he looked at her with wide gray eyes. He had survived as well.

Claire and Beth followed the crowd to the foot of a dolomite rock the size of a house. Red and Jenny stood on one side of Claire, Beth and DJ on the other. Frannie and Paul disappeared and Claire hoped Frannie wasn't planning anything unseemly.

The Forest Service ranger—Joseph Shields had been picked to do the honors—stood on higher ground. "Thank you for coming to the dedication ceremony for the memorial to the victims of the Hebgen Lake Earthquake."

Joseph talked about the magnitude of the earthquake, and the eighty million tons of rock that slid down one side of the canyon and up the other in less than thirty seconds. "The slide generated hurricane-force winds and a twelve-foot wall of water that rushed upstream, destroying everything in its path."

Claire's chest tightened, remembering. The land had been forever altered in those cataclysmic moments, and so had their lives. The Reilly sisters had lost each other, but found parts of themselves. Frannie found her faith, and Bridget discovered her courage. Claire had learned how to hope. They were stronger now—better sisters—and closer to each other even as their lives diverged. Even Dad had been changed by the earthquake. He hadn't stopped worrying, but he was learning to hold on to his daughters a little less tightly.

The bronze plaque on the memorial boulder was unveiled, and all bowed their heads as Father Donahue prayed for the souls of the departed. After the formalities, the crowd dispersed. Beth and Claire approached the memorial, their hands clasped, as close in spirit as they had been that night one year ago, holding desperately to each other.

Red came to stand beside them, holding Jenny high enough to touch the words engraved in bronze, while he read them aloud without hesitation. *"This boulder is part of the huge slide caused by the earthquake of August 17, 1959. It is dedicated to the memory of the men, women, and children whose lives were lost as a result of the earthquake."*

Below the words *In Memoriam*, the twenty-eight names were listed.

Claire traced the names of the couple she thought of every day. *Jeffrey and Dottie Gardner.*

"But for the grace of God," Beth murmured.

Dottie's act of generosity had been the difference between life and death for Beth, Jenny, and Claire. They would never be forgotten.

Suddenly, a voice sang out—clear and confident and unmistakably Frannie—swelling over the boulder-strewn slide, across the scarred mountain and the hushed waters of the lake.

"Amazing grace, how sweet the sound . . ."

Beth's grip tightened on Claire's hand. Claire's heart surged with remembrance of the hope that song had given her and Beth when they most needed it.

"That saved a wretch like me."

Paul and Mel joined their voices to Frannie's. "I once was lost, but now am found, was blind but now, I see."

As the echoes of the song died away in the canyon, Claire wiped the tears from her cheeks. Frannie bounded up, dragging Paul by the hand. "See, I told you she'd like it." Frannie and Paul said goodbye and promised to visit Riverside before the end of the season. Beth got a ride to West Yellowstone with Bucky after promising she'd come to the house later for dinner.

Claire wasn't ready to leave.

She took one of Jenny's hands and Red took the other. With their daughter toddling between, Claire and Red walked to the edge of the slide. Claire gazed over the silent mountain of rock, the memorial on the dolomite boulder, the lake with its drowned treetops—reminders of the despair and loss that night had wrought.

But looking closer, Claire could see hope.

Scarlet Indian paintbrush bloomed among the boulders, and purple harebells peeked through the rubble. Sage and grasses sprouted on the barren slopes. Above the placid waters of Earthquake Lake an osprey alighted on a nest built atop a flooded tree.

The Hebgen Lake Earthquake had brought destruction to the canyon, but it had also wrought a seismic shift in those who had survived. Courage arose out of fear, faith emerged from doubt . . . and hope transcended despair.

Claire rested her hand on her burgeoning middle. And weren't children the ultimate sign of that hope? Beth with DJ in her arms. Jenny, saved by a miracle. Soon, a brother or sister to add to her and Red's family.

It was enough—more than enough—to hold on to.

Claire turned to Red. "I'm ready to go home."

He smiled at her, those Montana-sky eyes filled with all their tomorrows. He took her hand in his and they clung to each other, holding tight to what they had almost lost—and to what they'd been given in their darkest moments.

Holding on to hope.

A Note from the Author

Dear Reader,

The inspiration for *The Fault Between Us* was twofold: the little-known history of the Hebgen Lake Earthquake and its aftermath, and the stories I grew up hearing from my mom and her sisters about their time living and working in Yellowstone National Park in the 1950s.

The Hebgen Lake Earthquake, combined with the 80-million-ton rockslide, hurricane-force winds, and a twelve-foot tidal wave, killed twenty-eight campers and formed a new lake 125 feet deep and six miles long. But that was just the beginning. As I researched this little-known but extraordinary event, it was stories of the survivors and rescuers that captured my imagination and inspired my characters. Their firsthand accounts told a story of heroism, resilience, and hope in the face of darkness, terror, and pain.

The stories of the heroes and heroines of the quake were nothing short of astonishing. My only regret is not being able to chronicle every act of courage and moment of grace that took place that dark night and in the ensuing days.

The family history set within the pages of *The Fault Between Us* made this my most heartfelt and personal novel. Many of the details of living in and around Yellowstone National Park come from family stories told by my mom and dad. Our family lore recounts my parents' brief courtship during my mother's summer as a savage at Old Faithful, as well as tales of bears on the porch, bar fights over babies, and my dad's beloved horses. Dad's work for the National Park Service and Mom's intrepid spirit later led them to national parks in California and the Pacific Northwest, but Yellowstone always held their hearts.

My favorite part of writing this novel was my many conversations with Mom, in which she talked about the early years with Dad—known as Red to his friends —who passed away ten years ago. It was during one of these talks that she told me about a young woman she had known whose husband drowned in the Yellowstone River. She explained how the pregnant young woman's in-laws were keeping her captive and how she and Dad devised a plan to rescue the girl and send her home to her parents. With that, Beth's story came to life! Mom will celebrate her ninetieth birthday soon, and each conversation I have with her leaves me profoundly grateful for her courage, wisdom, and enduring faith.

In addition, I was blessed to be able to personally interview my aunts, who did indeed travel from Minnesota to Montana to visit their adventurous sister. I thank the Lord for my telephone visits with Aunt Mary about her time as a nurse in Mammoth before she passed away in December 2023. Aunt Joan, also a nurse, vividly recalled the myriad ways tourists managed to get injured and killed in Yellowstone, and declared her sister was the bravest person she'd ever known to live in that awful place. My mom's youngest sister, Marlyn—inspiration for the reckless Frannie—regaled me with the hijinks teenagers got into after a day's work in Yellowstone, including dancing, hot-potting, and bear watching.

I have fictionalized this raw material of interviews, primary sources, and historical research for both clarity and storytelling effect. Readers who are interested in additional details of my research and personal interviews with family can find more on my website: stephanielandsem.com.

Discussion Questions

1. When Claire first met Red, his quiet nature struck her as romantic, but after they're married, she finds it frustrating. Whenever a topic comes up that Red doesn't want to talk about, he finds something else to do. Do you know anyone like this? Are you sometimes tempted to behave this way yourself?

2. Bridget tells Frannie, "God hears your prayers, even if you don't get what you ask for." Why does Frannie have a hard time believing this? What happens to start changing her mind?

3. Frannie says that when people die in accidents, like Buddy Holly and Ritchie Valens, it makes her think God isn't very loving. This is an age-old question, how could a good God allow bad things to happen? Have you had to wrestle with this question in your own life?

4. After the mix-up with the baby formula, Frannie says she told Claire she was sorry, but Red calls her on it. Why do we sometimes feel like we've apologized even when we haven't actually said the words? Why are the words important?

5. Red tells Frannie that growing up is mostly about doing things you don't want to do. Do you agree? What are some of the good things about growing up? What does Frannie eventually learn about this?

6. Throughout the book we see ways in which Daniel Reilly is overprotective of his daughters. Why do you think he's that way? How do each of the daughters deal with it, and what are the differences and similarities in the outcomes?

7. Claire tells Red she believes God created the wonders of Yellowstone to show us how much he loves us. Do you sense God's love through the wonders of nature?

8. At the end of the book, the adult sisters learn that their mother had tried to contact them after she left. How might this change their perception of her leaving them? Was their father right to keep this information from them?

9. In the 1960s it wasn't as easy to find people as it is today, but do you think the sisters will or should try to track down their mother after all these years? What's the reasoning behind your answer?

10. In her note to readers, the author says this novel is inspired by family stories and interviews with her mother and aunts. Are there any stories in your family history that would make a good novel?

About the Author

Stephanie Landsem writes historical fiction for women, about women. She's traveled the world in real life and traveled through time in her research and imagination. As she's learned about women of the past, she's come to realize that these long-ago women were very much like us. They loved, dreamed, and made mistakes. They struggled, failed, and triumphed. She writes to honor their lives and to bring today's women hope and encouragement.

Stephanie makes her home in Minnesota with her husband, two cats and a dog, and frequent visits from her four adult children. Along with reading, writing, and research, she dreams about her next travel adventure—whether it be in person or on the page.